Earth Quaking

Earth Quaking

Anelthalien Book Two

Written and Illustrated
By
H.A. Pruitt

H.A. Pruitt
Something Different Publishing
www.hapruitt.com

Earth Quaking

Published in the United States of America by H.A. Pruitt. For information visit www.hapruitt.com.

Cover and interior illustrations are created by and copyright of H.A. Pruitt.

Publisher's Note: This novel is a work of fiction. Names, characters, places, and incidents are either products of the author's imagination or used fictitiously. All characters are fictional, and any similarity to people living or dead is purely coincidental.

ISBN: 978-1-7372309-0-8 (Paperback)
ISBN: 978-1-7372309-1-5 (eBook)

TABLE OF CONTENTS

For my Maker, who holds me when I am shaken.

DEVIATION

Carmen shuddered as she drew in a deep breath. The air should have been warm. She was too far north for it not to be full of heat and water. As she traveled, though, the wind that blew past her deeply chilled her. Its biting edge was so icy that it shook her to a halt. In her frozen state, she considered her path. Her destination was not far, and her deed would take seconds. The bitter wind, though, pushed her to consider a different route to anywhere else. She tried to push away the glorious alleviation she knew turning back would grant her, but it grew into such a desirable option, she couldn't ignore it. Until that moment Carmen had known exactly where to go, but now her decisiveness crumbled. The wind cut deeper into her, and she gathered her whole entity to move from her paralysis and step in a new direction.

After only a few slow footfalls, the wind died and Carmen dove into her new course. As she rushed along, she kept all her senses heightened, searching for any irregular feeling, sight, sound, or smell. Much sooner than she had expected, something reached her keen perception, and she slowed. Not far ahead a carriage—a familiar carriage—was bumping along through the dark night. She watched it, trying to fathom the reason for its journey here through such a tense, terrible night. As no explanation entered her mind, a betrayed feeling slowly crept over her. In another second, Carmen burst inside the carriage then collected herself to face the woman occupying it.

"Carmen," Blenda gasped with a steadying hand on her chest. Once their eyes met and they exchanged slight, cordial smiles, Carmen suddenly regretted her split decision and stared out the window. An eerie glow bounced off the ground as the lantern light from outside passed over it. The lantern wasn't visible from the small window, so the lonely light and everything it brushed seemed ghostly. Not even the moon illuminated the night; every luminary in the sky was blocked by the thick clouds hanging overhead.

Carmen frowned as her eyes turned up to the thick cumulous towers. She couldn't feel them or the rain she knew to be churning in them. She shuddered, remembering the cold air that had frozen her not long ago, and turned her gaze down again. The soft, swift sound of the wheels turning was the only noise, and Carmen was content to throw all her attention on its repetitive lull. She closed her eyes and tried to forget everything—the natural world sweeping by so closely yet so distantly, her earlier intention, and the weight on her heart. The meditative sound and constant rocking of the carriage had almost stolen her consciousness when Blenda broke the silence.

"Carmen, what are you doing here?" Blenda slowly inquired.

Carmen kept her focus on the darkness behind her eyelids. She did not intend to answer.

"Car—"

"It's terribly late for a carriage ride," Carmen interrupted and, out of the corner of her now fully open eye, saw the queen swallow.

Blenda pursed her lips as she bowed her head but then shook away her tacit yet apparent discomfort and gazed at Carmen. "I thought you were at the castle."

"As I believed you to be," Carmen immediately responded and shot a sidelong look at her queen.

"Carmen," Blenda coldly reprimanded as she wrinkled her forehead, "what has … no, excuse me, you are right. It is quite late …

I couldn't sleep. I thought some air might clear my head."

When she spoke her last sentence, Carmen sharply turned her head and eyed Blenda, trying to determine if she was suggesting more than what she said. They locked stares, and Carmen saw nothing insidious in her light blue eyes. Feeling guilty for her suspicion, Carmen dropped her gaze.

"What's wrong?" Blenda softly asked. "Is it tomorrow?"

Carmen closed her eyes in an attempt to shut out her disquiet. She regretted her deviation from her original course even more now and desperately wanted to flow out of the carriage and back into the night. Her chance to end it all had been so close, and she knew if she would only lose herself in the sky again, perhaps …

"Carmen, you're not yourself. Is everything alright? Has something changed?"

"No," she almost choked out the word. "Nothing is wrong. Everything is as it has always been." Once she heard the words spill out of her mouth, Carmen knew they were a dangerous lie and guilt stung her again. "Everything is … as it should be," she corrected herself with a strained breath.

"Are you sure?" Blenda sounded incredibly concerned. "Because if anything has changed, you must tell me. It is not only one life depending—"

"I know," Carmen snapped, and before Blenda responded, a calming silence filled the carriage.

"I need to know," the queen very quietly but urgently commanded, "has he said anything? Does he know anything about …?"

Carmen compulsively shook her head over and over. Finding she couldn't stop the motion or flood of speech eager to flow out of her depths, she switched her words to another subject.

"I think it may rain." Her voice shook as she divulged the disgusting words, but she calmed herself with the knowledge that they had covered something much worse.

Blenda shifted uncomfortably but sighed, "I am sorry."

"You have no idea" —Carmen felt her hands begin to shake—

"what it is like to live like this."

"Carmen," breathed Blenda soothingly, "you must let go of your past wrongs. You could go back. You are different now, you are doing what is right—"

"Am I?" Carmen cried then whispered, "I don't believe I know what is right anymore … and, no, I will not ever go back." An impulse to act seized her, and she lifted her necklace up and over her head.

"Carmen what—?" Blenda started to ask but fell into wide-eyed silence as Carmen held out her hand.

When the queen made no move to take the four necklaces lying in her palm, Carmen dropped them on the cushion between them. Her whole entirety suddenly shocked with excruciating pain, Carmen gasped, "Send us help—that is all you need to say." Almost sure of what was coming, she placed her hand on the ledge of the open window. Fighting against the ripping pain terrorizing every inch of her being, she stretched her fingers to feel for any hint of moisture in the air. The moment Carmen found it, she lost control of her form and burst into a million droplets.

For a few horrifying seconds, Carmen couldn't sense where she had scattered, only the confusing air and earth hitting her from every direction. Summoning every iota of consciousness, she searched for familiarity. A few drops of her suddenly touched water—warm, flowing, and calm. She tried to will her entirety to the river but didn't hold the power. Then a very soft, caring wind blew her into the river's safety. The warm breeze guided all of her to the wonderful water, but despair overwhelmed Carmen. Even though she was now fully in the water, she was still painfully apart from her element and sensed her strength subsiding and the current taking command of her direction.

RECOLLECTION

"Unbelievable," sighed Ella, shaking her head. Tad and Kindle had just finished relating their experience from the night before to her and Andrew. Both of them appeared dumbfounded. Ella kept opening and closing her mouth as if she was too full of words to choose just a few, and watching her made Kindle feel glad they hadn't spoken during the night.

After she and Tad had realized that they had outstripped the hooded figure, Tad still had not allowed Nasah to ease her gallop. He only slowed when they reached the Gilded Goose, and then he had just briefly stopped in the stable to order Ella to jump on a horse and leave the city right that moment. Kindle had heard Ella begin to protest that it was too late to purchase a horse, but before she fully expressed her dismay at Tad's direction, he spurred Nasah into the street again. Knowing how opposed Ella was to anything unlawful, Kindle had doubted Ella and Andrew would find them that night. Before long, though, their companions had appeared behind them on a huge black steed. Once Ella had caught up despite Tad's attempts to stay ahead of her, she had commenced to bombarding them with questions and rebukes about their behavior. When they had reached the gate, though, and neither Kindle nor Tad had answered her in any way, her words ceased, and they rode side by side out of Iteraum and then east along the river in silence.

After a while of riding by the quiet water, Kindle had felt all of them relax, and the horses, not riled by their riders' urgency, grew tired and slowed to a walk on their own. Even then none of them spoke. Only when the sun broke over the horizon had any of them attempted to speak. Andrew had mumbled something about rest, and—in such a unified manner that it seemed planned—they all slowed to a halt and dropped to the ground. It was then that Ella had begun to half-heartedly chastise Tad for leading them to turn into criminals and lose a whole night of rest and Tad had cut her off and loudly defended himself with the battle in the castle garden.

"Unbelievable," Ella finally sighed again and lay back on the grass. "I've lived my whole life right near those black ghosts' home, and never once have I seen a trace of them, and now you two have chanced to encounter one twice."

"It wasn't a ghost," Tad grumpily replied. "That stupid thing was solid."

Kindle started to nod in agreement, but it made her tired head dizzy, so she voiced an affirmative as she stretched out on the ground.

"And it wasn't chance," he continued, squinting away from them.

His words ruffled Kindle's curiosity, but she too much wanted to sleep to chase his thought. She was ready to close her eyes just like Ella already had, but the surprise of hearing Andrew's voice pulled her away from sleep.

"What do you mean?"

Kindle rolled over to see Tad grin and lift an eye to sneak a peek at Ella. "You know that night Ella was tellin' us not to listen to Azildor and Naam talk?"

"You did," Andrew stated in a bland, unsurprised voice, and Tad frowned at him.

"How'd you know?"

Andrew shrugged. "I knew you would."

"Whatever. So you know what I'm talkin' about. They acted like that thing was gunna follow us."

Andrew scrunched his brow then debated, "Ella and I haven't seen it. If it was following us—"

"Aw, shut up," Tad interrupted. "They didn't say it was gunna *follow* us, they said ..." He glared at the ground as his voice trailed off. Then he pushed his heel against Kindle's shin. "Hey!"

"What? You don't have to kick me, I'm awake."

"Wha'd Azildor and Naam say about that thing? You remember?"

"Ugh," Kindle groaned and lay her cool hand on her warm face. She tried to make her sleepy mind think, but the task was like wading through mud. "I dunno, what you said—it knew where we were or whatever."

"Yeah!" Tad brightened. "That's what they said. It knows where we are."

Kindle watched Andrew's eyes roam back and forth then shift from her to Tad. "It knows where you are," he said in a strange, low tone, as if he hadn't meant to say it out loud at all.

"Yeah, that's what I said, Einstein," Tad grumbled then stretched and yawned before flumping onto his back. "That thing knows where we are, so we gotta figure out how to kill it."

Andrew, frowning at him, dropped his eyes and shook his head before walking to a sleeping spot away from everyone else. Kindle, still watching Andrew, murmured, "You're such a jerk to him. Why can't you just be nice?"

"Wha'd I do?" he retorted, looking genuinely oblivious.

Kindle huffed a sigh. "Just go to sleep." She heard him snort a laugh before she lay her head down and followed her own orders.

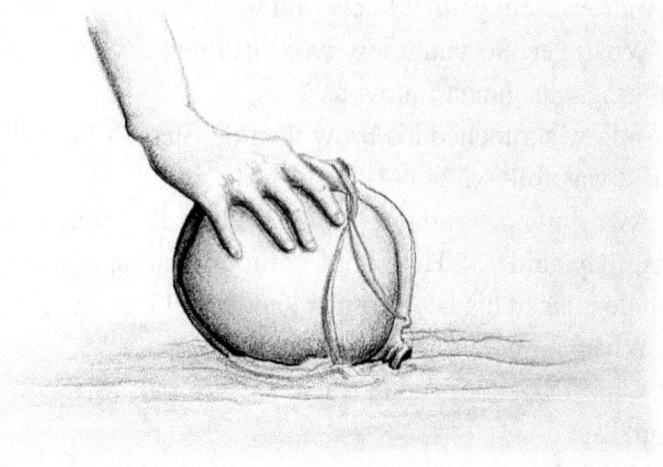

RIPPLES OF RIFTS

K indle blinked awake and blurrily surveyed her surroundings. The two horses and Ella, Andrew, and Tad lay scattered around her still asleep. Staring up at the sky, she tried to determine how long she had slept and, since the sun hadn't reached its zenith yet, guessed that it had not been very long. She almost decided to roll back over and resume her nap, but the uncomfortable dryness of her mouth pushed her to search for a canteen. Upon finding hers empty, Kindle slowly meandered down to the riverbank. Before she reached the soft mud, she slid off her boots and lazily tossed them over her shoulder so they would not become wet. Then she knelt down and held the mouth of her canteen at the surface of the water to catch it, just as she had watched Ella do. Once it felt heavy, she rocked back and took a swig.

"I wouldn't drink that," Andrew's voice quietly warned behind her, and with the water still in her cheeks, she turned to stare at him. He came and sat at the edge of the river.

"It isn't purified. It's probably not safe."

Kindle dropped her shoulders and begrudgingly spat her

mouthful back into the river. "Isn't this the same water we had in our canteens?" she argued, "It's the same river."

"It isn't purified," he blandly insisted.

"Well, it wasn't before either." She waded to him and moodily dropped her open canteen on the ground. Andrew picked it up and poured some of the water on his hand so that it trickled through his fingers and left dirt and other bits of sediment on his palm. Kindle wrinkled her nose at the thought of ingesting the gunk on his hand. "Ew," she mumbled, now glad he had stopped her.

"It *was* purified. It was hot when Ella gave it to us. Remember?"

Kindle plopped down beside him and avidly stared at him. "Yeah, did you ask Ella what she did to it? I totally forgot to ask you about it. Wha'd she say?"

Andrew turned his eyes to his feet. "I didn't ask."

"Ugh—Andrew," Kindle groaned. "Why not? Don't you want to know what's up with her making stuff get all hot and how she fixed my leg? She'd tell you—I *know* she would—if you asked her." She stared at him, waiting for a reply, but he didn't give one. After enough time had passed to convince her that Andrew didn't plan on continuing the conversation, Kindle loudly sighed and prepared to stand and return to her sleeping spot.

"She wouldn't tell me," Andrew resolutely stated, and Kindle stopped in mid-stand.

"What? I thought you said you didn't ask."

"I didn't." He dropped his forehead on his knees then tossed it back up. "She wouldn't talk to me that night after she healed you. She avoided me because she didn't want me to ask about it."

"Did she tell you that?"

"No."

"Well, how do you know, then? What if she was just, I dunno, tired?"

The straight face Andrew gave her told Kindle that both he and she knew her suggestion held no truth.

"Okay, so she was mad then. But she's not *now*. I think you should—"

"Quit bugging me about it," he unexpectedly interrupted and left Kindle blinking with her mouth agape. Before she could even try to compose a retort, Andrew pushed himself up from the bank, mumbled something about heading out, and walked away from her. As Kindle watched him travel to the horses to rouse them, she tried to justify her annoyance at him for rudely cutting her off, but she couldn't escape the truth that she had probably been fairly annoying herself. She shook away her guilty agitation, plucked up her canteen, and plodded over to help wake up Tad and Ella.

They spent almost the entire rest of their day riding along the river. Ella and Andrew took the lead on Nox, the large black stallion they had stolen in Iteraum, and Tad and Kindle followed on Nasah. Kindle, even though she had changed back into her leggings, rode sideways on the back of the saddle so she could stare off across the grassy plain. It wasn't the most exciting sight, in fact, the flat land hardly changed all day, but the vast openness and monotony of it gave her mind space and freedom to wander.

The previous night played over and over in her head like an unwelcome but catchy song that she wanted to remember and forget all at once. She still couldn't believe how the castle, Adlic, and the ball had seemed so amazing but had proved to actually be awful. The thought of Adlic and how he had tricked her made Kindle shake her head in embarrassed disgust for the hundredth time. His ruse—above everything else—sickened her the most. For a day, he had made her believe she wasn't painfully plain and unlikeable, but it had just been a lie to reel her into a trap. Without meaning to, she sighed aloud, and Tad glanced at her out of the corner of his eye.

"Bored?"

She sighed again. "No."

He sniffed as if he didn't believe her then offhandedly demanded, "Hey, check if we still got some toast."

Kindle dug through the large bags piled around her until she found the bread that she didn't have the heart to tell Tad was stale. When she handed it up to him, a victorious laugh escaped from his mouth before he shoved a crunchy bite into it. Kindle watched him, half amused, half disgusted, then felt a sudden freedom with him and blurted, "Tad, what's wrong with me?"

"Muh?" he grunted past the food in his mouth.

"Seriously, what's wrong with me?" she dismally repeated.

He swallowed. "You're short, you won't leave people alone when they wanna be left alone, you're annoying sometimes—"

"Okay, thanks," she quickly cut into his answer. She had not wanted nor expected him to actually list her faults.

"And I'm always havin' to cut somebody up so they don't kill you—"

"Okay, Tad. Forget I said anything," she firmly grumbled.

"And you're always trying way too hard to make everybody like you—"

"No, I'm not!" she protested, thoroughly annoyed with him.

"Yeah, you are," he retorted with confidence as his evil grin curled up on his face.

Kindle thumped his back. "Don't laugh!"

"Hey, you shouldn't hit your driver, you know. I could wreck."

"Oh, whatever," Kindle groaned, trying not to laugh. Then, urged by her curiosity and determination to prove him wrong, she challenged, "How do I try to make everybody like me?"

He shrugged but replied, "You're always sayin' sorry and just doing what everybody wants you to."

"That's called being *nice*. And I don't just do whatever people tell me to do. I never listen to you."

"Yeah, well, what about that punk prince? You didn't even know that idiot, and you did whatever he said."

His comment struck her hard, and she recoiled into silence. When Tad realized she wasn't going to return fire, he twisted around, laughing, "See, I'm ri—" Seeing her frown, the smile fell off his face. "What?"

"Nothing," she coldly replied, refusing to look at him.

"Okay, whatever," he mumbled and turned forward.

Kindle glared at the back of his head, angry that she had thought she could confide in him. "Ugh, you're a jerk," she sighed under her breath, and he swung his head back around to her.

"Wha'd I do? Huh? Or am I just a jerk because you say so?"

Kindle could sense that she had struck a tender spot with her name calling and almost blurted an apology but, remembering his earlier accusation, withheld it.

"Because I know I was stupid—you don't have to remind me!" Kindle hadn't intended to shout, but now that she had, she kept going. "I know it was my fault we almost got killed, and I was dumb to go to that stupid ball, and—" Her confidence broke, and she lowered her voice. "And to think anybody would like me. Okay? So, sorry I called you a jerk, but you didn't have to remind me I'm an idiot."

"Are you two alright?" Ella called from ahead, and Kindle leaned around Tad to see she had turned Nox to check on them.

"Yeah, fine," Kindle answered and waved for her to disregard them. Ella's face showed she wasn't convinced, but she pulled the reins to reset Nox on his course. Once her back faced them, Kindle prepared herself for the argument she knew had to be boiling up in Tad. However, even after Ella and Andrew had broken away from them, Tad didn't say a word to her. Kindle, disgruntled that he seemed to be ignoring her, crossed her arms and loudly huffed. Despite how irritating she found arguing with him, Kindle also too much enjoyed the challenge of proving herself right to let him torture her with silence. In another attempt to capture his attention, she cleared her throat loudly.

"What?" he grumbled in a surprisingly dark, deflated tone.

Kindle, suddenly afraid she had seriously offended him, felt the need to repair whatever damage she had caused. "I'm sorry. I didn't mean to say that—I mean, calling you a jerk, you know. I meant all the other stuff, but, like, I don't know why I said it. I dunno, I guess

I just got, like, mad."

Tad remained silent, and she felt worse than she had before her confession.

"Ugh," she sighed. "I'm sorry, just forget I said anything."

"I didn't call you an idiot," Tad mumbled in the same empty tone.

Kindle brightened slightly, glad he was speaking to her. Slowly and carefully, she began, "Well, you kinda did—well, I mean, I thought you did when you said I did whatever ..." She trailed off, unwilling to utter Adlic's name and her ugly mistake.

"Well, I didn't," he firmly cut into her silence. "That stupid punk was an idiot ... 'bout got us all killed."

"Yeah, but I believed him," Kindle pathetically sighed, and Tad whipped around to glare at her.

"What're you trying to do? You *want* me to call you an idiot?"

"No!" she cried, frustrated at herself, "I just, I dunno, I feel bad!"

"About what?!"

"Ugh—I told you! I was dumb enough to believe that guy! And think he liked me!" Kindle yelled, now unconcerned about who heard her silly thoughts, and then buried her face in her hands.

"That guy had the whole stupid city fooled," Tad snuffed. "You weren't the only one. And he didn't give a rip about any of 'em."

His words, even though they sounded angry, carried a suggestion of consolation and eased Kindle's humiliation. She bit her lip as she examined the back of his head, trying to think of how to communicate her thanks as covertly as he had given her comfort. "Yeah, I guess you're right," she decided to say. "He was kind of stuck up and all full of himself ... and he said he did all that just so that thing would leave him alone."

Tad gave her a confused glance. "Huh?"

"When you were stabbing that thing or whatever, he said that thing threatened to kill him if he didn't get me to go to that garden with him and tell him about our necklaces."

Tad raised an eyebrow. "*Tell* him about the necklaces? You

13

sure he didn't mean jack 'em?"

Kindle shook her head, "No, he said that creepy thing wanted him to get me to talk about the necklaces. I know it sounded really weird when he said it ... you think that thing wants to steal them from us?" Kindle understood that Tad knew no more than she did about the strange hooded creature but still hoped he would answer her wondering. Whether he intended to or not, though, Kindle never knew because at that moment Ella turned Nox and called them to her side.

"What's up?" Tad demanded, his voice full of ferocious anticipation.

Ella waved a hand. "Calm yourself. We're only pitching camp."

Kindle sighed in relief; she, just like Tad, had expected trouble.

"It's not even getting dark," Tad argued, "Why're we stopping?"

"Because," Ella claimed authoritatively then jumped down and began unloading Nox.

"*Because* isn't a reason," Tad spat. "Why do you get to decide what we do? Huh?"

Ella lay her head on Nox's rump for a moment then turned a calm face to him. "Because of exactly the way you are behaving. All this bickering must stop, and it isn't going to unless we all have a chat."

"Oh, we're gunna chat," Tad mockingly snorted.

Ella's lips snapped into a tight line. "Yes, chat." She returned to the task of disburdening Nox as Andrew dropped down to her side.

"This is stupid," Tad quietly grumbled but slid out of the saddle and threw his pack on the ground. Ella gave him a stern, slightly irritated look then turned away and asked, "Tad, do you remember the very first lesson Azildor gave us?"

Without looking at her, he defiantly replied, "Yeah."

"What was it?"

"Blocking with that stupid stick."

"No, it was before that when he took us to see the ruins of Bellalux. He told us that we must work together or else we'll

14

accomplish nothing." Now she faced him. "And as of yet we have proved his words—we've been so busy arguing that we have done absolutely nothing except make enemies among ourselves and all through the land. If we do not put an end to all of this nonsense, then we will soon be chopping one another apart alongside our enemies. It has to end." Ella shook her head in exasperation then sat right where she was. "Come, sit," she commanded just softly enough that Tad's defiance didn't rise, and he dropped down along with Andrew and Kindle.

"So, what? Are we gunna talk about our feelings and junk?" Tad sneered, glaring off into the distance.

"If feelings are involved in your disagreements, then yes," Ella quickly chimed.

"I don't have a problem with anybody but you," Tad retorted. "And I already told you what it was, so why do we have to do this? Argh! This is *so stupid*!" He started to leave their circle but stopped when Ella calmingly but threateningly whispered, "If you respect Azildor and if you honestly wish to be the hero that necklace claims you to be, you will sit and you will listen."

Tad and Ella steadily glared at one another long enough that Kindle impulsively spoke to fill the angry silence.

"We really are okay," she tried to effortlessly chuckle. "Like, me and Tad, I mean."

"Kindle, I know that is not true," Ella sighed, finally peeling her eyes from Tad. "You two were arguing just moments ago."

"See?!" Tad yelled, "That's why you're annoying! Nobody can be right but you! She's tellin' you the truth—why can't you believe her, huh? Aren't we supposed to get along with each other like you just said?"

Ella gave a long sigh. "My apologies, Kin, I thought you were arguing. You two always seem to be arguing."

"It's okay." Kindle gave her a small smile, but Tad grumbled something, and her hope of ending the argument dissipated.

"Do you have a word to put in?" Ella exasperatedly asked Tad.

"Yeah. I said it's not okay. You wanna know why? 'Cause you

said you'd quit acting like you're in charge of everybody, and you *never have*. You think we've all got issues and junk, but the only issue anybody's got is *you*."

For a while, they all sat in silence while Tad's loud, angry breath slowed to a normal pace. Finally, in a truly pained voice, Ella replied, "I–I never said I would change. I only said perhaps we would all have to … and it does seem that way. But, Tad, I've only been trying to care for you all and lead you to do right. Can you fault me for that?"

Tad sent a sneer her way. "Yeah. You're doing a really cruddy job."

Ella shook her head. "I know. I know I cannot—but we do need a leader. We do need someone marking our path."

"I thought that was Andrew's job," Kindle cut in, trying to be helpful.

Ella gave her a sympathetic smile. "Yes, Kin, he has our way marked out, but one of us must" —she searched for the right words— "give orders so we stop falling into danger by running whichever direction we please. Do you see?"

Kindle nodded. She understood exactly what Ella meant. As she looked around their group, though, none of them seemed to fit the role of leader. She knew Ella and Tad would never listen to one another and Andrew was neither confident nor talkative enough to tell anyone else what to do.

"Who?" she finally asked Ella, who gave her a sly grin.

"You, Kin," Ella answered.

Kindle's stomach twisted uncomfortably.

"Best idea you've had all day," muttered Tad, but no one heard him over Kindle's plea.

"But I don't want to—I mean, I just don't think, you know, I'll do a good job." Kindle dropped her eyes, trying to think of something more convincing to say. Truthfully, she hated the idea of being the one who everyone would blame for every mishap. Having the weight of her one mistake in Iteraum on her shoulders was already crushing her; the thought of carrying more responsibility made her feel sick. Before she could compose her emotions into a defense, Ella spoke again.

"You'll be fine, Kin. My papa, when he talks about the kings of Garrick, says that the best ones are not the men who wanted the power but the ones who were most invested in the people in the city. And, Kin, even if you do have a qualm with Tad, I know your heart is with each of us." Ella's smile softened. "I know if my papa knew you, he would say you're the one to lead us."

"Thanks," Kindle replied, unwilling to argue with Ella's papa. She peeked at Andrew and Tad, "Is that okay with you guys? I mean, I'll try not to be bossy or anything."

They both nodded, and she released a small sigh of relief then turned to Ella. "So … what do I do?"

"Well, it would be beneficial, since we are all here—" Ella began, but Tad loudly interrupted.

"Don't you tell her what to do!"

"I am answering her question," Ella defended. "Since we are all here, you could sort out any strife among us."

"Oh." Kindle had been hoping for something easier to do. "Um … okay. So are you, like, okay with everybody, Ella?"

"I haven't a problem with anyone—"

"Don't lie," Tad begrudgingly snorted.

"—as long as Tad works to diminish his rudeness," Ella finished, and before Tad could utter his comeback, Kindle put up a calming hand and interjected, "Okay. So you just have to be nice. *Okay?*"

Tad frowned against her forced smile but finally grumbled, "Yeah, okay. If she quits bossing me around, I'll try to be nice."

"Okay." Kindle took a deep breath and smiled, slightly more confident about the direction of their powwow. "Andrew, you okay?"

He didn't answer, but his eyes flicked Tad's way, and Kindle guessed his thoughts.

"Tad, you gotta quit calling him names, okay?" she apologetically said, trying not to rouse his anger, but he still threw up his arms in agitation.

"Why's everybody gangin' up on me?!"

17

Kindle put a hand over her face to cover her impulsive eye roll. "We're not ganging up on you. You just—just don't call him names and try to be nice, okay?"

"Okay. Nice. Whatever."

Kindle accepted his insincere promise and pushed ahead. "So it's your turn, Tad. What do you wanna say?"

He eyed her suspiciously as if he didn't believe she would actually allow him to speak then answered, "Okay, you know what? We're all being honest here, so I'll fess up—I got problems. I know you guys all hate me because I'm a stupid, rude, worthless jerk," he growled accusingly at each of them in turn. "But it's just how I am 'cause that's how you guys and everybody else my whole life's ever been to me, okay? So maybe if *you*" —he glared at Ella— "quit acting like everything's my fault and *you*" —now he turned to Andrew— "quit acting like I'm not worth anything, and you" —he only half-turned to Kindle— "quit calling *me* names, I'll quit acting like the useless jerk you think I am." When he finished, Tad crossed his arms and set a boiling glare past his shoulder.

Kindle felt obligated to find something to say, but her sudden sympathy for Tad and her own guilt rendered all of her words insufficient. She was sure they were about to endure a long, quiet night when Ella's voice broke the tense air.

"I'm sorry, Tad, I really am. And I'm sure Kindle and Andrew are as well." She paused to let them nod in agreement. "It will change … the behavior among us all. We'll start being a family, just as Azildor wanted us to be. We'll help one another, look out for one another …" Her voice trailed into silence as her eyes met Kindle's then flitted to Tad. "Excuse me. I didn't mean—"

"No, it's okay," Kindle stopped her, knowing she was only apologizing to keep Tad from exploding again. "You're right, we gotta be a–a family and be nice to each other and all that stuff. And we gotta talk to each other like this." Kindle bit her lip; she knew that she sounded nowhere near as eloquent as Ella and wished she could. The moment somehow felt pivotal, as if what she said would turn them either to greatness or failure, and she wanted to urge them to success.

Suddenly, something that her father lectured to her and Mikey every time they fought jumped into her mind, and she thankfully repeated it.

"We're a family, and we all have to take care of each other like we're one person. Because we need each other." Kindle blushed at the intimacy of her father's adage but smiled at its familiarity. She heard Ella make a throaty sound of agreement and peered up to see her grinning as well. Glancing around, she saw that Andrew also appeared satisfied with her words but Tad was still glowering away from her. Feeling that she still owed him a deeper apology than a nod, Kindle quickly pieced together an idea to talk to him alone.

"Hey, why don't you guys practice sword fighting?" she suggested to Ella and Andrew. Seeing Andrew's eyes begin to calculate her words, she added, "You know, like, it's not dark yet, and when we were with Azildor, he always had us practice around now, and just that—all that at Iteraum, you know—I think it would be good to practice." Kindle thought her explanation sounded flimsy, but to her relief, Ella's face perked up.

"Kindle, that's excellent. All along we should have been sharpening our skills each day." She sprang up and gathered her sword then tossed Andrew his. Andrew lifted it from the ground as if it was a fragile pane of glass.

"I can't," he pitifully argued.

"Oh, what rot, of course you can," she insisted then trotted off to a spot away from the horses. Andrew passed Kindle an unenthusiastic glance, sighed, then slowly plodded over to his eager opponent.

Kindle watched Andrew try to mime Ella's elegant blocks and flourishes until she was positive they were fully immersed in their practice then turned to find Tad.

He was gone.

With a huff of frustration, Kindle spun around to search the green plain stretched out behind her. Since nothing grew on the flat land except the short grass, Kindle soon spotted him and was on her feet jogging to catch him.

"Hey," she said once she was at his shoulder, "where're you

going?"

He shrugged and curtly replied, "Nowhere."

"Oh." Kindle nodded as if she understood but truthfully had no idea how to take his answer. She had thought their chat had resolved the problems between everyone, but Tad seemed more irked than before. As she kept pace with him, Kindle tried to determine what could have pushed him into such a standoffish mood but finally concluded it best to simply ask.

"Is something wrong?" she tried but received no answer. "Tad, I know something's wrong. What is it? If it's about what you said, I really am sorry for calling you a jerk. I didn't know it bothered you like that. Ugh—I know that sounds lame, but I really am sor—"

"It's not that," he interrupted her babbling in a flat, empty tone.

"Oh ... well, what is it? I mean, is it, like, Ella? Because I really think—"

"No." He heaved a frustrated sigh. "Just forget about it, okay? You wouldn't understand anyway."

His assertion only increased her determination to know and comprehend what was bothering him. "What wouldn't I understand?" She smiled playfully, hoping his joy of arguing would spark. When his face remained solid, she skipped ahead of him so she could turn and face him. "C'mon, you can tell me. Remember, we're fam—"

"It's that!" he suddenly exploded, and Kindle had to regain her balance. "It's that stupid word you guys keep throwin' around like it's supposed to make everything okay."

"What?" she started to ask, but he shook his head and gave a cynical laugh.

"See, you don't get it. I told you you wouldn't get it."

He tried to walk away, but Kindle cut him off.

"I want to," she assured him, boldly staring straight into his angry blue eyes. "I want to get it."

His face twitched through a few hints of expressions, as if he couldn't decide how he felt, then he grumbled, "Why? Why do you care?"

Without hesitating or thinking, she responded, "Because I do.

Because I do care …" Her brain caught up to her words, and Kindle's self-consciousness tried to stifle the rest of her sentence, but she brushed it away and quietly finished, "About you. So, why does it bother you?"

Tad looked away as he tried to stuff his hands in pockets he didn't have then crossed his arms instead. "Remember what I told you about my … family?" The last word was so saturated with disdain that Kindle also cringed at it.

"Yeah, you–you live with your grandma."

He scoffed, "And my brat sister. So you know what family is to me?"

Kindle had no idea how to answer but kept her pained eyes on him so he would know she was listening.

"It's people who keep you around so they can hurt you. It's people who use you to get whatever they want then tell you you're a useless failure while smackin' you around so much you can't move till the next day then act like nothing happened and you're an unholy liar if you say anything." He stopped his waterfall of words to swallow hard, and Kindle copied him to suppress her horrified sadness.

"That's … that's terrible," she shakily mumbled.

He sniffed and, trying to still seem uncaring, grumbled, "Yeah, tell me about it."

Kindle found herself shaking her head. "No, we're not gunna be like that to you. That's terrible and–and that's not what family's supposed to be. It's supposed to be, like, looking out for each other, just like you've been doing for me. You are part—"

"No, I'm not," he argued, "I'm not part of anything." Tad started to walk away, and understanding flashed through Kindle's mind.

"You're not or you're too scared to be?" she carefully asked, and he halted. "Is that why you keep running away every time something happens? You don't want to try to keep anything good or try to stay with us because you're too afraid it's all too good to be true or something like that?"

His heavy sigh and averted eyes answered her question.

"Because that's not how it's gunna be," she almost desperately cried then reeled her voice back to a softer tone. "We're really in this— you know, like I said at Iteraum. All this is really real, and you, me, Ella, and Andrew are all in it together to the end. And–and we're gunna stick together no matter what happens, you know? It's gunna be like that … like this, me caring about you. All of us caring about each other."

Tad slowly peeled his gaze from the ground to carefully examine her. From his stare, she could tell he was teetering on the verge of trusting her words but still wouldn't let himself believe her.

"I promise," Kindle breathed, eager to have his trust. "I promise, Tad."

His harsh frown faded, and he lifted his face to the sky. "You don't even know what's gunna happen. Or how long we'll be here."

"It doesn't matter. I'm not gunna leave you, and I'm not gunna stop caring," she resolutely replied and extracted a half-grin from him.

"I don't get you, Kin."

She smiled back. Then, eager to break away from the serious, deep air, suggested, "You wanna go watch Andrew drop his sword?"

DERAILED

The rest of the evening, they took turns sparring with one another until Tad had resoundingly beat each of them and they all fell exhausted around the small fire Ella had built. Kindle had forgotten just how sore and tired sword fighting made her, and a part of her wished she had never mentioned practicing. Thinking about how much fun and laughter it had created, though, led her to happily ponder how she could possibly team with Ella to overcome Tad's quick, fierce offense. She was sure she had crafted a solid plan, but when Kindle woke up the next morning, she had forgotten it completely.

As they crammed down their breakfast while they prepared to leave, Kindle noticed that Andrew, Ella, and even Tad were getting along much better than the previous day. Ella and Tad didn't argue about who should clean the fire debris or anything they usually did, and Kindle thought she heard Andrew ask Tad for a hand while loading the horses. Once they cleared the camp, they headed off with the river as their guide. Besides a few random conversations, the day passed uneventfully, and Kindle felt relieved to escape its monotony when she saw the sky begin to discolor and they stopped to make camp. Just as the previous night, Ella tried to reshape Andrew's clumsy form before he gave up and Ella, Kindle, and Tad challenged one another to playful frays until the sun finally set.

The next morning slid by just as smoothly and routinely. They quickly erased the traces of their night's stay, then climbed on Nasah and Nox, and recommenced their eastward trek. To keep herself from the aching boredom she had endured the day before, Kindle rode beside Ella so they could banter through the long hours. As the sun climbed higher and their stomachs started rumbling, their talk inevitably turned to food.

"Seriously?!" Kindle gasped at Ella, whose face was confused. "You guys seriously don't have chocolate here? Oh, man, I'm gunna die."

"Whatever do you mean? What is it? Is it some sort of necessity?" Ella questioned, still lost.

"Only if you're a girl," Tad laughed from the ground. He and Andrew were walking beside the horses, listening to Kindle try to explain their world to Ella.

"No, seriously, it is," Kindle insisted, ignoring Tad and Andrew's snickers. "It's, like, so yummy and … just, like, the best thing ever. Ugh, I wish I had some."

"Alright …" Ella seemed to be mulling over what Kindle had poorly explained.

"It's candy," Andrew helpfully added. "It starts as a cocoa bean, then people add sugar and milk to it to make it taste sweeter."

"Oh, it's a sweet." Ella smiled, finally comprehending. "I don't believe any place in Anelthalien makes chocolate, but from what I've heard, towns do have their own special sweets. Garrick is known for its ginger roasted peaches."

"You guys got ice cream?" Tad butted in and elicited another odd stare from Ella.

"Well, perhaps they have cold cream in Turner …"

"Forget it." Tad shook his head.

"Ooh! What about peanut butter? You guys have peanut

butter?" Kindle asked in a rush, full of excitement.

"Peas?" Ella hesitantly inquired, but Kindle shook her head.

"No, like, that awesomely nutty, creamy stuff you put on bread. Like, everybody loves peanut butter where we live."

"Crunchy's better," Tad argued.

"I've never had peanut butter," Andrew mumbled then smiled at Kindle's affronted gasp.

"Are you serious?! Like, do they not have peanut butter in New Jersey?" she blurted before she could evaluate how silly her question sounded.

Andrew shrugged. "I'm allergic to peanuts."

Kindle sighed in relief, but Tad eyed the thin blond boy beside him.

"You one of those kids that's allergic to everything?"

Andrew returned his inquisitive stare but replied, "Not everything. Nuts, pollen, dogs, and lactose or casein … I'm not sure which."

"Casein?" Tad made a sour face at him.

In a perplexed, distant tone Ella asked, "What is that?"

"A protein in milk. That's why I'm not sure if it's—"

"No, *that*," interrupted Ella as she pulled Nox's reins and reached for her bow. Realizing she meant something outside of their conversation, Kindle lifted her eyes to scan the plain. At the same time as Tad unsheathed his sword, she saw it. An indistinct bobbing mass of dark colors loomed in the middle of their distant path. Kindle leaned forward and squinted to determine what it was but gained nothing more about it except a sense that it was moving toward them.

"Is it … is it an animal?" Kindle guessed, hoping it was not.

"No," Ella slowly replied, "Men … Four men on horses."

Her answer didn't relieve Kindle's anxiety. She stared hard at the mass again to see if it truly was heading their way. Just then, a small rectangle appeared over the group, and Ella uttered a noise of understanding.

"They're from Aryl."

"The town near Xylina Forest?" Andrew knowingly asked, and

Ella nodded.

"Yes, but it's more of a small city, really. I don't believe they'll bother us …"

"You don't *believe*?" Tad glared at her. "'Cause I'm not gettin' cut up because you don't believe—"

"They raised their flag," Andrew calmingly interjected. "If they were enemies, I doubt they would have shown us who they were."

"Yeah, only if they were pansies," Tad argued and lifted his sword as if he was ready to fight the still distant approaching figures. "So I'm bettin' they're gunna cut us up."

Ella gave the back of Tad's head a disproving head shake then expectantly looked at Kindle and asked, "What do you say?"

"Uh …" Kindle grimaced, painfully aware that she would have to make a decision. To stall for time to think, she squinted at the horsemen again. They definitely were closer and riding straight to them, but as far as she could tell, nothing about them appeared threatening. The four men, who all were some degree of portly and carried quite dull expressions, were outfitted in the same midnight blue uniform and matching tams with ruby pink pom-poms. Overall, they looked like a team of mediocre, middle-aged golfers.

"Let's see what they say," declared Kindle, wishing she sounded more decisive. "I mean, they don't look like they even have swords."

Tad flashed a begrudging look back at her, but Kindle, knowing they didn't have time to argue, simply urged, "Put your sword away, okay?"

Frowning as though he had been robbed of a treat, Tad slid his sword into its sheath. "Happy?" he grumbled.

"Yeah," Kindle whispered, seeing that the men were almost to them. "So everybody act friendly, okay? And–and if they ask, we're just traveling through."

Ella seemed as if she wanted to protest Kindle's second command, but at that moment one of the men called out.

"Ho! Strangers!" The man with a beard called and raised a hand. Kindle sheepishly waved back, but wasn't sure how to respond, so kept silent. When the men came within feet of them, they finally pulled their horses to a halt. The bearded man urged his horse slightly ahead of the others and then eyed them haughtily. Even though his round face reflected his girth, he had a long, thin, pointed nose and dark, squinty eyes that gave him an air of sharpness. He turned his nose up higher as if sniffing them then asked, "Who are you? Where do you come from?"

Kindle bit her lip. Even though she had just told the others what to say, she was starting to doubt that she had made the right decision and couldn't bring herself to answer. To her relief and surprise, Andrew spoke.

"We're on our way to Garrick from Fluston."

The bearded man swiped his nose down to Andrew. "Fluston? You adolescents don't carry a semblance of Fluston citizens."

Without missing a beat, Andrew replied, "I didn't say we were native to Fluston."

The man scratched his beard. "Then what carried you down to Fluston?"

"We're doing survey work for Garrick Kingdom. We're on commission to scope the competition of other fishing cities in efforts to improve our own trade selection."

The man squinted so hard at Andrew his slit-like eyes almost closed. Then he twisted around to his three companions and hissed, "Have any of you heard anything about this?"

As they shook their bemused faces, Kindle caught Ella's eye and they also exchanged surprised glances.

"Have you any valid verification of this commission," the man curtly snapped, "or are you a troupe of lying ruffians?"

"Our findings are confidential," Andrew seamlessly lied. "If you would like to view them, you'll have to speak to the king."

"The king—fft," the mustached man behind him muttered in disgust. "Rip off his arms."

"Braon!" the bearded man scolded, and Braon rolled his shoulders and grumbled. "Only a suggestion, Wissen."

Wissen ignored him to flip his nose up at Andrew. "What you

may have or may not have does not matter. Your little excursion ends here."

"What?!" Tad burst, and Kindle saw him reach for his sword.

Out of impulse, she kicked her foot out to stop his action and loudly asked, "Why? Um, uh, we–we really need to keep going and get all of the, uh, important stuff to the king."

Wissen's hard glare didn't flicker. "Well, this is Lord Beryl's territory, so whatever directives that king up north has distributed to you are trumped by his, and he has cut off all travel for the time."

"Please, sir," Ella quickly jumped in, "I know our mission may not appear urgent, but it is. We really can't—"

"You can," Wissen interrupted, "and you will return to Aryl with us. Lord Beryl has ordered that due to a recent wild disturbance in Iteraum, all persons traveling this way are to be stopped and detained until questioned."

"You gunna make us?" Tad threateningly challenged, and Wissen raised his nose at him.

"Is that an intimidation or a dare, young man?" he curiously interrogated. "Because neither really pose a problem for my men Braon, Bard, and Ober." Wissen steered his horse back in line with the other men who puffed their less than impressive chests.

Kindle could see that Tad's hand was creeping toward his sword's hilt again, and her mind began to frantically search for a way to stop a fight from ensuing.

"No—yeah, I mean, it's not a threat or anything," she blurted. "We just don't know the way, so you'll have to take us—that's what he meant. We don't know the way, so are you gunna *take* us?"

Tad turned an incredulous face up at her cheesy smile, but thankfully, none of the men noticed it.

"Yes ..." Wissen slowly replied, obviously suspicious of her shaky words, "we will take you straight to Lord Beryl himself."

"Oh ... great," Kindle tried to enthusiastically reply but had the sense that following them would be the exact opposite of great.

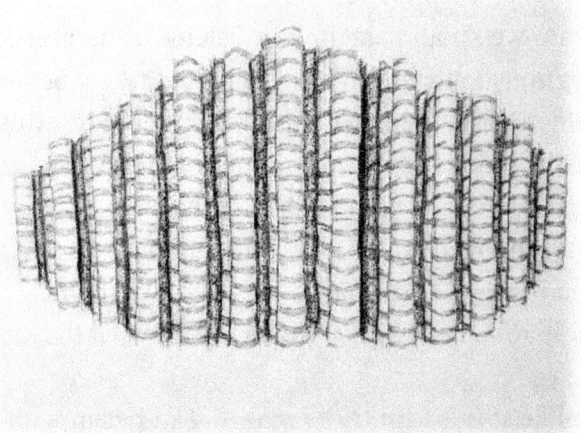

PRETENSE

"You should of let me cut 'em up," Tad grouchily whispered back to Kindle.

Kindle, not really keen on arguing if her impulsive decision was the right one, simply shook her head and sighed. After she had told Wissen they would follow him to Aryl, Tad and Andrew had taken a seat on the horses so they could travel at a faster pace. Since then, they hadn't stopped trotting along even for food and Tad had been muttering his grievances whenever he let Nasah lag slightly behind. Just as every other time this happened throughout the day, Wissen prodded one of his larger companions and, with a swing of his nose, sent him to nag Tad to increase his speed.

"Quit your hoof draggin', you!" Bard called as he rode back to them. "You got to keep up."

Tad gave him an emotionless stare. "Yeah, okay," he dully answered but kept Nasah at the same pace. Kindle huffed. If one of the other men had chastised them, she wouldn't have minded Tad's silent defiance, but through the day Kindle had discerned that Bard was the lowest and dumbest of all the men, and as his round, uncomprehending eyes stared at them, Kindle felt sorry for him.

"Yeah, we should catch up …" Kindle mumbled to Tad even though she grinned at Bard. "We don't want to get behind." She saw Tad's shoulders drop then felt Nasah turn her slow walk into a trot. Satisfied, Bard rode past them to rejoin his fellow riders. Once they had fallen back into step beside Ella and Andrew, Tad twisted around to give her an annoyed glare.

"You just gotta do what everybody says, huh?"

Kindle rolled her eyes. "Either we do what they say or they're gunna make us."

"I'd like to see 'em try to ma—" Tad began with his evil grin on his face, but Ella cut him off in a barely audible voice.

"Stop, Tad. They're likely able to hear you, and Kindle is right."

To avoid the argument Kindle knew Tad wanted to dive into, she quickly asked, "Do you think we're almost there, Andrew? I mean, I thought they said we needed to get there before sunset."

Andrew thoughtfully looked at the ground then softly answered, "I think so."

They all squinted at the horizon ahead to check his accuracy. The only sight in front of them was the forest that had appeared much earlier that day. When they had spotted it, Kindle had been sure something was skewing her vision, but now that it stood closer, she could see that the trees truly were tall, white birch-looking poles all standing oddly close together. Even though she could make sense of the trees, Kindle still could not see any sign of a city. When her mind started wondering if perhaps Wissen had tricked them, Ella let out a sound of sudden comprehension.

"Oh …" she breathed then leaned sideways so she and Tad could hear her whisper. "Do you remember what I told you about Xylina Forest?"

Kindle shook her head, and Tad scrunched his brow while asking, "That?"

Ella nodded and opened her mouth to explain, but Andrew spoke first. "You said … people don't go in Xylina Forest."

"Yes." Ella smiled. "Most of the travelers who come to Garrick pass around it entirely—they circle up 'round the mountains instead. They say it isn't worth the troubles to pass through it—that it has enchanted sounds, and they daze you into circles. I've heard more than one man say there's no way in or out of it, but traders from Aryl pass through it." Ella smiled as if she had disclosed the reason for the missing city, but Kindle felt clueless about Aryl. She considered embarrassing herself and asking Ella to explain again, but then to her relief, Andrew answered her unsaid query.

"The town is in the forest," he mumbled then, squinting harder, continued, "or they built a wall to look like it is."

Ella gave a short nod. "We must be staring right at it and not even know. It's quite clever if that's what they've done."

"So if no one ever goes to this stupid town, why's everybody know about it and why's it on our map?" Tad challenged Ella, and she waved her head at him.

"Now, I never said no one goes to the city—everyone who cares to have listened knows that Aryl lies just west of Xylina Forest, and I am sure that anyone who has given any thought to the matter and stood where we are knows the city lies behind a wall of disguise," Ella promptly explained. "I'm sure anyone could find the city. And many traders have told about their business excursions there. It's the forest hardly a soul enters."

Tad huffed but didn't continue to argue with her. Kindle felt compelled to congratulate him on restraining his pugnacious tendency but then realized the reason for his silence. Wissen and Ober, the largest of the four, were riding their way.

"Ho! Halt!" Wissen importantly called, even though his horse was blocking Nasah and Nox from taking another step. "From your little exchange, I see you have extrapolated the whereabouts of our city. It is obvious, though, as you, Miss … Green, have articulated," he deridingly noted, waving his nose at Ella.

"Ella," she corrected, "My name is Ella, and this is—"

"I do not care," Wissen stuffily interrupted. "Your names will not matter to Lord Beryl, so you do not need to waste my or his time disclosing them. Anyway, as you know, our city lies right behind this barrier. You will dismount and lead your horses through the barrier *right behind* Braon and Bard. Ober and I will tail you. If you move to escape while passing through the barrier, know that you will be apprehended. Now—dismount.”

At his command Kindle, Andrew, and Ella slid to the ground, but Tad remained seated.

“Boy. Off,” Wissen curtly snapped, but Tad suspiciously glared at him.

“Why?” he demanded, his voice full of distrust. “Why do we have to walk and you guys don’t?”

Wissen jabbed his nose in the air before answering, “We and our mounts are much more capable of navigating this barrier than you and yours. Your horses will undoubtedly panic, and without us you will find yourself lost. But if you insist on riding, do.” Without waiting to see or hear Tad’s response, Wissen called for Braon and Bard to press on. He and Ober waited until Kindle, Andrew, and Ella had walked and Tad had ridden past them then spurred their horses close behind them. As they trekked along in their new formation, Kindle knew that any chance of escaping from the men or talking without being overheard by them had definitely ended.

After a long stretch of silence during which Kindle had pondered whether Wissen’s words about the trees were true or just an empty, arrogant threat, they reached the edge of the tall white and brown striped poles. Now Kindle could see that the barrier did not consist of one line of branchless trees but of rows of carefully and closely staggered trunks that all appeared identical. Suddenly, Kindle understood and believed Wissen’s warning.

“Last chance, boy.” Braon smirked back at Tad. “Walk or get ready for a wild ride.”

Kindle peered up at him, internally willing him to jump down beside her. The barrier that separated them from the city of Aryl looked like a confusing maze, and she wanted all of them to see the other side of it together. Tad, though, seemed unaffected by the towering labyrinth ahead and remained motionless in Nasah’s saddle.

Kindle considered whispering a plea Tad's way, but before she formed a convincing sentence, Wissen snapped his fingers and called, "Go on, Braon."

Braon's smile widened, and he mumbled, "Alright then, boy." He and Bard turned their horses to the white maze and one after another rode into it. Ella gestured for Andrew to follow them as she sent an urgent glance back at Tad and Kindle. Immediately understanding the restrained dual desire in Ella to command Tad to obey and to direct Kindle to act as the leading voice to make him do so but knowing neither would happen, Kindle simply returned an apologetic head shake. Ella's stare hardened, but she broke it to lead Nox between two poles. As Kindle caught Nasah's lead rope to follow, she chanced one more nervous look up to Tad. She expected him to ignore her, but he noticed her upturned face, and a disgruntled frown crossed his own. After an agitated huff, he jumped down behind her.

"Happy?" he grumbled so only she could hear.

In the same moment, Wissen barked a triumphant laugh and taunted, "Not as bold as you tout, eh, boy?"

Quickly and quietly, Kindle whispered, "Don't listen to him. He doesn't even know you." She heard Tad release an angry breath, but to her relief, he said nothing. "C'mon," Kindle urged and hurriedly led him and Nasah along the same path Ella had just trod.

After they had zigzagged around just the first few trunks, the green plain behind them vanished and Kindle felt as if she had entered another world. All sound fell out of the air, and the soft pat of their footfalls and the tinkling clicks of the harnesses magnified into startling echoes between the trunks. The odd reverberations pulled Kindle's eyes off Nox's black coat ahead and to the tight forest around her. Suddenly, she felt dizzy. All the white and brown stripes surrounding them melded together into one depth-skewing optical illusion. The swatches of brown on one tree seamlessly connected to lines on the others that stood feet behind or in front of it, making them all appear adjacent. Kindle tired to distinguish one pole from the others, but the longer she stared at the pattern of white and brown, the more all the stripes melted into one spinning mass encircling her.

Unconsciously, Kindle stopped walking as she examined the swaying lines fencing her in, and she sensed panic creep into her mind. The fear that she was trapped in an endless spiral only lasted for a second, though.

"Hey," Tad's voice said, and the illusion of the trees dripped out of her focus as she turned to see him questioningly staring at her.

"Huh?" she replied.

"What're you doing?"

"The trees …" she began, gazing around at them again, "they all, like, swirl together."

"Eyes off the trees!" called Wissen, and they twisted to see him waving his lifted nose their way. "I warned you of their duplicitous nature, and now your miniscule, enervated mind sees why."

"Shu—" Tad started to growl, but Kindle loudly spoke over him.

"Yeah, okay, I get it! Don't look at the trees!" she practically yelled and caused everyone to jump except Tad, who frowned at her for pushing away his attempt to retaliate. "Sorry, okay? And thanks," she quickly breathed to him before resetting her eyes on Nox and resuming her walk.

For the rest of their winding trek through the maze-like barrier, Kindle determinedly kept her eyes from wandering. Most of the time she watched Nox's tail swish back and forth, but whenever the flag that Bard was carrying slipped into view, she examined it. The majority of the flag was the same dark blue as the four horsemen's uniforms, but the intrigue of it lay in the bright, wavy fuchsia line that drifted across the upper half of the rectangle interrupted only by a single off-center fuchsia hexagon. After a particularly long while of staring at the two contrasting tones, Kindle began to wonder if they represented the colors of the whole city, just as the white and green on Iteraum's flag had. She tried to picture a street lined with houses painted midnight blue and adorned with bright pink shutters. The image that her mind conjured looked ridiculous. Kindle closed her eyes to shake it away and, when she reopened them, saw a sliver of the real city of Aryl.

Just from her peek of it, Kindle could tell that no outrageous colors decorated the buildings, and once they twisted past the last few trunks, she saw the city actually appeared incredibly normal. Some houses were constructed of stone, others wood, and all held unique qualities but also seemed to fit together. The neat line of related houses did not run very far in front of them—after only about ten buildings, another tree barrier loomed—but rows upon rows of similar buildings spanned farther than Kindle could see. The structures and layout of the city felt familiar to her, like one of the many subdivisions sitting near her own home in Missouri, and Kindle breathed a relaxed, relieved sigh. With the afternoon sun sinking behind the scene, she almost believed that she was nearly home after a very long day and would enjoy the evening eating dinner with her family then falling asleep in her bed. Kindle wanted to hold that comforting image in her mind until it turned into reality, but Wissen's loud call yanked it away from her.

"You scoundrels, back on your mounts! Hurry it up! Lord Beryl won't sit up all night for you."

This time even Tad followed Wissen's order, and soon they were riding past the numerous streets. Kindle stared down each row of houses, hoping to spot some people. Secretly, she wanted to see a group that resembled her mom, dad, and brother. The city felt so like her home that she was sure she could find familiar faces in it, but the longer they rode, the more her high hope dropped. Hardly any living thing occupied the streets, let alone reminders of her family. When they finally turned down one of the short, empty rows, she exhaled a defeated sigh. Deep inside Kindle had allowed herself to indulge in the fantasy that this place was her home and her family waited for her somewhere in it. Now reality had resurfaced and thwarted her dream, and she experienced a hopeless nausea that she hadn't felt since they were in the Chokmah home. The disheartening prospect of never seeing her family or house again so overwhelmed her that she didn't notice they had halted until Wissen yelled right behind her.

"Braon! What's the delay?" he snapped and rode to the front of the pack. He lowered his voice to an inaudible whisper as he continued to wave his nose at Braon and Bard. Kindle didn't try to hear their conversation but instead gazed at the large, dark wooden building that stood before them. It was taller and longer than any of the other structures they had passed in the city, standing two or three stories and running the length of five streets. The building faced the rest of Aryl as if it was watching the city and was backed by the second tree barrier that Kindle assumed separated them from Xylina forest. Its size and position seemed very deliberate but also very out of place in the friendly-looking city, but its oddest and most ominous quality was the lack of windows on its dark exterior. The only sign that it was a building and not an impenetrable box was the single, simple door that Bard's horse partially blocked. Just as Kindle started searching the door for some sort of explanatory sign, a man, younger than the horsemen but dressed in the same uniform, slid through it.

The young man shook his head. "Lord Beryl does not want visitors."

"Ian," Wissen persuasively drawled, "we understand Lord Beryl's predisposition to shoo frivolous guests in the evening time, but these are *spies*." Wissen deliberately emphasized the last word, and as he did, Kindle noticed Tad and Ella defensively shift.

"We are not—" Ella started to correct, but Wissen energetically waved his nose her way.

"Uh-uh-uh. *Not* what your silver-tongued companion revealed. You four—by whatever title you care to call it—are spies." Wissen grinned at Braon then turned to Ian. "Transfer that message to Lord Beryl and then relate his answer to us."

Ian slowly ran his gaze over each of them, passed a squinty grin up to Wissen, and then disappeared through the door.

"That'll sway him," Wissen mumbled in a self-satisfied way. Braon then Bard began to snicker, but Ella broke apart their pretentiousness.

"You should be ashamed—lying to him. We are *not* spies, and it is an insult—"

"Miss." Wissen sliced his nose toward her. "You are insulting my keen memory with your accusation. I recall your wordy friend there explaining that you four are spies for the king of Garrick, but if you sincerely wish to recant that statement, then that would prove all of you to be twisters of the truth and neither we nor Lord Beryl have need for that sort of riff-raff."

"Yeah," Braon added, flexing his hands. "So which are ya'? Stinkin' spies or rotten liars?"

Without hesitation, Andrew emotionlessly replied, "Commissioned surveyors of aquatic merchandise."

"Cut the fancy talk!" demanded Braon, his face almost as bewildered as Bard's.

"Now, Braon, I wouldn't expect you to understand his colorful wording, but he only answered your question," Wissen mockingly chided then sneered down his nose at Andrew. "They are spies."

Kindle saw Ella heave a frustrated sigh and sensed that she wanted to object but knew it would not change Wissen's mind. Instead, Ella turned a searching face to Kindle, as if asking for help. Having no idea of how to escape their situation but feeling obligated to think of one, she bit her lip for a moment.

"It'll be okay," she decided to whisper, even though she still didn't know what Wissen intended or how to avoid it. Thankfully, Ian reappeared and she didn't have to explain her statement.

"So, has Lord Beryl revoked his prior statement?" Wissen questioned with a conceited grin.

Ian, even though he did not seem happy to, nodded and replied, "He wants to speak with the spies."

Wissen swiped his nose upward. "I suspected so. Braon, Ober, you two take the spies' horses around to our stable. Bard, you go—"

"Hold up," Tad rudely interrupted, "you jokers are not takin' our horses."

Wissen frowned at him. "Lord Beryl requested an audience with you, boy, and in order to do so, you must dismount your horses. I know a boy of your low intellect cannot comprehend—" Wissen began to mock but stopped when he saw Tad reach for the hilt of his sword. He whipped his nose to his fellow horsemen but kept his narrowed eyes on Tad as he commanded, "Eh, change of plans. Braon, you take these juveniles' weapons, and, Ober, you and Bard take their animals."

"Yes, sir," Braon replied, evilly grinning as he rode over to Ella and Andrew. "Hand over all your goodies nice and easy now," he chuckled, and Ella begrudgingly unloaded her sword and quiver into his arms. "Bow?" Braon raised an eyebrow at her as she alit on the ground.

"It's useless, really, without the arrows," she told him while handing him Andrew's sword. "Surely, you know that."

Braon puffed his chest and defensively retorted, "'Course I do." He wrapped a fist around one of her arrows and shook it at them then Ian. "Now, you two over there."

Once they had obeyed and Bard finally figured out a way to hold the flag aloft and lead Nox away at the same time, Braon pointed his arrow at Tad and Kindle. "Now you two's turn. Jump on down and lay out those shinys at your feet. And no funny business, boy!"

To Kindle's surprise, Tad immediately swung out of the saddle, donned his black jacket, and then tossed down his entire sword holster.

"Happy?" he spat and held up his empty hands.

"You too." Braon jabbed his arrow Kindle's way, and she slid down behind Tad and surrendered her weapon on the ground as well.

"Alright, then," Wissen impatiently snapped and also dismounted. "Now, you four follow me …"

Ian cleared his throat, "Uh, Wissen … Lord Beryl wishes to see *only* the spies."

"Only?" Wissen repeated, clearly irked. "Are you certain, Ian? Don't you think it would be the best precaution for me to accompany these spies? We have no idea what they are capable of. I mean, I understand you are only a novice guard, but surely you comprehend the hazard—"

"You've taken their swords," Ian firmly cut into Wissen's insult. "That is enough precaution. Now, whether it suits you or not, Lord Beryl has expressed that he wishes to speak to the four spies alone. If you would like to defy his orders, I will tell him—"

"No, no. You are correct," Wissen blurted in a rush.

"Precautions have been taken, all is well … just be sure to alert me when the meeting concludes. These spies will need their belongings returned."

"Just put their things in the stable. They don't belong in the guards' quarters," Ian slowly replied. Wissen flipped his nose at Ian's words but waved to his comrades, and they trooped down along the left of the wooden building. Once they were out of earshot, Ian stopped watching them and turned to Ella, Andrew, Tad, and Kindle.

"Come in," he firmly but kindly instructed and opened the door for them. Kindle had to nudge Tad, but after a few seconds, they all had congregated in a long, narrow, dim hallway. The only light flickered from torches fastened to the wall, but Kindle could see that the hall ran to their left and right almost the entire width of the building without crossing any other passageway. A door directly in front of them and a few others scattered along the slim passage were the only signs that the hall alone did not make up the entire interior of the building. The dim, empty hall reminded Kindle of a more intimidating and strangely colder version of the Tunnels. She shivered, now keenly aware of how much cooler the hall felt than the outside world and saw Ian glance at her.

"Lord Beryl prefers the cold," he quietly explained her way then addressed them all. "I gather you have not previously gained an audience with Lord Beryl. Before you speak with him, you must know a few … guidelines."

"Guidelines?" Tad snorted, and Ella sprang into the guard's awkward hesitation.

"Listen, please, we are not spies. We have not committed any crime or done anything to disturb your lord or the city, and we mean no harm. We're only passing through, and we really do need to return to our journey, so please, could we just go?"

Ian sighed as he shook his head. "No. Lord Beryl desires to speak with you, so you will speak with him. Now, do not speak until Lord Beryl addresses you, and when you do speak, address all of your comments to Sir Aryl, but never look at Sir Aryl when speaking, only Lord Beryl. Do you understand?"

"What?" asked Kindle, sure she hadn't heard him correctly. "Who's Sir Aryl?"

Ian gave her a sidelong look, as if analyzing her question, then replied, "It will be apparent. Do you understand?"

"Yeah, whatever—don't talk to Beryl, don't look at Aryl. We get it, okay? We're not stupid," Tad grumbled with more agitation than usual. Kindle glanced at him and saw his arms were locked to his sides and his hands were jammed so far in his jacket pockets that it was squeezing him. Apparently, he felt and hated the chilly air as well.

Ian gave him an odd look but tipped his head in a nod as he sighed, "Alright." He bent to unlock the inner door, pushed it open, and gestured them through. Kindle expected him to follow them through the doorway, but instead, Ian swung it shut as he whispered, "Good luck."

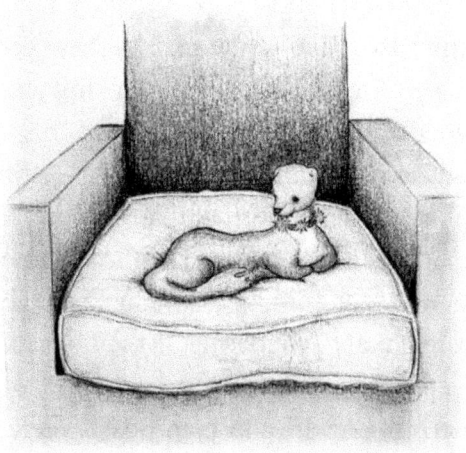

ARYL

"What?" Kindle impulsively asked, staring at the door, but Ella made such a careful shushing noise that Kindle forgot her query to stare around the room. Its square shape and the occupant sitting on one of the two simple wooden thrones directly across from them were the only differences from the hall they had just exited. Without warning, the man on the right throne boomed, "We have guests, Aryl! It must be those spies, Aryl! Wipe your face, Aryl, you look a mess!"

Kindle scanned the room, searching for who the man was talking to. Not seeing anyone, she squinted back at who she supposed had to be Lord Beryl. Even from far away in the poor lighting, she could see he was an extremely fat, ridiculous-looking man. Most of his face was hidden behind his thick brown beard and eyebrows and occupied by his large, square-ish nose. She couldn't see if his head was covered with matching hair due to the floppy blue tam with an especially puffy pink pom-pom engulfing everything above his ears and eyebrows. The rest of his clothing only added to his silly, eccentric appearance. White and mint green stripes ran over the shirt that painfully stretched over his midsection and gave the effect of an ugly, over-stuffed pillowcase. The same pale green covered the pants squeezing his meaty legs and the soft cloth slippers on his feet. The paramount of his bizarre outfit, though, was his enormous, furry midnight blue housecoat trimmed with fuchsia puff balls. To Kindle, he looked more like a circus performer than a ruler of a city. She gazed around the room again just to make sure the real Lord Beryl wasn't hiding out of sight. As she did, she saw her companions' faces and knew they too were likely wondering if they sat in the middle of a weird prank.

"Invite them in, Aryl!" the man bossily cried. "Tell them to step up and explain their reasons for coming to my city, Aryl!"

After a long pause, Ella hesitantly whispered, "I think we should do as he says."

None of them moved.

"Aryl, tell these spies to explain themselves or leave! Tell that tall girl in the vest to speak, Aryl!" Lord Beryl yelled, and Kindle, Andrew, and Tad all turned to Ella.

After lifting her eyes from her vest and momentarily returning their stares, Ella strode across the room to stand in front of Lord Beryl. Ella bent in a quick curtsy then kindly said, "Greetings Lo—uh, Sir Aryl. Pass our humble greetings and respect to Lord Beryl as well. Um, Sir Aryl, my friends and I—"

"Sir Aryl!" Lord Beryl interrupted, "Tell all of the spies to approach our thrones! I want to see them, Aryl, tell them that!"

Sir Aryl still said nothing, and Kindle wondered if he was possibly Lord Beryl's imaginary friend. The man certainly *appeared* loony enough to talk to someone who didn't exist. When she followed Tad and Andrew to Ella's side, though, Kindle realized that Sir Aryl was very real and Lord Beryl was crazier than she had thought.

A weasel perched on the cushion of the second throne. Completely forgetting Ian's rules, Kindle stared at the creature. It seemed to be a normal weasel—its size was ordinary and light brown fur covered its shovel-like head and back while white ran under its chin and long belly—except for the pink pom-pom collar around its neck and the absence of its eyes. At first Kindle supposed she just couldn't see its eyes from where she stood, but at the sound of Lord Beryl's voice, the weasel turned its head, and she clearly saw that black voids gaped where its eyes should have sat. The sight stirred her stomach into a knot, and she wanted to look away but kept staring.

"Hey," Tad hissed out of the side of his mouth, and Kindle, with a grimace still on her face, turned to him. Tad jerked his head at Lord Beryl, and she blinked at the fat man.

"Was she staring at you, Aryl?!" he incredulously asked. "Ask that girl if she was staring at you!"

"No, I wasn't staring at hi—you. I wasn't staring at you, Aryl," Kindle impulsively lied. "I–I was just looking at your throne. It's nice."

"Aryl, tell all of these spies that laying their eyes on you will result in their unhappy deaths!" Lord Beryl seriously shouted.

"We understand, Sir Aryl," Ella quickly replied.

For the first time, Lord Beryl turned his face to Aryl and commented in a low voice, "That is good, isn't it?" He scratched Aryl behind his ears for a few moments before retuning his attention to Ella.

"Aryl, tell them I am ready to hear their reasons for coming to my city."

"Sir Aryl," Ella steadily replied, and Kindle felt glad that she didn't have to speak to the ridiculous man or his weasel. "My friends and I are not spies, and we did not choose to come to your city on our own."

"Well, who could they be and why are they here, Aryl? Do you suppose these spies want to trick us, Aryl?! Take our minas and our thrones?! Find out who they are and what they want, Aryl—and be clever about it!"

"This is stupid," Tad grumbled under his breath, but Ella spoke over him.

"We are not spies, and we're not trying to trick anyone, Sir Aryl. We don't want anything but to pass through your city and into the forest. You see, we're travelers on a mission—a very important mission—and we need to reach the east of Anelthalien as quickly as possible to complete it."

Lord Beryl returned to petting Aryl as he loudly mused, "She's weaving us a story, Aryl. Oh, you know what I mean, Aryl. Ian told us these four were spies Wissen found for us, but this one's telling us something new ... we can't believe any of them. I know, I know, Aryl. I know we need spies. Yes, Aryl, I know we need them quickly—don't you think I know that better than you. That's right, I do. Now, Aryl, tell them I don't care about their stories or missions or who they're working for—what, Aryl? We should ask? Yes, it would show me their capacities wouldn't it? Alright, Aryl, ask them—the girl who admires your throne this time—ask her about this mission and who has sent them on it."

Kindle felt her cheeks redden. She knew Lord Beryl wanted an answer from her, but she had no idea what response to give. For a millisecond she considered continuing Andrew's false story, but just thinking about doing so roused her guilt and fear of misspeaking and pulling them into more trouble. Knowing she had no chance of crafting a believable lie, Kindle closed her eyes to collect her thoughts, took a calming breath, reopened her eyes to see Lord Beryl, and divulged, "We need to get through your city and the forest and all that to go east because we're going to stop an evil king. And, like, we're not gunna kill him or anything because we can't. We're going to destroy his throne because it's got this evil magic stone in it, and we have to do that because if we don't, the next evil king is probably going to destroy all of Anelthalien." She paused to sigh at his dumbfounded expression.

"I know all that sounds weird and crazy and stuff, but it's true and ... ugh, and we should have just told you all that in the first place because that's what we're supposed to be doing too, because if you and everybody else knows about this evil king and his throne, then maybe it won't happen. Like, if you know he's coming, you can be ready for him. You know? Um, Sir Aryl." Kindle tried to assess his face for understanding but saw no sign of it. Feeling as if she hadn't explained their mission very well, she nervously bit her lip.

Lord Beryl remained silent for a long time, and she began thinking of how to better communicate the truth that even she still had trouble comprehending even though she had its proof hanging around her neck. Remembering her necklace, Kindle fished it into her palm and held it for Lord Beryl to see.

"And the only reason we know we're supposed to do all that is because of these—we all have one. No person really sent us to do all that, well, kind of, but he said that these necklaces found us because we're supposed to get rid of the evil throne and tell everybody about it. So, I guess it's these that told us to do all that … and the queen who sent them to us. But … she's dead." Kindle sighed. When she had started talking, she had been fully convinced that their quest was founded on truth, but verbalizing their mission had made it sound far-fetched. Doubt that the story she had just told was true crept into her mind, and Kindle dropped her chin. The firelight bounced off her necklace and caused the little golden dragon to glitter. It seemed to sway in the pool of red as if trying to catch her attention, and as she watched it, intrigued, another thought entered her mind.

"These are the marks of the makers of Anelthalien. That's how we know this isn't all just made up." Kindle spoke the words more to herself than Lord Beryl. Even though her doubt was still trying to convince her that the whole tale didn't make sense, she wanted to believe every word she had uttered, and the longer she let her eyes remain on the glittering dragon, the more she believed every bit of her explanation.

"Marks of the makers of Anelthalien, Aryl? Is that what she said?" Lord Beryl finally muttered to his weasel.

Aryl twisted his unseeing sockets to Lord Beryl as he opened his mouth to squeak and show two rows of dangerously pointed teeth.

"No, Aryl," Lord Beryl replied as if the weasel had given an intelligible comment. "I don't know what they are either or what they prove, but they do look worth a few minas, don't they? Oh, yes, Aryl, those shinys would be nice to have, but what do you suppose we do?"

In the moment Lord Beryl paused to tip his ear to the silent weasel, Kindle noticed Tad's left hand slide out of his pocket and to his hip. Instantly, she understood why he had donned his jacket earlier and what he intended now. She knocked her elbow into his and covertly shook her head.

"We need to get outta here," he breathed out of the side of his mouth. They didn't have a chance to argue further, though, because Lord Beryl had apparently gleaned an answer from Aryl.

"That may work, Aryl!" he boomed. "And either way, we'll gain their valuables, won't we? Now tell them, Aryl. Tell them I've decided that they are skilled spies and will hire them if they wish or they may leave through the forest for the payment of those gems. Tell those spies that those are their only two options, Aryl—and don't let on to your plan to trap them in the prison."

For a few seconds, Kindle, mouth slightly agape, flicked her eyes between Lord Beryl, Ella, and Tad. She couldn't conceive an answer herself and wasn't sure if she should but also felt less confident about how Ella's honesty or Tad's anger would respond. Then they both fulfilled Kindle's fear.

"Dude, we can hear you!" Tad incredulously shouted.

"And we are *not* spies, and we will *not* give you our necklaces!" cried Ella. "We are leav—"

"Aryl!" yelled Lord Beryl and raised a hand with meaty fingers pinched and ready to snap. "Aryl, tell these spies that if they refuse to choose one of the options you have given, then they will choose to have their heads torn from their necks! Tell them, Aryl! Tell them to choose now, or I will snap my fingers, and you will execute the punishment yourself!"

"Pft!" Tad snorted. "I'm not afraid of a stupid rat!"

"It's a weasel, and you should be," Andrew quickly whispered as he carefully stepped back. "Weasels are known for being much more deadly than they look. They usually don't attack people, but … they could do a lot of damage."

Tad glared at Andrew as if checking him for honesty then turned his narrowed eyes to Lord Beryl and Aryl. As Kindle watched him, hoping he wouldn't do anything rash, she noticed Ella warningly staring him down. Realizing both of them were ready to pounce and seeing nothing except a thousand terrible possible outcomes resulting, Kindle dove into the first evasion plan that crossed her thoughts.

"Can we think about it?!" she cried in a more anxious, pleading tone than she had wanted. As all the pent-up energy around her froze, Kindle steadied her voice and continued, "I mean, like, could we have a while to talk about it and … and think about it? It's–it's kind of a big decision, you know, and we wanna make the right one … Sir Aryl." To her relief, Lord Beryl lowered his hand and laced it with his other on his belly.

"What do you suppose, Aryl?" Lord Beryl asked the unconcerned weasel. "Do you think the spy is lying? Yes, I see your point, Aryl—it doesn't matter, does it? Well, then tell them, Aryl. Tell them I am finished wasting my energy for the evening and will hear their decision in the morning. And, Aryl, tell them to exit and fetch Ian so you can inform him of the arrangement."

"Thanks," Kindle instantly replied before anyone else could object or change their mind. She let her feet travel a few hesitant steps backward to test if her desperate stab at freedom truly had worked. When Lord Beryl ignored her and turned to speak to Aryl, her confidence rose.

"C'mon," she urged the others as a smile lifted one side of her mouth. Then she spun and almost ran across the dim room with Tad, Ella, and Andrew close behind her.

"Yes, Aryl, I do hope those spies choose to stay!" Lord Beryl boomed as they reached the door. "They do seem more capable than those others we sent to that overly embellished—"

Ella snapped the door shut and silenced his voice. Ian, who had jumped sideways to make room for their sudden appearance in the narrow hall, blinked at them in surprise.

"What—?" he began to ask, but Tad grumpily interrupted.

"He wants to talk to you."

Ian blinked. "Excuse me?"

Slowly and rudely, Tad replied, "Crazy dude wants *you* to go in *there*."

Ella huffed in a parental way then kindly explained, "Lord Beryl wants to inform you of our discussion."

"Oh." Ian tipped his head and slightly distrustful gaze to each of them. "Wait here …" Still casting a searching look around, Ian slipped past them and into Lord Beryl's room. As soon as the door snapped shut, Tad reached for the knob that would open their way to freedom.

"Tad, what are you doing?" Ella interrogated before he could turn the knob.

Tad glared at her in disbelief. "Didn't you hear him? He's gunna lock us up if we don't get outta here."

"I really don't believe he will," Ella softly retorted. "He wants our help, and that would be no way to convince us to lend it. And also, we have to give him an answer tomorrow morning—we can't leave."

Tad turned his sneer from her to the door and attempted to twist the knob. Neither the bulb in his hand nor the door budged.

Kindle shot a sideways glance at Andrew, who returned her silent anxiousness then sighed, "It's locked."

After grunting and trying to turn it again, Tad wrapped both his hands around it and violently shook the unmoving knob.

"It's not gunna open," sighed Kindle then bit her lip. She had honestly believed that her plan had plucked them out of trouble, but now she could clearly see that it had not.

"Stupid door!" Tad yelled as he kicked it then spun to face Ella. "Now you believe he's gunna just let us go?"

"Tad—" Ella started to patiently reply but stopped as Ian cracked open the door and stepped into their group. He cleared his throat as he swept his eyes over them then took a deep breath and reported, "Lord Beryl has informed me of the situation and that you require time to consider your answer to his offer. He wishes to provide you with a room for the night. If you will wait here a moment, I need to fetch a guard with the keys to your room." Almost before he finished speaking, Ian took off down the long hall.

Kindle felt some relief wash over her as she watched him hover between a power walk and jog. Just seconds ago, she had been convinced that they were trapped, but now she smiled at the idea of sleeping in a real bed that night. Ian finally reached the single door at the end of the hall, hesitated a moment to unlock it, then disappeared.

"See, it's gunna be okay." Kindle smiled at Tad, whose frown remained unchanged.

"Yes, a room where we can talk this over." Ella nodded but sounded apprehensive. Unsure of what her tone meant, Kindle turned to examine her face, but Andrew's words caught her attention instead.

"He has keys. He's not getting keys."

Before any of them could say another word, Ian reappeared with Wissen, Braon, Bard, and Ober tailing him. Kindle's stomach dropped. If the horsemen's presence had not immediately alerted her that something unwelcome was about to happen, the evil grins Wissen and Braon wore would have.

"I told you," Tad angrily shot between his teeth while they were still too far away to hear him.

Even though Kindle wasn't sure why Ian had collected the four men, she knew she did not want to find out and began searching for an escape route. After a short survey of their surroundings, though, she submitted to the fact that they were definitely locked in the hallway.

"Salutations again, spies!" Wissen merrily called as he arrogantly lifted his large nose. "I hear you have persuaded Lord Beryl to open his abode to you for the night. He is a munificent man."

"Heh, heh, mew-nif-sent," Bard stupidly chuckled and received a brief annoyed sneer from Wissen. Full of fear and adrenaline, Kindle unconsciously eased backward and accidently bumped into Tad.

"Sor—!" she almost apologized as embarrassment burst into her already swirling emotions but lost her thought as Tad maneuvered around her, Andrew, and Ella. Now a barrier between the two groups, he crossed his arms and lifted his chin.

"What're you guys gunna do, huh?" he demanded as if challenging all the blue uniformed men.

Wissen, who shoved his way to the head of his pack, swiped his nose sideways and replied, "Escort you to your night lodgings, *boy*. Or do you have a dispute with Lord Beryl's hospitality?"

Braon and Ober chuckled with Bard this time, but Wissen ignored them to continue, "Because it is entirely in our power to allow you to sleep outside like a flea-ridden dog."

Sensing Tad was ready to lash out at the guard and wanting to avoid an uneven fight, Kindle blurted, "It's fine." She peeled her eyes off Tad's tensing fists and up to Wissen. "Wherever you want us to stay is fine."

Tad turned to give her a questioning glare, but Wissen knocked it from his face as he rammed into his shoulder to push past him. In the second it took for Tad to twist around and reset his hate-filled stare, each of the large guards yanked one of them into a chokehold. Almost simultaneously, a flurry of shouts and swinging limbs ensued. Kindle threw her elbows back in every direction and tried to stomp her captor's foot but only succeeded in allowing Ober to pin her arms behind her back. Vainly struggling, she watched Ella meet the same defeat after loudly chastising Bard while attempting to pull herself free. She also saw that Wissen had easily subdued Andrew, but from the clamor rising from somewhere out of her vision, she knew Tad was still fighting.

"Argh! Boy!" shouted Braon, then a wooden *thud* followed by a sickening *crack* sounded. Kindle tried to twist to see who was dealing and receiving the blows, but Ober began shoving her down the hall.

"Wissen!" she heard Ian yell, "Is this necessary?!"

Wissen swung his nose triumphantly over his shoulder and cried, "Do you have eyes? These spies are clearly dangerous! This is a necessary precaution." Wissen pointed his nose and squinty eyes Kindle's way. "Pick the girl up if you have to, Ober. You are by far heftier than her. You as well, Bard."

Kindle felt the floor drop away from her feet and kicked them wildly. The movement, though, intensified the tightness of Ober's enormous arm across her throat, and she soon stopped.

"Where?" Ella coughed and pulled her chin up. "Where are you taking us?"

Another thud and shout rang out behind them, and Wissen lazily turned to see what had caused them.

"Braon! What are you doing?" he griped, "Get that boy under

50

control!"

Braon didn't answer Wissen but grunted then panted, "Ian, his feet ... now!" Kindle heard Tad roar in frustration and knew he had finally been caught as well.

"I asked you ... a question," Ella struggled to remind Wissen, but he resolutely ignored her. Undeterred, she continued, "If ... if you harm us ... Lord Beryl will know ... know you disobeyed his orders."

Wissen had put a hand out to unlock the door in front of him but halted to laugh, "Miss Green, you have absolutely no perception of Lord Beryl's orders. We are executing his wishes exactly as he administered them." Then in one smooth twist, Wissen unlocked the door, shoved it open, and pushed himself and Andrew through it. Bard, still half-choking Ella, quickly followed, and then Ober, panting from carrying Kindle, waddled after them.

When the room opened around her, a constrained groan escaped her lips. Past Bard and Wissen, she saw a few wooden cells illuminated by torches hanging between them. The two in her vision were narrow wooden rectangles fronted with dark metal bars. Wissen peered in each one then turned left to continue his investigation. Bard and Ober herded behind him, and as they did, two long rows of the dim cells spread out in front of Kindle's eyes. She uttered another defeated noise.

"Here," Wissen announced and ended his search to unlock a cell. He cracked the bars open only enough to squeeze Andrew through then grandly slammed the door shut as if he had accomplished a difficult feat.

"Here," Bard repeated Wissen's word as he presented Ella to enter the cell next.

"No, Bard, you insipid fool." Wissen wagged his nose impatiently. "The spies cannot share a cell. They could wind their skills together and escape. We must divide them."

"We must—" Ella started but gasped to catch her breath and yank on Bard's restraining arm. "Choking!" she cried, and Kindle saw Bard slightly loosen his grip. Ella breathed deeply then resumed her statement. "We must discuss Lord Beryl's offer. He expects an answer

51

from us in the morning, and we cannot come to an agreement if you separate us."

Wissen's expression soured. He glared at Andrew peering between the bars of his cell then turned to point straight across the aisle. "Put that one in there, Ober," he ordered, and Ober promptly lugged Kindle to her designated cell. Wissen watched Kindle attempt to squirm and kick out of Ober's hold as he sauntered over to unlock the cell's door.

"Thanks, boss," Ober panted as he crammed Kindle into the crack Wissen created.

Wissen jabbed his nose into the air and declared, "These spies would not be such a difficulty if you were capable of apprehending them. Hmm … Bard! Lock Miss Green next to that young man. Ober, aid him if he appears inept." The arrogant guard dropped his key ring into Ober's chubby hand then drifted down the aisle. Almost positive he was after Tad, Kindle sent a seething glare at his back until he rounded the last cell and disappeared. The snap of the door to the hallway confirmed her assumption, and she sighed in frustration as she settled on watching Bard and Ober try to maneuver Ella into the cell just left of Andrew's. Each time one of them tossed her backward into it, the other would fumble with the keys long enough for Ella to dash to the opening and almost slide past them but end up tangled in one of their chokeholds again. The third time the cycle repeated, Kindle shouted to cheer on her friend's escape, but at the same time several other rackets overpowered hers.

A bang echoed around the prison, and a chorus of angry voices erupted. Then Bard yelped and flung Ella back into the cell as she cried out with what Kindle thought sounded like an apologetic tone. What Ella said, though, Kindle had no idea because Tad was very loudly shouting every insult he could at the three guards wrestling him down the prison aisle. Kindle gazed around at her vanquished comrades, trying to understand everything that was happening, and noticed Andrew also appeared bemused. He was steadily staring at Bard, who was wearing a tortured expression and holding his arm as if it was in great pain. Kindle watched as Ober finished locking Ella's cell, turned to his friend, dropped his jaw before he yelled Ella's way, and then rushed Bard along the row of cells. When the pair passed Wissen, Ober tossed him the keys, Tad threw a particularly violent threat at the men restraining him, and Ella, after crying his name in shocked disappointment, started adding her reproach to the clamor.

"Here! Over here!" Wissen yelled amid the chaos as he broke away from Tad and pointed his nose Kindle's way. Braon and Ian nodded as well as they could while readjusting their hold on Tad and then toted him to the cell next to Kindle's. She tried to watch the rest of the struggle, but the bars of her cell kept her from witnessing what resulted.

Wissen's metal keys clanked in the lock, and a metallic squeal raked through the room to tell her the door was open. Kindle hoped Tad would make an escape before they could pen him inside the cell, but a grunt from Braon, smash of the door, and a final curse out of Tad told her he was now also trapped. Silence, except for a chorus of battered breathing, melted across the prison. Wissen, Braon, and Ian slowly stepped into her view. All three guards appeared exhausted, but Wissen and Braon's faces showed triumph.

"Braon, Ian, douse the torches," Wissen ordered and received an affronted noise from Ella.

"You can't!" she cried, "We need light to see!"

"Miss, your stipulations on communication with your fellow spies included only proximity, not visibility," Wissen smugly construed as Braon and Ian began snuffing the torches. "And furthermore, Lord Beryl only ordered that you spend this night locked in his home, so it is interpretable *how* you spend it."

"Yeah, and we interpret you don't need no light," added Braon.

"Any light," Andrew mumbled, and Braon sneered at him.

"What? You got something to say, little boy?"

Andrew turned his eyes to the floor but repeated, "*Any* light."

Kindle understood Andrew was correcting the man's grammar, but Braon obviously did not. He only scowled at Andrew with a furrowed brow then returned to extinguishing the lights. No one else spoke until only one torch flickered between the two rows on the wall near the door. Ian reached to stifle its glow but stopped when Ella called, "Please. We need light to see. *Please.*"

Even though Kindle wanted Ian to leave the torch as well, she couldn't understand the desperation in Ella's plea. She cared much more about walking out of the cell and Lord Beryl's entire house than having a night-light.

"Douse it, Ian," Wissen's voice demanded before it and Braon's broke into evil laughter. A few seconds later, the slam of the door ended their disgusting chortling, and silence filled the almost entirely black room.

"Please!" Kindle heard Ella beg in a constrained voice. Her friend sounded so close to tears that Kindle felt compelled to help.

"C'mon, please. I mean, it's not gunna hurt anything," Kindle pushed. "You could, like, ask Lord Beryl if it's okay and then go by what *he* says."

Ian sighed, peeled his eyes from the torch, and squinted in their direction. "I will speak with Lord Beryl," he conceded then plucked the light from its bracket and vanished.

When the door clicked shut, a long sigh streamed through the darkness. Even though Kindle couldn't see who had breathed it, she was sure it belonged to Ella. Kindle felt like sighing as well, but due to her determination to maintain her leader role and façade of having everything under control, she bit her lips together and leaned her head against the wall. The resigned posture didn't relieve her inner distress, though, and she almost dropped her feigned calm and burst into tears, but a loud *crack* right by her ear sent her into a confused panic instead.

"Wha—?!" she cried and shielded her head as another *crack* resounded through the wall behind her.

"Tad! Stop!" Ella shouted, her voice still slightly unstable.

Suddenly, Kindle realized that Tad, just on the other side of the wall, was creating the noises.

"No!" his voice snapped back. "Don't tell me what to do 'cause you know what?! It's *your* fault we're in these stupid boxes!"

"My fault?" Ella angrily gasped. "Tad, how can you blame me for this? I didn't want this to happen. How could I know they were going to trick us?"

"I dunno, maybe you could of gotten a clue when they jacked all our swords and locked us in this stupid place!" he raged in return. "I'll kill those stupid—"

"No, you will not!" Ella firmly interrupted. "You will do nothing to those men! And you need to stop shouting those vile threats and vulgar names at them! Do you know that only contributed to the horrid way they treated us?! You need to—"

"Shut up, you—!"

"Stop it!" screamed Kindle, unable to stand their bickering any longer. "Stop it!" Her words echoed a few times, then quiet replaced them. Kindle inhaled a long, steadying breath then released it and told them, "You guys need to quit arguing, it's not gunna make anything better. We're gunna get out of here, and everything's gunna be okay, but you just gotta stop yelling at each other." Her voice and words sounded much more confident than she felt. Internally, she still felt very much like crying and whining about how hopeless their situation seemed. Hoping they wouldn't see through her empty assurance, Kindle waited to hear their responses.

She heard Tad exhale an angry breath and growl, but when he didn't argue, Kindle knew he at least was trying to follow her command.

Ella very quietly sighed, "I'm sorry, Kin. I'm sorry, Tad."

Kindle waited for more but heard nothing. The darkness seemed to extend the silence into an endless pit, and she wasn't sure how to climb out of either. Thankfully, a light appeared at the end of the room, and Ian carried it to the space between their four cells.

"What'd he say?" Kindle hopefully asked, smashing her face into two bars to stand as close as possible to the light.

"As to the light" —Ian shook his head and frowned— "Lord Beryl does not see a reason for it remaining here … but I do have some good news. Lord Beryl has elaborated on the details of his offer. He has decided that if you choose to serve him as spies, he will see that you each own a comfortable home in the city of Aryl with all provisions taken care of. If you choose to give him your, um, shinys, he will repay you with all of your belongings, two more fine horses, and ten minas each. He hopes you will consider his graciousness a gift and choose wisely." Ian sighed in a way that made Kindle wonder if he was hiding something, and his next words revealed the reason for his constrained breath. "That is all Lord Beryl said, but I personally would like to add that, although the offers are good and honest, I do not know if accepting either would be … wise." Ian nervously cleared his throat. "Uh, good night. I will leave now. I would also like to inform you that no one will watch your cells tonight, just … uh, good night." At his last word, he pivoted and quickly walked away, taking the torchlight with him and plunging them into the dark, deep, silent pit once again.

GLIMMERS OF FUSION

K indle waited for someone else to speak. The renewed offers coupled with Ian's strange warning had sent her mind spinning a thousand excited, confused, hopeful, and wary directions, but she didn't want to pursue any of them until she knew what the others were thinking.

However, trying to avoid the delightful guarantee of having her own house in a place that reminded her so much of her own town proved too difficult. As the silence extended, Kindle considered the offer more and more. She knew that accepting a house in Aryl would mean probably never seeing her real home or family again, but she wasn't sure if she would ever return home anyway. The idea of never needing to worry about school or getting food or anything also pushed her to secretly grin. Her mom and dad were always talking about money and nagging her to do well in school so she could find a good job and not have to worry like them, and Lord Beryl's promise to take care of everything obliterated all that worry and difficulty.

In her mind, snatching Lord Beryl's offer to be his spy seemed like the right decision. It was safe and sure. *And* it really seemed like the only good route, considering their options. Kindle knew they couldn't just walk away and finish their mission; the weird weasel would kill them before they could run out of town. Also, if they sold their necklaces to Lord Beryl, they definitely would never leave Anelthalien. If they took the houses and kept the necklaces, though, maybe they would be able to pretend to spy for Lord Beryl but really find the evil throne and return home.

Even though no one could see her, Kindle nodded. They had to become Lord Beryl's spies. Certain it was the right path, Kindle walked over to the bars of her cell and called, "Hey, guys. I think I know what we should do."

"What?" Tad asked then sarcastically added, "Dig a hole out of here?"

"No," she almost laughed. "I'm serious. Andrew, Ella, can you guys hear me? Are you awake?"

Kindle heard footsteps, then Andrew replied, "We can hear you."

"Okay. I–I think we need to be his spies," she declared.

"What?" Tad argued, "I'm not working for that idiot."

"No, listen. We have to be his spies or give him our necklaces and—"

"Or Sir Aryl will tear our heads off," added Andrew, completely serious.

"Um … yeah, but I don't really, um …" Kindle tried to recollect her thoughts but couldn't help visualizing the weasel munching on Andrew's ear.

"I don't care," Tad mumbled and interrupted her mental repulsion. "Let that stupid rat try to get me."

"No. Guys, c'mon, listen. Nobody's gunna get their head chewed off or anything. You heard Ian say that if we become spies for Lord Beryl, he's gunna give us houses and everything we need, right? Well, we could get all that and then just pretend to be his spies but really go and find Letum and the evil throne and all that." Kindle waited for a congratulation on her plan but instead received a skeptical tone from Tad.

"What? You mean just tell him we'll do whatever he wants then leave?"

"Um, yeah. Kind of."

"I don't think so ..." Andrew's voice mumbled.

"Yeah, Kin, dude's right. It won't work. Crazy people like that Beryl dude always think people are out to cheat 'em even when they're not."

"He'd know," Andrew agreed. "If he sent us somewhere, and we never returned or couldn't bring him a believable story, he'd know we were lying. And ... from what Ian said, I don't think we should stay here."

"Then what are we supposed to do? Give him our necklaces?" Kindle retorted, frustrated that both of the boys had dismissed her idea.

"No," Andrew meekly mumbled, and Kindle immediately felt guilty for snapping at him.

"Ugh, sorry. I just ... I thought it was a good idea, and now it's not, and I dunno what to do."

"I say we break outta this stupid place," Tad grumbled, and Kindle heard him kick the wall.

"We can't," she sighed, her frustration giving way to desperation, "there's no way—"

"There is a way," Ella interjected, and Kindle realized that she had been completely quiet until now. Kindle wanted to ask her exactly what that way was, but Ella's uncharacteristic silence and nervous tone prompted her to give her friend space.

Tad, though, either didn't sense or didn't care about Ella's discomfort. "And what's that, huh? You got some dynamite or something?"

"No," she calmly replied.

Kindle expected her to divulge her plan, but when Ella did not elaborate, her curiosity surpassed her patience. "Well, what is it?" she excitedly asked. "Do you think you can get the doors open or ... or is there a window? What do you mean there's a way out?"

Andrew's, not Ella's, voice answered, "We could see some light if this place had windows, and ... the bars are metal. Ella, I don't think there's any possible way we can get out."

Ella sighed very heavily. "No, Andrew, you and Kindle and Tad cannot escape these cells."

Tad snorted. "Are you sayin' *you* can get outta here?"

Before she could answer, Andrew cautiously asked, "Ella, what did you do to Bard?"

"I didn't mean to!" she defensively cried, "I didn't mean to–to hurt him … I only, I couldn't help it. That's never happened before, and I didn't know …" Her voice trailed off, and Kindle hugged the bars of her cell, waiting for her to continue.

"What?" Kindle urged when it became apparent she was not going to finish her sentence.

"This," Ella almost sobbed as blazing fire suddenly illuminated the prison. Kindle had drawn back in shock, but once she realized the fire wasn't spreading, she returned to her cell door. Not believing what she saw, Kindle stared agape into Ella's cell. A large twisting column of yellow and orange flames was dancing over Ella's hands. Slowly, it dwindled until only a small handful of fire sat in Ella's cupped hands. "I didn't know this could happen on its own. I've always thought I could control it."

Kindle caught sight of Andrew's bemused face between two bars, trying to determine where the light was emanating from.

"Show him," Kindle directed and heard apprehensive disbelief in her voice. "Show Andrew what you're doing."

"Kin, please don't be afraid. I know this is terrible, but I can't help it. It's … it's how I've always been."

"Whoa, wait a minute. You could always make fire shoot out of your hands, and you never told us?" Tad complained but also sounded somewhat delighted. "You could have smoked those idiots!"

"No," Ella emphatically retorted. "That is exactly why I never told any of you. I don't want to use this to hurt anyone or for any evil reason." She reached out of her cell and lit the torch hanging between her and Andrew. Still staring up at the flame, she asked, "Tad … do you remember what Azildor told us about witches?"

"What? No," Tad replied, sounding confused.

Kindle searched her memory for anything about witches and why Ella was suddenly interested in them but remembered nothing. Ready to ask Ella what she meant, Kindle looked up but saw deep thought running over Andrew's face and knew he was about to answer.

"They fought the elves in the war," he slowly recalled as Ella closed her eyes and nodded. "And he said the fire spirit made them and ... no good was in them."

"Yes," Ella sighed. "And I try so hard to not let that be who I am."

"What?" Tad asked, and Kindle was sure a confused grimace covered his face. She felt the same puzzlement as she continued to try to piece together everything Ella was saying. As she squinted back at the flickering fire then Andrew's wide eyes, comprehension dawned over her.

"You're a–a witch?" Kindle gasped, the last word sounding odd coming from her mouth.

"No, I'm ..." Ella blew out a steadying breath and blinked at the ceiling. "I suppose I should have told you what I am when we first met, but I was ashamed ... and afraid. I haven't lied about anything—everything I've told you about Garrick and the Lighthouse and my papa, it is true." Ella stopped, her face much more strained and sad than Kindle had ever seen it. She wanted to understand what was bothering her friend and what she was trying to explain but struggled to string together a question that wouldn't probe too deeply.

Finally, she discarded her restraint and admitted, "Ella, like, I dunno what you mean. Are you a witch or not or something else? And, like, why were you afraid to tell us? Did you think we wouldn't like you?"

Ella tilted her head at her and replied, "Don't you know what it means to be a witch?"

"No," Andrew answered, "we don't have real witches in our world. They're just imaginary."

"Well, they are real here ... or were. You know Azildor said they fought in the Great War against the elves, yes?"

Kindle encouragingly bobbed her head, now remembering

when Azildor had spoken about the war.

Ella nodded then began to pace as she continued, "Well, after the war, all the witches who were left—because the fire spirit abandoned them—they all were under the rule of the elves. Of course, the elves didn't care for them at all, and from all I've studied and learned or heard, everyone hated them. I suppose it was with good reason, though … they did almost destroy Anelthalien, or would have if the elves hadn't stopped them. But anyway, everyone despised them. The elves forced them into lives as slaves and peddlers—the witches were not allowed to work for minas or own homes or anything. They could just exist miserably … and soon they began dying. Men and elves began killing them because they didn't see them as people but dangerous creatures that needed to end. Everyone was so afraid of their power over fire that they just killed them. And today I still hear men say how awful the witches were and what a favor their ancestors did by killing them."

"But that was a long time ago," Andrew quietly reasoned, "How can you be a witch?"

Ella suddenly halted her pacing. "I'm not–not sure." She bowed her head for a moment then lifted her eyes to the torchlight again. This time Kindle sensed that she was staring past it to somewhere she, Andrew, and Tad couldn't see. In a very distant voice, she almost whispered, "I remember, a long time ago, a woman sang a song while she held me. She was a very old woman with such strange white skin … and her song, I didn't understand it, but it was so sad. When she finished singing it to me, she told me, 'Your mummy and daddy love you so much, but they cannot be together, and you cannot stay with them.' Then she told me goodbye, and that's all I remember of her. I didn't know what it meant—I didn't understand it at all, and honestly, I tried very hard to forget her and what she said, but … *things* started happening."

"What?" Tad immediately urged and startled Kindle. He sounded totally absorbed in Ella's words, which had never happened before.

After blinking in surprise at his interest, Ella smiled faintly and answered, "Well, I had always been warm, but we lived in Garrick—one of the warmest cities in Anelthalien—so I thought nothing of it until my papa took me to school. When the other children would touch me, they said my arms and hands were so very hot, and I burned a few of them in a chasing game. My papa never made me go to school with the other children again but taught me himself during the day. It didn't stop, though, and I found I could make little flames in my hands if I tried very hard. I never let papa know ... but then one day I was playing in the garden, and a poor little bud was dying, so I picked it and ... and it got better, right in my hands. It recolored and blossomed in a moment, but I heard my papa call my name, and—and I don't know how I did it, but I burned the flower to nothing. My papa, he had seen it all and seemed so afraid. He took me inside and told me I could never let anyone know about the fire I could make or the plants I could heal. He said it would frighten people and they would harm me. So I never let anyone know.

"When he went down to work in the evening, I would stay up in my room and practice making little fires just to stop them and began growing a little houseplant. The older I grew, the more I realized I could do, and I tried more and more ... until my papa taught me about the Great War. He didn't tell me much—he didn't want to—but I read books and listened to customers and found out about the elves and witches and all they could do and how much they hated one another. And then I stopped practicing ... because I realized what I was, and I knew my papa was right."

Kindle, who had been listening so intently her mouth had dropped open, now let her eyes flicker back and forth as she registered all Ella had explained. When understanding clicked in her mind, she slowly concluded, "So ... you're a witch *and* an elf?"

"Yes," Ella reluctantly admitted.

"Well, that's, like, really cool, though." Kindle smiled. "I mean, that's how you fixed my leg, isn't it?"

"Kindle, it is not good. All of Anelthalien would want me dead if they knew."

"But we're not from Anelthalien," Andrew reminded her, and

Kindle nodded.

"Yeah, we're not from here, and we don't care if you're a witch and an elf, Ella. If you weren't, then I might not have a leg or be dead or something. It doesn't matter that you're like that … um, I mean it matters but it doesn't change anything. We're not gunna start hating you. We still like you just the same as we always did, and we still need you."

Ella peered at her with uncertainty. "Truly? Are you sure, Kin? You do understand what I am, don't you?"

"Yeah," Kindle assured her, "It really doesn't matter."

"You can heal things and make fire," Andrew pointed out. "What you can do is … amazing."

"Yeah, and you can get us outta this dump," added Tad with much less tact than Andrew. "So why don't you burn this place down already?"

Ella sent a genuine grin Tad's way but shook her head. "No, I'm not burning anything down."

"Then how are we gunna get out of here, huh?" he argued.

Instead of answering, Ella walked to her cell door and cupped her hands over the lock. Sure an explosion of fire would soon erupt, Kindle walked back a few steps but kept her eyes pinned on Ella. The sound that caught her attention, though, wasn't a resounding boom but a muted *plink*. Kindle searched for the source of the noise but didn't locate it until it repeated itself and she followed Andrew's stare. On the floor under Ella's hands, a small, shiny mass reflected the torchlight. As she watched it, wondering what it was, a rapid series of silver drops rained from above, and Kindle realized that the liquid was falling from the lock.

"You're melting it!" Kindle gasped in awe, and Ella flashed her a shy grin. Another moment later, Ella unwrapped her hands from the metal, releasing a small cloud of smoke, and swung open the cell door.

"Sweet," Tad laughed, and Kindle let his joy spread over her as well.

"Ella, that incredible," she cried, "now we can get out of here!"

"We can't leave yet," Ella replied somewhat apologetically as she started melting Andrew's lock.

Kindle rolled her eyes. "Yeah, I know you have to get us out first, but then we can just go and not worry about Aryl or Beryl or whatever."

"No, Kin, we can't. We need all of our things—our swords and supplies and Nasah and Nox."

"The guards have them," mumbled Andrew, looking somewhat nauseated as he stepped out of his cell and plucked the torch off the wall.

"So we go give 'em a beat down!" Tad viciously snarled, and Kindle saw his hand slash Natzal out of his cell, nearly catching Ella with it.

"Tad, really, put that away," Ella chided, neither fazed nor amused. "We are *not* going to hurt anyone."

Tad retracted his dagger as Ella went to work on his cell but grumbled, "Then what's your plan, huh? 'Cause I don't think those idiots are just gunna hand it over."

Ella sighed, "No, they won't. So we'll just have to take it."

"Oooh Miss Goody-goody wants to steal, huh?" he snickered, and Kindle saw Ella give him a serious stare.

"No. I want to retrieve what was taken from us in the least violent manner possible."

"Whatever," Tad snorted as he strode out into the aisle with Andrew and Ella. Kindle hadn't clearly seen him since the tussle in the hall, and so was surprised when she noticed a large bruise under his left eye. The sight of it also caused a flutter in her chest and a corner of her mouth to lift. Immediately embarrassed by the involuntary reactions, she tried to wipe away every trace of them, but Ella's eye glinted as she walked to Kindle's door.

"Glad to see you smiling," Ella slyly whispered.

Kindle dropped her eyes to avoid Ella's knowing gaze. "I'm just–just really happy to get out," she mumbled.

Ella nodded in return but didn't say a word. As they both silently watched smoke twirl out from between Ella's fingers, Kindle hoped Ella wasn't thinking what she *thought* her comment suggested. Kindle bit her lip and promised herself she would talk to Ella about it once they weren't in Aryl anymore. The jolt of the unlocked door shook Kindle out of her worried thoughts, and she stepped over the pile of melted metal and into the circle of her companions.

"Okay, so now we go get our stuff, right?" she asked Ella, glad to focus on their mission.

"Well, yes and no." Ella's cheer was fully back in her voice now. "I think it best if a few of us stayed here. The guards might come 'round, and if they discover we're gone, they'll come looking for us."

Andrew nodded in consent, but Tad crossed his arms and resolutely declared, "I'm not stayin' here."

"That's fine, I thought you and I would be best to go," Ella agreeably replied.

The comment, though, caused Kindle to frown. It made her wonder if Ella thought she was weak, and in a slightly offended tone, she complained, "Well, I don't want to stay here either. Why can't I go?"

"Kin, you and Andrew are much more convincing than Tad or I. If the guards *do* come, I'm sure you two can say whatever will appease them and keep your temper under control."

Tad sent a disgruntled sneer in Ella's direction, but it broke into his half-evil grin. "C'mon," he laughed, "I'm ready to go shank 'em."

"I'm going too," Kindle interjected. Her hurt had evaporated, but her determination had not. "The guards aren't gunna come around to check on us—Ian *told* us that—and if they do and nobody's here, it's not like they'll know where we are."

"They'll know we're somewhere in Lord Beryl's house," Andrew noted, and Kindle turned wide, agitated eyes at him. Andrew lowered his gaze and added, "They will. All of the doors are locked …" His voice trailed off, but his eyes continued to calculate. Knowing that whatever he would soon say—despite how annoying it might be— would probably be right and helpful, Kindle waited for him to piece his thoughts together. After a few moments, his stare traveled to the gaping cell door behind Kindle.

"If they do come, they'll bring lights just like Ian did," he slowly deduced. "They'll see these doors open and know we can get through the other locked doors. They'll look for any doors that are open. They'll know where we are."

"So, what, you want us just to forget it and not do anything 'cause they'll find us anyway?" Tad angrily snapped at him. "That's a pansy move."

"Stop," Ella chided, but Tad threw his hands up in exasperation.

"Fine, whatever! If you don't want to get out of this stupid place, that's *your* problem." He unsheathed Natzal and started to stomp to the door.

At the same time, Andrew very lightly murmured at his shoulder, "That's not what I said."

Kindle, hearing him, sprang after Tad and, once she stood in his way, urged, "Wait, okay? That's not what he meant. We're all gunna get our stuff and get out of here together, but you just gotta wait so we can figure out how."

His lips twisted as if he wanted to object or snarl, but he finally exhaled and grumbled, "'Kay."

"Okay." Kindle smiled, relieved he had complied, and they walked back to Ella and Andrew. "Okay," she repeated. "So we'll all go." She noticed hesitation cross Ella's face and shook her head. "No, Ella, we've got to go together—every time we've split up so far, it's been bad. A–Azildor told us to stay together, remember? So that's what we have to do." Kindle paused to send a nervous glance at each of them, hoping to gain some sign of consent. Even though they had elected her as the leader, she was still afraid to decide anything that made any of them mad. Once a grin crept onto Ella's face and she nodded, Kindle breathed in relief and continued, "Okay, so we're all going. And we'll just get our stuff and go and not let anybody see us or stab anybody ..." She glanced at Tad, who rolled his eyes but sheathed Natzal. Then Kindle peered at Andrew and meekly asked, "So ... how do we do that? You know, and not get caught?"

Andrew didn't immediately reply or move, but after a few moments, he turned his head back and forth, squinting as if he was examining something invisible. When he peeled his eyes from their search and turned them to Kindle, he answered, "When we were outside and Wissen took the horses, I noticed this whole building is attached. This prison is at one end, and the guard room, which is where they put all of our stuff, is at the other end. We need to get to the other end of this building without using any doors."

"Um … okay. So what *do* we do?" Kindle urged.

A corner of Andrew's mouth lifted. "We go around outside. All of the doors are locked from both sides, and this building doesn't have any windows, so I doubt that any guards patrol outside, especially at night."

"But what about Ian?" Kindle warily asked, "Wasn't he outside when we first got here?"

"No, Braon did have to knock, didn't he?" mused Ella. "And no one was anywhere near this place except us. That's brilliant, Andrew, to go outside. None of them will know to look there."

Tad crossed his arms and wrinkled his nose. "Yeah, real smart. How do we get outside? You forget about that?" he negatively interrogated.

Andrew, with subtle disgust perched on his lips, steadily stared at Tad. As the boys glared at one another, Kindle wondered if Andrew was finally going to snap and attack Tad, but soon Andrew broke the face-off to peer hopefully at Ella. "Can you get us out?"

A pained expression crossed her face as she replied, "Andrew, if you mean burning down a wall—"

"No," he interrupted. "If you could burn a hole by the ground just big enough for us to crawl through, you could build it back."

Ella blinked at him, shaking her head slightly. "I don't understand. I can't rebuild walls."

Andrew dipped his head then squinted back up at her. "You said when you picked up that dead flower, you made it grow. The walls are wood. They're just dead trees, and you can probably make them grow back also."

"That was a long time ago, though," she argued, "and it was the only time I ever revived anything dead. I really don't—"

"Why's it matter if you fix the stupid wall?" Tad interjected. "Just burn a hole in it and forget about it."

Ella sent a hurt glare his way. "Didn't I already say it? I don't want to destroy things. I don't want to become what the witches were long ago, burning and ravaging against everyone."

"Ella, you won't be," pleaded Kindle, desperate to salvage their only escape route. "It'll just be a little hole, and it'll be helping all of Anelthalien, remember?"

At Kindle's last word, Ella stared down at her hands and sighed, "I hate having this power."

"Oh, come on, get over yourself!" groaned Tad, "They're right—you can get us out of here and do the right thing and all that junk, but you standing there crying about how much you don't want to do anything isn't helping anybody. You know what it *is* doing? It's giving those stupid guards more time to find us and lock us up again and that stupid evil guy time to do whatever he's gunna do to your stupid home. So shut up and use your stupid power for something good."

The whole time Tad had berated Ella, she had stared wide-eyed at him. When he finished and she kept her green eyes locked on him, Kindle was sure she would return a much more eloquent but equally stinging fire. Ella said nothing, though. As the tense silence lengthened, Kindle found herself wishing someone else would speak, but when it became apparent that the others had no words, she peeped, "Could you just … try?"

"Huh?" Ella furiously blinked as if awakening from a dream. "You're right, Tad. If I don't use my power now for good, I'm allowing more evil into the land." With an unsettling expression of fear on her face, she gazed at each of them as she whispered, "How long have we all sat useless like this?"

"Too long, okay?" Tad growled, grinding his teeth in impatience.

Ella decisively nodded and snapped into a determined

demeanor. "Where should I burn the hole, Andrew?"

Instead of answering, he disbanded from the group to enter the cell Kindle had been trapped in. He walked to the wall and held the torch down near the floor. As it illuminated the contents of the cell—a pile of hay and a rusty bucket—Kindle felt even more grateful that she didn't have to reside in it all night.

"Here." With the torch, Andrew directed to the area behind the bucket.

Ella entered the cell, politely scooted the bucket aside, and held one finger up to a spot just a few inches up from the floor. Kindle started to approach her but decided to hang back at the bars to watch. Just as a thin stream of smoke began to twist from the spot Ella had chosen, Tad leaned on the opposite side of the bars beside Kindle and whispered, "This is gunna be insane if it works."

Suddenly, a small fire breathed into existence, and the wood of the prison wall cracked under its power. Kindle flashed a smile back at Tad and laughed, "It's gunna work." When she returned her attention to Ella, who wrapped her hands in a circle around the flame as Andrew slightly retreated, Kindle felt joy lift her heart. Even though anyone else viewing the scene would have probably only seen a bunch of teenagers vandalizing someone's home, she saw what was really happening. For the first time, they were all unified. All four of them were intently watching the fire together, hoping for the same result, waiting to pursue their shared goal. The sense of unity felt unfamiliar and somewhat unsettling but also so refreshing and empowering that Ella's earlier question replayed in Kindle's mind: how long had they been useless by arguing with one another? Azildor had told them what seemed like so long ago to work together, but until now the importance of doing so hadn't struck her. Now, as they all stared hopefully at the darkening wooden circle, Kindle was confident that they could actually accomplish what they had set out to do.

FIRE KINDLED

"This is awesome. This is so awesome," Kindle practically squealed in delight. The wooden circle that Ella was burning in the wall was beginning to crumble away to reveal a moonlit patch of soil.

Still carefully corralling the fire, Ella asked, "Once we're outside, what is your plan?"

Kindle suspected she was speaking to Andrew, so she eagerly peered at him. At the same time, though, he looked to her for an answer. They each stood silent, using their eyes to urge the other to declare a plan, but neither voiced one. Finally, Kindle gave in and guessed, "Well, I thought we'd just go around to the guard room and get everything and go." The process seemed so simple to her. She wondered why Ella even wanted her to outline it.

"We'll need to go around front," Andrew added, his voice expectant.

Kindle realized he wanted her to keep explaining, but having nothing to add, she shrugged.

Andrew sighed. "We'll need to go around front," he repeated, "because I think the back of this place sits right by the forest. The moonlight looks bright enough that we can see, so we'll put this out and leave it here." Andrew nodded at the torch.

A change in light swept Kindle's eyes from the torch to the wall in front of Ella. Her fire had disappeared and left a substantial hole just above the floor. Kindle smiled, and Tad banged the bars by her head before laughing, "Sweet." He strode into the cell and toward the hole, but Ella held up a hand to stop him.

"Wait." She grinned at Tad before turning to Andrew. "After we make it 'round the building, then what? Do you suppose I'll need to burn another hole?"

Andrew thought for a moment then slowly shook his head. "I'm not sure. When Wissen took everything, he didn't go through the hall to the guard room, so it must have some kind of outside entrance."

"I thought you said we couldn't use any doors," Tad challenged but sounded intrigued. Kindle eyed him, wondering if the idea of breaking through a door was exciting to him.

"We might not have to," Andrew answered. "He also took the horses, so they're probably tied up outside or in a stable. If we can just get to them, we might find everything else. But if that's right, it means we can't use your fire. It would scare the horses." He gave Ella an apologetic shrug, but she beamed back.

"The plan sounds fantastic, Andrew, and I'm sure we can find another way inside if it comes to it." Ella turned a sly smile Tad and Kindle's way. Unsure of what she meant, Kindle almost asked, but in the next second, her friend whispered, "Alright, Andrew, put that out. Tad, you go on first, then Andrew, and then Kindle, and I won't be long behind."

Andrew nodded and stuffed the torch into the bucket near his foot. Almost instantly, its light faded, and he carried the smothered torch out of the cell. Kindle squeezed her eyes shut to help them adjust to the darkness, and when she opened them, Tad was already partially outside.

"Tad," Ella urgently whispered.

He finished his exit before poking his head back inside.

"What?"

"Wait for us once you reach the other side. And ... don't do anything rash."

Without answering, he retracted his head and vanished. As Andrew clambered out next, Ella shook her head at Kindle. "I hope he listens," she sighed with a half-grin.

Even though Kindle didn't think Tad would, she replied, "I think he will."

Once Andrew had finally unartfully tumbled through the hole and dodged out of sight, Ella waved to Kindle. "You go on."

Kindle followed her direction and walked up to the cavity as Ella backed away from it. Before Kindle dove through, she glanced sideways and saw a trace of concern flit across Ella's face. When she fully turned to stare at her, though, the nervousness had gone.

"What?" Kindle probed, anxious to know what had caused her usually cheery, confident expression to falter.

Ella peered away from her, as if trying to fabricate an answer but then shook her head and locked eyes with Kindle. "I don't know if I can fix it, Kin," she admitted.

Comforted by the fact that nothing more was wrong, Kindle almost laughed as she replied, "Well, why not? I mean, you're an elf, right?"

"Yes, but ... I've never done anything like this."

Kindle ducked and crawled through the hole as she thoughtfully retorted, "Well, I've never snuck out of anywhere, or re-stolen a horse, or talked to a weasel ..." She stood and stepped aside to make room for Ella. As she broke into the moonlight, Kindle noticed that her skin looked almost white. Without letting Ella see, Kindle peeked at her own hand to see if it appeared just as fair but found it was almost invisible under the cover of the darkness. Returning her stare to Ella, who was contemplating the hole, Kindle wondered why she had never really noticed how strikingly unique Ella's fair skin and dark auburn hair were. Until now her companion had seemed so normal compared to the onslaught of strange creatures and people in Anelthalien that she hadn't realized her differences.

Seeing her in the new light made Kindle wonder if she really knew Ella at all, and an uncomfortable feeling wound through her, pressing her heart to yearn for her familiar home again.

She rubbed her neck to calm her sudden fear and inadvertently brushed her fingers across the chain of her necklace. The warm little metal string seemed such a part of her now that it eased her tumultuous mind and stomach. She twisted it around a finger to comfort herself further, and the reassurance that she had come to know it to deliver filled her. Without knowing exactly where her words blossomed from, Kindle continued her earlier thought. "But we *are* here, doing all this crazy stuff we never thought we would ... or could do. So, I think you can do this, Ella. I think I know you can."

Ella twisted to curiously peer at her. "You don't sound like yourself. Are you alright?"

Hearing the same voice that she had always known as Ella's returned Kindle's mind to the stable reality around her. "Uh, yeah ... yeah. I'm fine. I just, I dunno. I kind of spaced," she bumbled as she knelt beside Ella, who eyed her with a grin.

"Thinking of someone?"

"Uh—" Kindle realized what she meant and had to exert effort to not yell. "No. Ella, I don't—just, you gotta fix this so we can go."

Ella nodded as she refocused on the wood. She reached a hand to the blackened edge of the circle and ran her thumb along it.

"Kin ... I'm not sure what to do. I don't know how I healed that flower, and I don't know—"

"Ella!" Kindle gasped, excited at her epiphany.

"What? What is it?" Startled, she drew her hand away from the wall.

"You said when you healed that flower, you felt sorry for it. And remember when you healed my leg? You were really scared. Maybe if you feel really sorry about the wall or really afraid about somebody finding it, you can fix it."

"Kindle," she seriously responded, "I wasn't afraid when I healed you, I was doing what I thought was right. And I'm not even sure why I did what I did or how ..." Ella scrunched her brow and tilted her head at the hole. Closing her eyes, she stretched out her arm again. Kindle bit her lip, sure something was about to happen. When Ella's fingertips met the singed wood, the black ash dropped away and the edge of the severed plank slowly crept down. The new wood continued to follow her hand as if Ella was wiping it into existence across the opening. Once the wood connected, she raised both of her hands to repeat the process. Amazed almost into disbelief, Kindle unblinkingly watched until the hole had been completely replaced with new wood. Then Ella opened her eyes, gasped in exited wonder, and beamed at Kindle.

"How?" Kindle began, but Ella grabbed her arm.

"We have to hurry—Andrew and Tad are waiting."

Still connected, they dashed along the side of the building. When they reached the corner, Ella released Kindle so she could sneak a glance around the avenue fronting Lord Beryl's house.

Ella grinned and breathed, "Not a soul. Quickly now." Not waiting another second, Ella broke into a half-crouched sprint, and Kindle followed, copying her posture. Every few steps, Kindle's eyes jumped down a street or over her shoulder to check for onlookers, but no one except Ella existed in her sight. She stumbled slightly after one nervous backward glance and decided to pin her eyes on Ella and the wall beside her. The length of the tall wooden house was longer than Kindle had estimated, and coupled with her terror of being caught at any moment, the span felt like miles. By the time she jogged around the corner, her thighs and side were on fire and she was sure half of Aryl could hear her gasping for breath.

"Took you long enough," Tad snorted, and she spun to search for him. Due to his dark features and clothes, Kindle almost didn't see him sitting by the wall.

"Andrew—where's Andrew?" panted Ella, scanning the area for him.

"Around back," Tad lazily answered, pushing his chin toward the line of white trees.

"Why?" Ella asked, her breathing nearing its normal pace.

"A stable's back there. Just like Einstein said."

Ella trotted past him to check for herself. Kindle remained where she was, still trying to refill her lungs. After sniffing at her, Tad stood, snickering.

"What?" she tried to defensively whisper but simply panted the word.

He shrugged and turned his smile to where Ella was standing at the end of the wall. "What took so long?" he suspiciously asked.

Kindle grinned as she leaned on the wall beside him. "She fixed it."

His head swiveled back to her. "Nah."

"Yeah, she like …" Kindle raised a hand to mime Ella's action but, seeing it didn't carry the same effect, quickly lowered it again. "I dunno *what* she did, but the wood, like, grew back."

He made a somewhat impressed face but quickly erased it as Ella ran back to them.

"Come on, you two, Andrew's found Nasah and Nox," she excitedly whispered, and Kindle, catching her delight, pushed off the wall to follow her.

Tad, though, squinted at Ella and interrogated, "What'd you do, huh?"

Ella glanced at him before hurriedly answering, "Tad, it's not a matter now. If you want to know, I'll explain once we put some distance between this place and ourselves, but at this moment we need to see about our things."

She tried to turn away, but he dared, "Too scared to talk about it now?"

Ella turned an exasperated but good-natured face to him. "You are so insistent. If you come along, I'll tell you as we walk, alright? But we don't have time to spend idling."

Eager to move out of such a conspicuous spot, Kindle bumped Tad's elbow and then bobbed her head as she started walking backward toward the tree line. Ella joined Kindle, slowly expanding the space dividing them and him. Tad glared at each of them but fell in between and grumbled, "Okay, now talk."

"I'm really not sure how I did it," Ella quietly began, "but,

Kindle, when you mentioned how I felt that night I healed you, I remembered that I wasn't scared because somehow I knew exactly what to do. But it wasn't as if *I* knew what to do. I … I could hear the steps running through my mind, telling me exactly what to do."

Tad raised an eyebrow along with a corner of his mouth. "You got voices in your head?"

"No," replied Ella, clearly missing his suggestion that she was crazy. "It was only one small voice, but it was so clear, as if someone was standing right beside me but their words were inside me all at once. But anyway, I remembered hearing that voice when I healed Kindle, and I knew if I could just hear it again, it would tell me exactly what to do."

The more Ella divulged, the more skeptical Kindle grew. What she was explaining did sound somewhat insane and unbelievable. Any time Kindle had heard people talking about voices guiding them to do something, they were mentally unstable and acting ridiculous. However, as she considered how odd those kinds of people were, Kindle knew Ella didn't match that description. The fact that she had seen proof of everything Ella had claimed also decreased her disbelief. Wondering if Ella was actually both fully honest and sane, she peered at her past Tad. Other than appearing very thoughtful, she looked calm and normal. Still not completely sure if she could believe Ella, Kindle readied herself to dig deeper into what Ella had professed, but Tad cut into her investigation.

"Like somebody told you to do somethin' you didn't know anything about?" he questioned in such a strange tone that Kindle puzzlingly squinted at him. His face was squished into even deeper thoughtfulness than Ella's. Kindle, feeling as if she was being excluded from some unsaid knowledge, gaped back and forth. She wanted to stop and confront both of them, but they had reached the end of the wall, and Andrew suddenly poked his head around the corner right by her face.

After stifling an impulsive, terrified gasp, Kindle hissed, "You scared me."

He shrugged then squinted at the others. "Everything except

our weapons is out here. They must have taken them inside."

"Are you sure?" Ella quickly responded as they turned the corner and entered an open stable. To Kindle, it looked much more like a roofed porch than a place to keep animals. The sides of the structure were a simple continuation of the building's walls, and the sloped overhang above jutted out just high enough to allow the horses to stand under it. No stalls separated or penned the few horses. Each one remained in the enclosure only by the power of their lead ropes tied to a single wooden post running from the roof to the floor. A tinge of sadness ran through Kindle as she crossed the boards to Nasah.

"It's okay, girl," she whispered and stroked her mane. Wanting to release her horse from the small prison, Kindle reached to untie her, but Andrew waved a hand to stop her.

"We have to get our swords first," he almost inaudibly insisted.

"She needs to eat," Kindle replied and tried again, but this time Ella stepped up to block her motion.

"He's right—we don't want to take a chance of them running away. We must get our swords, and we can't predict what sort of clamor that might raise."

Kindle sighed; she knew Ella's argument was true. Squinting around in the darkness to check for any sign of an entrance, Kindle anxiously wondered, "So what do we do?"

"We get in the guard's room to search," replied Ella as if it was an easy task.

"How?" demanded Tad, still at the edge of the makeshift stable, and a muffled voice, different from any of theirs, asked, "Wha'd you say?"

The all froze, breath held and ears hopefully attuned for an answer. After a few seconds that felt like hours, someone grumpily answered, "You're dreamin', you oaf, hush up and sleep."

Kindle slowly blew out her fear and, too afraid to speak, gave Ella an exaggerated shrug. Without answering, Ella stepped away from Kindle. As she neared the wall, a small fire ignited on the end of her finger, and she lifted it to better light their surroundings. Andrew wound past her to the back corner and waved for Ella to join him. She, along with Kindle and Tad, all gathered behind him to see what he had discovered. The small but very bright flame Ella carried showed them that Andrew had located a door. It was extremely plain, and Kindle was sure she wouldn't have noticed it if Andrew wasn't outlining it with one hand and miming a pushing motion with the other. Ella carried her light closer to it, waving it around to illuminate every inch of the wooden rectangle and soon turned a puzzled face to Andrew. As he shrugged and resumed his pushing motion, Kindle quizzically squinted at the door. She could tell something about it was baffling Ella and Andrew but didn't understand what. The thought that it had to be locked crossed her mind, but she didn't think either of them had attempted to open it. Believing she would solve the mystery, Kindle reached for the doorknob and realized the problem.

The door had no knob. No knob or handle or any opening device existed anywhere on it. Now Kindle also understood why Andrew had continued to mime pushing. After a brief glance at Andrew and Ella, who were totally invested in a silent conversation, she curiously lay her hand on the wood and tried to move it. She felt the door budge very slightly under her touch but ceased as a soft metal *clink* sounded. Quicker than Ella could spin to shine the light on her, Kindle retracted her hand and turned her wide eyes to meet the others' shocked and reproachful stares.

Kindle mouthed a silent apology but knew that it wouldn't amend for her noise if anyone else had heard it. They all stood perfectly still, waiting for the sleepy voices on the other side of the wall to speak. Kindle's heartbeat had almost calmed its pace when Nasah loudly snorted and tossed her head. Even though the unexpected input from her horse terrified her, Kindle was glad to see the other three impulsively jump as well in the millisecond before Ella's light vanished.

Once again, they waited to hear if anyone would respond. Feeling slightly less terrified this time, Kindle reached through the darkness to tap Andrew's shoulder. By his movement, she could tell she had startled him and so was glad that Ella relit her fingers to show him what had touched him. Blinking somewhat offended eyes at her, he furrowed his brow and turned his face as if to ask what she wanted. From her precarious experiment, Kindle had determined that the door had to be secured by some sort of hook lock, and she wanted to convey that information but wasn't sure how. After a moment of thought, she turned her hand as if she was locking the door.

Andrew shook his head as he pointed to where the knob should sit, and she knew she had failed. Rolling her eyes in frustration, Kindle turned to Ella. She tried her key motion again, but Ella only gave her a confused stare. Desperate to be understood without creating any noise, she turned to her last hope: Tad. When her concentrated stare met his, she pointed at the door. He raised an eyebrow. She pointed at the place where a knob should sit then waved her hands back and forth. His eyebrow remained raised, but his expression changed to disgust. Sure she had lost him, Kindle made an ugly face back then huffed at the door. She wanted to scream at him that the door was clipped shut but, knowing that would only accomplish announcing their presence, restrained herself.

A movement from him caught her attention and brushed aside her frustration. He put out his hand to carefully push the door, and when nothing happened except the metallic *click*, his half-evil grin crept up on his face. Instantly, Kindle knew that he now also understood how the door was locked. For a brief moment, she felt relief that at least he knew what she had been trying to communicate, but his next move drained that hope out of her. Tad drew Natzal from his side and spun it in his left hand. Kindle stepped aside, afraid he was going to do something very loud and very stupid. Out of the corner of her vision, she saw a wide-eyed and tight-lipped Ella move to shove his arm from its destination. Just inches from impeding him, though, she stopped. Tad had not chucked his dagger into the door as Kindle, and apparently Ella, had feared. He had noiselessly slid it into the crack between the wall and door. As if he routinely practiced this action, Tad steadily and methodically raised his dagger to about his eye level, very lightly pushed the door as he flicked his wrist, slowly lowered his weapon to halfway down the slit, and wriggled his blade again. Then he turned his devilish smile to Kindle and tilted Natzal sideways. At his last move, the door swung away from them a few inches, revealing the foot of a bed. Ella almost instantaneously curled her flame into her fist and left them in nearly total darkness.

As they all allowed their eyes to readjust, each of them remained rooted where they stood. The first sign of life came from Andrew, who tapped Kindle then Ella's shoulder. They pivoted to squint his way and saw he was waving them on into the guardroom but slowly backing away himself. Ella began to follow him, but he adamantly shook his head and pointed at his chest and then the horses. Knowing he usually kept his distance from Nasah and Nox, Kindle wondered if he truly wanted to stay with them or just wanted to avoid whatever danger waited in the guardroom. Regardless of his motive, though, Kindle almost appreciated him staying outside. She knew how clumsy he was and was sure that if any of them would trip over, bump into, or drop something, it would be him. Holding out an arm to catch Ella's eye, Kindle nodded an assuring face at her. Even though Ella hadn't heard her thoughts, she seemed to know them as her expression changed to understanding and she waved to Andrew.

When she turned back to the door, Kindle's stomach dropped. Tad had vanished. The gap in the door had widened, and she guessed that he must have already snuck through it. She peered sideways at Ella and saw her very likely arrive at the same conclusion as she shook her head but grinned. After a sigh, Ella met Kindle's gaze, nodded, and slipped into the room as well.

Kindle knew she should follow but hesitated. In the prison the idea of sneaking past guards to recapture their belongings had seemed exciting and simple, but now that she stood so near to the task, it seemed exactly the opposite. Besides the danger of multiple light-sleeping guards, Kindle now also knew that the darkness, complete unfamiliarity with the room, and her cluelessness of where their swords might be would also prove problematic. After realizing all the potential difficulties ahead, she considered staying with Andrew. Kindle glanced back to see him untying Nox's rope, nervously peeking at the large stallion every few seconds. Seeing his pitiful anxiety redoubled her determination to bravely face whatever stood between them and escaping, and she slowly, carefully stepped into the guard room.

Without the moonlight Kindle couldn't see anything. She remembered that a bed sat very close to her right and so eased left with the door behind her as her guide. When her fingertips left the moving wood and brushed a solid wall, a single distant flame let her assess the room in front of her. Just like all of Lord Beryl's home, it was a dark, cold wooden room. Kindle squinted to determine what had been blocking the torch from her view and realized that it was a partial wall. Its presence sent her questioning eyes around the room, and happy realization swatted away some of her fear. The room was arranged exactly like the prison, with the cells running along the opposite walls and an aisle between them. As far as she could tell, the only difference was the absence of the bars fronting each cell. Now almost positive she could safely walk a straight line down the aisle, Kindle tiptoed away from the wall and began her search.

The walls partitioning each cell did a very good job of screening the torchlight at the far end of the room, and so Kindle couldn't quite discern what sat in each one. From her encounter of the one right beside the door and the sounds of large noses snoring and grunting, though, she guessed each one held a slumbering guard on his bed. Not wanting to even chance waking one, she maintained her straight path and did her best to visually search for any shape or glimmer of their swords.

About halfway down the room, the single light started to penetrate farther into each cell, and the outlines of bed and trunks swam into view. Kindle slowed to peer in each one more thoroughly. Nothing attracted her attention in the cell on her right. She turned to inspect the space on her left and almost fell over in shocked terror.

A figure was standing beside the bed.

Kindle felt a wave of hot fear ignite every inch of her as her wide eyes stared at it. Slowly, she started to retrace her steps. Every thought had left her except to escape, and she had to use all her self-control to keep from sprinting to the door. Just when she had almost backed far enough to exit the person's range of sight, he moved and she knew she had been caught. Ready to dash for the exit as soon as her legs remembered how to move, Kindle started to pivot, but the person suddenly ran at her, and in her fright she tripped sideways. Certain that the next second would bring a chorus of pain and noise, Kindle squeezed her eyes shut to prepare for the explosion of it all.

Neither pain nor noise met her. Instead, an arm wrapped around her stomach to interrupt her fall, and a hand clapped over her jaw to silence her oncoming cry. For a moment she hung in midair, too stunned to react to or know what had happened. Then, to check if she was safe or in more danger, she shuffled her feet to support her and twisted to see who held her. When she saw who it was, her first impulse was to swat his shoulder, but Tad uncovered her mouth to block her hand with his wrist. He immediately released her and flipped his hands in a defensive shrug. She knew what he meant—he didn't know how stopping her fall and the noises that would have alerted the guards of their presence had earned a swipe from her—but he had scared her, and so she felt justified in her action. Ignoring the shrug, she pointed past him to the cell she supposed he had been searching. He frowned and shook his head then tilted it and his thumb to the next one. Kindle nodded, and they silently parted ways. Tad returned to rummaging through the guards' quarters, and she remained in the aisle, glad that he was willing to take on the more nerve-wracking exploration. As Kindle turned back to her hunt, she saw Ella curl around one of the walls on her right. They met one another's stares long enough to see the other was still empty-handed, and then Ella vanished into the next cell.

Now that Kindle knew Tad and Ella were closely inspecting every cell, she quickened her casual scan of each one and soon reached the wall under the torchlight. She had seen no sign of their weapons, and as Tad and Ella rounded into some of the last few nooks, she began to doubt Andrew had been right. Nauseous disappointment chilled her even more than the room's cold air as she wondered if the guards had hidden their swords in another room or possibly multiple rooms in the horrid house. She leaned against the wall to soak up more of the overhead fire's heat and desperately stared at the door she knew led to the thin hallway. It looked exactly like the prison door at the other end of the hall, and she was sure it was also locked. Kindle sighed at it; their venture was looking more and more like a miscalculated, risky failure, and she was ready to return to her cell, wait for morning, and tell Lord Beryl she was his new spy. What frustrated her even more than their obviously wrong decision to escape was the fact that not long ago she had been so sure that their new unity had signaled a productive and correct turn of their journey. Now none of that exhilarating assurance existed in her. Once again they were all blindly wandering around for nothing.

Kindle rolled her head away from the door to pessimistically watch Ella sneak into the last cell in the row. As she waited for her friend to reappear defeated, a glimmer in her peripheral pulled her attention further left. No cell stood in the corner of the room, just an area blocked in by the last cell's wall and another perpendicular to it. Kindle lazily squinted at it, the weight of hopelessness exacerbating her tiredness. The glint had come from this direction, but now she saw nothing except the wooden wall. Dismissing the shimmer as her imagination, she pushed away from her repose to trudge back outside to Andrew. Before she could take two steps, though, the glimmer twinkled again, and in annoyance she turned to confront it.

Immediately, her anger diffused. At her new vantage point, she could see that the corner was not totally blocked off; a slit just big enough for someone to pass into the area behind the walls sat at the front corner of the square. Abandoning her original course along with her deflation, Kindle snuck to the opening and poked her head through it. Unlike the other enclosures, this one contained a torch that lit everything inside it. The walls were lined with a row of identical short swords hanging over a row of shields. The swords didn't appear incredibly sharp but were sturdy and shiny, and Kindle guessed that the torchlight reflecting off the one nearest to her had created the glimmer she noticed.

She slid in the shimmering room to better examine the swords and shields. Each sword's hilt was wrapped in dark blue and its three extensions capped with pink hexagons. The shields bore the same colors but were decorated with the same design as the flag Ober had been carrying. She walked a few steps along the wall, gazing at the repeated shapes, then turned to scan the rest of the room. Her eyes grew wide as they zipped to the spot under the torch where all their weapons lay in a messy pile. In a few strides, she crossed the floor and knelt down to check that they really were her and her companions' swords and shields. A smile lit her face as she saw the twinkle of her red and gold hilt and the soft brown leather of Ella's quiver. She wanted to snatch them up and victoriously dash out of the guard room, but the layers of metal were so jumbled she didn't dare touch any of them. Instead, she hurried back to the opening and peered out. Just as she had expected, Tad and Ella had finished searching the cells and were standing under the flickering torchlight with disgruntled expressions. She excitedly waved, and Tad's eyes glared her way. His anger quickly dissipated, and he passed Ella to stalk over to her. Ella, also spying Kindle, followed him, and soon they all stood grinning at their treasured weapons.

"Excellent, Kin," Ella very quietly sighed.

Tad moved to pick up his sword, but Ella threw out an arm to block him.

"What?" he hissed. "We came in here to get 'em, so let's get 'em."

Ella listened for any sounds from the guards before replying, "Yes, I know. But we must be careful not to cause a racket, or we'll be had."

Even though he didn't look happy to, Tad backed a step. He crossed his arms and frowned at them as he grumbled, "So what do we do, huh?"

"Start at the top," Kindle suggested.

Ella nodded, adding, "And whichever of us isn't picking from the pile, be ready to still anything that falls, alri—?" She abruptly stopped and caught her breath. Kindle had heard the groan that had silenced Ella and bit her lip as she also held her breath. The bothered utterance had seemed close, and Kindle guessed that their whispers had disturbed the guard on the other side of the wall that all three of them were now staring at. An incoherent mumble floated through it then the squeak of a depressed mattress as well. Kindle waited for footsteps to hit the wooden floor, but when a minute passed and none came, she slowly turned a fearful but hopeful grimace to Ella.

Ella cautiously lifted her chin then lowered it at the weapons. Understanding her motion as a sign of all-clear, Kindle tiptoed closer to the pile. Her sword rested atop the mass, so once Ella and Tad had taken their places beside it, Kindle very gingerly eased her fingers under the blade and hilt so she could lift it without knocking any other metal surface. Once she had secured it back at her side, she smiled at Tad, and he took his turn. After him, Ella carefully extracted Andrew's sword, handed it to Kindle, and plucked up her own sword and quiver. They exchanged relieved grins at their quiet success, but as Kindle returned her eyes to the shields still jumbled at their feet, apprehension filled her throat. A very small part of her yearned to propose that they leave the bulky metal shields. She didn't really *want* to abandon them but felt sure that they couldn't move any of the overlapped sheets without causing resounding clangs.

A wave of movement pulled Kindle out of her musings, and she blinked up at Tad. He stopped shaking his palms at her to point at her and himself at the same time; then hold up one, two, three fingers in quick succession; and finally mime snatching up his shield. The meaning of his actions was undeniable: he wanted them to grab the shields at the same time to avoid any crashes. Kindle wanted to shake her head. The thought of the secrecy of their mission depending on her ability to move as deftly as Tad seemed like a horrible idea.

Before she could object, though, he spiked his pointer finger into the air between them. Knowing she had only two more seconds to collect her nerves, Kindle tried to plan the spots where she would grab her shield, but his thumb popped up, and she forewent planning to focus on steadying her breathing. When his third finger jumped into the air, Kindle squatted and yanked her shield as quickly as she could, but as Tad lifted his out from under hers, her grip faltered, and she dropped the heavy metal rectangle onto Ella and Andrew's shields.

"Oh, I'm sorry, I'm sorry!" she yelped as a great cacophony of metallic clangs shot through the quiet.

"Forget it!" Tad shouted back as questioning yells filled the room. "Just grab it and *go!*"

They all quickly bent, snatched a shield, and then dashed out into the aisle of the guard room. Kindle almost immediately froze when she saw the scene spread before them. The room was neither dark, silent, nor empty now. A torchlight shone from almost every cell, and unsteady guards still in their sleeping clothes were wandering out into the aisle. Completely at a loss of what to do, Kindle stood gaping wide-eyed at all the sleepy men.

"C'mon!" she heard Tad urge, and before she could turn to find him, he shot right down the middle of the room with a shield over one arm and a sword in the other.

"Oy! Oy!" one of the guards cried, pointing at Tad. "That's one of them spies, Wissen! That's—" Just as Kindle discovered that the man yelling was Ober, he also saw her. "And that's them!" Ober frantically yelled, waving his pudgy arms in every direction. "Get 'em! Get 'em!"

Every guard in the room sprang into action. The three nearest Tad tried to block his escape, but he evaded them only to face another set of angry men. Kindle didn't see what happened to him, though, because a crowd of guards running at her stole her attention. Without thinking, she drew her sword and waved it back and forth.

"Get away! Get away from me!" she cried, trying to figure out what to do next. The group halted for a moment but, after exchanging a few nods and grins, restarted their approach more carefully.

"Don't believe we can't see through your pretense," one laughed, and she glanced to her right. Wissen's nose was lofted upward, and he sliced it at another guard who nodded and tried to dodge around behind her, but Kindle ran backward until her back hit the wall.

"Smart, smart," Wissen chuckled. "But really, Little Miss, you can't pretend that you can deflect all of us. Ober, take that from her."

"No!" Kindle objected and jumped into the defensive stance that Azildor had trained into her muscle memory. At her action, Ober recoiled from his approach and glanced at Wissen.

Wissen frowned and aimed his nose at him. "What are you doing, Ober? Take it! Disarm her!"

Ober pulled his wary face from his commander to Kindle. Reaching out, he started to sidle toward her. Impulsively she swiped her sword at him, and their arms instantly snapped in opposite directions.

"I'm sorry!" Kindle gasped, truly aggrieved that she had sliced open his palm. Hearing a snicker, she swung her sword back at the group. "I'm sorry, but I'll do it again, okay?!" she yelled as threateningly as she could. "I told you to get back, so … so get back!"

Ober did retreat into the line of guards, but none of the others moved. As they all eyed one another, Kindle desperately tried to think of how she could escape without hurting anyone else. Her thoughts were interrupted by the explosion of cheers and shouts at the opposite end of the room. The ruckus sounded so jubilant that Kindle feared Tad had been caught, and her adrenaline pumped all of her reasoning aside. After a deep breath, she rushed the line of guards with her sword leading her charge, and to her great surprise and relief, they scattered to avoid her weapon.

Realizing that she had created no plan beyond escaping the ring of men, Kindle skidded to a halt and hurriedly scanned the room. Several sleepy men were still standing wide-eyed at the end of their cells, but most of the guards had gathered near the door to the stable. One man tripped away from the rest of the mob and grandly pumped his fist along with Tad's sword in the air.

The second she recognized Tad's sword, Kindle bolted into motion. As she sprinted past the cells, she had no thought except to do whatever necessary to extract Tad from the grasp of the guards. When she was almost to them, she swung her sword over her shoulder as if she was about to hit a home run and was about to smash it into the nearest target when a hand grabbed her wrist. Her arms stopped, but her feet kept moving and ran out from under her. She twisted then slammed onto the floor. Gasping to recollect the breath that had been knocked out of her, she tried to find her sword and who had caused her to drop it. Before she could locate either, Kindle heard a *clink* and a man's voice mock, "Not your lucky day, huh?"

Still panting, Kindle rolled onto her back and saw a man holding the point of her sword over her.

"No!" she gasped, waving a hand and trying to slide out from under it. He laughed and raised it higher. Kindle knew that in the next second he would plunge it into her and did the only thing she could think to do: scream.

Even though her breath was still half gone, her scream rang out loud enough to shock the man above her into temporary stupefaction, and she started to scramble to her feet, but in the same moment, an incredibly loud, wrathful voice rang out.

"STOP!"

Kindle, along with everyone else, shuddered to a silent halt. Now on all fours and more terrified than she had been all night, Kindle lifted her eyes to search for the source of the command.

"No one move!" the voice roared again, and Kindle blinked, unable to believe her realization. She flipped her head up to see if the angry voice really did belong to Ella and saw her friend standing under the mounted torch looking far more fierce than Kindle would have imagined possible. Ella was seething at all the faces staring at her with her bow loaded and pulled to a dangerously quivering arch.

"Drop their swords and let them go!" she demanded, switching her aim between the man by Kindle and where she guessed Tad was.

Kindle waited for someone to comply but heard nothing.

"Lay their swords *down*!" Ella boomed so forcefully that Kindle ducked her head. As she did, she heard several scattered thuds.

"Now, now. Miss Green," Wissen began, and Kindle turned her incredulous stare from her sword beside her to Wissen, who was approaching Ella with lifted hands. "We all know you will not and—heh—cannot pierce us all with that single, impotent projectile of your—"

Ella swung the head of her arrow at his nose and threatened, "Not another slimy word."

Wissen halted for a moment, but as a low murmur floated

89

through the air, Kindle saw him smile and tilt his nose to the rest of the room. "They see your inability as well," he deridingly sighed. "It really is a shame … your bold act almo—oh!" Wissen stumbled backward then turned and ran into one of the cells. At his last word, Ella had sent her arrow whizzing by his ear and, before it had struck a wall, had reloaded with three arrows that instantaneously burst into flame. Ella directed her ball of fire to the ceiling, and the chatter among the guards vanished.

"Let them go, or I will burn this house down," she warned, her voice low and serious. The man near Kindle nudged her sword closer with his foot then retreated. Slowly, Kindle curled her hand around her hilt and stood. She gazed around the room at the frozen guards, amazed. A hand suddenly hit her arm, and she spun, ready to attack, but hunched into a relieved sigh.

"I didn't know it was you," she apologized to Tad even though he didn't seem surprised or offended at all.

"C'mon," he mumbled as he steered her around him.

"Wait—what about Ella?" Kindle tried to turn back to see her, but Tad pushed her to face the other end of the room.

"Seriously?" he snorted. "I think she's gunna be okay."

Kindle blinked at him but then realized how true his assertion was and let him steer her past all the immobile guards and out into the night.

RUSHING

Before Kindle's eyes had time to blink the dark stable into focus, Andrew hurried to meet her and Tad.

"What happened?" he anxiously whispered, his round eyes evaluating them.

"Ella went nuts, that's what happened," Tad laughed and leisurely strode past him.

Andrew stared at Tad then turned a confused face to Kindle. She reached over her shoulder to find his sword and shield that she had tossed onto her back in the chaos.

"Here." She handed him his belongings. He simply gawked at them. "Hey, it's okay. We got everything back, and Ella's gunna be here soon, and then we can leave," Kindle encouraged him with a smile, but Andrew's face didn't lighten.

"What? How? What happened?" he questioned, peering at the door.

"Hey, what'd you do with the horses?" Tad demanded, and Andrew turned to him.

"I untied them. They're just around the corner," he quickly

explained then returned his attention to Kindle. "Where's Ella?"

"She's coming," Kindle reassuringly insisted, but a clamor surged in the guard room behind her, and her confidence plummeted. Frightened by the noise, she stepped to the open edge of the stable.

Andrew, who looked as anxious as she felt, followed her and breathed, "I don't think everything's okay."

"What?" Tad stuck his head around the corner to squint at them, but his eyes snapped to the door as the racket grew and it flew open. Kindle was ready to run until she saw Ella tumble through the opening and smash into the wall.

"El—!" she started to happily cry, but her friend swung a pained, worried face to her.

"No, Kin, here," she panted, waving Kindle to her. "I need help. And we must go *now*. Lord Beryl is coming."

Although she was terrified to go near the door again, Kindle rushed to Ella's side. "What? What? What do you need help with?" she babbled, having no idea what to do.

"Hey, I got this," Tad grumbled as he appeared at her shoulder. "You and Andrew get the horses."

"Uh, okay," Kindle assented, flabbergasted that Tad would ever choose to help Ella. Staring over her shoulder to see him help Ella hobble away from the wall, Kindle dashed to Andrew, grabbed his elbow, and yanked him around to the side of the building. Just as he had said, Nasah and Nox were peacefully searching for grass to nibble. Kindle slowed as she neared them so she wouldn't spook them and helped Andrew clamber onto Nox. The face he wore showed his great discomfort. He never rode alone and probably had no idea how to guide the massive animal, but the alarm whirring through Kindle's mind blocked the idea to tell him what to do. Almost instantly forgetting him, Kindle climbed onto Nasah and steered her closer to the house. Soon she heard Ella's voice, and she and Tad appeared.

"No, it was *not* awesome," Ella was chastising in irritation, "I did what I had to do, and that's all. I did not enjoy it, but I was sure they were close to harming you or worse."

"Here," Kindle called to them as she rode over and held out a hand. "You can ride with me, Ella."

Ella nodded and started to move to Nasah but glanced sideways and stopped. "No, I'll go with Andrew," she insisted and, with Tad as a crutch, started limping his way. "He looks terrified."

Kindle nervously peered at her. "Are you sure? I mean, like, can you? Are you okay?"

"Once I get in the saddle, I'll be fine," she assured Kindle with a smile. "It's my leg is all. That horrid weasel bit into it."

Kindle glanced down at Ella's leg then back at the stable; she thought she had heard a shout echo out of it. Nasah snorted and pawed the ground under her, and Kindle tried to relax, but another much more distinct yell reached her ears. Her anxious eyes jumped to her friends. Tad and Andrew were working together to lift Ella onto Nox.

"C'mon, guys," called Kindle, her voice quivering.

A squeak sounded behind her, and she twisted to see Aryl bounding toward Nasah's legs.

"Guys!" she yelled as she snapped the reins and Nasah bolted forward, escaping Aryl's terribly sharp jaws.

"Hey!" Tad shouted from the ground as she flew past him.

"They're coming!" she called back, jabbing a finger behind her at the gang she knew was pouring out of the stable. Without slowing Nasah, she looped back around to face everyone. Ella and Andrew were now both safely on Nox and, with Ella at the reins, were racing around the front of the house. Tad was running toward her, just a short distance ahead of Aryl, who despite his blindness seemed to know his direction better than the guards still grouped by the wall. Keeping one eye on Tad and the other on the guards, Kindle saw that two of the men had finally boarded some horses and were heading her way as well. With just seconds between her and Tad, Kindle yanked the reins back, causing Nasah to toss her head and skid sideways. In the next second, Tad leapt up behind her, and she spurred Nasah into a mad dash again.

"Sorry, girl!" Kindle sighed to Nasah's mane, but before she could promise her treats, Tad pulled her arm, throwing Nasah into a hard turn. "What?!" she demanded as she reset their course to the tree line.

"Go–go," Tad panted.

"I *am* going!" she retorted.

"No–not trees … river, Andrew said … follow the river … into the forest."

"What?" Kindle couldn't make sense of what he was trying to communicate. Tad let out a frustrated growl, leaned forward to grab her hands, and drove them into a hard turn. "Hey!" Kindle objected and tried to shake off his hands, but his grasp was unrelenting, and he maintained their new path back to the front of Lord Beryl's house. "What are you doing?" she cried, her hope of escaping decreasing with each hoof beat. "That's our way out of here! *Go back*!"

Tad's only response was his ragged breath in her ear.

Sensing that he was done talking, she simply watched the white trees disappear from view as Nasah turned the corner. When she rolled her gaze forward, though, some of her hope returned. Almost at the other end of the long building, Andrew's shield was catching the moonlight each time Nox's hooves crashed against the ground. Kindle wasn't sure why, but just seeing that they were all heading in the same direction eased her fears. Even though she had no idea *where* they were speeding to, Kindle now felt content to go there as long as they all arrived together. She ended her fight against Tad's grip and slipped her hands out from under his to hold the saddle instead.

Suddenly, a loud voice shouted from behind, and in her attempt to see who was tailing them, she lurched sideways in shock. Before she could slide very far, one of Tad's arms wrapped around her, and she met his gaze.

"Be careful," he grumbled, but his furrowed brow seemed concerned, not annoyed.

"Uh, uh, sorry—" she started to stutter, but another yell yanked her eyes back to their original target.

"You won't get away!" she heard Braon threaten as he shook a sword in the air. His horse was slightly ahead of another, and she guessed it was due to the fact that two passengers were riding it. Kindle twisted forward again and curled both hands around the saddle.

"It's Braon," she reported as Tad returned both hands to steering, "and there's another horse, but I can't tell who's on it."

Tad sniffed. "Doesn't matter. They can't catch us."

Unsure if he was certain or just prideful, Kindle decided to ignore the horsemen behind them and focus on the outline of Andrew's shield ahead. As she squinted at it, she sensed that it was slowly veering left. Kindle blinked and tried to discern if her eyes or the dark night was skewing her perception, but when the round shield began to wane, she knew Nox's path was truly not straight. Soon all traces of Nox, Ella, and Andrew slipped out of sight. Kindle wanted to ask where they had disappeared to but decided to hold her query while Nasah ran the last few feet along Lord Beryl's house. As soon as they blew past the end of the building, Kindle relocated the group speeding along the tree line.

"They're over there. Do you see them?" she asked Tad.

He didn't give an answer but steered them toward the tall white poles.

"Tad, where are we going? What are we gunna do?" she questioned in a rushed breath. "We've gotta get out of here, those guys aren't gunna quit chasing us, and Braon's got a sword."

"So?" Tad didn't sound worried at all.

"So ... I mean, like, we can't run forever, so what do we do if they catch us or—?"

"They're not gunna, okay? And if they did, even you could probably take down all of those jokers."

She hesitated, not sure if he had complimented or insulted her, then replied, "Well, where—?"

"Hey," he interrupted and pushed his chin forward. Kindle followed his motion and saw the answer to her question. Far ahead Ella and Andrew turned and broke into the white wall of trees. Seeing their maneuver, Kindle's first impulse was to argue that fleeing into the forest had been her earlier intention and that waiting until now to do so had wasted time, but a faint sound reached her ear and erased her agitation.

"The river," she whispered back to Tad, and his half-evil grin curled onto his face. A smile flicked onto her own but fell off just as quickly as a distant voice yelled.

"Aryl! The traitor spies are heading into the woods, Aryl! Tell that guard to follow them!"

Kindle twisted her neck to see Braon's horse slow down to let the second riders, one of which she knew had to be Lord Beryl, catch him. They trotted alongside each other for a few moments, then Braon broke away and rode into the trees.

"Braon went after them," Kindle worriedly told Tad as she turned forward. "He went into the forest."

Surprisingly, Tad laughed, "What an idiot. That's what Andrew said they'd do."

"What? What do you mean?" she returned, slightly confused and irritated.

He snickered again. "You'll see."

Frustrated, Kindle rolled her eyes but sighed, "Okay." She wanted to be more annoyed with him for keeping the plan from her but found that she trusted him enough that his secrecy didn't bother her. Resetting her gaze on the river nearing them, she tried to think of what could be running through Tad's head. Suddenly, a muffled yell shook her out of her pondering, and she scanned the area for the reason for it.

"Hold on," Tad commanded in her ear, and she clutched the saddle tighter as the momentum of their turn pulled her sideways. Once they were riding in a straight line again, Kindle lifted her eyes to their surroundings. The maze of staggered trees was flying past them on one side, but the river stretched out on the other.

"Oh …" sighed Kindle, now understanding. "There's no trees here, so we get through quicker."

"So we don't get lost or whatever," Tad corrected in a distracted tone as she felt his arms shift.

"What?" she questioned, sensing something was wrong.

She started to look back at him, but he abruptly demanded, "Hey, you drive."

Before she could give any sort of response, he dropped the

reins and, in the second that Nasah slowed, jumped onto the ground.

"Tad!" Kindle yelled as she tried to gather the leather in her shocked hands while turning to watch him land and ungracefully tumble into the river. Worry for his safety almost caused her to turn Nasah back, but he immediately unsteadily stood and shook his wet head.

"Go!" he yelled. "Keep going!"

As she gaped back at him, the ruckus of thoughts spinning through her mind all at once—to stop, retrieve him, tell him he was a crazy boy, reprimand him for leaping off Nasah, pout about being left alone and unaware of what to do, leave him to his insane ploy, or keep going—kept her from doing anything. She simply stared at him as Nasah carried her farther away. Tad also watched her but, after a few moments, turned and ran in the opposite direction.

"Tad!" she cried, seriously worried for his sanity and then, as the horse carrying Lord Beryl whipped around the corner, his life. Deciding that she had to help him, Kindle slowed Nasah and was halfway through a turn when a voice spooked her.

"Kin!"

"Ahg!" yelped Kindle and whipped around to see Ella jogging to her along the narrow strip between the trees and the river.

"Kin, come along!"

"No, Ella, Tad went back, we gotta—"

"Yes, and that is what he was meant to do, so come along," Ella insisted.

Kindle blinked at her, back to Tad, and then at Ella. "Wait. How'd—?" she began, but Ella had reached her and climbed up in front of her.

"I'll tell you everything, but you must come out of sight first," Ella sighed as she flipped the reins she had taken from Kindle. They rode to the end of the mass of white trees, then Ella turned Nasah around the corner. Where the barrier stopped, the space between the trees widened and became irregular. A quick look up told her that since these trees still held their natural branches and leaves, they were actually out of Aryl and in the forest now. Kindle didn't examine the forest long, though, because Ella soon slowed Nasah to a stop where Andrew and Nox were waiting.

"Alright." Ella hopped to the ground and smiled at Andrew. "You were right, only one horseman followed them."

Andrew grinned slightly then turned his face to Kindle and asked, "Did the other one go in the trees?"

"Yeah, but …" Kindle shook her head. "Like, what is going on, you guys? Tad's still back there and …" A frustrated huff replaced her jumbled thoughts, and she scrutinized their faces, impatient for answers.

"Kindle, everything is alright," Ella calmingly insisted. "When Tad was loading me on Nox, he asked how we would …" A thoughtful grin slid on her face, and she swung it to Andrew.

He saw her expression then dropped his eyes to the ground he was sitting on and finished, "He asked how we would shake the guards."

"Yes." Ella brightly nodded. "And I suppose that means escaping from—"

Her voice broke off as a wild shout rang through the air. Knowing it sounded like Tad and suspecting he was in danger, Kindle started to turn back to the white barrier, but Andrew's even tone and next words stopped her.

"That's the sign—we need to get ready," Andrew stated, and Ella immediately began untying Nox. He stood to watch her and, seeing Kindle's confused and incredulous stare, shrugged and explained, "He asked how we could get away from the guards. I told him we wouldn't be able to navigate the barrier, but if we could make it to the river, we could just follow it through. I figured the guards would try to go through the trees, and that would slow them down enough for us to get away, but I told him that if they did keep following us, we'd have to lure them into the barrier. He said he would do it."

"And he'd give us a yell when he had," added Ella with a smile. "So pop up on Nasah, and we'll be off as soon as he joins us."

Taking in all Andrew had explained and melding it with all she had just witnessed, Kindle slowly nodded. Everything made much more sense now. She put a hand on Nasah's back to aid her remount but paused. "What about your leg?" she questioned Ella, "Wasn't it hurt?"

"Oh, yes." Ella grimaced as she boosted Andrew onto Nox. "That weasel took a nasty bite out of my calf, but it wasn't hard to patch up—nothing at all like that hole in your leg."

"Oh … you mean you, like, did all that grass and fire stuff?"

Ella gazed at her leg before slowly answering, "Yes, only not so much of either."

Peering down at the spot where Ella had mended her own leg, Kindle just as thoughtfully wondered, "And did you … did you hear, um, the voice?"

The next second didn't bring Ella's answer. Andrew's eyes had just enough time to curiously glance at her before loud, fast footfalls pulled all their stares backward. Tad was sprinting full force toward them. Remembering their need to flee, Kindle jumped onto Nasah's saddle and walked her to meet Tad. As he clambered on behind her, he shook his head and panted, "Go … go."

"Yeah, I know, just get on," Kindle almost chuckled, but his urgency slowly stirred a speck of worry into her thoughts. She shook Nasah into a full gallop behind Ella and Andrew then almost unwillingly asked, "Is something wrong? Like, are they still following us or …?" Knowing he was out of breath, she didn't push for a response. For a while she bit her lip in concentration and worry as they sped along the uneven riverbank and she pondered what could have rattled him. The moment a long stretch of level ground appeared, she twisted to check for the guards, but only quiet trees stood behind them. Slightly appeased but still unsettled, she returned her gaze to their path and whispered, "Tad? *Is* everything okay?"

"I don't know," he panted, "but I ain't never seen anything like that."

TRUST SHAKEN

Too afraid to ask what Tad meant, Kindle gulped and let the oncoming ground ahead of them hold her attention. Before much time passed, she noticed Andrew glance back and Nox slow to a trot. Kindle let Nasah almost catch the large black horse and then also relieved her to a slower pace. Without the task of steering over the dips and lifts along the bank to distract her, Kindle's mind wandered back to all the events and words fresh from the night. Most of their time in Aryl had passed so quickly that she hadn't really digested all that had happened. Now as all the scenes replayed through her mind, Kindle realized that the evening and night had been a roller coaster full of terrifying, perilous, revitalizing loops and hills. Kindle tried to count the times she had sincerely believed she was inches from the end of her life but stopped when the image of Aryl's eyeless little head sent a queasy shiver through her. To keep the disturbing weasel out of her thoughts, she rode up beside Ella and asked, "Are we gunna stop for the night or … or just keep going?"

Ella glanced back at Andrew, and then together they squinted back along the bank they had just dashed over. Kindle stared in the same direction and discovered that they had ridden far enough to eliminate the great white barrier from sight.

"Nobody's following us," Andrew decisively affirmed, and Ella dipped her chin in agreement.

"Yes, I really do think we left them wandering through that mess of trees," she happily sighed. "Let's do stop. Go on up the bank a bit, Kin."

Kindle gladly took Ella's direction and steered Nasah to a cluster of trees surrounded by some tall grass. She slid to the ground to tie Nasah to a tree so she could graze and as she did, peered up at Tad. He sat atop Nasah completely still except for his head, which kept suspiciously swinging in every direction.

"What're you doing?" muttered Kindle, causing Ella and Andrew to look their way.

"I'm not gettin' down," he defensively replied. Kindle felt too tired to argue with him and almost left him to spend the night on Nasah's back, but a disagreeable sound from Ella told her she would have to derail their oncoming debate.

"Tad, why not?" Kindle groaned, "It's really late, aren't you tired?"

"Yeah, but I'm not sleepin' on the ground," he quickly replied. Kindle squinted at him. Something in his voice sounded unfamiliar. It wasn't his usual lazy yet heated and argumentative tone but a resolute and somewhat anxious one.

"Tad, we've gone through this once already," Ella sighed but maintained her smile. "You are not above sleeping on the ground, and unless you return to Aryl—"

"Why?" Kindle interrupted, still staring at Tad but with his nervousness on her face now.

He stared back for a few seconds then looked to Ella. Pointing a finger at her accusingly, he interrogated, "You said this place was haunted, didn't you?"

"What?" Ella gaped at him, startled. "Tad, no. I never said Xylina forest was haunted. I only said that most men avoid it."

"Why? Huh? Why?"

"Tad, really, what's stirred you up? Why are you acting like this?"

"Hey, you didn't see what I saw, okay? That back there was messed up."

"What happened?" Kindle pleaded, desperate to know what had managed to scare him.

He glared at each of them, leaving Ella until last. "You really don't know what's up with this place?" he demanded.

Ella shook her head. "I have told what I know. Men say the forest can be confusing, but beyond that no one's ever given a clear reason why they avoid it. They just do." When Tad continued to glare at her, Ella sighed and put up a hand of surrender. "Alright, Tad. If you would like to stay on that horse all night, that is your choice. But I am going to sleep on the ground. Good night." Once she had said her last word, she retrieved a blanket from Nox's back and walked a short distance to find a place to lie down.

Andrew quietly peered at Kindle then Tad. Kindle wondered if he wanted to know the reason for Tad's snappy mood as much as she did, but he proved her wrong when he shrugged and mumbled, "Um, good night." Andrew sent one last look Kindle's way before he also found some bedding and wandered away to claim his sleeping spot. Kindle watched him until he stretched out on the ground a few feet from Ella then lifted her eyes to Tad.

"What?" he grumbled. "You gunna act like I'm an idiot too?"

Kindle rolled her eyes and whispered, "No, I'm gunna stay right here until you tell me what happened back there."

"I should've known you wouldn't leave me alone," he sniffed, but Kindle saw the hint of a grin on his face.

"So what happened? Because I know something did."

"You're not gunna believe me," he muttered as if he really doubted she would.

"Uh–yeah, I will. We've seen so much really weird stuff here that I think I'd believe anything, and I ... I know you're not gunna lie to me."

"Really?" he slyly challenged.

"Well, I know you wouldn't seriously lie to me," she clarified and then, unsure if she should, added, "I trust you."

For a few minutes, neither of them said anything. The silence caused Kindle to worry that she had said too much or something wrong, and she began to desperately piece together a cover explanation. She had almost wound one together and was summoning the courage to deliver it when Tad suddenly asked, "Why?"

"Huh?" she responded, unable to believe he was still talking to her. In her mind his silence had meant her words had pushed him into upset or awkwardness toward her.

"Why do you trust me?" he repeated, obviously unaware of her distractedness. "I'm not … loyal or good or whatever. People don't trust me. People don't even *like* me."

"Well, I like you," Kindle retorted without thinking then stuttered, "I mean, I, like, trust you because, I dunno, I do. You're always right there when I'm about to get stabbed or whatever. It's … well, I'm gunna believe you, okay? So tell me what happened."

Her babbling had caused his ambiguous grin to appear, and Kindle feared what it might mean. She very much hoped he wouldn't keep asking questions that made her give stupid answers and so was relieved when he nodded and agreed, "Yeah, okay." Tad leaned forward on Nasah's back so he could whisper but she could still hear him. "So I bailed, you know, to get those idiots to chase me into all those trees. And I ran past a couple trees and snapped sideways, and those idiots ran right past me. It was that Wissen idiot and the nut job. Didn't even see me, just kept goin'. I was gunna wait till I couldn't see 'em anymore so they wouldn't see me double back, but …" He grimaced. "You sure you gunna believe this?"

Kindle avidly nodded.

"The ground ate 'em."

She stared at him, waiting for him to say he was joking, but he was carefully watching for her reaction. Trying her best to sound confused and not doubtful, she questioned, "What do you mean it *ate* them? Was it like a hole in the ground or an earthquake or—"

"Nah. It ate 'em. See, I told you you wouldn't believe me."

"No, I do," she insisted. "I just—how did it eat them?"

"It—" Tad pushed himself upright so he could use his hands to demonstrate his words. "So they rode past me and a couple more trees, and then right in front of 'em the ground piled up like a big wave and smashed 'em." He snapped one viciously curved hand over his other then flattened them both. "Then nothing. The ground went flat, and those idiots were gone like they were never there."

Kindle stared at him, unsure of how to respond. The seriousness in his voice assured her that he wasn't joking, but the idea of the ground eating people seemed completely ridiculous. Just to remain true to her promise, Kindle threw aside the doubt in her mind and tried to believe what he had told her. As she considered it and imagined Lord Beryl disappearing under a mound of hungry dirt, another thought clicked into her mental movie. With a slightly worried face, she asked, "Do you think it ate Braon too?"

"I dunno," Tad scoffed, then a grin showed his teeth as he laughed, "I hope it did."

"No, I think it really did," Kindle, now fully believing Tad's story, fearfully whispered. "Like, right after he went in the trees, I heard somebody yell, and I thought it was somebody else, but what if it was him getting eaten? You heard it too, didn't you?"

"Yeah ..." he mumbled, his seriousness back. He glanced away from her for a moment, then very quietly asked, "You think Ella's holdin' out on us?"

"No—what?"

"I think she knows more about what's up with this place than she's tellin' us."

Kindle let his suggestion sink in before she replied, "Why? I mean, why wouldn't she tell us if she knew something?"

"I dunno, but she's the one who wanted to go through this stupid forest even though everybody else says it's haunted."

"I don't know ..." Kindle hesitantly murmured, trying to remember if it actually *had* been Ella's idea.

"And she lied about being an elf witch," Tad resolutely added.

"She didn't lie about it," Kindle defensively retorted.

"Yeah, well, she didn't tell anybody," he grumbled. "So I bet she's not been tellin' us a bunch more she knows."

His argument almost swayed Kindle. She was still slightly unnerved about Ella's secrecy, but remembering her earlier inner debate and conclusion about the matter, she shook her head. "I don't think so. I mean, she just got us out of the prison and stopped all those guards from killing us. If she wanted to kill us or something, she could of just ran off, you know? I just don't think she's up to anything."

Tad shook his head, and she knew he wasn't convinced. Pushing away the urge to tell him he was being paranoid, Kindle sighed, "Okay, we'll ask her in the morn—"

"Nah, I already tried that," he grouched.

She rolled her eyes in frustration. "Well, I dunno what to do. I'm just really tired, and I want to go to sleep."

For a while Kindle enjoyed the resulting silence. Then she shook her mind awake and, seeing that he had turned away, pleaded, "I'm sorry, I'm just really tired—"

"Okay, whatever," he grumbled without looking her way.

"Hey," Kindle apologetically said as she walked around to stand in his line of sight, "I *am* sorry. I wanna know what's going on with everything too. And I know it's really stupid she didn't tell us about all that stuff a long time ago, and I really just want all this to be over so we can go home, but ... but right now we can't do anything about any of it, so let's just go to sleep, okay?"

She saw his eyes flick to her then away again before he accusingly questioned, "You really want out of this?"

Her face fell. "What? That's not what I meant."

"Yeah, well, it's what you said. You don't really care about any of this or us or ... you just wanna go home."

"Tad," she groaned, irritated at her tired mind for vomiting out all her agitations. "I do care, and I don't want to go home, but I do, but ... ugh. I dunno, I'm tired. I just—" Kindle heaved a deep sigh. She knew she couldn't say all that she felt; the cacophony of thoughts ringing in her brain simply couldn't all be confined to words. "Can we just go to sleep and talk about this tomorrow?"

"Whatever," Tad curtly replied.

Knowing he was hurt but also that she couldn't say or do anything to help him, Kindle numbed all her frustration and asked, "Are you gunna sleep up there?"

"Why do you care?" he growled back.

"Okay." Kindle heard her voice pinch to a higher pitch and quickly gathered up a blanket before any more of her emotions leaked. She had almost made it halfway to Ella and Andrew when she stopped. An urge had seized her to look back and say something that would instantly and fully mend whatever she had broken, but no magical words came to her. Instead, she stared at her shoulder and called back, "Good night."

A reply didn't reach her ears, but she didn't expect one.

SKIPPING ROCKS

Consciousness slowly dawned over Kindle. Wanting to stay cocooned in her sleep, she rolled over and tried to bury her face under a corner of her blanket. Her fight to remain asleep had already been lost, though. Questions about how long she had slept, what time it was, and if anyone else was awake yet blossomed in her mind, and before long she nudged aside her cover to search for answers.

Brilliant sunlight dazzled her eyes, and she retreated behind a palm to save her vision. After a minute of allowing bars of light to filter through her fingers and greet her eyes, Kindle removed her hand and gazed at the scene around her. She knew she still lay in the same spot in Xylina Forest where she had bedded down the night before, but in the morning light, everything looked incredibly different. The tall, thin white and brown striped trees that she had considered empty now displayed beautiful yellow leaves that created a shivering golden ceiling of endless layers. Many of the yellow leaves also decorated the forest floor around her and covered a great deal of the rich brown soil and short, sparse green grass.

Now much more interested in her surroundings than sleep,

Kindle sat up to take in the entire view. With awed wonder, she let her eyes drink in the endless golden and ivory palace that seemed to have magically grown during her hours of sleep. The concentrated rays of bright sunshine she spied piercing the canopy added to the elegant beauty of the forest and caused a smile to skip onto her face. Her eyes ended their tour when a disruption in the white and yellow color palette appeared.

Not too far from her, Ella and Andrew were standing by a tree, staring up at its branches. Kindle, drawn by curiosity of what held their attention, stood and walked over to them. Before she could discover what was so interesting, Andrew noticed her and held up a hand. Understanding the motion, Kindle halted but sent a confused grimace to him. He held a finger to his lips then very slightly pushed it upward. Kindle almost followed it but saw Ella's hand start to slowly rise and switched her gaze to it instead. Just as she did, Ella snatched an arrow from her quiver, loaded it in her bow, and shot it into the branches.

"Did—?" Andrew began to ask, but a ball of feathers dropped by his feet, and he silently sidestepped away from it.

"Ha!" Ella triumphantly cried and plucked up the bird using the arrow projecting out of it. "Now we have breakfast."

Andrew gave her a queasy smile, and as Ella turned her way, Kindle tried to wipe her similar expression off her face.

"Kin, you're awake!" Ella brightly greeted her and lifted the dead bird. "Look, I've just caught us breakfast. Isn't it wonderful?"

"Um … yeah," she replied, trying to avoid the sight of the animal's blood.

Ella laughed as she turned her eyes from Kindle to Andrew. "Alright, you two, I can tell I'll have to prepare it myself." To Kindle's relief, Ella lowered her quarry and happily made her way to a spot out of their direct vision. Kindle watched her back for a moment then turned to Andrew.

"That's gross," she whispered. He glanced Ella's way but didn't voice his opinion. They stood without speaking long enough that they both began examining the forest around them. Kindle was considering drifting away from their increasingly awkward group when a realization struck her. To make sure she hadn't overlooked any space nearby, Kindle turned a circle then, when she faced Andrew again, asked, "Where's Tad?"

He shrugged as he also scanned the forest.

"You haven't seen him at all?" she pushed.

Andrew ended his visual search to lean around Kindle. As she turned to see what had snagged his attention, he reported, "He isn't on Nasah."

Peering through the trees, Kindle saw he was right: Nasah's saddle was empty. She leaned to find Nox and, just as she had anticipated, saw Tad wasn't sitting on his back either.

"Okay," she sighed to Andrew, "I'm gunna go look for him." Glad that Andrew didn't ask why, Kindle started over to the horses. She hoped she was wrong but imagined that their argument had spurred Tad to run off on his own like he always did when upset. When she reached the horses and saw no sign of him, worry also settled beside her guilt. His adamancy about remaining atop Nasah so the ground wouldn't eat him caused her to wonder if his fear had happened during the night. She bit her lip and examined the earth between the tuffs of grass at her feet. It didn't *look* monstrous, but Tad had said once the ground had devoured Wissen and Lord Beryl, it had returned to normal.

Feeling uneasy about the ground and the whole forest, Kindle almost spun around to relay her alarming speculation to Ella and Andrew, but a faint sound tugged on her attention. It was so quick and soft that Kindle waited to hear it again to make sure she hadn't imagined it. Before long the sound, repeated this time, touched her ears. Something about it was so familiar and friendly that she waited to hear it once more then slowly walked in its direction. As soon as she saw the riverbank slide into view, the sound connected to an action; someone was skipping rocks. The *plink-plink* noise began again, and Kindle detected the bouncing stone a short distance down the river. She swung past the last few trees to the river's edge and saw Tad stoop to pick up another rock.

Fear of rousing his anger or saying something dumb almost

convinced her to conclude her search and report his whereabouts to Ella and Andrew, but she noticed him briefly glance her way and knew if she left now, he'd never believe she really cared. Putting on a grin, she walked down to where he stood. Even when she stopped only feet away, he didn't let his glare deviate from the rocks around his shoe. All of her small hope that he had let their argument die dissipated. Not knowing what to say, she decided to be casual.

"Hey," she greeted him as cheerfully as possible.

He didn't reply.

Her smile faltered, and she searched for a question he would have to answer. "So, um, did you get any sleep?" Kindle waited, but he remained silent. "Ella's cooking breakfast," she tried, sure the subject of food would elicit some kind of response from him.

"Great," he grumbled then selected a rock, tossed it in his hand, and sent it skipping over the water.

"Are you gunna—" Kindle started to ask, but he suddenly rudely interrupted.

"Why're you down here? Did Ella make you come get me?"

Surprised and hurt by his outburst, Kindle crossed her arms and mumbled, "No."

He sniffed a sneer onto his face. "Really? 'Cause I know you don't care what the rest of us do. Bet you wish we'd leave you alone. Bet you wish I'd get lost."

"Ugh!" huffed Kindle, now offended. "No! I came down here by myself, okay? Nobody told me to. I just wanted to, like, I dunno, say I was sorry, I guess. But now I don't know why, because it's not like you wanna hear it."

Now Tad faced her to return her angry stare. "No, I don't want to hear you acting like you give a rip about any of us when you don't. When all you care about is going home. Pft, I don't wanna hear you bein' fake anymore. Just leave me alone, okay?"

They glared at one another, and Kindle felt as if they had returned to their first explosive argument at Azildor's farm. Remembering how she hadn't given in to his anger that day and the good that resulted, Kindle collected her mass of flailing emotions to retort, "No. I'm not gunna leave you alone. Don't you get that? Like, I'm the only one who ever comes after you when you run off. Doesn't that mean anything?" She paused to let him answer, but when he simply continued to glower at her, she heaved a sigh. "Ugh. I'm not gunna just leave you guys. And not just because I can't. Because– because it's like I told you, you guys are like my family now. You *are* my family now. And just because I said something stupid when I was tired doesn't change that. I just—I dunno why I said it. I mean, I *do* want to go home, but I also want to be here and do this and get rid of this evil guy and his evil throne, but I … I really want that part to be over, you know? Like, just the whole 'everybody depending on us' thing." Kindle halted her flowing words. She hadn't meant to take their argument in this direction or to release all of her thoughts and fears, but spilling them out into the space between her and Tad felt relieving.

Hoping her release wasn't having the opposite effect on Tad, she checked his expression. His face didn't carry a distinct emotion, but since it definitely held less anger, she continued, "You know what I mean? It's just, like, really hard feeling like everybody's depending on us and we don't even really know what to do. And–and that's what I wish was over, not hanging out with you guys all day. But I know we can't just quit—like, I know we can't go home and might not ever go home and all that—because we're the ones who're supposed to do this, and so we've got to, and we've all got to do it together. So … I guess I want to go home because … I dunno, it's, like, where I've always lived, but I really do want to be here and do all this stuff because this is … *right*. It's what we *need* to do. And we've got to do it together, and … and that makes it a lot easier to want to keep going."

Knowing her babblings very likely sounded like nonsense, Kindle examined her hands while she waited to hear Tad's response. Too much time passed before he spoke, though, and unable to restrain her nervous embarrassment, Kindle sputtered, "I'm sorry, I know I said a bunch and—"

"Nah," Tad calmly mumbled, and she picked up her face in surprise. He wasn't fuming at her or restraining any mockery but staring very thoughtfully across the river. Kindle followed his gaze, sure something had distracted him. Before she had a chance to look, Tad spoke in a constrained, quiet voice. "You wanna know somethin'?"

Even though Kindle considered that her answer might depend on what the "something" was, she nodded. "Yeah."

"Azildor said somethin' when he gave me this," Tad told her as he put a hand on Natzal. "He said that we're gunna do this—take out the evil guy and all that junk—but we can't get all stupid and think about being scared and stuff. He said if we're gunna do this, we gotta forget about not being able to do it and being scared and mad and gettin' hurt and just do whatever we gotta do."

For a while, Kindle simply stared at Tad, unsure of what to say. She remembered how she had been carefully listening to Azildor when he presented Natzal to him, but since then, most of their words had faded into vague wisps. As Tad had reminded her of their conversation, though, Azildor's powerful words refilled her mind like voluminous clouds. All that time his words had only *seemed* important, but now that the truth within them was mixing into her current reality, they rained understanding and peace over her.

Suddenly, Kindle knew that her fears of never seeing her home again and being responsible for Anelthalien's annihilation were the very culprits keeping her from truly diving into their mission and achieving their goal. She hadn't known the restraint of fear had even existed in her or had been the reason for her and Tad's argument, but now that she understood that it did live in her and saw all the setbacks and difficulties it caused, she wanted it gone. Letting the rain of comprehension wash away her anxieties, Kindle sighed.

"Thanks," she breathed, glad to finally let all her worries slide out of her mind.

Now Tad shot her a confused look.

"Um, I mean for saying that," she clarified. "I was just worried about everything, and that's why I said what I did last night. I was just worried … but you're right, I shouldn't be, so thanks, and … and I'm sorry."

Tad shrugged. "It wasn't me who said it. It was Azildor."

"Well, I'm glad you remembered," Kindle replied, determined to give him thanks.

"Yeah," he mumbled, and she considered it a sufficient acceptance of her gratitude. Still not completely sure if he had taken her apology, though, Kindle waited to see what he would say next. When he silently returned to skipping rocks, Kindle knew she would have to wrestle his thoughts out of him. Picking up a stone to skip, she bumbled, "So, um … are, um … do you—?"

"What?" he laughed but not deridingly.

She blinked at him and saw none of his hostility remained, only puzzlement. "Do you believe me?" Kindle worriedly blurted. "I mean, I said I was sorry, but I didn't know if you believed me."

With slight confusion on his face, he eyed her then answered, "Yeah."

"Really?"

"Yeah," Tad repeated then half-grinned as he slung his rock. "I guess since you still won't leave me alone, I have to believe you."

Deciding that his answer was far better than what she expected, Kindle also let a smile raise one side of her face. In the joy of their repaired friendship, Kindle forgot to focus on skipping the rock in her hand and instead pathetically tossed it into the water not far from their feet.

Tad barked a laugh. "Don't you know how to skip rocks?"

"Um, yeah," Kindle replied, humiliated but still grinning. "It's just been a while."

Tad snuffed in amusement but then proceeded to instruct her in the art of rock skipping. Kindle knew exactly how to send a rock bouncing across the water's surface, but she let him roll out directions, laugh at her exaggerated failures, then reinstruct her over and over. When she had just decided to allow some of her true ability to show, a yell from down the bank startled her and her rock zipped straight to the bottom of the river. As Tad laughed, she spun to see who had called.

"Tad! Kindle!" Ella shouted as she waved them to her. After she dropped her handful of stones and Tad tossed his out over the river, they jogged along the water to Ella.

"The birds have been ready for ages," Ella sighed as they met her and all trekked into the trees together. "Have you two been tossing rocks this whole time? Andrew and I have searched all about for you. We were beginning to believe you had disappeared."

A debate on how to answer commenced in Kindle's mind. She didn't want to lie to Ella but also didn't want her to know they had argued. While she was still weighing her options, they reached the little fire Ella had created.

"Go on, you two, I shot one for us each," directed Ella, pointing to the four roasted birds skewered over the fire. "Just one to split among us all didn't seem enough. I suppose I'll find Andrew before he wanders too far." Swinging her head back and forth, she trailed past the fire and between the white trees. Kindle watched her leave and considered waiting for her and Andrew to return before eating, but Tad was already trying to select his breakfast.

"Fft!" he hissed, and Kindle fully faced him and saw he was shaking his hand and glaring at the fire.

"What'd you do?" she asked, hoping he hadn't tried to snatch a bird from the fire. He turned his angry, pained face to her, and she rolled her eyes.

"You have to take them *off* the stick before you eat them."

"Yeah, I know," he defended himself but let her carefully pluck up the end of the spit and lean it against a nearby tree.

Kindle saw him greedily eyeing the little roasted birds and with a giggle cautioned, "Just wait a minute so you don't burn your hand again."

A grumpy frown took over his face. "I didn't burn myself."

Kindle just rolled her eyes and sat beside their cooling breakfast. Tad plopped down on the other side of the birds and hungrily glared at them.

"How long do I have to wait?"

Kindle shrugged. "I don't know. Until they're not super hot or—"

"What's wrong? Are they not good?" Ella interrupted Kindle's thought as she reappeared with Andrew behind her.

Tad shot a disgruntled face her way and explained, "They're hot."

"Oh, well, of course they're warm. I've just cooked them," Ella laughed then strode to the skewers and slid off the top bird. Handing it to Kindle and then the next to Tad, she noted, "They don't seem to be warm now."

As Kindle passed her meal from hand to hand, she turned a puzzled stare up at Ella. The bird she held was definitely almost hot enough to burn her. As she peered at Tad to see if he also felt the overwhelming heat still in his bird, he returned a disgusted glance then asked, "What do you mean it's not hot?"

At his question Andrew, who had been ready to receive his breakfast from Ella, lowered his hands and stepped back from Ella as she twisted to see Tad.

"What?" she inquired, flipping her confused eyes to each of them. Tad sat his bird on the ground, crossed his arms, and suspiciously glared up at her. Ella stared back but with bemusement covering her face. As Kindle flicked her eyes between them, she realized neither was going to provide the other with the answers they each wanted. Heaving a sigh, Kindle resolved to clear Ella's trouble first.

"Ella, these *are* still hot," she apologetically explained, laying hers aside as well. "Why did you say they weren't?"

"But, Kin, they're not," she insisted, glancing at the one in her hand. "I suppose you might feel a bit of heat in them ..."

Behind her Andrew pinched his brow together and, in his strange way of both asking a question and stating a fact, wondered, "You can't feel them."

"What?" Ella asked, turning back to him.

"You're too hot—" Andrew halted at Tad's snicker, but Ella, with understanding now on her face, nodded.

Somewhat uncomfortably, she admitted, "I can't feel its heat like you can. Fire and other things people say is hot has never felt so warm to me, so I suppose I'm just too warm to feel its heat. And cold things as well. They have never seemed unpleasantly stinging or refreshingly cool as anyone says, and I can never hold them without making them warm. At the Lighthouse the complaint I endure more than any other is that a drink is too warm." Ella turned sad eyes to Tad. "I didn't mean to lie to you, Tad, if that's what you're sour over. I honestly had no feeling of its heat."

"Yeah, whatever," he grumbled. "Just like you don't know anything about this forest."

"What is that—Tad, do you still believe I am keeping secrets?" Ella quickly retorted, but before Tad could return fire, Kindle dove into the escalating debate.

"Wait. Guys, calm down, okay?" she urgently pleaded then rested her nervous eyes on Tad. He met her expression, sneered at it, but settled against the tree. Satisfied that he would let her explain his frustration to Ella, she meekly peered up at her friend.

"Um, Ella, I ..." Having no idea how to delicately demand that Ella spill all her secrets, Kindle huffed and quickly divulged, "Ella, it's just, like, Tad and I ... ugh, you know you *just* told us about you being a witch and an elf and everything, and that's totally fine—it doesn't creep us out or anything—but it's just, like, it just kind of makes us wonder about what *else* you haven't told us. So ... we just want to know." Kindle could see her confession had punctured Ella and wanted to apologize. She also sensed Tad watching her, though, and suddenly remembered the reason for his suspicion.

"I mean, Tad just saw something really weird last night," Kindle tried to explain, "and you know everything about Anelthalien, so it's not like we don't trust you—" She ignored Tad's snort. "It's just that we wanna know what's going on."

Very slowly, Ella turned her betrayed face from Kindle to Tad. At first Kindle didn't think Ella would answer. She opened her mouth several times without uttering a sound but finally found her voice. "What did you see?" Ella quietly asked Tad. They all cautiously peered at him to hear his answer.

All they received was a stony glare.

Shaking her head, Ella sighed, "I don't know how you can

expect so much when you give nothing. Tad, I've already told you I know nothing about this forest except that men do not prefer to enter it, and that is why I know so little. And I cannot reveal something about it which I have no inkling of." She paused to shift her eyes to Kindle. "And, Kin, this—all of this suspicion and demanding of every bit of my life—is exactly why I did not plan to tell you and never planned to tell anyone of my … my curse. I'm not like anyone else, and people would want to hurt me for it. Can't you see why I kept it from you? Not to trick or harm you, but to keep safe. And now those men in Aryl know, and they'll want to find me and do away with me. So can you understand, Kin, why I said nothing of it for so long?"

Ashamed, Kindle dipped her head in a nod and left it bowed. "Yeah, I'm sorry. I just—I'm sorry."

"Kin, it's alright. I only wanted us not to be at odds with one another."

"So you don't know anything else?" Tad pushed, ripping the bond that had almost mended.

Exasperation cracked Ella's calm, and she huffed, "Again, Tad, why do you expect so much? Of course I am aware of things I haven't told you—the dinnerware at the Lighthouse is stored in the bin beside the kitchen door, the traders from Turner have the most reliable medicines, and my papa has a nasty wart on his right foot—but I do not see the reasoning in telling you those things or everything I know. Isn't it enough that I have told you everything I know of this forest? But, since you expect me to inform you of all of my life, why don't you share your own background? Because how can I trust anything you say until I'm certain you are not an ogre or a troll?" Ella's voice had been rising in volume and offended anger, but after it peaked at her last word, she inhaled a deep, calming breath then sighed, "No, excuse me, that is ridiculous to demand so much. Instead, could you please tell me what you saw?"

Kindle wasn't sure if Ella's words or the now mashed and smoking bird in her fist convinced Tad to answer. Either way, the steadfast defensiveness on his face melted slightly, and he mumbled something to the ground. Fearful that he would explode if Ella asked him to repeat himself, Kindle hurriedly interpreted.

"He said he saw the ground eat those guys who were chasing us." From the shock that snapped onto Andrew and Ella's faces, Kindle knew they hadn't expected her statement and likely didn't believe it. She swept a sidelong glance at Tad then declared, "And I believe him."

Disbelief softened to curiosity on Ella's face, and she wondered, "How exactly did the earth eat them?"

Kindle turned to Tad for an explanation, and reluctantly, he pulled his glare up to Ella. "So you said you live by the ocean, right? It was like a wave—a big wave of dirt—smashed over 'em then went back flat."

"A landslide?" Andrew wondered aloud, and Kindle could tell by his squinty thoughtfulness he was struggling to picture what Tad had described.

"No, not a landslide, genius," Tad snarled. "Do you see any hills around here?"

Andrew didn't answer but dropped his abashed but still calculating face to his feet.

After glancing at Andrew, Ella urged, "Then what *do* you mean?"

"What do you mean what do I mean?!" Tad snapped back. "I told you what I saw, okay? And I'm not sayin' it again. If you don't believe me, that's your problem."

"Do calm down," Ella ordered, then guilty realization jumped onto her face, and she added, "Please. I did not say I did not believe you—I've heard *much* stranger tales than that—I only asked what you meant. Do you mean that the ground of this forest welled up and over the horsemen? Not that a riff in the earth opened or something natural?"

Tad's blue eyes bored holes into her as he slightly shook his head and scoffed, "It wasn't natural."

The way Ella tilted her head then peered over her shoulder to catch Andrew's eye led Kindle to wonder if Ella *did* know something about what Tad had witnessed. She started to question Ella, but her friend suddenly switched her focus to the bird in her hand. Staring at it, Ella mused, "I have a feeling, and I think it best if we all had a chat … but we must start moving. Here." She handed the spit with the last bird on it to Andrew. "I hope it really has cooled now."

Once Andrew prodded the roasted animal and nodded, Ella hurried over to Nox and Nasah. Kindle stared after her for a few seconds then blinked between Tad and Andrew. Ella's sudden insistence to leave their campsite bemused her, and she wondered if she had missed the reason for the necessity of their flight. When puzzlement also dawned over Andrew and Tad, though, she felt less uninformed.

With a shrug, she hesitantly suggested, "Um, I guess let's go." As she plucked up her breakfast, Andrew immediately meandered over to Ella. Tad, though, only stood after Kindle did and then blocked her path to the others.

"She's up to somethin'," he hissed.

Kindle, although she sensed something was wrong, shook her head. "I really don't think so. Like, I think what you said might of reminded her of something, and now she's scared or something like that, but I don't think she's up to anything."

"You sure?" he interrogated as he evaluated her face with narrowed eyes.

"Yeah, I'm sure. She just wants to tell us something." She peered around him to avoid his penetrating stare and find Ella, who was boosting Andrew onto Nox. "C'mon, they're ready." Kindle stepped around Tad before he could respond, and soon they both reached Nasah and climbed onto her back. Without a word, Ella spurred Nox into motion and steered him away through the trees. Tad gave Kindle a challenging look then shook Nasah's reins to follow Ella and Andrew.

As they hurried to keep pace with the others, Kindle wondered if Tad was right—if Ella was hiding some sort of malicious plot. When they did pull up beside Nox and all turned to ride along the river, though, Ella's expression cleared her suspicions. Alert worry covered her face, and her keen, quick eyes were examining the forest.

"Ella, what's wrong?" Kindle slowly questioned, afraid of what her answer would reveal.

Without breaking her search, Ella responded, "I'm not sure, but something is … something is not right."

Kindle scanned the empty, serene space between the white trees. "What? I mean, do you see something or is it what Tad said?"

"No. I … I felt something." Finally, Ella made eye contact with Kindle as she spoke. "And, Kin, I know this sounds strange, but I felt something in the earth."

Kindle sucked in her breath then whispered, "Was it gunna eat us?"

"An earthquake?" Andrew almost simultaneously guessed, but Ella waved her head at them both.

Then, to Kindle's great surprise, Tad seriously concluded, "You heard somethin' again."

"Yes," Ella replied as her face turned to him. "Quite like before but instead of words only a … I suppose a notion that something else in this forest—in the ground of this forest—was quite near us and it was not something good."

Now Kindle and Andrew exchanged confused glances.

"Um, guys …" Kindle began as she tried to determine what to say.

"Did you hear or see something?" Andrew filled in her silence.

Ella sighed and tilted a smile to him. "No, Andrew. See, I've told Kindle and Tad, when I repaired Lord Beryl's home in Aryl, I listened to this voice, and it led me to mend the wood, and the same had happened when I mended Kindle's leg with the grass. And just then it was that same sort of voice, only not a voice, but I still understood it well enough."

Thoughtful confusion wrinkled Andrew's brow. "I thought you knew how to do those things because you're an elf."

"No," Ella quickly replied, "I've always been an elf but have never had any inkling of how to do any of that. It's that nudging voice telling me. It's as if the plants and earth are speaking to me, as if I'm connected to them …"

"What?" Andrew mumbled, and Kindle saw a glimmer of comprehension light his eyes.

"I know, that sounds absolutely blathering, but—"

"No," Andrew interrupted. "You said ... Ella, it's your necklace."

Kindle, Tad, and Ella twisted to fully stare at him. Andrew shifted uncomfortably and dropped his eyes, but Ella prompted him to explain. His gaze flicked up to her then back down again, but he mumbled, "You said you felt like you were connected to the ground. Lord Rex and Lady Luna told us that the necklaces connected the elemental spirits to their makers and the elements. So it makes sense that *we* are connected to the elements and the makers."

While he had explained his conclusion, Kindle let her eyes fall on her own red gem. What Andrew said followed logic and, in a very strange way, sounded perfectly reasonable. Ever since Kindle had first noticed her necklace, she had known it was significant, but until now she had considered its significance to only exist in the past. The thought of it still holding its ancient ability to connect her to something so vast as the sky and so mighty and mysterious as a maker caused her to feel very small but also very close to an incredible amount of time and power. Kindle picked it up and squinted at it, hoping she would hear the voice Ella had described. After a few moments of disappointing silence, she let it fall against her shirt.

"Are you sure?" she sighed as she peered at Andrew. "I mean, it's just ... I can't hear anything from mine. I never have. And, Ella, you're the only one who *has*. Maybe it's just yours ..."

Ella glanced back at her with a grin then switched her focus to Tad as she slowly divulged, "No, it's not only mine. You've heard it too, haven't you, Tad? When I mentioned it in Aryl, you understood. I know you did."

"I dunno. Maybe," he grumbled.

A smile lit Ella's face as she breathed, "When?"

His silence gave Kindle time to try to recall Tad's words in Aryl. She remembered that he had said something curiously perceptive after Ella had confessed about the guiding voice but couldn't pull his exact sentence from any corner of her mind. "You did ..." Kindle quietly mused as she thought. "You said—or I think you asked her something—and it was like you knew exactly what she meant." Kindle saw his shoulders roll, and she understood that he did know what she and Ella were referring to but didn't want to talk about it. "C'mon, Tad, please tell us," she softly begged in the most kind and personal tone she could.

Turning his face to her so Ella and Andrew couldn't see it, he met her pleading eyes. After searching them for a long minute, he mumbled, "'Kay."

Facing forward to steer Nasah but speaking to all of them, he admitted, "Yeah, I know what you meant. I didn't hear no voices, but it was like somebody naggin' me to do somethin'."

"What? When did it happen?" encouraged Ella.

Tad passed a grumpy face her way before he groaned and relented the whole truth. "Back in Iteraum. When you told me to go to that stupid castle. And you told me to follow Kindle around. I didn't want to go in that stupid tutu show, and I wasn't gunna 'cause I knew nothin' was gunna happen except a bunch of snobs were gunna drool over that punk prince. But ... it wasn't a voice. It was, I dunno—I got a bad feeling, and it wouldn't leave me alone. I got a feeling somethin' bad was gunna happen in there, and I went in the stupid place just so it'd leave me alone."

"Is that how you knew where I was?" interjected Kindle, remembering how wonderful and perplexed she had felt when Tad had appeared to save her that night.

"Yeah," he replied, sounding perturbed. "I saw you and that punk dodging through that door, and by the time I got through it, that punk was tryin' to get back through." Tad sniffed. "I almost had to break his stinkin' leg to get him to talk."

A smile lifted Kindle's mouth at the memory but disappeared as soon as Andrew argued, "But that *doesn't* make sense."

Immediately, Tad defensively retorted, "Yeah, well, it's what happened!"

As he continued to grumble about Andrew only ever believing

Ella, Andrew rolled an exhausted face to him and clarified, "It doesn't line up with what's happening to Ella. She heard about her element. What happened then had nothing to do with an element, especially fire or water, which are the only ones your necklace could possibly connect to."

"There was a fountain!" Kindle cried, excited she had possibly linked the facts into an answer. Andrew gave her a doubtful glance, so she explained, "No, seriously, there was a fountain in the garden where that creepy thing attacked me. What if that was the water that told Tad something was wrong?"

Squinting an unsure face at her, Andrew inquired, "Was it *in* the fountain?"

"What, the creepy thing?" she replied, and he nodded. Closing her eyes to recall the layout of the castle garden, Kindle twisted her lips in thought. Finally, she shook her head. "No, it wasn't. I don't know where it was hiding. It *did* fall in the fountain after it attacked me, but it got out really quick."

"It wasn't the water …" concluded Andrew, and Tad glared back at him.

"So, what? When *I* hear stuff it's 'cause I'm stupid, but when *she* does it's 'cause she's all magical and awesome? Pft—I should of known you were just gunna—"

"Tad, stop," Ella calmingly broke into his grumblings. "He only said it wasn't the water that spoke to you—"

"Nothing talked to me!" he angrily interrupted.

Ella patiently sighed and smiled. "Alright, *nagged* you, then. So it wasn't the element of water that nagged you, but what about fire? That is what you said, isn't it, Andrew? His necklace either connects him to water or fire? Was there any sort of fire about?"

"This is stupid. Why's it matter?" growled Tad.

Kindle guessed that he was tired of Andrew invalidating his every word and therefore done with the conversation. Curiosity about his nagging feeling, though, urged her to keep diving deeper into the mystery. "No," she answered Ella, "There wasn't any fire in the garden, not even torches or anything. It was all open so the moon lit it."

Ella thoughtfully huffed, "Well, I don't know, then. There had to be something there, though, Tad. You knew all too well what it was like whenever I told you two about that voice and just now when I felt that disturbance in the earth. Wasn't there anything else in the garden?"

"No," he spat. "Just plants and that stupid fountain … and that creeper."

"Tad!" Kindle gasped and caused all of them to jump and twist to see her. "That–that thing, it said something to me right before you threw Natzal at it! It said … it said, 'It is close,' and I didn't think about it then, but …" Unable to find words to explain her sudden epiphany, Kindle simply stared wide eyes at Tad, willing him to understand.

"What?" he demanded, his face scrunched.

"Ugh … okay, um, so do you remember what Azildor said when we …" She glanced sideways at Ella, who immediately deciphered her hesitation.

"Kin, did you listen in on him and Naam?" Ella began to chide, but Kindle quickly continued.

"Yeah, when we did that! You remember what he said about that thing?"

"Somethin' about it knowing where we are," Tad replied. "What's it—"

"Yeah! He said it was like that thing knew where we were," she breathlessly repeated, and the others blinked as if her point was beginning to dawn over them.

"Do you think …" Andrew slowly mumbled, his eyes calculating, "that thing can sense where our necklaces are and … and *we* can sense where *it* is?"

Ella's eyes bugged, and she swept the group with them.

Kindle, though, shook her head. "No, well, I mean, yeah, but only kind of. I think that thing knows where *Tad's* necklace is, and he can tell where *it* is."

"Are you thinking that black ghost isn't a black ghost at all?"

whispered Ella.

Instead of telling Ella that she had never thought the creepy hooded monster was a black ghost, Kindle replied, "Yeah, I think it's one of the spirits."

After uttering a small gasp, Ella argued, "But it can't be. All the spirits have gone. They lost their power."

"They lost their forms," Andrew added.

"Yeah," Tad agreed. "And that thing keeps goin' after *you*, not me."

Kindle raised her hands in defense at all of them. "Okay," she sighed, addressing Tad first. "So, it hasn't come after me. Just wait a second—you remember what it did on the tower? It went for my boot. Back then I just thought it wanted to eat my leg or something, but that's where your necklace was. I stuck it in there when you didn't want it. You know, at the library? Then at Iteraum it *did* attack me first at the garden, but when you showed up, it, like, totally forgot about me and went for you. And it knew you were coming! Right before you showed up, it said that: 'It is close.' It *knew* your necklace was close."

As she caught her excited, rushed breath, Kindle examined each of their faces. Andrew seemed to be thinking at high speed, the part of Tad's face she could see appeared wary but almost convinced, and Ella looked dumbfounded.

"See?" Kindle persuasively urged mostly to Tad since he was the only one who had experienced the creature besides her. "It's connected to your necklace."

"Then why don't you guys have weirdos followin' you around too, huh?" Tad questioned, and Kindle rolled her eyes at his determination to argue.

Seeing her, Ella interjected, "No, Kindle, he's right. It can't be one of the spirits. They've all gone. All of their power was in these necklaces, and now we have them, so they've lost all of their power."

"And their forms," Andrew logically reminded them again. "They aren't in their forms anymore."

"But what if they are?" Kindle persisted. "I mean, who said they died or lost their forms or whatever? *Who?*"

She waited for an answer, but even Andrew eventually shook his head and concluded, "No one said that. The Cifra and Azildor never said what happened to them … but that's what makes sense."

Kindle eyes brightened. "But what if it's not what happened? What if they're still out there somewhere? Like, just the bodies they made without their power?" She paused as a realization crept into her brain then whispered, "You know what they'd wanna do if they were still out there … with no power?"

"Oh my," murmured Ella, and Kindle knew from her hand that protectively curled around her gem and her frightened tone that she understood.

Before Kindle had a chance to dramatically announce her discovery, though, Tad, in a tone that sounded like he was challenging them to do so, growled, "They'd want 'em back."

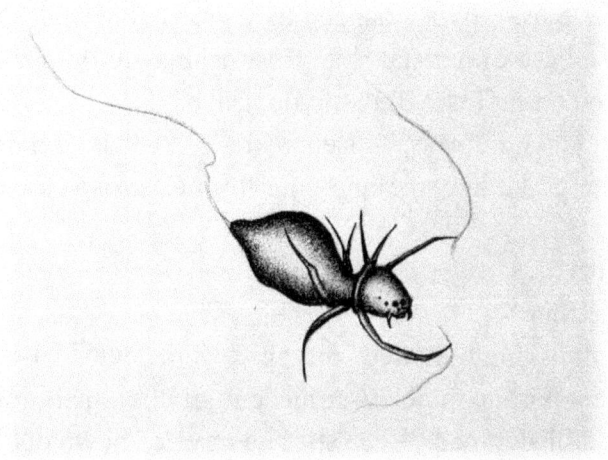

DISTANT IN SPIRIT

"What?" Menthoshine spat as she snatched her staff. "You better have something extraordinarily fascinating, Bennickle!"

As his face materialized in her orb, a low snickering issued from behind her, and she violently twisted.

"You filthy wretch, leave!" she wrathfully shouted. "I do not want your stench anywhere near me!"

"Flattery, Men-tho-shine," Bennickle gradually cranked out of his jaw, "is more powerful than … insult."

She sneered at his face and hissed. "Flattery is *slow*."

"Effective," countered Bennickle in an especially low, gravely tone.

Another laugh from Castrosphy echoed through the room, and Menthoshine whipped around to face him, propelling the spider that had been steadily spinning at her side.

"Ma'am!" the arachnid squealed as she flew in one direction then the other.

"Leave us, Olivia," dangerously growled Menthoshine as she slammed the base of her staff into Castrosphy. He flumped sideways and remained crumpled. "Both of you, leave."

"They are near," Bennickles's voice reported, and Menthoshine broke her snarling glare from Castrosphy and tied it to the orb.

"What?"

"The four."

Menthoshine's hatred morphed into evil delight as she gathered her skirt to quickly stride out of the small room where Castrosphy still slumped. When she had traveled down one long, dark hall and tuned down another, she halted and demanded, "They are in the forest? Do you have them?"

Menthoshine writhed in annoyance as he slowly lifted his face, slid his eyes back and forth, then eventually but decisively answered, "It is difficult."

"What is difficult?" she fumed, practically shaking her staff. As she resumed her walk through the dark, she avidly but more quietly questioned, "What is difficult, Ben? What could possibly be difficult about knowing if four disgusting, inept children tramp over your soil or if you hold them captive?"

"They travel … the river," he simply responded.

She huffed then snarled, "I do not care where they are in your forest. If they are near you, *get them*."

"It is difficult."

"You useless troll!" she exploded. "If it is so difficult, perhaps I should come and fetch them."

"Insult slows processes," Bennickle evenly responded.

"Stupidity and trepidation slow processes!" she screamed back. "You worthless fool! I should have known better than to entrust your pebble of a mind with any task! Just tell me where they are, and I will complete what is too *difficult*."

Unmoved by her screams and insults, Bennickle unconcernedly replied, "You will remain."

Menthoshine's nostrils flared at his words, but she stormed along the dark hall for a long time before snarling, "I am not a child. I will not be told what I can and cannot do."

His answer came immediately but lasted too long for her short temper. "Cir-cum-stan-ces bar us more than … desires free us."

"To rot with your circumstances and desires!" she cried, glaring at his solidly expressionless face. "I know what you are capable of, and the only factor that bars that is your desire to treat me like a CHILD! Now let me out of this sordid prison before your slow talk and mind ruin everything!"

"It is diff—"

A horrible, raging scream from Menthoshine drowned his last word. Before the last echo of her anger faded, she wiped her thin, pale hand over her orb, and green swirls then crackles of light immediately replaced Bennickle's face.

"CASTROSPHY!" she boomed. "Castrosphy, you rotten cretin! Find me at once!"

Instantly, his thin, airy voice hissed, "Yesss?"

Menthoshine spun to find and shine her soft green light on his cloak. Finally, she discovered him in a heap beside the wall. Slamming her staff into him, she rumbled, "You filthy roach, I command you to cease your sneaking. Now listen: that ogre Bennickle has exceeded his usefulness. He has run dry of answers and ability. So tell me what you know of his forest."

Slowly and quietly, Castrosphy hissed, "SSSylina Foressst isss dissstant."

"Yes, and that is no matter to you, you incompetent wretch. Now tell me something I am not aware of."

"Not dissstant in ssspace. Dissstant in ssspirit."

Menthoshine, who had been watching the green electricity, narrowed her eyes and let them drift his way. "Explain yourself."

"The air isss difficult there. Difficult to dissscern."

"What is difficult, Castrosphy?" Menthoshine hungrily demanded. "What is so difficult about the air in Xylina Forest?"

Three short hisses issued from his form, and Menthoshine

129

violently kicked and pinned him against the wall.

"How dare you laugh! Answer me!"

Castrosphy exhaled a wheeze-like chuckle then whispered, "Water."

UPHEAVAL

After Tad voiced Kindle's thought, they all fell silent. Kindle was sure, though, that all their minds were just as busy and loud as hers. All her memories, thoughts, and speculations were zipping across one another so quickly and erratically that they tangled into one anxious, exited, confused ball. Yanking her mind to a standstill, Kindle took a breath and then slowly unraveled all the thoughts.

First, she tried to find the strands of truth. They each had a necklace—she knew that for certain—but only Tad and Ella had heard or felt anything from them. Also, despite what the others believed, Kindle knew that the creepy thing knew where Tad's necklace was and was probably the water or fire spirit. Kindle tried to detect more solid facts from their conversation but couldn't see any.

Next, she hunted for all the guesses they had presented and almost immediately felt too overwhelmed to pursue any of the theories. Kindle closed her eyes to calm herself, trying to focus on the fact that possibly all their ponderings were false. However, her instincts told her some of it had to be true, and her determination to understand what was dancing just out of her comprehension reeled her back to the cacophony of hypotheses.

Something was communicating with Ella and Tad, and it had to be either the makers, the spirits, or maybe even the elements. As she wondered which it could be—or if it was all of them—the question of why nothing had communicated with her and Andrew entered her thoughts. The fact bothered her. It seemed to imply that she was somehow less than Ella and Tad, as if she was not as skilled or worthy of receiving any revelations. Shifting uncomfortably on Nasah's back, Kindle tried to switch her thoughts to a different track.

The hooded figure pushed into her consciousness, and she gladly welcomed it. Even though she found the creature horribly eerie, the mystery around it intrigued her. Kindle reminded herself that it had to be one of the spirits. At least in her mind, nothing else explained its awareness of and hunger for Tad's necklace. Which spirit it was, though, she couldn't decide. After a while of sifting through what she could remember of Azildor's story about the crazy fire spirit and considering that Tad's necklace *was* blue, Kindle decided that the strange creature tailing them was the water spirit. However, as soon as she determined that conclusion, it tripped over Andrew and Ella's speculations about the dismal fate of the spirits. Maybe the spirits really had lost all their power and their forms. Kindle *did* recall Lady Luna saying that they had lost something. Wanting to dismiss her friends' suggestions, Kindle shook her head. If the spirits were gone, then the creepy thing had to be something else, and she did not want to accept the consideration that something unknown was hunting them.

Done with her even more entangled and worried thoughts, Kindle sighed and stared past Ella and Andrew to the river. The peacefully flowing water held her attention and kept her frenzied thoughts from overtaking her until she noticed Andrew curiously peer her way. Switching her gaze to him, she sighed, "What do you think?" Convinced that he, Ella, and Tad were just as overwhelmed and confused as her, Kindle did not expect Andrew to answer, but after a shrug, he revealed a very decisive conclusion.

"I think there's a lot more going on than we know about."

Ella curiously tilted her head as she asked, "What do you mean, Andrew? You sound as if you've worked something out."

He sighed and rocked his head to indicate his postulations were not solid truth.

Not really caring if he was sure about what he very likely had rightly guessed, Kindle urged, "Well, what? What do you think's going on?"

"I'm not positive," he began without confidence, "but I don't think what's following us is one of the spirits."

"So what is it?" grumbled Tad as if he didn't care how Andrew would answer.

As Andrew's eyes began roving around the air, he explained, "The Cifra and Azildor never said what happened to the spirits—they never even said how they lost their necklaces—but they did say what the spirits were before they got power.

"The elements themselves," Ella chimed in, her voice full of proud discovery. "The makers created the spirits from their elements and then gave them power. So do you mean to say that when they lost their power, they didn't die but only returned to the element from which they came?"

Andrew nodded. "That makes the most sense."

"No, it doesn't," argued Kindle. She didn't see how Andrew's logic explained the voices speaking to Ella and Tad or the hooded figure. "How does that make sense with everything else going on?"

Andrew dropped his face as if dejected but mumbled, "It explains almost everything."

"How?" Kindle insisted, growing impatient with his resistance to speak his thoughts.

Andrew pointed his face to the river but finally divulged his full network of logic. "If the spirits went back into their elements, that explains why Ella has been more attached to hers than the rest of us. We've been on or under the ground the whole time we've been here. And I think it also explains what you saw last night, Tad,"

"What?" Tad sneered at Andrew, who ignored him.

"Ella, you told us that an abandoned mine is on the other side of this forest, and you said everyone avoids it, but it isn't on our map."

Kindle and Ella exchanged confused glances but returned their eyes to Andrew when he continued.

"That means that mine was created sometime in the last one thousand years … when the earth spirit went back in the earth. I think that spirit made that mine and he lives there and under this forest. That would explain why no one ever comes here or goes there, why you've been more attuned to the earth here, and how the earth could eat someone here."

Ella sadly shook her head. "But … but that would mean they still have power, Andrew. And they don't. They simply can't."

Raising and lowering his shoulders, Andrew bowed his head and quietly responded, "Maybe not."

"Nah!" Tad burst out. "Dude, don't let her tell you what to think. You're finally makin' some sense."

"Oh, Tad, really, I'm not—"

"Yeah, you *are*," he cut into Ella's defense then lifted his chin to Andrew. "So how's that stalker freak fit in?"

Andrew, obviously just as shocked as Kindle that Tad would defend him, blinked wordlessly. When he dropped his stare to his knee, Kindle decided to also encourage him.

"Yeah, all that does really make sense, but what about that … that thing? I mean, it knows where we are, so it has to be one of the spirits."

A thoughtful expression crossed Andrew's face as he turned it to Kindle. "It might be one," he mused, "or it might be working for all of them."

"Now you lost me," interjected Tad without taking his eyes from the path ahead. To stop Andrew from frowning at Tad, Kindle eagerly signaled for him to keep talking.

"If it is one," Andrew slowly reasoned, "it's the fire spirit. Azildor said that she disappeared when Ignalus disappeared, and then whoever took his place burned down Bellalux. If she took the evil throne, she might not have actually died after her one thousand years on the throne. The stone might have given her enough power to stay alive without the necklace, but because she wasn't a human, *that* might have given her enough power to not die with the end of her reign. Maybe you *are* right about her, Kindle. Maybe *she* isn't dead. Maybe she's somewhere in Anelthalien with just a body and no power ... but she wants power back, and so she's tracking Tad down to get it."

"You mean Tad's necklace is the mark of the fire maker?" Kindle questioned, unwilling to accept what Andrew had deduced. She not only hated to think that her guess about his blue gem had been wrong but also that a wrathful, half-undead fire spirit was hunting them and such a horrible being was inextricably tied to Tad. "Well, what if it's not her? What if it's ... whatever else you said?"

Andrew didn't seem to notice the objection in her voice to his first explanation as he bobbed his head and agreed, "That is a lot of 'what ifs'. I think it is something else but it knows where we are because it's working for the spirits. If they are alive and stuck in their elements, they will want their power back, but they can't get it, so they need someone else to do it for them."

"Who?" Kindle demanded more forcefully than she intended. Reeling back her nervous anticipation, she more calmly asked, "Who do you think it is?"

Andrew shrugged. "I don't know. It has to be someone who has some kind of stake in all of this ... someone who would get something for helping them."

Ella gasped, causing Nox to halt and stamp the ground. Once she had settled him and brought him back into step with Nasah, she whispered, "You don't suppose it's the heir, do you? The one in line to take the evil throne? I can't think of anyone else who would willingly enter such a wicked contract."

"Told you we had to kill that thing!" Tad triumphantly cried as he twisted to shoot his half-evil grin at Andrew and Kindle.

"Tad, you cannot kill it—what if it's a person who doesn't even realize—" Ella began to chide, but her words caused Kindle to remember something she couldn't keep to herself.

"You said it wouldn't die," she breathed to Tad then looked to Ella. "It's not just some person. Tad stabbed it like fifty thousand times, and it didn't even act like it was hurt. Oh! And remember at Azildor's? When you kicked it? It just disappeared."

"Yeah." Tad sniffed in hatred. "That thing's not human, and I'm gunna kill it."

"Tad," Ella pleaded, "don't you recall what Azildor told us? He warned us not to become killers."

"Yeah, but he also told us to track that thing down and make sure it didn't get on that throne," retorted Tad.

Ella avidly shook her head at him. "*No*. He told us to destroy the stone and … Tad, anyway, none of this is sure. The creature following us could be anyone."

"Or anything," added Kindle then snatched her opportunity to end their unsettling debate. "I mean, I don't really know what it is, but I don't think it's a person. It's not big enough, and it sounds … I dunno, it sounds weird. Remember, Ella, you thought it was a ghost when I first told you about it? But, it doesn't matter. Could we, like, stop and eat something? I'm getting really hungry."

Ella turned an apologetic face to her and replied, "I don't think we should stop. Regardless of the details of the fact, something is not right about this forest. Just dig about in the bags and hand us all a bite."

Even though Ella's answer had stirred Kindle's fears, it had also settled their arguing, and so she accepted it as she nodded and began hunting through their packs. After a long, increasingly disappointing search, Kindle sighed and held out the last of their stale bread. Tad, once he saw what she had found, grinned and snatched most of it. He was the only one who appeared even remotely excited about her discovery.

"Is that all we have left?" Ella hesitantly questioned. Neither she nor Andrew moved to take the few last bites from her hand, and Kindle knew they, unlike Tad, understood it was old, not toast.

Before Kindle could admit her answer, Tad eyed all of them then the bread and snorted, "You guys too dumb to eat?"

"Take it," sighed Kindle as she dumped every crumb into his palm.

As Tad poured his handful into his mouth, Ella, with a

sympathetic smile, chuckled, "Tad, you know that bread is past its time, don't you?"

"Tastes fine to me." He shrugged, examined his hand for more crumbs, then wiped it on his pants.

Ella ended her pointless conversation with him and turned her slightly concerned but still smiling face to Kindle. "Are you sure there's nothing more?"

Kindle reluctantly nodded. As she did, Tad twisted to view her response and realization slipped over his face.

"What? There's no food at all?" he demanded, eyeing both her and Ella.

To keep another fight from blossoming, Kindle shook her head. "No. It's okay, though, I'm not really hungry."

Andrew wrinkled his nose and mumbled, "I thought you just said—"

Quickly, Kindle shot him a protesting frown, but neither of their words nor actions mattered; Tad was already loudly blaming Ella.

"You were supposed to buy food," he accused. "What'd you do, forget?"

Smiling patiently but with a glimmer of fire in her eyes, Ella retorted, "Of course not. I *did* buy provisions in Iteraum, just as I told you I would, but only enough to last us a few days."

"Well, that was stupid," he snorted.

"If I had bought any more, you would have been yowling over the rotten stench, and we would be dumping it," she confidently returned. "And I never believed Aryl would prove so hostile. We *ought* to have traded there."

"Oh, okay, why don't you go back and ask that crazy dude and his weasel if they wanna share?"

"Oh, Tad, stop. I do not want to bicker with you. What happened with those guards could not have been avoided. They had heard of the upset in Iteraum and were primed to obstruct anyone who passed their way."

"Whatever. You know we could of gotten away if Einstein hadn't of told 'em we were spies."

"I never said we were spies," Andrew mumbled, but Kindle was sure only she heard him.

"He never said anything about us being spies," Ella replied in a tone that told Kindle she was finally losing her patience with Tad. "And his idea was brilliant."

"Oh, what? And I'm—"

"Quit!" Kindle shouted, knowing no other way to stop their fight. "Just quit, okay? It doesn't matter what happened back there."

"Matters that we don't have any food," Tad grumbled, and Kindle had to restrain her urge to punch him.

Instead, she rolled her eyes and exasperatedly sighed, "Well, we can just stop, and Ella can shoot something again." Kindle softened her expression to beg Ella, "I mean, it won't take long, and we can wait until it's later and we're really far from whatever was creeping you out."

Returning a sad smile, Ella contended, "It is not safe, Kin. We can't stop."

"Ugh," she groaned, let down by Ella's answer. "We have to eat."

"We could turn south," Andrew suggested, and each of them gave him a questioning stare. He uncomfortably shrugged and mumbled, "It would get us out of the forest ... and we eventually will have to veer south anyway so that we avoid the mine."

Cheerfulness climbed back on Ella's face as she assented, "Yes, Andrew, you're right. That's brilliant. If we turn now, we may find our way out before nightfall." Ella turned to Tad and, with eager apology in her voice, avowed, "And if we do, I'll hunt you three birds for supper."

Kindle watched Tad glance at Ella's expression to assess her sincerity.

"Honest," Ella promised then reined Nox to a halt. "Now, to head south, we must cross this river. Isn't that right, Andrew?"

As Tad pulled Nasah around to face the water, Andrew confirmed her question with a nod.

Swinging her gaze to the wide, swiftly flowing river, Kindle bit her lip. She didn't mind the idea of swimming; in fact, Kindle especially enjoyed playing in pools and occasionally a river during the summer, but the river beside them was much larger than any wild, unknown body of water she had ever ventured into. Worries of how deep it might be, how they would transfer all their packs, and if their horses could or would swim filled her mind.

"Is it safe?" she blurted, peering at Ella. "I mean, do you know how deep it is or anything?"

Ella twisted her lips in puzzlement, and her eyes filled with apprehension as she examined the river. "I don't really know, actually," she admitted. "I never considered it as unsafe to cross. Do rivers go very deep? I always supposed they were shallow how the traders speak about them."

Kindle heard Tad utter an annoyed sound as Andrew informed Ella, "Rivers can be very deep, and judging by how wide this one is, it probably is pretty deep."

"Oh," Ella replied, "well, do you suppose we *can* cross it, then?"

Andrew shrugged then asked, "Can you swim?"

Ella and Tad immediately, simultaneously responded. "Do you mean flailing about in the water?" Ella cried with sincere aversion as Tad shouted, "I'm not swimmin' anywhere!"

"What do you mean?" Kindle questioned Tad as Andrew addressed Ella.

Tad jumped down from Nasah and frowned at her. "I mean I'm not swimmin'," he repeated. "So unless we find a boat, forget it."

"What?" Kindle, glad for the opportunity to stretch her legs and not wanting to shout down at him, slid off Nasah as well. "There's no boat around here. I mean, I know it's kind of far, but Ella's not gunna let us stop and eat until we're out of this dumb forest. C'mon, it won't be that bad."

Tad didn't respond but moved his glower to the river. For a moment, Kindle thought he was mulling over her argument but understood another emotion occupied his mind when he disgustedly sneered at the river.

"Hey, what's wrong?" she whispered. Kindle knew he wouldn't talk to her if he knew Ella and Andrew could hear them.

"Nothing," he muttered and proceeded to stalk up the bank and into the trees. Kindle rolled her eyes but scurried after him. As she reached the first tree, she heard Ella shout her name and momentarily halted to call back, "No, it's okay, we'll be right back!"

Not waiting for Ella's response, Kindle dove between the tall, thin trees and soon caught up to Tad.

"Hey," she sighed. "Okay, so I know something's wrong because you do this every time something is wrong, so why don't you just tell me what's wrong so we don't have to fight and stuff?"

He eyed her as he smirked and asked, "So you think you got me all figured out?"

"Ugh, no. That's why I'm *asking* you what's wrong."

His defensiveness melted slightly, and after a few seconds, he grumbled, "I don't swim."

Kindle blinked in surprise. "I thought you lived in Florida."

"That doesn't mean I'm a stupid fish."

"Well, I didn't say you were a fish. I just thought that people who live by the beach go swimming and surfing all the ti—"

"Tad! Kindle!" Ella's voice rang out, and they turned to see her swiftly nearing them. "What are you two doing? Come back to the bank."

"We were just taking a walk," Kindle quickly lied then, so she felt less guilty about her fib, added, "We've been riding all day, and we're just, like, really stiff."

Ella's face did not appear convinced, but she shook her head and insisted, "Well, that is fine, Kindle, but do come back to the bank and walk, alright?"

"Why's it matter?" Tad defiantly demanded. "We've been walking in this stupid forest and nothing's happened. How do we know you're not just trying to get us to do whatever you want?"

"Oh, Tad, stop. *You're* the one who saw the earth devour those men, so I do not understand why it is so hard for you to believe something is not right here. Now, just plea …"

Kindle waited for Ella to finish her last word, but her friend's mouth and eyes slowly dropped open into a shocked, fearful face. As the seconds passed and Kindle continued to hope Ella would snap back into her usual cheerful mien, she chewed her lip. She had never seen Ella with such a terror-ridden expression and dreaded to discover what was causing it.

"What?" Tad suddenly disrupted the silence and startled Kindle. She slapped his arm, and he loudly protested, "*What?!*"

"Kin, Tad ..." Ella whispered and drew their attention back to her. Now her mouth had closed, but her green eyes, still wide and fearful, were sliding back and forth and staring past them. Kindle whirled around to see what she was watching but saw only golden emptiness between the white trees. The *shing* of Tad's sword sliding out of its sheath caught her ear, and she also pulled her sword from her hip.

"What is it?" she nervously wondered, not truly wanting to know but also desirous to be prepared. "Is it that thing? That black robed thing?"

"I think ..." Ella breathed, and Kindle, after glancing at her face and seeing she was staring right at her feet, pivoted to see her.

"What?!" Tad angrily demanded, and Kindle tugged his shirt to direct him to also watch the ground. When he had spun, Ella lifted her eyes to them. "I think we should—"

A noise pulled all their eyes to the circle of yellow leaves resting between them. The soft crackle of the leaves sounded again as they shifted to reveal three thick cylindrical rocks, squirming as if they were waving in the wind. Slowly, they sank back under the golden carpet, and Kindle snapped her stare up to meet Ella and Tad's.

In a rush Ella gasped, "I think we should ru—ahhh!"

Without any sound of warning, a boulder had somehow smashed up through the ground at their feet, knocking them each in a different direction. Dazed, Kindle watched from the base of a tree as Tad sprang up and prepared to slam his sword into the boulder. Before he let his blow fly, Ella appeared on the other side of the large rock.

"Tad, stop!" she cried. "You'll only damage your sword!"

He glared at her but lowered his weapon. The next moment, though, another almost identical boulder crashed into sight a few feet away, and he defensively raised it again.

"What—?" he began, but Ella cut him off.

"Never mind what! Kindle, get up, we must go!"

Nodding, Kindle scrambled to her feet. She nervously began to edge around the first boulder when it and its twin suddenly exploded. Squealing, she ducked, but hearing no clatter of rocks against wood, peered up. The boulders hadn't exploded; they had opened. Now she could see that they were two five-fingered, rocky hands. The giant fingers, which were each at least as big as her leg, flexed then stretched in unison. Just as she realized that the hand standing between her and Tad was as tall as him, both palms slammed forward, and the ground began to quake. Struggling to maintain her balance on the shifting earth, Kindle ran to Ella's side.

"What? What?" she panted, not really sure what question to ask.

"Never mind," Ella hurriedly returned as she began pulling Kindle back toward the river.

"Wait!" Kindle freed her arm and spun to search for Tad. Before she spied him dashing around one of the rock hands, two sickening sights nabbed her attention. The glint of her sword, still lying by the tree where she had stumbled, first made her stomach drop, and then the thick grey arms rising from the crumbling dirt petrified her. Rooted to the spot, she greatly desired to run to the river with Ella but also knew she could not leave her sword. As she stared at the blocky arms, Kindle feared that she would have to retrieve her sword by evading whatever monster was pulling itself out of the ground.

"Kin!" Ella cried behind her, and she felt her friend's warm hand tug at her elbow.

"No, my sword!" Kindle explained, shaking off her fingers as she gathered her courage to sprint forward. Tad, though, had reached them, and after a quick glance in the direction she was grimacing toward, he scoffed, "Really? Urg—you guys go, I'll get it."

"No," Kindle insisted, again escaping Ella's pull. "I'm sorry, it's my fault. I'll—"

"I said I'll get it, so get outta here, okay?" Tad snapped, and Kindle backed a few steps before she turned to sprint away with Ella. They ran together until they reached the last trees near the riverbank. Ella continued to run to where Andrew stood, trying to both avoid and calm the nervous horses, but Kindle whipped around to watch Tad rescue her sword. To her amazement and relief, he had already recovered it and was rounding the giant arms. She almost shouted a victorious cheer for him, but it transformed into a scream as a pile of earth suddenly mounded around the arms and an entire rock creature burst up from the ground. The eruption occurred so quickly that Kindle couldn't tell what stage of it threw Tad sideways, but as the reverberations of the monster's landing shook the trees around her, Kindle knew he had been knocked unconscious. As her hands flew to her mouth in horror and shock, Kindle sensed Ella return to her side and heard her gasp as well.

The giant rock monster shaking soil from its flat, rectangular head was so terrifying and yet so strange that Kindle couldn't do anything but gape at it. Its disproportionately large head that hunched forward at its shoulders connected to the top of the hunk of rock that was its angular mountainside of a body. Its long ape-like arms that ended in massive fists swung freely and smoothly as if they were playground swings rather than heavy rock. What most astounded Kindle, though, were the stubby, very unevenly stacked piles of mismatched rocks under it that seemed to be functioning as very capable legs. She watched them stomp until the monster turned its huge, dull face Tad's way. Its tiny black eyes only considered him for a second, and Kindle sighed in relief as it swung its head in the opposite direction.

"Perhaps it can't see," Ella happily breathed.

Enjoying the idea that the monster was as dull-witted as it appeared, Kindle nodded and whispered, "What is it?"

"I haven't the faintest idea," Ella replied. "I've never heard of anything like it."

Kindle nodded but sucked in her next comment as the rock

143

monster turned its face their way. It tilted its great head, and the long, uneven line under its eyes cracked open. A low, gravely growl escaped from it as its wobbly-looking legs started carrying it toward them.

"I think it can see. I think it sees us," Kindle squeaked to Ella and prepared to scramble out of the nearing monster's path, but Ella hooked her elbow.

"Wait, Kin," she quietly directed. "Wait until it's almost to us, then we split and confuse it."

"Uh—" Kindle tried to give words to her thoughts but found that fear was the only occupant of her mind. Instead of answering, she simply watched the giant rock creature. Kindle thought it would have already reached them but saw the trees stood as cumbersome obstacles for it. At the moment, it was attempting to squeeze between two of the white trees while avoiding their branches. It stepped forward and back several times, failing to fit both of its hulking arms through the space. The scene was entertaining to Kindle, and she almost declared that perhaps the rock monster was harmless but held her thought as it turned to sidle through the narrow gap. Its mouth split again, and it let out a satisfied, "Murrr."

The sound suddenly broke into angry grunts as the monster swatted a branch out of its eye. As it stomped its legs and swung a destroying fist at the top of the tree, Kindle discarded her previous assumption about it and exchanged a fearful glance with Ella.

A loud crack pulled her eyes back to the monster, and Kindle watched with renewed fear as it threw aside the trunk it had uprooted and snapped. Then it swung its body back around to face them and proceeded to smashing a path their way. Again, Kindle impulsively attempted to run, but Ella hugged her elbow tighter and chanted, "Wait, wait, wait …"

Just when Kindle decided she would not wait any longer, Ella released her arm and shouted, "Run!"

Already primed to follow Ella's order, Kindle broke from her friend and sprinted off along the tree line. She heard the monster utter an irritated growl and felt its quaking stomps but refused to look back or stop. Only when the noises behind her faded and the earth stilled did she slow then lean against a tree to scan the river and forest. Andrew still stood on the bank with the horses, but Kindle couldn't detect any sign of Ella or the rock monster. Leaving the tree line and jogging back into the forest, Kindle peered past all the slender white trunks for a hint of grey rock or green fabric. Neither appeared, but the circle of disrupted soil created by the monster stole her attention. Remembering that Tad had been knocked down by the mound, Kindle switched her direction to it. As she sped past the trees, Kindle tried to see if Tad really did still lie ahead. When she reached the fresh earth, his black hair finally slid into view and relief filled her. Feeling the pain of the splint in her side, Kindle decided to walk the remaining distance between them.

She gulped down precious oxygen as she stepped around the pile of dirt and examined it. The earth was dark and soft just like the kind used for planting, and the amount of it caused Kindle to wonder if a hole sat hidden somewhere. Now wary of it and the ground she walked on, Kindle put more distance between the dirt and herself. Her foot bumped a tree, and still eyeing the dirt, she placed a hand on the trunk to steady herself.

The moment her skin touched the wood, something whipped her back, and before she could twist to see it, she felt the ground disappear out from under her. Looking down, she saw her feet rising and kicking and also noticed something white at her waist. Before she could assess it, the forest spun and she found herself facing a squinting, frowning tree.

Kindle blinked wildly at it, sure she was imagining the face, but no matter how many times her eyes reopened, the narrowed black eyes and unhappy brown mouth remained on the trunk. Suddenly, she flew backward a few feet and saw exactly what was happening. The tree truly did have a face right under the jagged broken wood that crowned it as well as muddy root legs and two branching arms, one of which was wrapped around her waist. Too stunned to react, Kindle simply stared at the tree as it inspected her. It looked her up and down as if *she* was odd then, in one swift second, flipped her sideways and tucked her under its arm.

Now Kindle let out a scream, partly out of fear and partly to alert the others of her capture. The tree person glared down at her, rapped her head with a twiggy finger, and began loping through the forest. Terribly disoriented by her horizontal position and the painful tap, Kindle ended her scream and instead used her energy to support her head. The second she discovered which way was down, she saw the tree person's dirty root feet step over Tad.

"Tad! Tad!" she yelled, hoping to wake him up. All she received from her call, though, was another strict swat as Tad's motionless body slipped out of sight.

"You stupid tree!" she cried, angry at it for capturing and punishing her. Kindle tried to kick and smack the tree from her awkward position, but after only a few hits, it halted and grabbed her.

"Let me go!" she shouted as it held her away from its body and disgustedly frowned. "Let me go!" As Kindle repeated her demand, she yanked at the branch holding her. The tree person groaned then quickly wrapped its other hand around her arms. Kindle struggled against its grasp but couldn't budge its wooden fingers, and it apparently understood that fact as well because it transferred her back under its arm but this time with her arms locked at her sides.

"Ugh!" she complained, dizzy again, but the tree, who had placed her head behind it, either didn't hear or didn't care. "Ella!" Kindle called, careful to not be loud enough to earn a third rap. "Ella! It's got me!"

Not even two seconds passed before Ella burst into view, swung her head around, and then sprinted her way. For a brief moment, victory filled Kindle, but just as quickly defeat replaced it. From the same spot where Ella had appeared, the rock monster lumbered into view. It took only a second to detect Ella and then joined the chase.

"Behind you!" Kindle yelled, "It's behind you!"

Even though Ella didn't reply, Kindle guessed that she was probably fully aware of the rock monster smashing through the trees behind her. Wishing she could provide some sort of real help, Kindle tried to think of a plan to shout. As she attempted to fabricate an escape for them, though, the scene grew more and more perilous for Ella, and nothing but distress swam through Kindle's mind. She could see that soon Ella would catch up to the slow progression of the tree person and then the rock monster would catch all of them. Ella did soon reach her, but unlike Kindle anticipated, she continued between the tree's root legs and out of sight.

"Ella?" Kindle asked the ground, wondering if perhaps Ella had not seen her. No answer came, but the tree person suddenly jolted to a stop, and Kindle's focus switched to keeping her head from painfully bobbing up and down. With difficulty she lifted her eyes to peer around and, seeing the rock monster was only a few thundering strides away, screamed.

Another strained cry rang out as hers did, and then the whole forest swirled by, and Kindle found her brain dizzy once again. She blinked hard, trying to orient herself and find the rock monster, but saw only waving trees.

"Ella!" she yelled, hoping the other scream had not come from her. The horrible shriek rang out again, and the arm wrapped around Kindle trembled. Its movement informed Kindle that the tree person was the one shouting, but the reason why was a mystery to her. Then a terrible thought struck her.

"Ella, where are you?! The tree guy's got me, and the rock guy's got him!"

"No, he doesn't, Kin!" Ella's voice replied nearby, but Kindle still couldn't find her.

"Where are—"

"Be ready if he drops you!"

"What?" Kindle cried, extremely confused. Then all at once, the tree person shrieked, warmth swam around her feet, the smell of burning wood hit her nose, and Kindle understood. Ella was lighting the tree person on fire.

"Get him!" Kindle encouraged and wriggled her arms to test the tree's grip. His hold had not eased. Suddenly, the forest swirled past her again, and once she had steadied her vision, Kindle's hope sank.

Now she faced the rock monster, who was blinking at what Kindle guessed had just been shoved into its fist: Ella. The rock monster and Ella simply stared at one another for a few seconds, but when Kindle felt the tree person resume its determined walk, the beady black eyes of the monster's face turned her way, and it began tottering along as well.

"What do we do?" Kindle cried to her friend, who was gazing at the creature's huge fingers around her.

Ella momentarily glanced at Kindle, gave her a wink, and returned her focus to the stone hand. Kindle gaped at her in disbelief. Not only was Kindle offended by being ignored, but she also knew that they were not in a situation that called for winking. A suspicion that perhaps Tad had been right about Ella not fully being their ally began to slide into her mind. Panic and a feeling of betrayal also rose up in her as she wondered if Ella had summoned the rock monster and tree person and was now going to destroy her, Tad, and Andrew. With a face full of mortified sorrow, Kindle looked up at Ella.

At once her doubts fell away, and she smiled. Smoke was squeezing out from between the monster's fingers and curling up around Ella's head. Now Kindle understood Ella was attempting to burn the rock monster and eagerly watched to see if she could. For a few minutes their two captors moved through the forest completely aloof to the smoke, but just as a very repulsive odor reached her nose, Kindle saw the rock monster sway its head in irritation. It turned its flat face to the hand gripping Ella and drifted to a stop. Vaguely gazing at it and the smoke issuing from it, the creature raised its hand up to its face. Suddenly, it howled in pain, and its legs stamped the ground, shaking everything. Kindle felt the tree person halt and prepared for him to spin around to search for the reason of the commotion. In the second before the trees swirled past her eyes, the rock monster yowled even louder and slammed its smoking fist and Ella into the nearest tree.

Kindle inhaled a pained gasp, terrified that Ella had been crushed, but before she could verify her dread, the tree person whirled around and left her facing an empty forest. The two monsters growled and chattered for a moment as Kindle shut her eyes to regain equilibrium. Just when everything had stopped spinning, the tree person pivoted once more and sent Kindle's head into resurged misery. Through her dizziness and newly acquired head-throbbing, Kindle squinted around to find the rock monster's hand and check her friend's condition.

Kindle sucked in a sharp breath as she bit her lip; Ella's head was freely lolling back and forth face down on the monster's finger.

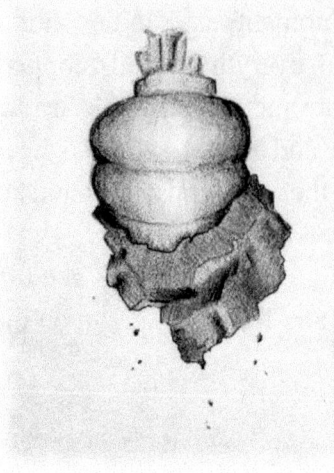

DARKENING DOUBT

K indle stared at Ella for a long time, wanting nothing more than for her to stir. As the minutes and then what seemed like hours melted by, though, only the motion of the rock monster moved Ella. Finally succumbing to the pain in her neck, Kindle let her own head bow and sway to the slow rhythm of the tree person's wide gait.

As she watched the dead golden leaves pass below, despair filled her. Everything had turned so wrong so quickly, and Kindle felt that each of their fates was still suspended in a dreadful fog. She had no idea where the monsters were carrying her and Ella, if Ella and Tad were unconscious or worse, and what had happened to Andrew and their horses. Above all the uncertainty plaguing her, the fact that their group had been shattered scared Kindle the most. Through the journey, she had acclimated to not knowing exactly where they were heading or what insane situation they would fall into next but had not ever considered continuing alone. Kindle knew just feet separated her from Ella, but since her friend was as silent as death, she felt completely isolated from the only three people and all the security and certainty she knew in Anelthalien.

With all of them together and even when she had been with just one of the others, Kindle had always known they could figure out how to somehow dodge danger and keep pressing on. Now, though, she truly felt completely devoid of hope. She sighed, partially due to her thought, partially to try and fill her slightly constricted lungs.

As time continued to pass just as uncertainly as the distance they traveled, Kindle let her mind construct a variety of unfortunate ends to her own story as well as Ella, Tad, and Andrew's. When she was churning up Andrew's death by a two horse stampede, a low rumbling pulled her out of her dark imaginings. Bending her sore neck up to see the rock monster and Ella, she hunted for the cause of the sound. Nothing struck her as different from when she last looked at them. The rumbling began to increase, and the trees even shivered under its influence, but neither the rock monster nor the tree person reacted at all. They simply kept walking.

"Hey!" Kindle called then, recalling the tree's quick, sharp fingers, wrestled the sass out of her tone. "Hey, tree guy, what's that noise?"

No answer, not even a grunt, came.

"Hey, can you hear me?" she asked the tree's back then faced the rock monster. "Can you understand me? Do you know what that noise is?"

The rocky line of his mouth didn't crack, but his little black eyes flicked down to her. Sensing she had its attention, Kindle opened her mouth to question it but abruptly forgot her words.

Cool air wrapped around her feet as a dark shadow fell over her and the rock monster. She twisted her face as far as she could to see what had blocked the sunlight. A curved arch of dirt cut into her view of the trees. As she wondered what it was, some loose soil dropped from it and landed on her cheek. Kindle shook it off and almost returned her gaze upward but realized that the earthen wall was surrounding them and gradually curving down behind the rock monster as well.

"No! No!" Kindle desperately cried, her fear reawakened by the dwindling light. "No—ow!" She smashed her eyes shut against the swat the tree person had delivered. When she opened them again, everything was black. The smell of deep, rich, moist earth and the new chill in the air were all she could sense.

"Where are we?" Kindle whispered. She did not expect an answer but simply wanted to force her growing anxiety out of her consciousness. "I think we're in a cave. Maybe we'll just be down here for a minute. Maybe we won't die." Feeling silly about talking to herself, Kindle switched her focus to awakening Ella. "Ella? Can you hear me? Are you even there anymore? You gotta wake up. I don't know where we are or where we're going or what we're gunna— OW!"

The tree person had adeptly struck her head. Kindle wanted to yell at him but knew he would continue to strike her unless she kept quiet. Even though she hated to, Kindle ended her ramblings and let the dark silence become a dense reality.

For a long while, she heard and saw nothing. She could tell from the movement of the tree person and the increasingly cold air breezing by her face that they were traveling but never heard a footfall. The only explanation she could fathom was that they were journeying over very soft soil. In the silence she concentrated on imagining what the space around her might look like. As she deduced that it had to be something like the Tunnels—giant arching dirt passageways running in every direction—a sound stirred her wandering mind. When the dull *click* repeated and then took up an endless pattern, Kindle guessed she was hearing the rock monster's footsteps. She hopefully inhaled, excited for the possibility that Ella might still be nearby.

"Ella?" she whispered then sighed in disappointment. Either Ella was not close or still completely unconscious. Renewed, heightened desperation and loneliness instantly overwhelmed her, and she felt tears collect in her eyes. She didn't want to cry but didn't know what else to do. Andrew was surely lost, Tad was likely still sprawled on the forest floor, Ella was probably dead, and she was on her way to some kind of horrible, dark end. They would never reach Letum or destroy the evil throne or even see one another again. Kindle's dreary predictions circulated through her mind and pushed more and more wet sadness out of her eyes. Since she couldn't wipe away her tears, they ran down her cheeks and nose, and that made her feel even more tragic and pathetic. Nothing, not even the tree person, hindered her depressive spiral, and her mood sank lower and lower.

While she was still sobbing and feeling sorry for her friends and herself, the tree person halted. Kindle almost didn't notice the pause, but the rock monster's resulting grunt pulled her out of her mire. Curiously but not hopefully, she raised her head. The dense dark still surrounded her, impeding her sight, but she could hear every sound. A light shuffling followed by a mumble from the tree caught her ears. Kindle sniffed back some of her waterworks to hear more but suddenly left the tree's side and a second later hit a cold, hard surface. Coughing, she rolled off her sore side. Then, close enough to cause her to shake in surprise, a loud *flump* sounded. The chatters and low grumbles of their captors floated slowly away and then, all at once, every noise except her own groaning hushed.

"Ugh," she moaned as she attempted to move. Kindle wanted to stand or at least roll over, but her stiffness and the pain in her left hip and shoulder dissuaded her from doing either. Instead, she remained on her back and wiped her face dry with her sleeve. Once she finished that task, Kindle closed her eyes and listened.

Nothing. Absolutely nothing. No footsteps, grunting, or any sound of life existed in the pure darkness. She was alone. As that fact sank into her mind, Kindle almost broke into tears again, but as she slid her hand off her face and it fell onto her neck, her eyes popped open. Her fingers had fallen on her necklace, and it felt warm. Thinking that her hand might just be very cold, she ran it along the chain until it touched the smooth gem. When her fingertips met it, she knew that it truly was generating some heat. She wrapped her hand around it, glad for its warmth. The gem felt so nice in her cool hand that she didn't question its heat but simply enjoyed it.

As she switched hands, a slight smile eased onto her face. Her warm gem made her feel less alone, as if it was a small friend trying to keep her company. Kindle's smile grew as she considered the idea of it as a friend. At first it seemed silly to think that the necklace, which was probably just metal and stone, could have feelings or a personality, but the longer she thought about it with nothing to distract her, the less far-fetched the idea became.

Kindle knew that Ella and Tad had heard something from their necklaces, so it didn't seem impossible that she could feel something from hers. Picking it up and holding it close to her face, Kindle fixed her eyes on the spot where she thought it was. She waited, hoping to hear it now that only empty black existed around her.

"Why can't I hear you?" she dejectedly sighed after a few seconds. It didn't seem fair that she still couldn't hear any kind of voice but could just feel its warmth.

"I can't even see you," Kindle mumbled and let it fall back against her chest. Several times in the past, the glimmer of it had caught her eye and had helped her somehow. Now she couldn't see it and felt abandoned. As that thought entered her mind, the gem seemed to grow warmer and drew Kindle's cold hand back to it. The heat on her skin hushed her negative thoughts and reminded her that even if she still couldn't hear or see the necklace, it was still with her. It had not left her alone.

Kindle wrinkled her nose. She had known it wouldn't— someone had told her that. *Naam* had told her that. Squishing her face, Kindle worked hard to recall when Naam had told her that. It had also been dark then but not totally dark. The fire was heating a big pot beside them, and the wheaty smell of mush was close. As soon as Kindle remembered that it had been the morning she received Nasah, Naam's exact words also bloomed in her mind as if the gentle mother was right beside her.

"You will not be alone."

"Yeah I know, Ella—" Kindle had started to sigh.

"No, closer than your three friends, you have a tie to the creator whose mark you wear."

"Hux?" Kindle breathed just as she had that quiet morning. Ignoring the pain still in her hip, Kindle sat up and held her gem tightly. In one moment she vividly remembered that when she had almost quit or had been lost for direction, the sight of the little dragon on the curved red jewel had spurred her to remember their mission or know exactly what to do or say. Kindle realized that she *had* heard Hux. He had been reminding her and guiding her the whole time she had worn the necklace. Now instead of trying to hear a voice, Kindle tried to wipe away every thought and remember what the little golden dragon looked like.

Her memory wandered over the dragon's upturned head that always seemed to be gazing at her with its shining eye. Its neck was long and grand just like its curved tail and claws that seemed to lie against a rock. Kindle ran her finger over the almost smooth gem. Even though no rock actually existed under the dragon, she had always imagined it to be sitting on one. His talons rested right on one of the striations in the gem, and so when she could see the dragon, it was easy to pretend the slight texture was a rock. Kindle placed her own hand on the rock she actually sat on and slid it over the rough surface. As she did, a determination to search her surroundings seized her, and believing the notion was a cue from Hux, Kindle released her necklace and ran both of her hands over the floor. Renewed hope swelled in her as she swept her palms in a circle. Suddenly, she froze. Kindle couldn't help but feel ridiculous; she was sitting in the dark, rubbing her hands on the dirty ground because she thought that a maker who she had never met might want her to.

Wrapping her arms around her legs, Kindle shrank in embarrassment and confusion. She wanted to search for an escape but felt silly for believing one existed. She wanted to listen to the nudge from Hux but also felt silly for believing he had actually spoken to her or was even real. A demoralized sigh blew out of her nose as she leaned forward to sit her chin on her knees. The movement caused her necklace to bump her leg, and Kindle straightened up. The little gem that had seemed so friendly not long ago was now beginning to annoy her. Grabbing it, Kindle almost threw it off but stopped. Its warmth had instantly taken her back to the morning beside Naam: the fireplace, the hot bowl of mush in her hands, and again Naam's words.

"You have a tie to the creator whose mark you wear."

If she carried out her intention of flinging her necklace away, she truly would be alone. Kindle heavily sighed. More than she didn't want to feel crazy or embarrassed, she did not want to be alone.

"Okay," she whispered to herself and, truthfully, the necklace as well. Kindle spread her hands back on the ground and immediately collected some more confidence.

Azildor had said it would become hard to believe. He had told them that their journey would be difficult and it would be easy to doubt everything and give up. Kindle recalled that she had wrestled with the same thoughts—trusting that everything was real—in Iteraum. She bit her lip, now feeling silly for falling back into the same dismal ensnarement of disbelief and whispered what she knew to be true.

"It's real. Hux is real. This is all really real."

Assured of her conclusion, Kindle resumed her blind search. She carefully leaned one direction, ran her hands over the rock, then tilted the other way. At the arch of her swipe, her fingers hit something soft and warm. A surprised yelp escaped from her as she simultaneously scooted back from the unexpected thing and covered her mouth. Waiting for whatever it was to pounce, her mind snapped to recalling all large creatures that lived in caves. Not enjoying the list compiling in her brain, Kindle kicked a foot out toward her unwelcome discovery. The toe of her boot connected with the soft entity, but it didn't seem to react at all. Kindle stretched out her other leg as well and pushed against it with her feet several times. It still neither moved nor made a sound. Almost sure that it wouldn't hurt her, Kindle slowly crawled to it and quickly poked it. When nothing bit off her hand, she reached forward again to try to determine what it could be. As soon as her palm fully rested on it, Kindle realized that it was an arm—Ella's arm. Overjoyed that Ella had been so near her the whole time, Kindle gasped a laugh. Then she ran her hand along her friend's arm until she found her shoulder.

"Ella! Ella! You gotta wake up!" she urged, shaking her. The fact that Ella's skin was still very warm informed Kindle she was still alive, just unconscious. "C'mon, you gotta wake up! Wake up, wake up, wake up!"

Kindle continued to yell variations of her demand until it

became clear that volume would not rouse Ella. Squeezing her eyes shut, Kindle tried to think of what nurses or people on TV did whenever someone had been knocked unconscious. Recalling boxing trainers slapping around fighters to awaken them, Kindle hesitantly felt for Ella's face and tapped her cheeks. When that proved fruitless, Kindle simply pressed her cold fingers against either side of her friend's face.

Amazingly, a sharp inhale sounded, and Ella's hand touched Kindle's.

"Ella?"

"Kindle?"

"Oh! You're alive, and now you're awake, and everything really *is* gunna be okay!"

"Kin? Whatever do you mean, and … why is it so dark?"

"Oh, yeah," Kindle replied, realizing Ella had not been awake during most of their imprisonment. "Okay, so you remember the rock guy had you, right?"

"Of course. That tree toting you did not enjoy my burning it and handed me off to him."

"Yeah, and—"

"One moment, Kin, we don't have to sit in the dark like this," Ella cheerfully interrupted, and a sliver of orange light appeared not too far from Kindle's elbow. "There, that's much better." Ella smiled and let the flame grow in her hands. As she did, Kindle's mind wandered away from the narration of their capture to examine what surrounded them.

The floor was stone just as Kindle had assumed, but it did not extend as far as she had suspected. In fact, only a few feet of ground spread out on either side of her and Ella before it turned up to form a craggy rock arch over them. Kindle examined the rock surface rising nearest her. It, unlike most cave walls she had encountered, was quite jagged and uneven. Following the walls in front of and behind her, Kindle saw that as far as Ella's fire lit the hall-like space, the walls never ceased to appear dangerously uneven. Just as Kindle began to wonder about the dryness of the cave, Ella spoke.

"What is this place? Do you suppose we could be in a rock or a sort of mountain?"

Kindle peered at her, wondering if she was still slightly disoriented, then shook her head and decided to explain. "No. I don't think it's a mountain. But, anyway … okay, so remember burning that rock guy?"

"Yes, and it did not sit well with him, did it? Kin?" she asked, gathering her fire and standing. "Do you believe we should see what lies down this passageway?"

"Um, no." Kindle also rose and frowned at Ella, now almost positive she was still addled. "Do you remember what that rock guy did, Ella? He slammed you against a tree."

"Oh, that is terrible."

"Uh, yeah. And it knocked you out … and you've been out for a really long time."

"Really?" Ella responded, but her tone sounded completely uninterested. "Are you sure we shouldn't just see where this leads to?"

Starting to feel ignored and frustrated, Kindle crossed her arms. "Can I just, like, tell you what happened first and where we are?"

"Oh." Ella finally peeled her eyes from the distant darkness. "Of course I want to know, Kin. I only became curious is all. It just seems as if we ought not linger here … but, no, go on. Where are we?"

Too eager to relate her knowledge to dwell on her own perturbation or Ella's odd behavior, Kindle explained, "So the rock guy knocked you out, and I really thought you were dead, but I couldn't do anything. You know? And then the tree guy walked for, like, ever, and the rock guy followed him, and then the ground ate us."

"Really?" exhaled Ella, now truly interested. "Do you mean we traveled underground?"

"No, well, yeah, but it was just like Tad said. The ground came up over us like a big wave, and then we were down here … well, not *here*. They carried us for a long time before we got *here*."

"And then they left us here? Just dropped us off without a word?"

"Um, yeah. I don't think they talk. The rock guy only ever

grunted … but, um, yeah. They just left."

"That is odd," mused Ella as she returned her eyes to the unlit passageway.

"Yeah, I know," Kindle sighed, glad Ella was showing some understanding. "I couldn't believe that rock guy. And the ground eating us. I mean, it really did *eat* us."

"Well, yes, all that as well, but Kindle …" Ella turned a very hesitant, confused face to her. "Don't you think it odd they toted us such a great distance just to drop us and walk away?"

At her question, Kindle felt trepidation arise on her own face. "Uh … yeah. What do you think …?" Kindle didn't want to finish her sentence. She suddenly feared what the answer would be.

"I don't know, but it does not seem to be safe to continue standing about," Ella breathed and lifted her fire to dispel slightly more darkness. Kindle glanced behind them then nodded in the direction Ella was facing. Without a verbal consent, they both started forward. Kindle let Ella drift slightly ahead so she could hold her light over their path but stayed within inches of her. As they quickly but carefully wandered past the dark, jagged walls, Kindle kept her eyes bouncing between Ella and the empty space ahead. Internally, Kindle begged the darkness to remain devoid of any other life, even a bug, because she knew her adrenaline was wildly flying and she had no weapon. She let her eyes travel to Ella's back to reassure herself with the bow and arrows that always hung there, but when she did, her stomach dropped.

"Ella!" she gasped as she caught her shoulder to stop her.

"What? What is it?" Ella breathlessly responded as the fire in her hands flared to a new intensity.

"Your bow and all your arrows are gone," moaned Kindle. "What are we gunna do if … if … Do you have your sword at least?"

Ella reached over one shoulder then the other. Heaving a sigh, she admitted, "I was afraid I lost them in the scramble, but I never stopped to look. Oh, that rotten rock. I stumbled and almost knew I had lost them, but he was already nearly to me, and I just couldn't stop. Oh, Azildor would be so disappointed. He told me to hang on to those like treasure." Ella huffed and patted her belt. "My sword's still here, though. Here, Kindle, you take it in case—"

"But what about you?" Kindle quickly interjected, not wanting to hear what Ella imagined would happen. Even though she still had her head bowed in dejection, Ella grinned slyly, and the fire in her hand danced.

"I think I will be alright."

"Oh, yeah," Kindle started to laugh, but her cheer fell as she glanced down at the sword in her hand. Turning her eyes up to Ella, she slowly asked, "Do you think, um, Andrew and Tad are okay?"

Confidently, Ella replied, "As long as Andrew finds Tad, they will both be fine. Andrew's not got rocks in his head, and even if he did, Tad's a bit rash, but I've no doubt he can fend for the both of them."

Kindle nodded, hoping Ella was right. Then a desire to reunite with them pushed her to command, "Let's keep going."

"There you are, Kindle!" Ella heartily encouraged and smiled as they returned to their careful pace. "And perhaps one of those boys will find my bow. Wouldn't that be lovely?"

"Yeah," Kindle agreed and squeezed the hilt of Ella's sword.

No new sound or sight met them. So much time passed without any disruption to their walk that Kindle slipped Ella's sword into her own sheath and both girls relaxed their cautious creeping to a leisurely amble.

"These walls are really weird," Kindle commented. She was bored and tired and was desperate to start a conversation about anything.

"I don't know, "Ella replied. "I've never thought of what rocks would look like under the earth."

"You've never been in a cave?"

"Well, besides the Tunnels, no. No caves or underground anything lies around Garrick. It's too close to the sea, and it rains quite often. I've heard Papa say that's why the Lighthouse can't use the cellar—it would no doubt have all of our things underwater before long."

"Oh. Well, where I'm from, we have lots of caves, and the walls are usually pretty smooth like the floor is."

Ella stared at the flat rock walkway under her feet. "Do people in your land have a way to make it so smooth?"

"Um, no. Well, I guess they do, but people don't usually make caves. I think water does, like underground rivers and lakes, and all that water makes the rocks all smooth."

"So are your caves all full of water, then?" Ella asked, obviously a bit confused.

"No, water *makes* caves," Kindle clarified, "but then it pretty much goes away and just leaves big holes and tunnels."

"Oh, I see. They're dried river ways, only under the earth."

"Yeah, I think so. They're still really wet, though. Like, they drip and make stalactites and stuff."

"Stalactites?" Ella curiously tried the word in her accent.

"Big rocks that hang from the ceiling."

"Your land sounds so bizarre," Ella laughed as she turned her face upward.

Kindle giggled to herself. It amused her that Ella found such ordinary things strange but carrying fire in her hands perfectly normal. She also gazed up at the arch of angles overhead, trying to think of something else to talk about, but a noise brought her attention down again.

"What was that?" she quickly whispered as she drew Ella's sword. Ella didn't reply, but Kindle could tell from her searching eyes that she had heard it as well. The noise came again and this time persisted. It sounded like rock crunching against rock and seemed to fill the whole space.

"Where's it coming from?" Kindle nervously wondered aloud and felt Ella nudge her arm. She whirled around and immediately saw the answer to her question. Part of the wall near Ella was gradually slipping out of sight as if it was a sliding door. Even though Kindle couldn't see anything moving the rock, she feared another monster would soon appear and pulled Ella back against the opposite wall. Just as her back hit a terribly sharp rock, the noise ceased and Ella's fire disappeared.

Kindle sucked in a frightened breath but heard Ella's voice whisper, "Perhaps it hasn't seen us, whatever it is."

Restraining her desire to argue that she had not seen anything so maybe *nothing* stood in the new opening, Kindle instead wrapped her hand tighter around the hilt at her side.

"Re-kin-dle your light," a deep, slow voice commanded, and Kindle's heart jumped at the sound of her name. Widening her eyes, she tried to catch a sign of the speaker but saw only darkness. She turned to where she knew Ella stood beside her and tugged her arm. As much as she dreaded to see the speaker, she feared even more the possibility he would attack unseen. Ella's fire, though, did not reappear. Kindle yanked her arm harder, growing more anxious as each dark second slid by. The warm arm she held began to escape her grasp, but Kindle hung to it tightly. It pulled away again, and Kindle realized that Ella was attempting to sneak them away from the dangerous spot. Ready to flee, Kindle allowed Ella to guide her a few steps but then froze.

The footsteps, heavy but soft ones, had not stopped her, but the sight of what had entered her peripheral vision had. An eerie white-grey orb that seemed to be floating at her eye level had slid into view. Kindle, entranced by its oddity, turned her face fully to it. The globe seemed to be glass, and its dull white aura appeared evanescent and distorted due to the misty clouds very slowly churning inside of it. Even though Kindle could see it clearly, she had no idea *how* she was able to in the dark passageway. Ella hadn't generated another flame, and no other light source existed.

Another tug on her arm reminded Kindle that she should be fleeing, but Kindle ignored it. She wasn't sure why, but she desired nothing more than to stare at the swirling grey clouds.

"Re-kin-dle your light." The order was louder and closer this time and startled Kindle back into fright.

"Do you mean to harm us or to help us?" Ella bravely interrogated.

The speaker uttered a low hum as if thinking then announced, "Business."

"Business?" Ella asked in a surprised tone. "We aren't traders, and we haven't any minas. What sort of business do you mean?"

"Re-kin-dle your light."

Kindle heard Ella sigh and knew she felt conflicted. Then to her surprise, a fire illuminated all three of them. After briefly glancing at Ella's hard, suspicious squint, Kindle found the speaker.

He was not the rock monster she had anticipated. The firelight revealed that he was a real human being but was quite unlike any man Kindle had ever encountered. He was massive. Kindle's head was about level with his elbow, and his bald, angular head almost touched the rock curve overhead. The size of his body, which was garbed only with a crisp white cloth around his waist that reminded Kindle of what ancient Egyptians wore, matched his enormous height. Every inch of his smooth, dark brown skin encased threatening, geometric muscles. His whole appearance was grand, as if he was a statue of a king or pharaoh sharply carved from the rock wall he stood near. Even his sculpted face held a calm, distant aloofness that suggested he was someone to be respected.

Suddenly, Kindle realized she was staring and, terrified to offend him, dropped her gaze to the ground. When she did, she noticed that his feet were also bare. Just as her eyes began to drift to the foot of the perfectly cylindrical staff that supported the orb, Ella spoke.

"I've done what you asked," she quietly informed him. "Now would you please explain what sort of business you mean?"

Kindle checked her friend's face and saw she was still somehow maintaining a bold, unshakable expression.

"Greetings first," the man very gradually insisted. Kindle covertly peered at him as he spoke and noticed his jaw seemed reluctant to form words.

"Oh, well, alright, then," Ella acquiesced, obviously taken aback by his request. "My name is Ella, and this is Kindle."

When Ella told her name, Kindle tried to smile but wasn't sure she achieved a happy face.

The man bowed his head at each of them then responded, "An honor. I am Bennickle."

At his announcement Kindle found herself disappointed. She had expected a long proclamation of what he ruled and his accomplishments or at the very least a title of honor to precede his name. The name that he had uttered seemed much too simple to sum up his impressive stature. Kindle glanced up to check if he was about to tell them more, but his face was stoic.

Ella broke the silence. "Hello, Bennickle. If I may ask before we talk about the business you have, Kindle and I would like to know where we are."

"Tor-tuosus La-by-rin-thos." Bennickle took a long time to exhale the two words, but once he had and Kindle pieced them together in her mind, she decided their ominous weight made up for his simple name. Hoping she could somehow move the subject to the glowing orb, Kindle decided to enter the conversation.

"So, um, is it a cave?" she inquired then squirmed as he turned his dark brown eyes on her. "I mean, if it's okay to ask, um, sir."

"Titles are … unnecessary," he replied.

"Uh–uh, okay," Kindle stuttered as she reconsidered her decision to speak.

"It is my home," Bennickle explained as he lifted his eyes to stare around the rocky hall.

"So were those—the rock and the tree who brought us here—do you know them?" Ella wondered.

Bennickle respectfully inclined his head to Ella. "Apologies for … the roughness."

"It's okay," Kindle automatically replied. Truthfully, she did not believe that rock and tree monsters that pounded and swatted whatever they pleased *was* okay, but she thought accepting his apology would make him happy. However, Kindle saw Ella send her an argumentative glance and again regretted her words.

"You know about them and how they treated us, then?" Ella carefully inquired, and her voice told Kindle she was piecing the bits of information into understanding. "Did you tell them to grab us up and bring us here?"

"Sincere apologies," he replied then, after a deep breath, explained, "Meeting is imperative."

"Because of the business you mentioned?" Ella quickly asked.

Bennickle raised his chin. "You are discerning."

Kindle stared back and forth between them. Something about their conversation caused her to believe that they both knew more than she did. She wasn't sure if it was Bennickle's way of uttering the fewest words possible or Ella's perceptive questioning or something else. Whatever the reason for her slight confusion, Kindle wanted to overcome it.

"So why's it so important?" she questioned then, realizing she sounded far from discerning, added, "I mean, what kind of business is so important we had to come down here?"

"Trade," he simply replied, and Kindle thought one side of his mouth twitched into a momentary smile.

"Of what?" interrogated Ella in a defensive tone.

Kindle stared at her. She wasn't sure why her usually calm and open friend was so guarded. Bennickle looked fairly intimidating, but so far his demeanor seemed so congenial and subdued that Kindle wondered if he was actually a friend. As Kindle turned her puzzled eyes to him to watch his chin work up a response, the massive man moved for the first time.

Bennickle took a half-step closer to them and raised his hand to the pinnacle of the cave tunnel. Even though Ella lifted her fire to illuminate his action, Kindle didn't know what he was doing. His dark brown hand ran over the rocks, studying the shape of each one before it moved to the next. Finally, his fingers ceased searching, wrapped around a rock, and forced it from its hiding place. A few pebbles rained down, and Kindle instinctively shielded her eyes. When she lowered her arm, she saw that Bennickle held more than just a rock. Something that resembled a short, fat purple carrot was sticking up out of the dark stone in his hand. As he gently shook the funny plant to remove some of the soil from it, he expounded, "You require … refreshment. I have … abundance."

"What is it?" Kindle curiously wondered. Bennickle offered the rock to her, but before she could accept it, Ella raised an elbow to block her arm.

"And what must we give you to have it?"

Bennickle turned his eyes to Ella, and Kindle feared that she had finally reached the end of his patience. Her anxiety only lasted as long as his inquisitive silence, though. When he answered, his voice was still its gradual monotone rumble. "A taste is free." His arm remained exactly where it was, offering Kindle the root. She checked Ella's expression. It was still wary, but when she noticed Kindle silently begging for direction, her mouth twitched into a brief soft grin.

Kindle hungrily snatched the rock and the strange purple carrot and repeated her earlier question. "What is it?"

"Medela," answered Bennickle. "A deep growing root."

"It is food, isn't it?" wondered Ella, some of her interested curiosity back in her voice. "It won't harm us, will it? It isn't poison?"

At her query, Kindle ended her battle to free the root from the rock.

"It brightens," Bennickle assured them and then, as if to prove his statement, reached forward, snapped the top of the medela into his hand, and ate it. She and Ella watched him slowly chew then finally swallow and sigh, "Brightening."

Totally convinced that what she held was not only food but tasty food, Kindle returned to her fight to acquire it. Bennickle and Ella silently watched her for a while, then Ella abruptly asked, "So you would like to give us more of these medela as a trade for something we have?"

"All my medela … and more."

"More food?" Kindle happily panted. She still had not extracted the root and was close to simply eating it out of the rock.

Bennickle shook his head. "My home."

Ella inhaled in surprise, and Kindle, once she took her eyes off the medela and registered his words, felt the same shock.

"You mean, like, this place?" she wondered, sure she had misunderstood. "This cave tunnel?"

"All of Tor-tuosus La-by-rin-thos."

Unsure of what to think, Kindle turned to Ella. The offer he had given didn't really interest her. She did not particularly like the dark tunnel they stood in and did not know if it was the entirety of Tortuosus Labyrinthos or not. The tone in which Bennickle had announced his offer, though, suggested that it was much more significant than she knew. As Kindle weighed all of the possibilities of accepting his home, she watched Ella's expression shift in thought.

Before Kindle had come anywhere near a conclusion, Ella asked, "Why would you like to trade your entire home? We do not have any need of it, and, quite honestly, your ease of giving it seems a trifle underhanded, as if perhaps it isn't worth very much to you at all."

Bennickle raised his chin. Kindle worried that Ella's comment might have offended him, but if it had, his stoic face didn't show it.

"Its value … is immense," he eventually replied, "when traveling."

A questioning expression clouded Ella's face. "Its value is immense when traveling?"

"It links Xylina … to the east."

Realization burst in Kindle's mind, and excited to at last understand the shaded conversation, she gasped, "It's the mine, isn't it? Well, I mean, we thought it was a mine, but it's that big hole or whatever between this forest and the other one, isn't it? That means we wouldn't have to go all the way around." Kindle breathed her last sentence to Ella and expected glad agreement to wash over her as well, but she remained unmoved.

"Does it really go so far as Ignancia Forest?"

Bennickle slowly raised and lowered his head.

"And how do we know it's not just one large twisting tunnel?" Ella continued in a questioning tone. "Or that it really does go as you say?"

"Your thoroughness … is admirable," Bennickle surprisingly complimented. "And therein lies … the last offer."

Kindle felt lost again and snuck a glance at Ella. Her friend stared at the fire in her hands as she inquired, "You mean to tell us the way through this Tortuosus place? From here to Ignancia?"

Bennickle shook his head but responded, "Every way. Through, down, up, … and out."

Kindle smiled at his last word. "You'll tell us how to get out of here?"

He lifted his head, but before he could bring it down in assent, Ella quickly quizzed, "So you would like to trade us these medela as well as your entire home *and* tell us how to navigate through it all?"

Bennickle finished his nod.

"But what could we possibly have that would balance such a large trade? We haven't anything of value—your rock man carried us far from all of our supplies. But even if we had our packs, we've all but emptied them of food and minas."

As Kindle listened to Ella, she realized she was right. The only possessions they had that were worth anything were their horses and swords. Now worried that the large man might want Ella's rapier, she twisted to hide it.

"All I seek," he finally worked out of his mouth, "are the marks."

"No," Ella immediately responded and stepped farther from him.

The same reaction had pulsed through Kindle's mind, but instead of denying him, she explained, "Well, I mean, we'd really like to, but we need these. They, um … help us know what to do. Maybe we could trade something else?"

"No. The marks," he insisted then added, "You do not … need them."

"We do," Ella confidently refuted him. "I suppose you already know, but they do help us to know what we must do. They let us hear the elements. Or the makers."

"The makers are dead," Bennickle coldly replied, and Kindle

168

blinked in shock. She had not long ago concluded that her necklace really could help her hear Hux, but now this man was very resolutely asserting that possibility was impossible. While her mind was still reeling, Ella spoke what Kindle wanted to be true.

"They are not dead."

"You have not … seen them." Bennickle had not asked the words but stated them as truth. Kindle felt her stomach drop as she realized he was correct. They had only *heard* about the makers but had never actually *seen* them.

"They are not dead," Ella repeated, but Kindle could sense from her tone that her belief was also shaken. "They can't be dead. We've heard them … or, I suppose, I have at least."

"Yeah, I have too," Kindle interjected, and Ella's eyes brightened as they flicked to her.

"You hear … your thoughts," he slowly, calmly replied.

"Well, regardless of what you suppose, we would not like to trade these," Ella decisively told him.

"I witnessed … their end. I am sorry. They are … gone." Even though Bennickle's three short sentences took him a long time to utter, both girls endured them with wide eyes.

Once he finished, Ella shook her head but didn't verbalize her thoughts. A long silence opened, and Kindle tried not to frantically sort through all that the Cifra and Azildor had said about the makers to determine if anyone had mentioned if they were alive or dead. Just to distract herself, she returned to her task of acquiring the medela. As she struggled with it, she sensed Bennickle's eyes watching her. An urge to ask him to stop crept up in her but melted away when he held out a hand. Kindle ceased her fight. Guessing his upturned palm indicated that he wanted the medela back, she sighed and relinquished it. Bennickle did not yank it out of reach as she expected, though, but wrapped a tight fist around the rock to crush it. He shook the rubble off the medela then handed it back to her.

"Consider: … all you need … I offer." He inclined his head to each of them then pivoted to exit from the opening behind him.

"Wait," Kindle cried. "What are you gunna do to us? I mean,

since we didn't want to trade."

Bennickle turned his proud profile over his shoulder. "Nothing."

Kindle wrinkled her nose, glanced at Ella, who appeared concerned rather than confused, and then raised her face to question Bennickle, but he had disappeared. Surprised that he had gone so quickly, Kindle blinked at the solid rock where the dark hole and majestic man had stood seconds ago. Questions slowly rose into her consciousness, and once too many occupied her mind, Kindle, still staring at the wall, asked, "Ella … what do we do?"

When a few minutes passed and Ella's bright voice still hadn't answered, Kindle tore her attention from the rock and her boiling thoughts to look at her friend. Ella was gazing at the fire she held. Her face did not show sadness or anger but also held no joy; it was quite blank. The lack of expression concerned Kindle, and despair suddenly pushed a multitude of questions out of her mouth.

"Ella? Are you okay? Do you think we're gunna be okay and— and what do you think he meant? I mean, about leaving us alone? Do you really think he's not gunna do anything? And … and …"

"I don't know if he was telling the truth, Kin," Ella softly answered her last unspoken query.

Too scared to talk about what was clearly at the forefront of both their minds, Kindle commented, "I mean, he sounded nice, and all that stuff he wanted to give us was pretty helpful."

"I just can't bring myself to trust him," Ella replied then looked straight in Kindle's eyes. "You told him you had heard one of the makers as well. Did you honestly mean it?"

"Well, I thought I did. But, I dunno, it could've just been me thinking I did."

Now Ella's face did fall into disappointment.

Kindle bit her lip. "I mean, we can't hear them if …"

"But Kin, how could I know in my own thoughts so certainly how to do things I never even knew I could do? Things I never knew could even happen? How could it be only our own thoughts we heard?"

"I don't know," mumbled Kindle, not really wanting to mull over such a confusing, frightening possibility.

"No, Kin, I could not have been doing all that."

"I dunno, maybe … maybe it was one of the spirits or your element like we said it might be. Remember? We said it could be any of them that you heard."

"Kindle," Ella replied with such a pained voice and face that Kindle had to avert her eyes. "Kindle, you were so sure not so long ago that you had heard a maker. Not an element or spirit, a *maker*. He could be lying, Kin. He could be lying about the whole lot of it. He did tell us he wants our necklaces and …" Ella's voice drifted into nothingness, and Kindle let her eyes flick to her face. Ella's mouth hung slightly open, but her eyes were racing back and forth like Andrew's did when he was calculating.

"What?" Kindle urged, her curiosity now stronger than her discomfort.

"Kin …" Ella's fire danced as she pursed her lips in thought for a moment. "Also in the forest, you said that if the spirits were alive, they would want our necklaces."

They momentarily locked gazes, but Kindle vigorously shook her head.

"No. He can't be a spirit. He was too nice and … and he didn't look anything like that creepy thing. I mean, you even said that the spirits probably don't have any power."

"I know what I supposed, Kin, but it was only a supposition. Think, who else would so readily give so much for them?"

"Lord Aryl, um, Beryl—"

A slight grin drew up Ella's mouth. "He was a rotten, greedy fool and hadn't an inkling of what they were. That Bennickle—he knew all about them without us uttering a word about them. He knew they were marks of the makers. No one else we have met our whole journey has even heard of the makers. Don't you see, Kin? It all aligns."

"But … I dunno, why didn't he just take them, then? I mean, if he really is one of the spirits, why didn't he just grab them and kill us? That creepy thing keeps trying to kill us."

"No, Kin, it's not. You told us that as well in the forest. The black beastly thing is after Tad's necklace." She paused to let Kindle reluctantly nod. "And now Bennickle is after ours. So you see, that beast is a spirit connected to Tad's mark and Bennickle is a spirit connected to mine."

"How do you know he's connected to yours?" impulsively argued Kindle, her pride jumping at Ella's final conclusion.

Ella gave her a sympathetic smile. "Honestly, Kin, are we flying in the air or under the earth?"

"Oh ... yeah, sorry."

"It's alright, don't worry over it. But do you see? All you said *must* be right. The spirits are after these." Ella pulled a hand from her fire to lay it on her gem. As she did, Kindle stared down at her own shining jewel. She too desired to place a protective hand over it, but at the same time felt new, uncomfortable distance from it. Until Bennickle's assertion, she had considered it a friend, but now it appeared that it was not a tie to a guiding maker but just a deceitful bond to a wicked spirit. Now she wondered if she should guard it, trust it, or even keep it.

"Maybe we should give them to him," she sighed miserably.

"What? Of course we should not give them up," Ella incredulously replied.

"Well, why not? I mean, if the spirits are just gunna keep bugging us and the necklaces don't really do anything—"

"Kindle!" cried Ella. Kindle shrank back from her reproachful tone. Ella shook her head, and Kindle hoped she had recognized her rudeness, but she did not. "We cannot give them up. These necklaces—they've chosen us, they want us to complete the task they have given us, and if we do not need them, if we could do it all on our own, don't you believe they would not have even come to us at the beginning of all this? If we didn't need them, don't you believe the makers would have chosen a pack more ... able? We do need them, Kin. We must keep them; they *are* changing us. I know I can feel the change in me ... I've never known and done so much—and done so much that's helpful—with this fire. And I know it is not just my doings, Kindle. I *know* it is whatever power that is in this necklace and the maker connected to it. We do need them, Kin, and we cannot simply go and hand them over because we feel a bit of persuasion or struggle. We cannot be thrown off our course." Ella determinedly waved her head. "You can't listen to him, Kin. He wants you to give it up, but you can't. I don't intend to boss you, I truly don't, but surely, you've felt it as well? I know you understand that these necklaces are powerful and are changing us. I know you've heard its direction."

Ella's last few sentences pushed for a reply, but Kindle felt too emotional and confused to give one. She did trust Ella and wanted to believe everything she had claimed, but Bennickle's words were still echoing in her mind.

"But ... what if the makers *are* dead?" she weakly asked.

"They're not. I know it as well as you. They can't be. We've heard them, haven't we?"

Kindle gazed down at her necklace and sighed heavily. She almost voiced a question of its reliability, but Ella's firelight reflected off the dragon, and it seemed to twist its neck even more to peer right up at her. In its small perhaps real, perhaps imagined movement, it reminded her of the truths it had stirred up in her along their journey.

It was real. Everything about the throne, marks, spirits, and makers was real.

The marks proved it all was real.

The makers used the marks to help them.

And the marks and the makers had not left them.

"Yeah," Kindle finally breathed. The comprehension in her word caused her to smile. "Yeah, you're right. I have heard it the whole time, but not like you have. I mean, it's not like a voice I can hear like you said, but ... but when I see my necklace, I always remember stuff. But, I mean, it's not like *I* remember stuff, but my necklace reminds me. Do you know what I mean?" She peered up at Ella to see she was beaming.

"I knew you had, Kin. I knew you had heard it as well. And yes, I do suppose I see what you mean." Ella's bright eyes slid sideways, and Kindle sensed an idea was forming in her mind.

"What?" she urged.

"Oh, I only wondered … Kin, do you believe we all hear them differently? The marks and the makers?"

"Um, yeah … I guess so," Kindle replied, puzzling over Ella's reason for asking. "I mean, it seems like it. Why?"

"Well, I only supposed that if you and I hear our marks and makers in a different manner, then Tad and Andrew may as well … and perhaps they've been guiding us all more than we know."

Kindle thoughtfully wrinkled her nose. "You mean, like, telling us what to do without us knowing?" She didn't like the idea of being unknowingly controlled.

"Well, in a sort. Not told but … you do remember how Tad said that in Iteraum he felt odd and so decided to check on you?"

Kindle quickly nodded, focusing hard on Ella's logic so she wouldn't grin.

"I suppose it's that sort of guidance—as if our makers place a thought or idea or feeling or action in our mind so we mull over it and hopefully do what's right with it. Do you see?"

"Oh, yeah. Like they don't make us do whatever they want but try and help us out?"

"Yes, they guide us if we let them … if we listen. And they speak in different ways because we all listen in different ways."

"Oh …" Kindle nodded as she realized not only what Ella meant but that her assumptions possibly explained some of her actions. She could recall several times on the Chokmah farm feeling the need to return Tad to their group without understanding why and wondered if the urges had been from Hux. The thought of participating in such a transcendent communication caused an excited but anxious sensation to crowd over her whole body. She tried to think of another time a similar unexplainable compulsion or idea had struck her but could recall none besides the few times her necklace had led her to remember something.

"Kindle, are you alright?" she heard Ella ask and blinked out of her thoughts. Her friend's face was concerned, and she wondered if she had spaced out more than she realized.

"Is it cold in this tunnel?" Ella wondered, and when Kindle gave her a confused stare, she inclined her head and explained, "Your arm has those cold bumps."

Kindle gazed down to see that she had unconsciously lifted a hand to toy with her necklace, and in doing so her sleeve had drifted down.

"Oh, no—well, I mean, yeah, it *is* cold ..." she replied as she pulled the cloth back over her arm, "but I was just thinking about what you said, and it, I dunno, kind of made me feel weird—but not bad weird—just like ... like it's weird that I can hear somebody I don't know, and it's somebody really important, and that they want to help me out."

Ella grinned as if she understood exactly how Kindle felt and sighed, "The enormity of it all *is* strange ... but wonderful."

Even though they stood silently staring at Ella's fire for the next few minutes, Kindle felt a new closeness between them. Working out such a resounding, undeniable understanding of their marks and makers together seemed to have connected their very souls. Kindle was sure she and Ella were rolling through the same thoughts and feelings and then digesting and fully comprehending them in unison. Just as she began to wonder if the makers would breathe help to them soon, Ella announced, "Kin, we should go."

"Because—?"

"Yes. Something about this whole place is not right. And Bennickle as well." She spun and returned to their walk that Bennickle had interrupted.

"So you think this is the right way? You know, *out?*" questioned Kindle even though she was almost positive she knew the answer.

"Yes. I just keep hearing that small voice telling me to go this way."

"You did when you first woke up too, didn't you?"

"Yes." Ella flashed her an apologetic smile. "That's why I was so distracted. I absolutely wanted to know what that awful rock creature had done."

"And you knew about him too, didn't you? I mean, before he ever popped out of the ground?"

Ella nodded but her smile faltered. "It wasn't the same, though. It was this horrible, dreadful feeling just the same as I felt this morning about the grou—"

Kindle halted as Ella's voice did. The tunnel they were traveling had come to an end. The wall blocking their way, though, was unlike the jutting arch Kindle had learned to be normal. In fact, the longer she squinted at the smooth, light grey convex surface, the less she thought it was a wall. Kindle slipped a suspicious glance at Ella, who was holding her fire up to the obstacle and wearing a wary expression.

"It's not a wall?" Kindle half-stated, half-asked since she wasn't certain what it was.

"If it is, it isn't natural," whispered Ella, and Kindle felt the urgent need to lower her voice as well.

"Well, what do you think it is? Do you think we can move it?"

As Ella began to turn around, she murmured, "I don't know, it would be—oh!"

Kindle whirled around as well, ready to toss aside the medela and draw Ella's sword. When she saw what had caused Ella's surprise, though, her readiness morphed into dismay. Another identical rock had appeared just feet behind them.

"We–we just—" stammered Kindle to Ella, whose expression of wariness had become alert distrust.

"He's trapped us, Kin. That Bennickle's trapped us," Ella confidently avowed.

"Well, what—?" Kindle started to ask, but her frantic thoughts shifted. "But didn't he say he wasn't gunna do anything to us?" She quickly scanned the cage of rock, fully expecting to see Bennickle or something awful lurking in a corner.

"He did claim that, but he claimed quite a lot else I didn't believe either." Ella also searched the walls but much more calmly.

"What are you looking for?" Kindle whispered, her panic

easing slightly. "Do you think we can get out?"

Ella's eyes reached the peak of the arch above then dropped to Kindle. "Now, don't fret, but those two great rocks could very possibly be some more of those inconsiderate rock creatures, and even if they are not, I can't imagine moving them will be likely," Ella quickly whispered. "So we must work another way out of here, and I believe …" She lifted her eyes, and Kindle followed them to the dangerous ceiling. "That going *up* is our best chance."

"Up?" Kindle incredulously repeated. She turned her eyes back to Ella's face. Her confident, sly grin told Kindle that she was not only serious but had a plan. "How are we gunna go up?"

"I'm not quite sure how, but when Bennickle extracted that medela, it had soil on it, so I'm supposing that all those rocks above us here are embedded in soil as well."

Not sure how Ella's assumption would help them escape, Kindle lifted her gaze to the rock arch. It was at least five feet above her head. "How do we get up there, though?"

"Kindle," Ella sighed, and Kindle lowered her eyes to see she was shaking her head but grinning. "You keep forgetting …" The fire she held danced, and Kindle nodded. Even though she still didn't fully understand what Ella intended to do, she knew her fire could reach the rock above them.

As Kindle backed as far as she could from Ella, she asked, "So … what are you gunna do? I mean, you can't burn a hole in the rock, can you?"

Ella shrugged and brightly replied, "I suppose we'll see."

Realizing Ella actually had almost no plan, Kindle felt compelled to ask more questions or try to convince Ella to devise one, but instead, she bit her lip to remain quiet. Ella's face had fallen into deep concentration, and Kindle did not want to be the reason for the outbreak of an uncontrollable fire. For a few moments, they both stood in perfect, breathless silence, Kindle watching Ella, and Ella watching her small flame. Suddenly, a huge column of orange fire twisted up from her hands and smashed into the rocks overhead. The flames bubbled over and licked the cold, dark stone but did not appear to alter it at all. Kindle watched it as long as she could stand its light and heat then covered her face.

"Is it too much, Kindle?" called Ella over the sweeping roar of her flames.

"No, I'm okay," she truthfully replied. The blaze's intensity wasn't much different than a bonfire worthy of marshmallow roasting.

"Alright," she heard Ella's not quite convinced voice reply. "Do tell me when it is."

"Okay," Kindle promised then almost immediately felt the heat grow uncomfortable. Not wanting to burn alive but also desperate for Ella's fire to make some sort of progress, Kindle shifted a few fingers aside to see what was happening. After only a brief look, Kindle covered her face again and spun to hide as much of herself as possible in the jagged wall. Ella's fire *had* grown in intensity. It had changed from flailing orange tongues to a concentrated blast of white flames encircling wicked blue fire. As she squeezed more and more of herself against the still somewhat cool rock, Kindle tried to think just how hot fire had to grow before it turned blue. Her mind was too consumed by the stifling heat to concentrate, though, and she considered shouting at Ella to stop. Then, before she could bring herself to end their only chance of escape, the overwhelming heat vanished.

Very slowly, Kindle uncovered her face. Everything was dark.

"Ella?" she asked, worried the fire had been too much for her friend. To her great relief, Ella's cheerful voice sounded from across their enclosure.

"Yes. Are you alright?"

"Um. Yeah. Where are you?" Kindle began to edge to Ella's voice, but when her first step hit the stone, Ella cautioned, "Stay where you are for a moment, Kindle. I haven't gone anywhere, and I'm alright, but I'm not so sure if everything's settled."

Kindle wrinkled her brow, trying to decode Ella's statement. Then a hopeful thought struck her. "Did it work? Did you break it or melt it or whatever? Did you make a hole?"

A few seconds of silence passed. Then she heard soft footfalls, and much nearer to her, Ella answered, "I think I have melted enough for us to nip through. Here, where are you? Your medela's a bit cooked, I believe."

Kindle felt the wind of Ella's hand sweep by her and reached out hers to find it. When they finally collided, Ella quickly stuffed the medela into Kindle's palm. Surprised by its heat, she almost dropped it to the floor but instead created a hammock for it with the end of her long shirt.

"You think it's safe to eat?" she questioned as she bounced the hem of her shirt to cool it.

"Yes. I have heard of medela. The older traders sometimes chat about them and act as if they're the most wonderful things to eat but the hardest to find. Most everyone else who hears them claims that their old minds are boggled and no such thing exists, but now seeing where one comes from, it's no surprise why hardly any man's seen one. I only questioned *that* one because I was sure that Bennickle was out to kill us. Is it cooler now?"

"Huh? Oh, um, I think so …" replied Kindle, wondering how Ella knew she was attempting to fan the medela.

"So you don't mind a small light, then?" Ella asked as a pinpoint of light brushed back some of the darkness. "I don't want to burn you up."

"Oh," Kindle laughed as she realized Ella had been asking about the room's temperature. "Yeah, it's fine in here now."

Ella allowed her flame to grow until they could see one another then curiously stared at Kindle's medela pouch. "What are you doing?"

"Oh." Kindle quickly plucked the root out of her shirt. "I was just trying to cool it down. It was pretty hot."

Ella's smile shrank. "I didn't know. Are you sure you're alright? Not burned at all?"

"No, I'm fine," Kindle insisted. "And you had to so we could get out of here." To move Ella away from her remorse, she broke the softened medela in half, gave one piece to Ella, and then bit into the other part as she walked to the other end of their rock cage.

"Hey, it is good!" she happily remarked. Truthfully, Kindle hadn't expected the funny root to be greatly appealing, but it was sweet, earthy, and a little crunchy like a roasted carrot, only much better.

"It is," Ella agreed as she carried herself to Kindle's side. They both turned their munching chins upward to see what Ella's fire had accomplished, but the high ceiling hid in darkness.

"Can you make it a little brighter?" asked Kindle, and when Ella consented, she breathed a quiet, "Wow."

A circle about the size of a manhole of dry, ash-white soil sat back away from the rest of the now much less jagged rocks around it. Turning her eyes to their feet, Kindle saw a smooth, slightly smoking black lump and guessed that it was the rock Ella had melted.

"Wow," repeated Kindle, then she beamed at Ella. "You did it! I mean, you really melted rock!"

To her surprise, Ella very meditatively replied, "It's these necklaces, Kindle. Like I told you before, I've never been able to do much more than heat a pot of tea or light a candle. These necklaces are more powerful than we know."

Kindle tried to seriously nod. She did believe Ella but was determined to in no way dampen her own glee. "So, either way, we can get out now, right?"

Ella stared upward. "Only the rock's melted away. We'll have to break through that dirt, and then I suppose we'll have a route up."

"Well, how? It's way up there. I mean, it's not like we could just dig—"

"Do you have my sword?" Ella thoughtfully interjected, and Kindle slid it out of her sheath.

"Yeah, why?"

"Hand it here," replied Ella. Kindle squished her face in hesitation but finally relinquished the weapon. Ella's mouth twisted as she examined and weighed the sword in her hand as if appraising it. As she peered up to the hole, she confessed, "I don't know, Kin. This may not be the most sane thought."

"What?" Kindle anxiously questioned, beginning to form a

suspicion in her mind.

Ella laughed to herself. "But I suppose if Tad were here, he would have already done it."

"What? Are you—?"

"You best stand back," Ella suggested to her. Then she bent back, engulfed her sword in flames, and launched it like a spear into the dry soil above. Kindle ducked and dodged back a few steps as flaming bits of soil rained. Eager to see what would happen, though, she trotted back to Ella's side. They stared up together as the fire evaporated and the rapier remained lodged in the dirt.

"Well ..." Ella began to sigh, but cracks suddenly webbed through the circle, and Kindle and Ella scattered as the sword tumbled down in a shower of dusty earth.

"Ugh! Bleck!" coughed Kindle as the cloud rolled around her in the darkness.

"Is it—uff, uff—is it cleared?" Ella wondered as she also choked on the dirt. Kindle bumped her arm as the dust settled away from her nose. In the next moment, Ella pulled away, a fire lit the space again, and they both eagerly squinted up.

Kindle gasped in delight. "It worked! Ella! It worked!"

"Yes, Kin, I can see!" she replied with a jubilant smile. "Now, get on my shoulders."

"What?" Kindle brought her eyes down as her glee also fell. "What do you mean?"

"One of us has to climb up if we're going to work a way out of this cave, and you're smallest, so climb on my shoulders, and I'll boost you—"

"But then how will you get up?" Kindle interrupted, her triumph now fully replaced by unwelcome realization. "If only one of us should go up and find a way out, it should be you. I mean, I won't even be able to see, and you'll know what to do, and—"

"Kin," Ella calmingly stopped her. "Don't fret over it. You're smaller, and I can lift you. You'll take my sword, and you'll know what to do just as well as I would. Remember? It's not me hashing out things, it's the necklace."

"Oh … yeah, but—"

"Listen to it," Ella gently insisted then spun and crouched down in front of her. "Hop on."

"Um …" Kindle bent to retrieve Ella's sword but made no move to stand on her friend. She wasn't sure if she feared squishing her or falling or poking her head into a dark room, but her entire being felt completely opposed to complying with Ella's direction.

"Kin," Ella sighed as she twisted to see her. "Don't make me boss you. You'll be fine. Now, come along."

Feeling as if she *had* been bossed, Kindle heaved a sigh and tried to gingerly step onto Ella. After placing only one foot on Ella, Kindle wobbled slightly and announced, "I'm sitting first. I'm gunna sit until you stand up, then I'll stand up."

"That's alright, Kindle, just don't fret."

Glad that she didn't have to try to hold her balance on Ella, Kindle readily threw her legs over her friend's shoulders.

"Set?" Ella asked.

"Yeah—whoa!" Kindle leaned forward and wrapped her arms around Ella's head as she stood.

"Kin! You're alright!" Ella's muffled voice called up to her.

"You have to hold on to my legs or I'll fall off!" she retorted.

"Kin, I'm holding the fire. If you want light, I can't hold on to you."

Knowing she was right, Kindle huffed.

"Now, look, are we under the hole?" asked Ella, still ensnared by Kindle's nervous hold. Kindle gained her balance, slowly released Ella's head, and cautiously peered around.

"Okay, um, you're gunna have to go forward a little bit, but be careful because there's that pile of … melted rock."

"Alright, hold steady now," Ella ordered and walked a few careful steps.

"Okay!" Kindle called when they stood right under the hole. She gazed up and shakily sighed, "You're gunna have to help me. You're gunna have to hold on to my legs."

"It will be dark."

"I–I know."

"Alright. Call down when you've made it." At Ella's last word, darkness engulfed them. Kindle bit her lip then closed her eyes to focus on what her hands could feel and her task rather than her unwilling, frantic mind. She found Ella's shoulders under her legs and then carefully, one leg at a time, she transitioned to a doubled-over stand. Before she could cry for help, Ella's warm hands found her ankles. After a deep, calming breath, Kindle focused every thought and muscle on straightening up and raising her hands to search for the hole. To her surprise and gratefulness, her fingers bumped rock when level with her neck. Quickly, she slid her hands along the sides of the opening up past her head. Before her arms were fully extended, cool empty space surrounded her hands. A very small bit of her fear gone, Kindle's mouth lifted slightly.

Raising her arms as high as she could, Kindle discovered that her forearms were able to bend out over the sturdy soil above.

"I think I can get up," she quietly called down to Ella. "Just push my feet up when you can."

Kindle didn't hear a reply but felt Ella shift her grip and knew she understood. Mustering all the strength she possessed, Kindle pulled the rest of her arms and head into the dark void above as well. As she did, she felt Ella's steadying hold leave her ankles but soon return as a pushing force under her feet. With the help from below, Kindle managed to drag then kick and twist her entire body up through the hole. Once the toes of her boots were the only parts of her not laying on firm ground, she exhaled all her intensely wound determination. Exhaustion from the short battle waved over her, and she dropped her cheek on the cool dirt to rest.

"Kindle?" she heard Ella's distant voice call.

"Yeah," Kindle answered as she reluctantly sat up. When she did, she saw a faint glow rising from the hole and knew Ella had relit her fire. Peering down into the illuminated space, Kindle reported, "I made it up. I'm fine."

"Good," Ella replied. "Go on and have a search 'round to see if you can find anything at all that might help."

"Um …" Kindle squinted at the darkness all around her. Finding anything, even the walls, didn't seem possible. Also, the longer Kindle stared at the unknown world spread imperceptibly out on every side, the more and more she feared what could be living in it. "I can't see anything," she finally called down.

Ella dropped her gaze to her surroundings then replied, "I'll do what I can here, but you must try to find something—even if all we can do is pile a load of rocks here. Alright?" Ella turned her face up, and Kindle saw her cheerfulness was not fully genuine.

Knowing she couldn't leave Ella stranded, Kindle nodded and, in a tone much more confident than she felt, promised, "I'll find something."

Kindle waited to see Ella smile and drift out of her view before she blew out a frustrated, tired breath and stood. For a while she remained beside the circle of dim light. Even though she truly did want to rescue Ella and find a way out of the Tortuosus Labyrinthos, she feared the means of those goals. Adventuring around a completely dark cave that could be full of monsters or pits or anything scared her, and trying to feel around in such a dangerous, unfamiliar place seemed like a horrible idea. The longer she remained rooted to her somewhat lit spot, the more her fearful predictions multiplied and convinced her to stay immobile. Kindle considered calling down to Ella that she couldn't find anything and couldn't keep her promise, but when she let her eyes travel down, the sight of her necklace stopped her.

As she stared at it, she remembered what Ella had claimed about their necklaces not very long ago. She had said that they were the power causing things to happen and had urged Kindle to listen to hers. Somewhat nervous that she may not hear anything, Kindle bit her lip and tried to silence her tumultuous mind and listen. She didn't know what to listen for, but as she focused on pushing back the roar of fears echoing in her mind, a very soft memory rose among the noise.

At first the little bubble of thought was fuzzy; it was something connected to all her fear and blowing about in it but was also distinctly its own. Suddenly, the bubble popped into clarity and rained its distinct truth over the last of her imagined wariness.

The memory was Tad. The picture of him standing by the river was slightly misty, but his words were so distinct that it was as if she was truly hearing them for the first time.

He had said to forget about being afraid and just do what she knew she had to do. Kindle allowed the memory of his words to replay until it faded to let the present collide with its truth.

As she blinked herself back into the dark cave, Kindle understood that she had to act. She had to just forget being scared, go into the darkness, and know she would find something. Determined but still aware that she had no understanding of what existed around her, Kindle stretched out her arms and carefully began to venture through the dark.

BORING

After a few wide, awkward steps, one of Kindle's hands hit a dirt wall. She quickly sidled up to it and took up a more normal pace along what she assumed was a tunnel. Not really sure how to conduct her search, Kindle simply walked along with one palm tracing the wall and the other waving through the open space beside her. Every few seconds she twisted to check if she could still see the circle of light behind her. The only clear plan she had created was to not stray too far from the hole so she could easily find her way back to Ella.

Even after the opening's glow grew dim and small, Kindle hadn't encountered any sort of change in her surroundings. From all she could sense, the passageway remained the same. The wall passed smoothly by her skin, the floor continued flat and level, and her slowly waving hand caught nothing but cool air. She began to wonder if the Tortuosus Labyrinthos was actually just one long, straight underground passageway and if she just walked long enough, then she would eventually find the end. Her thoughts traveled to pondering over how long it might take to reach the end of her walk and if she would simply hit a dirt wall or emerge into the forest when she did reach it.

With her mind occupied, Kindle forgot the initial purpose of her walk until a distant noise caused her to halt and whirl around.

As she searched for any sign of the sound's source, she realized that complete, uninterrupted darkness was all she could see. Checking for Ella's light had escaped her busy thoughts. Kindle turned and trotted back a few feet but still saw only black. Torn between running back or continuing her search, she lifted her heels and chin as high as possible to check for the light at a higher view. When she finally accepted that she really had traveled too far to see it, Kindle sighed and leaned against the wall. Keeping Ella's light in her vision had been her primary goal, and she wanted to stick to it. Now that she knew how unchanging and empty the tunnel she stood in had proved, though, she wasn't sure if she should maintain that plan. Even though she couldn't see the untraveled path ahead, Kindle turned her head to stare at it. She chewed her lip in thought for a moment then made a decision to continue.

Resolved to follow the wall at her side until it ended, Kindle hurried along beside it. She didn't want to give up all of her progress and greatly hoped and almost believed that the tunnel would soon end in a slope that led above the ground. When she had jogged for several minutes without any sign of a slope or change, she slowed to a walk. As she did, she felt her tiredness and wondered if she really should keep going. She had spent so much of her energy climbing through the hole and wandering in the dark that she doubted her body would possess enough to carry her back if she walked much farther. Kindle almost decided to stop and retrace her steps, but a sudden change in the wall caused her to forget the impulse.

It had disappeared. Kindle kept her feet rooted and stretched as far right as possible to make sure she hadn't accidentally drifted from the soil wall. Her fingertips brushed only air. Slightly alarmed at the sudden loss of her guide, Kindle pivoted to search for it, but when she did, a new sight stole her attention. At first she thought it was a light, but when she squinted at the distant white glow, she realized that she had encountered it earlier. It was the mysterious orb that had appeared with Bennickle. Captivated by it, Kindle began to slowly wander to it but halted in mid-step.

Approaching it was stupid. She knew that any time any person in a movie walked up to a shiny thing they shouldn't, it always ended badly. Also, the misty orb had sat on the staff Bennickle had held when he met them, and he was very likely holding it now as well. Considering the giant, powerful man could be staring right at her, Kindle retreated a few steps. She waved her hands around to find a wall but felt nothing. As she did, the orb's glow brightened and she froze. The grey clouds grew and swirled faster for a few seconds then returned to their original state.

Trying not to breathe loudly in her fright, Kindle put a hand on the hilt at her side and continued to carefully retreat with her eyes on the orb. Suddenly, her shoulder hit something, and she squeaked, spun, yanked out Ella's sword, and slashed. A dull puff sounded as she made contact with a soft but impenetrable surface. Kindle blew out a breath of relief and agitation as she placed a hand on her enemy. She had attacked the wall.

"Stupid wall," she grumbled, but then as her voice echoed behind her, her annoyance faded. She whipped around so her back touched the wall and held out the rapier, sure that Bennickle knew where she stood. For a few moments, she quietly prepared herself to face him and demand that he release her and Ella. Eventually, though, she realized that she had not heard his voice or steps and that the orb was not moving closer to her.

Her heart still racing from her scare and preparation to fight, Kindle cautiously lowered the sword and called, "Hello?" Hearing the fear in her voice, she cleared her throat and more forcefully repeated, "Hello?"

Bennickle's voice did not reply.

"I know you know I'm here," she nervously called. After a span of complete silence, during which she chewed her lip, Kindle whispered, "Is anybody there?"

Still no voice answered. However, the orb, as if it had heard her, brightened again. She blinked at it, curious, and then even though Kindle could hear half of her brain warning her not to, she headed to it. With each step the clouds thickened and swirled faster and faster. When her nose was only inches from it and she could see that it sat in a nook in the dirt wall, the atmosphere inside the orb had reached a tornadic velocity. The light grey clouds had rolled into one dark storm force churning wildly in the glass. It appeared so angry and tumultuous that Kindle hardly believed it wasn't creating any noise. Wondering just how thick the glass had to be to contain such a violent wind, she raised a hand to touch it.

In the instant her finger met the glass, a multitude of results charged and overwhelmed her senses. The swirling storm froze, lightened to dazzling white, and thinned into a glistening mist. At the same time, a whisper began and very gradually rose into a gusting sound. It was not the angry whooshing she had expected from the storm but a long, lonely whistling that filled her imagination with a sparse tundra and tall snow-covered mountains. She shivered but not just from her vivid, icy thoughts. The glass connected to her skin was cold—so cold that it caused her entire body to feel as if she had been doused in ice water. Even her lungs felt the immediate change and struggled to inhale the brisk air. As the whistling wind reached a ringing pitch that stung her ears and skin, Kindle fought against the immobilizing cold in her free arm to sweep her whipping hair out of her face. The impulsive motion popped open Kindle's eyes, which had shut against the chilling assault. Seeing the glittering orb behind her thrashing strands of hair told her that the wind was not only a sound but a tangible, present force. She attempted to break away from the orb, but the tip of her finger remained on the glass as if it was welded to it.

Fighting against the very real blizzard gusting around her, Kindle grabbed her captured hand and pulled. The motion did not detach her finger but propelled the entire orb from its shallow dirt nook. It tumbled down and yanked her whole arm with it. Just before it landed, her knees hit the hard, frozen soil and she squeezed her eyes shut in pain. Her hope that the orb had broken or at least cracked pushed her eyelids immediately back up. In a second she saw that it had not suffered at all and that her necklace had escaped her shirt and was swinging toward the orb. Then, as a light *ding* of metal on glass hit her ears, Kindle screamed.

A pain—a cold, deep, ferocious wrenching unlike anything she had ever encountered—had filled her whole being. Void of thought and any sense except the horrible ripping, she screamed and writhed on the ground. The agony seemed to tear down into her soul and relentlessly surged on for an unthinkably long time. Then, after what also felt like only seconds, it all ended.

Warmth returned. Kindle remained still and let the beautiful sensation wash over her. It wasn't just an absence of the horrible cold but a blanket of heat like sunshine pouring over her. The warmth also dove into her skin like the icy wind had, but instead of ripping and cracking, it seemed to melt everything that comprised her into a pool of peace. When her lungs finally filled with the amazing summer-like air and her breathing evened, she blinked open her tired eyes. All Kindle could see was brilliant golden light. Before she could lift her head, a distant yell rang out and the light vanished.

"Kindle!"

Rocked by the sudden, drastic change from blinding gold to almost complete black, Kindle shut her eyes.

"Kindle, what's happened? Are you alright?" the same voice asked, and she knew it belonged to Ella. Kindle tried to answer but realized that she felt very weak and instead uttered a groan.

"What's gone on?" Ella asked, close now. "I heard you screaming, Kindle. What's he done to you?" She felt Ella gently shake her arm and, glad for her friend's warm hand, Kindle placed her fingers on it to keep it there.

"Kin, you're shaking terribly. What's happened?" Ella questioned but seemed to be speaking to herself more than prodding for answers. "Come, open your eyes if you can. We're leaving."

Kindle did as Ella had directed and saw her kind but worried face peering down at her.

"There's a good girl. Now, come along, stand up." Ella didn't wait for Kindle to move but extinguished the flame in her palm and pulled on Kindle's wrists.

"If you can get your feet about …" Ella instructed, and Kindle gathered her legs so she could push up from the ground. Together they worked Kindle up into a standing position, and then Ella propped them beside one another as if Kindle had a broken leg. As soon as they were stable, a small flame lit the darkness.

"Now, let's come along, Kin, as quickly as you can, alright? That scream of yours was wretched enough to let Ledyard know your whereabouts."

Kindle nodded and they started forward. After only a few dragging steps, though, Ella stopped them.

"This isn't going to crack it … here, stand for me, Kin. Can you do that just for a pip?"

Wishing she had the energy to reply instead, Kindle bobbed her head. Without warning, Ella's steadying support left, and Kindle teetered. She tried to will herself to stand, but strength to do so simply did not exist in her. Thankfully, Ella returned in only a few seconds and pushed something into her arm before ducking under the opposite one.

"Lean on that as well, Kin, and you'll be alright," Ella directed and started carrying them forward again. Kindle found that if she did use the object and Ella for support, she could walk at Ella's urgent pace. With Ella's flame illuminating the soil cavern around them, they quickly exited the room and dove into the tunnel that Kindle had been traveling. As they turned out of the room, Kindle squinted back to find the strange orb but didn't spy it. Mystified, she dropped her gaze, and a sparkle from the object supporting her caught her curious mind. The twinkle had come from one of the number of large emeralds embedded in the smooth, dark metal capital on the long staff. She followed it down to the soil and realized what it was when she saw its matching foot.

"Wha—?" she slowly started to ask, but Ella broke into her weak voice.

"Kin, I absolutely promise to explain all of how I reached you when we're safely away from this horrid maze," she divulged in a rushed breath, "but now, please, let's just stay silent."

Kindle possessed neither the desire nor energy to argue, so she complied with Ella's plea. Her mind, though, did not restrain its questions. It chewed over the possibilities of how Ella had escaped, what had happened when she touched the orb, where the storm and light had come from, how Bennickle's staff had found itself as her crutch, why she was so weak, and a million other puzzles. None of the events made any sense and only caused anxiety to well up in her, so Kindle did her best to focus on walking.

Unlike she had supposed, the dirt tunnel was not similar to the rock one in size. Ella's light only lit the wall right beside them and left the height of the arch above in darkness. Its apparent enormity led Kindle to wonder if it was the same path that the huge rock and tree monsters had carried them along earlier. She watched the soil pass by under their feet to see if a footprint told her that she supposed rightly. After a few minutes of staring at only dirt, she gave up her search.

With nothing to occupy Kindle's mind, it began to reach back to its impatient questions. Determined to avoid them and their overwhelming, unexplainable mysteries, she whispered, "Far?"

Ella twitched at her voice then, after a few moments, reluctantly answered, "I'm not fully sure of how far we have to go. But I am positive this *is* the right direction. Are you feeling any better?"

Even though Kindle did not feel stronger or warmer, she nodded then willed herself to ask, "Bennickle?"

Again, Ella seemed hesitant to reply but finally sighed, "I don't really believe now is the time ... but, well, I suppose if they didn't come running at your yowling ..."

Kindle turned an apologetic but defensive face to Ella. She wanted to explain that she did not intentionally scream and to describe the horrible pain that had caused her to do so, but as Ella met her stare, Kindle saw that she seemed to already understand.

"Oh, Kin, I didn't mean a mark against you for it. I know you weren't howling for the fun of it, I only meant to say that was a horrid noise you made. I thought ... Kin, I thought for sure you were at an end." Ella sighed but then grinned at her. "But you're not. You're here and … and anyway, about Bennickle. He hasn't cropped up since he left us. I haven't an inkling of where he is or if he knows where we are, and I'm quite content to leave it …"

Ella's voice and expression faded into thoughtfulness, and Kindle followed her stare to see the reason for the change. She didn't see Bennickle, monsters, danger, or anything. Nothing except darkness and soil existed ahead of them. Kindle turned a puzzled gaze to her friend as they slowed to a standstill.

"There's another way," Ella murmured to herself and lifted her flame. The fire grew and lit the left and upper portions of the cavernous tunnel. Kindle peered around the entire space for another opening but couldn't find what Ella meant. The straight tunnel only continued unbroken in the same direction that they had been traveling.

"It's there," Ella confidently stated as if she knew Kindle was wondering where this other way was. With her tall light, she gestured slightly ahead to the left. Kindle ran her eyes over the area again but saw only smooth brown soil.

"Come along," Ella brightly urged and walked them to the wall. Once they reached it, a smile broke over her face. "Kin, there's another tunnel here. It's the one that will lead us out."

Kindle felt on the verge of telling Ella that she was seeing things or going crazy when she ducked out from Kindle's arm and lay a hand on her necklace. Suddenly, Kindle understood: Ella was listening to her maker. Not wanting to appear weak while Ella beamed at the dirt, Kindle tried to casually lean against the wall. Thankfully, Ella was too captivated by her discovery to notice Kindle wobble and then use the staff to slide down to the ground instead. She watched Ella examine the wall for a while then slowly asked, "How …?"

Before she could finish her question, Ella assured her, "There's another tunnel beyond this wall, and the wall itself isn't so thick."

"Fire?"

"No … Ki—" Ella stopped in surprise as she spun to talk to her and found she was sitting. "Are you sure you're alright?"

This time Kindle didn't feel like lying and so huffed a tired, frustrated breath.

"Of course not." Ella sympathetically frowned but quickly returned to her original thought. "Anyway, Kindle, do you suppose that if I—or this necklace or the maker tied to it—mended that wooden wall in Aryl, then it could carve a hole in this one?"

Sensing that Ella was voicing her thoughts rather than seeking an answer, Kindle shrugged and suggested, "Try."

A new sly and determined smile slipped onto Ella's face. She returned her gaze to the wall and then her fire disappeared. Immediately, Kindle wanted it back. Some of the cold that had already left her returned, and she pulled her knees up to her chest to huddle against the chill. As she did, a circle of warmth pressed against her leg, and Kindle thankfully gathered her gem in her hands to ward away the unwelcome iciness. Feeling greatly consoled and even somehow less cold, Kindle hunted for sounds from Ella. She could hear a faint sliding sound and imagined Ella was running her hands over the wall. Supposing that she would do some action similar to the quiet, careful miraculous wood-growing, Kindle listened for shifting soil. Instead of hearing the earth move, she heard Ella breathe, "Please, what do I do? We need your help."

Kindle waited to hear a gasp of understanding or the sound of dirt crumbling, but nothing alerted her ears of a change. As the dark silence lengthened, her mind began to wander. At first it roved to the waterfall of questions still roaring just under her consciousness, but Kindle determinedly pulled it in a different direction: the smooth jewel in her hand. The small bit of heat flowing from it calmed her and reminded her that soon they would be out of the horrible, dark, cold cave and back in the light. She ran a thumb along the necklace's metal back and, with her other hand resting on the dirt to stabilize her, suddenly smiled.

The familiar sensations under her fingers along with the leisurely position had roused a distant but happy memory. It was from a summer day when she and Mikey had still been young enough to enjoy playing in the dirt together. They had found their dad's shovel, and Kindle held it importantly while she gave orders to Mikey from the ground. She had told him to start watering the dirt with their garden hose, and while he obeyed, they argued about where the biggest hole ever would take them. Mikey had insisted they would go to China, but Kindle remembered that she was old enough to know they would get to the center of the earth where lava lived. They argued until Mikey had thoroughly soaked the middle of the backyard and Kindle ordered him to stop. Then he had stared at her and asked, "What do we do now?"

Kindle had held up the shovel and explained, "Duh, Mikey, it's dirt. Dig."

As her kiddish response played vividly in her mind, Kindle started to laugh, but her growing smile froze, and she blinked in realization. "It's dirt," she breathed and then, as Ella's light appeared, explained, *"Dig."*

"What?" Ella squinted at her with a wrinkled brow.

Kindle, in the joy of her incredibly simple epiphany, tried to stand but remembered her weakness and instead held out her necklace and repeated, "Dig."

Ella stared slyly at Kindle as if she had told a joke she didn't quite understand. Just when Kindle began to worry if she did sound silly, Ella laughed, "Alright, we dig."

ℰℚ

After Ella discovered that Bennickle's staff was useful for pounding away the tightly packed surface of the wall, the digging went smoothly. At first Kindle tried to help, but Ella insisted she could handle moving dirt on her own. Kindle did let her independently tear at the wall for a while but soon became impatient since Ella kept stopping to light her flame to check her progress.

"C'mon, let me help," Kindle whined, genuinely feeling somewhat warmer and stronger.

Ella must have noticed the longer sentence and turned an

inspecting face to her. "Are you sure you're up to it?"

"Yeah," Kindle insisted and stood without the help of the staff. The movement did make her head spin, but she hid the dizziness by stretching her arms and neck. Once she gained her composure, Kindle smiled. "See?"

"Alright, come along," Ella happily consented. "Now, let's try to break a hole through before we go to widening it," she instructed, and once Kindle nodded and stuck a hand in the dent Ella had already created, Ella extinguished her flame and they began digging. As Ella had explained, the hole was deep, not wide, so for a while their hands continuously collided as they scraped aside the soil. Eventually, though, they wordlessly fell into an agreed pattern of clawing while the other scooped the loose dirt and switching every so often.

To Kindle it felt like they dug and dusted for hours. However, she knew that the time was probably only dragging by since their expedition was incredibly boring and the darkness was disorienting and kept their progress invisible. Finally, she heard Ella gasp in delight, "Kin, we're through!"

"Really?" Kindle excitedly asked. "Let me see."

Ella retracted her arm as Kindle started to slide hers into the hole. As Ella lit a flame, Kindle watched her finger poke through a tiny opening and felt warmer air surround it.

"I can feel it!" cheered Kindle, pulling her whole arm out of the long hole. "I can feel warm air on the other side!"

"Ye—" Ella started to reply, but in the same instant, the entire tunnel began to shake. "What?" Ella breathed instead, bracing against the wall for balance.

"It's him!" squeaked Kindle. Her high emotion had switched to panic. "It's Bennickle, Ella!" She also hunkered against the wall as the quaking increased and clods of soil rained on them. They both stood in stupefied silence, staring between one another and the slowly dissolving ceiling.

Suddenly, Ella cried, "Oh!"

Kindle squinted at her, trying to make sense of what was wrong despite the moving space and flickering fire.

"Kindle, our hole!" Ella cried, "It's going to collapse!"

With difficulty she twisted to see that her friend was right; just as the large, solid tunnel around them was crumbling, so was the miniature one they had just dug. Seeing the quake erase all their work caused a determined defiance to flare in Kindle.

"No," she protested and began wildly brushing the newly fallen earth out of it. Dirt kept falling over her arms, though, and she knew her attempt was vain. "No," Kindle adamantly repeated, and Ella shook her head at the dirt falling from the unseen arch above. Kindle dropped her face; she did not want to watch the tunnel cave in over them. When her gaze fell, Bennickle's staff, shivering near their feet, caught her attention. As quickly as she could with her mind wobbling, Kindle snatched it up and shoved it in the opening they had created. Her motion grabbed Ella's attention, and she too put a hand on the staff. Together they mashed it into the hole again and again, pounding and pulling soil out with each pass. Their action soon broke through the far side of the wall, and all at once the quaking reached a furious intensity, they both dropped the staff, and Ella's fire quivered into nothingness. As Kindle stumbled into a lump on the ground, a horrible crumbling noise erupted and she curled into a ball, ready to meet the crushing force of the tunnel's broken ceiling hitting them. Just as she threw her hands over her head, though, the shaking ceased. Not sure if she had died without knowing it or if the earthquake had truly ended, Kindle twisted around in the dark and called, "Ella?"

"Here, Kin," her voice whispered close by as her fire returned. Kindle blinked at her and then up to where the tunnel apparently still vaulted over them intact.

"It stopped," she breathed in mystified relief.

"Yes ... oh, Kin," Ella mournfully sighed, and Kindle followed her stare to see that their escape route had been the source of the crumbling sound. It was completely refilled. Desperate to find out that perhaps it only *appeared* full of dirt, Kindle slowly rose and rubbed away some of the soil.

Ella sighed and stood beside her. "Kin, let it alone. I believe you're right—Bennickle was behind all that quaking. He must have known we broke through and wanted to keep us all caught up, and now that he's got his aim, he's left us alone. That must have been what he meant, how he wouldn't do a thing to us. Hmph, not a thing but leave us to wander about alone. Kin, really, leave it," Ella finished in a sympathetic tone. The whole time she had been pondering aloud, Kindle had kept digging. Everything in her simply refused to accept that Bennickle had won.

"Kin," Ella more forcefully urged and caught one of her frantic hands.

"No!" Kindle whined and continued pathetically wiping the dirt with her other hand.

"Stop."

"No!"

"Kin, co—"

They both froze their squabble over Kindle's hands. Her last swipe had revealed the end of Bennickle's staff. Ella turned surprised eyes at her, and Kindle knew the same thought was filling both of their minds. Just as simultaneously as they had frozen, they snapped back into unified action.

"Okay, are we gunna push or pull first?" Kindle asked as they dug out enough of the staff to each wrap a hand around it.

"Neither." A sly smile crept up on Ella's face, and she gave Kindle a wink. Kindle almost asked her what she meant, but Ella ordered, "That's enough. Step back a bit now."

Kindle held her ground.

"I assure you that I will only do the opposite of hindering our digging this out. Now please, Kin, do step back a bit." The flame on her fingers danced, and Kindle slowly nodded as she put more space between them. She wasn't certain exactly what Ella was about to do, but she knew it involved fire and was glad they stood in a large tunnel. When she had traveled beyond the edge of the firelight, Ella dropped them into darkness.

"What're you gunna do?" questioned Kindle, suddenly feeling alone and nervous.

"Well," Ella thoughtfully replied, "seeing as how that

Bennickle knows when we damage his wall, we have to be quick in making this hole"

Kindle waited a few moments for her to continue before pushing for a less vague answer. "So … what?"

"So." Ella grunted and a dim orange glow surged into existence. Kindle drifted sideways to see it better and realized that the eerie illumination was Bennickle's staff. Ella grunted again, and Kindle jumped as an odd, heavy *flump* reverberated through the air. She waited to hear soil shifting or see flames, but all that resulted was a satisfied sigh from Ella.

"What?" Kindle urged.

Ella lit her palm and smiled. "Come along, I need your help now."

As Kindle followed her direction, she gazed at the wall behind Ella. A circle of parched, ashy earth spread a few feet in every direction around the staff.

"Did you …?" She wanted to ask what Ella had accomplished but wasn't sure how.

"I remembered how the earth dried to a crisp and cracked away so willingly when we escaped that rock tunnel and supposed that would work just as well here. Now, grab a bit of this staff, and we'll—"

Kindle hissed as her skin brushed the hot metal, and Ella grimaced. "Oh, Kin, that was thoughtless. It's still blazing, isn't it?"

She nodded. "It's okay … so what are we gunna do when it cools down?"

"Well, I believe that when we give this a right strong tug, it will disturb all this dry stuff around and we'll have a way through."

Kindle eyed the wall warily. Shaking loose so much dirt seemed like a bad idea; nothing guaranteed that the wall wouldn't completely fall away and, if it did, where and how much of it would fall. An image of them being crushed and suffocated played in Kindle's mind and caused her to hesitantly question, "You think … you think it'll work?"

Ella inspected the wall then turned a serious face to her. "To get through, we have to snatch through quickly. It's really the only option we have … and, yes, I do believe it will work."

Chewing her lip, Kindle nodded. She still very much wanted to escape Tortuosus Labyrinthos and defy Bennickle's attempt to stop them but did not feel the confidence Ella held about the plan. Wondering if Ella's necklace had assured her of the success, Kindle covertly eyed her green gem. She so rarely examined anyone's necklace except her own that she had forgotten Ella's dragon was unlike her golden one. It was copper colored and seemed to be running rather than sitting. As she tried to secretly gain a closer look at it, Ella tapped the staff and murmured to herself. "It feels alright … Kin?" She spoke the last word louder, and Kindle tried to appear invested in the wall as Ella looked her way.

"Kin?"

"Hm?"

"Has it cooled? It doesn't feel a bit warm, but …"

Very carefully, Kindle waved her palm over it. When she didn't sense any radiating heat, she cautiously tapped and then held it. The metal had not completely cooled but was endurable. When Kindle kept her hand wrapped around the staff, Ella stepped to the other side of it and also placed her unlit hand on the metal.

"Alright," she seriously said, "we can't depend on having time to mull about, so one strong tug, and then, whatever happens, dodge through as quick as you can."

Kindle wanted to ask what she meant by "whatever happens", but Ella's flame disappeared, and Ella's voice commanded, "All hands on. Now, on three. One."

Kindle latched her other hand on the metal as she frantically wondered how she could run through the hole if she couldn't see. Before her busy mind could find a solution, she heard Ella call "three". All her worries snapped into oblivion as the urgent thought of pulling with all her strength filled her. Using every inch of her being, Kindle yanked the staff and felt Ella's warm hands bump hers as they half-ran, half-tumbled backward with surprising ease. While their momentum was still carrying them away from the wall, a deafening crumbling ensued. Almost instantaneously, a muffled *thump* sounded as the staff jolted to a stop and the tunnel began quaking again.

"Go, Kin, go!" Ella shouted as her wonderful illuminating flame appeared.

Her heart pounding with fear, hope, and excitement, Kindle dropped the staff and dashed forward. She attempted to run into the huge, dusty cloud ahead, but the shivering floor and shifting pile of rubble that her feet found made every movement except stumbling impossible. The choking cloud around her made even seeing where she was going difficult, but when her roaming arm hit something that felt solid, she guessed it was the wall.

"El—" she tried to shout, but the dust sent her into a fit of coughs instead. Suddenly, she felt Ella's warm arm link around her own and pull her sideways then farther ahead. Kindle tried to peer through the dim, misty cloud enveloping them, but it stung her eyes, and she chose instead to blindly let Ella lead them to safety. Soon the shaking earth felt more solid, and Kindle lifted an eyelid. To her relief, the cloud had almost settled, and she quickly assessed their surroundings. The rubble scattered the ground only under her tripping feet, and the wall and enormous pile of quivering grey soil sat behind them.

Ella caught her staring around and panted, "Alright?"

Kindle gave her a quick nod, and they unlinked elbows. Joy almost filled her as she realized that they were truly past the wall, but as she watched Ella sprint ahead and felt a sluggishness sway her, slight worry rose in Kindle. Then Ella's light vanished, and a true terror welled up in her.

"Ella!" she cried as she ceased her struggle to keep moving. No answer came, and the darkness, earthquake, and sense of helpless abandonment overwhelmed her. Kindle's already ragged breath turned into panicked gasping, and in a tearful voice, she yelled, "Ella! Ella, where are you?!"

"Just keep going!" her friend's voice urgently replied.

"Can't—" Kindle panted and sank to her knees. "I can't!"

"You *can*!" Ella shouted, and a very small circle of something that wasn't light but was an illumination in the darkness appeared. "You can!" Ella cheered again, and the circle widened. "You can, Kindle! We're almost out!"

Encouraged by her words and the break in their dark prison, Kindle began to push herself up. A sudden enormous explosion of sound and flying lumps of hard, dry soil behind her brought her back down into a fearful crouch.

"Kindle?" Ella cried, concerned, and her bright fire lit the scene. Kindle had only a moment to see that Ella was not far ahead of her at the top of the dirt slope with one hand reaching up through the ceiling before another boom resounded behind her, and she twisted to see what it was.

At the bottom of the slope where the ruined wall sat, a huge rock arm was grasping at the rubble. Knowing that the arm had to belong to a rock monster that was searching for them, Kindle restrained a scream and instead kicked her feet to crawl up to Ella.

"It's–it's–it's," she stammered hysterically as Ella bent to help her stand.

"Stop, Kindle, stop," Ella soothingly commanded, her eyes wide and watching the monster as well. "You must calm yourself, we're almost out. Help me dig."

Her light subsided, and Kindle tore her gaze from the dark, quaking, broken wall that she hoped the monster couldn't finish shattering. A bit of cool, moist dirt rained on her, and she stared up at the widening hole.

"Dig," begged Ella, and after a second of watching her punch and claw at the earth above, Kindle willed her tired arms to mimic the action. The more soil, grass, and leaves they tore down, the more the land shook. Finally, it reached such a ferocious rumble that large dirt clods began to shake loose on their own.

"Alright. Kin, it's big enough," panted Ella. "You first."

Kindle didn't object as Ella netted her hands together to create a step for her. She placed a foot in the boost, and Ella lifted as she pulled at the sides of their hole. A booming roar from below caused them to momentarily freeze and stare breathlessly at one another. Ella quickly regained her composure, though, and heaved Kindle higher. After a few more frantic seconds of climbing, Kindle collapsed on a bed of trembling leaves. Every muscle fiber begged her to remain on her stomach, but she heard Ella shout and scrambled upright. She snatched Ella's hands clutching the edge of the hole and together they managed to pull her up into the night as well. Once her feet emerged, Kindle leaned back, exhaled a joyful noise, and incredulously laughed, "We did it! We did—"

"Not yet we haven't," Ella hurriedly breathed. "That creature's broken through."

"Uh!" Kindle squeaked as Ella swung her head around.

"Kin!" She grinned and pulled Kindle's arm to help her stand. "This is where he first popped up! We can make it to the river!"

"Uh—" Kindle anxiously peeped again. Her mind was so frightened and boggled and her body so weary that she couldn't think to do anything but allow Ella to drag her off through the forest. As they stumbled between the tall, thin trees, Kindle twisted back and saw the large mound of earth the rock creature had launched into existence what seemed like days ago. Without comprehending why, Kindle scanned the area but saw only quaking trees. It wasn't until they broke out onto the bank and Ella gasped that Kindle understood her search.

ACCORD

"They're gone!" Ella gasped, and Kindle's throat tightened. Tad had not been laying beside the mound of earth, and neither he, Andrew, nor the horses occupied the long riverbank.

Fearful that they too had been captured, she began to ask, "Where are—?"

Both girls shrieked as part of a tree flew over their heads. Kindle heard it splash into the river but turned to see the rock monster that had speared it at them. The creature seemed larger than the last time she had seen it, but before she could assess its features, Ella yanked her arm.

"We have to get to the river," she insisted as she pulled Kindle into the shallows.

Staring across the wide river, Kindle shook her head and admitted, "I can't swim across—I'm way too tired."

Ella flipped a worried face to her, then the monster progressing through the trees, and finally the river. A slight relief broke over it, and she questioned, "Can you make it to that branch?"

Kindle saw she was pointing at the partial tree slowly floating downstream. "Um ... yeah, I—"

"Good. Hand over my sword and go on."

At that moment the rock monster smashed the last tree blocking it from the bank. In a terror, Kindle drew the rapier into Ella's hands and splashed into the water. Trying to forget the sluggishness of her mind and body as well as the chill of the water, Kindle stroked and kicked through the river as fast as she could. The current helped her forward, and soon she reached the large branch. As Kindle found a place to securely wrap her arms around it, she twisted to see how close Ella was. However, the water behind her was undisturbed. Kindle swung her gaze all around the river. Her eyes finally froze at the bank. Ella was racing along the water's edge with the rock monster tailing her. Kindle almost abandoned her float to return to her friend, but after a few seconds of watching them, she remained.

Ella looked like a tall, slender Olympian runner racing against an overgrown toddler. She was quickly putting more and more distance between them while the rock monster nervously tottered along the bank that its two feet barely fit on. To Kindle it appeared momentously concerned about avoiding the water. Realizing that Ella, who had faded into the night, was not in danger, Kindle curiously watched the monster.

Each wobbly step it took seemed unwilling, and every few seconds he stopped to peer ahead and release a mournful roar. Eventually, Kindle even began to outstrip him, but she kept her inquisitive stare locked on the sad creature. It seemed so resoundingly defeated and opposed to continuing that she almost felt sorry for it. In her mind its behavior stemmed from Bennickle's harsh orders rather than its own wishes. She began to wonder if it would ever end its already defeated pursuit when it came to a particularly narrow part of the bank and halted.

The creature lifted its stare up then slowly down as if considering its options. Kindle had just decided that it would end the chase when it grabbed a nearby tree for balance and attempted to sidle past the close river. It almost crept to safety but lost its balance and stumbled back into the water. As soon as its rock foot hit the river, it bellowed out a pained roar and ripped its balancing tree right out of the ground. Even though Kindle was sure she was too far to catch the force of the monster's flailing arms, enormous splashes, or swinging tree, she shrank closer to her branch for safety. While it continued to thrash in its terror, Kindle tried to see if the water was actually hurting it but couldn't spy any reason for its fit. Kindle reluctantly chuckled— she didn't want to make fun of the creature if it really was in pain, but the thought of something so apparently invincible being afraid of water seemed ridiculous to her. Seeing that the rock monster finally composed itself enough to slosh out of the river and into the woods, Kindle let her eyes drift ahead to search for Ella.

The night had fully fallen, and Kindle knew that finding anything smaller than the rock monster would not be easy. For a while she tried to carefully scan the bank nearest her, but as she watched the strip of sand and rocks, she realized her branch was slowly drifting farther from it. Fear washed over Kindle. The possibilities of losing Ella, growing cold and tired and sinking, or being nibbled to death by whatever insane things might live in the river all scared her, and so she tried to kick the wood in a new direction. The branch, though, resolutely, steadily flowed along the current. Suspecting and dreading that she would soon reach the middle of the wide river and have no chance of being seen or heard from the bank, Kindle began yelling as loudly as she could.

She called Ella's name for a while and then shouted any plea for help that popped in her mind. Soon her throat became so dry and her exhausted gasping so heavy that Kindle ended her attempts. Readjusting her weary arms to find a more secure hold, Kindle desperately scanned the shrinking bank. Not expecting to spy anyone, her heart leapt in joy when a living being entered her vision. Kindle squinted hard, trying to discern who or what it could be. She held back her cry for help until the incredibly fast and dark racer made sense.

"Hey," she attempted to shout but found that her weak breathlessness minimized her call into a gasp. Taking a moment to calm herself and gather her voice, Kindle watched the rider continue to rush along the bank. She was positive the dark horse was Nox but couldn't tell if Andrew or Tad sat on him. Due to the speed of Nox, she guessed it had to be Tad and shouted his name as well as she could. Whether Tad was sitting on Nox or not, though, the horse and the rider never slowed at all. Kindle tried to alert the rider a few more times, but soon she knew he was too far to hear her.

Feeling as if her last hope of rescue had just barreled out of sight, Kindle huffed and lay her forehead against her arm. Irritated, she wondered if Ella had known her idea would leave her in the middle of the huge river and how much time would pass before Ella returned to look for her. A bitter feeling toward her friend began to creep through her tired, frustrated mind, but Kindle sighed it away. She knew Ella probably had not meant to trap or abandon her but had thought only about escaping the rock monster. Digesting the knowledge that Ella truly had saved them more than once through the day helped Kindle lift her face to keep watch for Ella's return.

For a long while, nothing stirred except the water flowing around her. Kindle's hope of seeing Ella and her will to stay awake gradually ebbed into a fight to remain conscious enough to maintain her hold on the branch. Her battle had almost ended in defeat when a noise startled her into a fit of splashes and babblings. Quickly, she remembered where she was and what she had established as her goal and shook the water from her face to examine the bank. Almost immediately, she spied Andrew sliding off Nasah. His yellow shirt and hair almost glowed in the moonlight and clearly identified him, but Kindle could not understand why he had dismounted. He wasn't facing her, so she knew he hadn't stopped to help her. As she watched him simply stand by her horse, Kindle began to wonder if something was wrong with him or Nasah.

"Andrew! Nasah!" she cried, glad to hear her short rest had strengthened her voice. Andrew remained motionless, but at her call Nasah reared up on her back legs and whinnied. Realizing that Nasah knew she was near, a pleased smile broke over Kindle's face, and she started smacking the water and yelling Nasah's name. The more noise she created, the more Nasah neighed and stomped. Kindle hoped Andrew would hear her or understand Nasah's agitation, but she could see even from far away that his fearful attention was locked on Nasah.

"Nasah, come!" Kindle desperately shouted, and to her great joy, her horse trotted around Andrew and splashed a short distance in her direction. Finally, Andrew turned, and Kindle feverishly waved her arm.

"Andrew! Help!" she cried with what felt like all the energy and air left in her. He didn't call back but his next action showed her that he understood her situation. Andrew peeled off his shoes and waded to Nasah. Even though the night and her constant movement made his actions difficult to discern, Kindle thought he had started a search through their packs. Whatever Andrew had begun, he took a while to accomplish it. Every few minutes he would look up from Nasah's saddle, lead her to stand even with Kindle's branch, and then return to his work. Through his entire process, Kindle yearned to know what he was doing but waited in hungry silence to store up as much energy as possible.

At last Andrew jogged back to the bank, dropped off his sword and shield, and led Nasah out as far as she would walk. Then he dove into the water. Realizing that Andrew was going to attempt to swim out to retrieve her, Kindle felt her hope sink. Everything she knew about him told her that he could not possibly contain the strength, courage, or skill to accomplish such a task. Kindle nervously eyed her branch, wondering if it could support both of them if necessary. Fearing that it wouldn't, she returned her gaze to Andrew to yell for him to turn back. Her words, though, dissolved at the surprise that rocked her mind.

Andrew was not floundering or splashing a pathetic doggie-paddle as she had anticipated but was actually swimming. In fact, his fast, graceful freestyle stroke seemed too confident and strong to belong to him. Almost to make sure that it truly was Andrew swiftly making progress toward her, Kindle shook the grogginess out of her brain and blinked the tiredness from her eyes. Neither his appearance nor his steady stroke changed, and she finally accepted that it had to be Andrew and he was a great swimmer. When he finally did reach her, he was panting and did lean on the branch to catch his breath.

"I didn't know you could swim, well, you know, really good," commented Kindle.

He didn't answer but instead twisted and fished around in the water.

"What—?" she started to ask, but he handed a long, frayed piece of fabric to her.

"Rope," he gasped then took a moment to fill his lungs. "Hold it … swim back … to Nasah … right behind."

Even though his directions were sparse, Kindle understood. The other end of his mocked-up rope was tied to Nasah, and he wanted her to use it to swim back to the bank. Kindle tried to smile at the rope but wasn't sure if it would be enough help. She still felt cold and weak and not at all ready to swim the distance that had left Andrew so winded.

"Can … you swim?" he questioned, and Kindle bit her lip. After a glance at his calculating stare, she nodded. His amazing show of ability pushed her to avoid appearing weak and useless. With a deep breath, she released the branch and began traveling along the rope.

Very soon, Kindle realized she had made an incredibly silly, prideful decision. Paddling through the water while pulling herself along the rope proved nearly impossible, and her head kept dipping under the water. She struggled for a while, growing more and more embarrassed, clumsy, and panicked. Just when she was ready to forego holding the rope, it stretched taut and rose to the surface.

Wondering what had caused it to transform into a tight, helpful line, Kindle peered back to Andrew. He was still clinging to the branch but had wrapped all the rope's slack around one of his hands. Kindle grinned back at him, grateful for his calm, endlessly working brain. A corner of his mouth slightly lifted, but with a bob of his head, he urged her to return to the path he had created. She nodded then resumed a much less humiliating swim along the rope.

Before Kindle could drag herself very far, another force pulled the wonderful line. A jolt of fear jumped through her, but when she lifted her eyes to see what had happened, a new warm gush of thankfulness drowned the fear.

Nasah had joined her rescue. She was smashing through the

shallows back to the bank, toting the rope tied to her saddle. With renewed joy from the abundance of help, Kindle practically laughed as she continued to walk her hands along the rope. It felt much looser, so she supposed that Andrew had released the branch so Nasah could reel him in as well. The slack didn't frighten Kindle now that she knew she would soon reach the bank even if she just simply held the rope. To focus on keeping her head above water, Kindle locked her eyes on Nasah. Her horse finished kicking back the river and trotted onto the bank. She pranced around as if to check how far she and Andrew still floated from the bank and then leaned against their weight and galloped up and away between the trees.

Only a few more moments of rushing through the water passed before Kindle's foot hit a rock and she found her footing on the soft river bottom. For a few steps, she tried to cling to the rope and match Nasah's pace but found it too fast. Sure she was safe, she unwound her hands and sloshed to the bank on her own tired legs.

As soon as she cleared the water, Kindle sank down onto the bank. She sat up long enough to watch Andrew float close enough to stand, then she dropped down on the rocky ground. Sleep almost covered her, but a drop of water on her face led her to open her eyes. Andrew, looking much more like his usual nauseous, nervous self, was dripping on her.

"Call her," he said, turning his eyes to the forest.

Although Kindle did not want to move or speak, she even more did not want to lose her amazing horse.

"Nasah!" Kindle yelled from her back. "Nasah, come back! We're okay." She quietly sighed the last two words and saw Andrew cautiously, curiously peer down at her before she let her eyelids shut. "We're okay," Kindle repeated after a few seconds of silence. She knew from Andrew's face that his mind held a series of questions he probably wouldn't ask and thought it best to let him know Ella was safe also. "We're all okay."

"Ella?" he questioned, and Kindle knew he had caught her hint.

"Yeah."

"Where …?" Andrew slowly wondered, but Kindle angled her

arms into a momentary shrug before letting them flop down again. He didn't question her further but let the quiet night fill the air.

INTERLACED AROUND NOTHING

Kindle was walking. She wasn't sure where she was walking because the world around her was dark. Somehow, though, she knew her destination lay straight ahead. A slow voice began to speak behind her and spurred her into a run. She couldn't quite distinguish its words but did not try to hear them. A circle of light sat in front of her, and she knew if she could reach it, she would be safe.

The indistinct voice grew louder, and she tried to run faster, but her legs just couldn't seem to find earth to push against. Looking down, Kindle realized she was underwater. Bringing her alarmed gaze back up, she noticed that the gap between her and the circle of light had shrunk. Determined to reach it and leave the horrible voice, Kindle wildly kicked and pushed against the water. The light, which she knew would let her escape the water and the speaker who she could feel edging closer and closer, slipped farther away. Kindle thrashed harder against the water as a spiral of despair wound up into her throat.

Suddenly, she broke over the surface of the water and out onto a vast, dim beach. Everything beside and above was black again, but the ground rose and fell in endless dunes of ashy rubble. Kindle turned to see if the water and her pursuer existed behind her but met a black wall. Her eyes roamed up its incredible height then left along its unending length. She started to examine it to her right but froze.

A nook holding a beautiful, glittering orb had appeared inches from her nose. Kindle reached up and slid it into her hands. It was beautiful and bright, and she knew it could help her find the other light that would help her escape. She turned back to face the beach. A small gasp flew out of her mouth and echoed around the darkness. With her new light, she could see a person—a hulking person—stood a short distance away. She wanted to run but felt anchored to the spot. Kindle knew who it was even though his back was turned to her, and she did not want to stay near him. While she was still hoping to flee, the slow voice spoke very distinctly.

"They are dead."

"No!" she heard herself yell even though she hadn't meant to.

"They are dead."

Kindle felt her hands shake and stared down to see that the orb had lost all its light.

"No!" she sorrowfully cried down at it. "No! Come back!"

"They are dead," Bennickle insisted, and as Kindle looked up to defy him, he turned his profile over his shoulder and, in a new and much more frightening, airy voice, whispered, "It is close."

Her own scream filled her ears, and she dropped the orb to use her palms to block the bloodcurdling sound. Her scream continued as the orb smashed onto the rubble and shattered into a million shards that blasted in every direction. Then all noise and movement abruptly ceased. All the deadly diamonds of glass hung in the dark, empty space between her and Bennickle. Very slowly, they began to twist and spin all around her. Kindle lowered her hands and tried to run out of the glass tornado forming and gaining speed, but it surrounded her. She heard one more chilling whisper slide out of Bennickle, but before Kindle could determine its meaning, the breath transformed into a howling wind. The tornado and the screaming wind rose faster and higher and closed nearer and nearer around her. Terrified and trapped, Kindle hysterically cried, "They're not dead! They're not dead!"

Just as the shards wrapped close enough to rip at her skin, a bright, hot light blasted them away. Kindle peered around, eager to find the source of the golden blaze, but saw only the brilliant light. She spun and searched for anyone or anything without success. The light grew hotter and brighter, and she almost understood from where it radiated when a very distant but solid voice spoke and dragged her away from it. She desperately tried to remain in the light, but it quickly faded as consciousness spread over her mind.

"Hey."

The word pulled Kindle out of her dream and into reality. As her eyes snapped open to see the night sky, she sucked in a shocked breath. For a few seconds, Kindle let her eyes roam while she tried to steady her ragged breath and beating heart.

"Hey."

Even though the voice was familiar, it startled her, and she lost all the progress she had made in calming herself. She heard Tad snicker at her jump and sat up to find him. First, she saw Ella sleeping a short way down the bank, then noticed Andrew curled up closer to the grass and trees, and finally found Tad sitting on the softer ground behind her. He appeared tired and slightly disgruntled but also entertained.

"What?" she asked, not sure if she felt glad or annoyed to see him.

"You woke me up."

"I had a bad dream," she quickly, defensively admitted.

He sniffed. "Yeah, I know. I'm surprised you didn't wake them up too."

Kindle dipped her head in embarrassment. The dream and all the fear it had stirred in her were still too real for her to feel like arguing.

"What happened to you guys?"

His question pulled her eyes back up to his face. Tad was still wearing an agitated frown, but his tone was curious. Believing that he had no intention of mocking her, Kindle turned to face him and asked, "Didn't Ella tell you?"

"Pft, no." His lip curled into a slight sneer. "You really think she'd tell me anything?"

Kindle quietly digested his response as she wrapped her arms around her legs. The chill inside her still hadn't left, and she wanted to block out it and her memories of the horrible blizzard.

"What's wrong with you?" Tad indelicately asked, and Kindle blinked up at him. She hadn't realized she had drifted into her thoughts long enough to show how much they distracted her.

"I–I dunno," Kindle confessed and saw Tad squint in suspicious confusion. Not wanting him to believe she was trying to keep him uninformed, she sighed, "I mean, I know what happened and everything, but … but I dunno what it all means or what was really going on. You know?

He shook his head.

Kindle sighed in frustration. She did want to divulge everything about the Tortuosus Labyrinthos and her dream but did not know if she could explain it well enough for Tad to truly understand. After checking his face for any sign of mockery and seeing it was clear, Kindle decided to try.

"So you saw that rock thing and tree guy?"

"What?" he interrupted, and she almost felt too abashed to continue. "You mean that hand thing?"

"Oh," Kindle breathed as she remembered when he had been knocked unconscious. "Yeah, a whole rock monster came out of the ground, and then a tree monster came too, and they caught me and Ella and carried us for, like, ever—"

"That's what Andrew thought. He saw all the broken trees, and we followed 'em."

"Yeah," Kindle smiled slightly, glad to know that they had tried to find them. "But they took us underground—the ground ate us just like you said—and they left us in this really dark rock tunnel. Well, once Ella woke up we had her light, but—"

"Pft, she fell asleep?" he snorted. "Bet she—"

"No. She … she was trying to melt the rock guy, but he got mad and smashed her into a tree … I thought she was dead."

"Oh."

"Yeah, but she wasn't, so when she woke up and lit her fire, we were in this weird rock tunnel and walked for a while, but then this guy came ..." Kindle's thoughts surged beyond her articulation, and she struggled to think of how to explain Bennickle.

"What guy? It wasn't that weasel freak, was it?"

Kindle's laugh at his insult quickly faded. "No, it ... okay, so he said his name was Bennickle—"

"That's a stupid name."

"But I don't really know, like, who he really was. I mean, he was huge and looked like some kind of seriously mean wrestler guy but was kind of nice and had this staff thing and acted like some kind of king, and Ella thought he was one of the spirits because he wanted our necklaces, but ..."

Seeing Tad's expression change as he tried to locate her necklace, Kindle found it and held it aloft.

"We didn't give them to him, but it was weird because he wanted to give us all kinds of stuff for them. Like, he said he's got tunnels that go all the way to Ignancia Forest and would give us all of them and tell us how to get through."

"Yeah, right."

"Yeah, Ella didn't believe him either," Kindle agreed as she resolved to withhold how much she *had* believed Bennickle. "But it was just weird how he talked. It was ... I dunno. It was weird."

"So, what, did he try to get 'em?"

"Huh?"

"Your guys' necklaces—did he fight you for 'em?"

"Oh, no. He ... he just left."

"Pansy," mumbled Tad but smiled. "So then you guys left?"

"Um, kind of. We, well, Ella said her necklace knew the way out, so we walked for a while, but then these big rocks trapped us, and Ella melted the rocks over us to get us out—yeah, it was pretty cool—but only one of us could get up to it, so she made me stand on her shoulders, and I went to go get ... I dunno, a rope or something, I guess. But I ... um ..."

Tad narrowed his eyes at her hesitation. For a moment she

worried he was feeling slighted and struggled to find the courage and words to keep talking, but he seriously and gravely asked, "That creeper show up again?"

"No," Kindle replied and shivered at the memory of the cold, whistling wind that still seemed to live inside her.

"What, then?" he interrogated, and the discernable but dark concern in his voice caused her to turn her face back to his. As she did, his jacket fell at her feet, and she blinked at it then him.

"You're cold. Wear it," he bluntly demanded then pushed, "What happened?"

"You're not cold?" Kindle questioned as he folded his arms in what could have been chilliness or annoyance.

"No. What happened?"

Kindle considered how to explain the orb as she put his jacket over her shoulders. "Um … well, so I was walking, and it was all dark, and then I saw this thing that was kind of like a fishbowl, you know, and it, and … this is weird, isn't it?"

"Not as weird as the ground eating people."

She took a moment to soak up all his comment held then, feeling less self-conscious, continued, "So it was glass and all round like a fishbowl but didn't have a hole at the top or water or fish in it. It had … well, they looked like these really thin clouds all floating around it, and they were really eerie but pretty, and when I got closer they started spinning faster like they knew I was there. And … and I *know* I should of just left it alone, but—and I don't even know why—I touched it." Kindle shivered again and ashamedly turned her pained face to stare down the bank. Admitting her action made her feel as if she was horrible and silly and brought the awful storm and ripping pain vividly into her mind. She did not want Tad to see any of the myriad of weak emotions on her face and expected him to belittle her vague confession with a sarcastic stab.

"Did it hurt you?"

Kindle was so surprised by his completely serious, understanding question that the sting of the icy wind evaporated from her mind. "Um, yeah," she quietly replied then chanced a peek at him.

His face was slightly angry but in a different way than usual. "Um, it … I touched it, and it changed. The clouds went away, and it got really bright, and I heard the wind that made me feel cold, and then it really *was* wind, like, a real wind was really there. I could see it blowing my hair, and it was so cold … and I tried to get away from it, but I was stuck to it, and it fell, and I fell, and then …" Kindle swallowed hard and unconsciously wrapped a hand around her necklace.

"Then it hurt you."

"Yeah, well, I dunno what did it, but it was like something was trying to rip out everything in me, and it was so cold, and—" Her voice squeaked, and she paused to settle herself. "And I know that doesn't sound that bad or anything, but I dunno how to explain it. It didn't just hurt like getting stabbed—it made every part of me *feel* bad like … I dunno. It was just the worst thing ever." Kindle bit her lip and stared down at her necklace, waiting for Tad to respond.

When a few minutes passed and he still remained quiet, Kindle peered up at him. He was glaring off into the distance with an unreadable expression. Without realizing she did, Kindle stared at him until he noticed her and grumbled, "Like you were nothin'? Did it make you feel like you were nothin'?"

Stunned by how accurately he had defined the pain, Kindle nodded and simply replied, "Like I was gunna be nothing."

They sat in silence for a while, staring off in different directions. Even though they did not speak, Kindle felt as if they were sharing something—something deep, momentous, and intertwining just as she and Ella had in the Tortuosus Labyrinthos. She couldn't define in her mind exactly what the something was, but Kindle knew it bridged a previously untouched area in their friendship. As she closed her eyes to try to focus on the something tying them closer, Tad spoke and reeled her into the present.

"You got away." His tone was so strangely empty but full that Kindle began to dig through the layers of it but instead restrained herself to keep his unsaid thoughts private.

"Yeah, it was awful, and I thought it would, you know, make me nothing, but this warm light appeared and made it go away. I don't know what it was, but it made me feel so much better, and then it went away too, and Ella showed up."

"Was it her?"

"I don't think so … I think she came *after* it went away, and it wasn't like her fire. But when she came, that globe thing was gone, and we got away. Well, I mean, we had to walk a bunch and dig through a wall, and then there was this earthquake, and Ella had to, like, dry it up so it would break, and then this rock guy came after us, but we dug through the roof and ran away, and he chased us, but when we got here, he got scared of the water and ran off."

Tad slowly nodded at her one long sentence. She knew it probably sounded confusing but was also sure in the morning she would have to retell the story in detail with Ella to Andrew.

"Who died?" he finally questioned and caused Kindle to wonder just how confused her explanation had left him.

"Nobody died. I didn't say anything about anybody dying."

"Yeah, you did. You were yelling about somebody not being dead when you were asleep."

"Oh." Kindle almost retreated into silence but, after a glance at his serious face, divulged, "Well, nobody died down there, but that Bennickle guy told us, um, the makers were dead."

Tad raised a skeptical eyebrow but didn't comment.

"Yeah, it was when he was trying to get us to give him our necklaces. Ella told him we couldn't because they're how the makers talk to us, and then he said that. And he said he saw them die."

Again, Tad did not verbalize his thoughts but sniffed deridingly.

"What?" she eagerly but anxiously probed.

"You gunna believe some psycho caveman?"

His answer made her giggle and feel thankful Ella had convinced her otherwise. "No, I know he was just trying to get our necklaces, but it just kind of … I dunno, I wish he hadn't said it."

"Why? Who cares what some idiot says?"

"Have you heard it—um, your maker—talk to you? I mean, I know you said in Iteraum you—"

"I'm not hearin' voices."

"I know, but down there Ella said she thinks all of the makers talk to us in different ways, and … I think she's right. Like, hers actually *talks* to her and mine …" Kindle didn't think Tad would understand or believe that Hux spoke to her through memories as readily as Ella.

"What? Does yours sing a song?" he sarcastically asked, and Kindle rolled her eyes to him.

"No, and I'm being serious, so if you don't—"

"Okay. Serious," he interrupted and leaned back on the grass.

"Are you gunna believe me?" Kindle suspiciously inquired as she tried to see his face.

"Nah," he replied, but his tone was so emotionless that Kindle sensed he meant the opposite but was growing annoyed with her.

Staring fondly down at the little golden dragon, Kindle explained, "Hux helps me by helping me remember things. It's usually stuff Azildor said or what, um, somebody said, but I know down in that cave place he reminded me of just something that happened. And I know it's him and not just me thinking of stuff because it always happens when I look at or think about this dragon and what I think of is always something I had forgotten or wasn't thinking about at all, and … and it's always really helpful, like exactly what I need to know." Kindle tried to round up more words to help him see what she knew to be true but found none. To check if he understood, she craned her neck to see his face, but his knees blocked her view. Determined to know his reaction to her words, she stood, wrapped his jacket tighter around her, and walked over to him.

Tad's eyes were closed. A flutter of agitation ran through her. He was asleep.

"Does that make sense?" she loudly questioned.

To her surprise, he immediately answered, "No, but nothin' in this stupid place does."

Unsure of what to say or how to feel about his reply, Kindle folded her arms and stared off into the forest. He was right—almost nothing about Anelthalien, the makers, or the marks made logical sense. A land full of people who knew nothing about and really didn't seem to care about who made or ruled it, mysterious makers who could talk to them through their necklaces, and the power-hungry spirits who wanted the necklaces all seemed bogus and insanely contradictory but also somehow very unignorably plain. Everything that seemed impossible about Anelthalien had and still was playing out all around her. The trees, cities, and ignorant people really did exist. The makers speaking to and guiding them was a continuously occurring fact. Even the spirits were showing themselves as a very real, very powerful threat. Remembering Bennickle compelled Kindle to instinctively step back from the white trees.

Tad must have sensed her movement because his eyes snapped open and he sat up. He appeared ready to question her, but Kindle decided to explain her frightened eyes by turning them to the forest. Catching her action, he pivoted as he stood to face it as well.

After a few seconds of silence, he whispered, "What?"

"We can't go in there," breathed Kindle, "because even though all of this seems crazy, it's real."

She saw his slightly puzzled face turn her way and met his blue eyes.

"The spirits are after us, Tad … and the only way we're gunna do this is to trust the makers. We *have* to listen to them."

He eyed her face for a moment then glared into the forest. "I dunno," he vaguely grumbled.

Kindle huffed, exasperated by his resistance. "We really do. The makers *do* talk to us and we *do* have to—"

"I get it," he interrupted but not harshly. In fact, he almost sounded yielding. Crossing his arms and glaring away, he huffed. "I get that the makers or whatever tell us what to do, but how do we know we can trust 'em? And even if we can, how do we know it's them and not just some idiot caveman or one of the spirits?" When Tad finished his string of questions, he turned a hard expression to her.

Feeling like she had to give him answers, Kindle opened her mouth but slowly shut it again as she realized she had none. Then she shrugged and let out the only words she could think of. "We just do."

Tad's face fell flat, and he shook his head. Desperate to not seem completely void of thought, Kindle scoured her mind to understand why she had said the three words.

"I mean, ugh, I didn't mean to sound stupid."

"You're not stupid," he grumbled, and Kindle felt her confidence lift.

"I just meant that, like, well, it's like when Hux helps me remember something—I *know* it's him. I don't know how I know … I just do. You know what I mean? It's like when you talk to somebody you know really well on the phone—you can't see them, but you know what they sound like and the stuff they usually say—and I don't know how people's brains know how to know who's talking to them either, but it's just like that—they just *do*."

Kindle waited for him to give a sign of understanding, and when his eyes hesitantly slid back on her, her mind snapped to his initial question.

"And I guess we know we can trust them because they're them. I mean, why would the people who made Anelthalien want bad things to happen to it and everything in it? If they're telling us something, there's no way it's anything that's gunna mess Anelthalien up. If they're telling us something, it's got to be something that's gunna help us get rid of the evil guy and his throne and tell everybody about all the stuff that's gunna save them."

Tad examined her out of the corners of his eyes. "That's how we know we can trust 'em?"

Kindle ran her own words through her brain. She had just let them spill out of her mouth in a rush to prove the makers were reliable, but the more she processed them, the more she realized that they did make plain, simple sense. "Yeah," she finally sighed, "that's how."

A snarl then a frown rolled over his face. Kindle almost sighed to surrender the battle to help him understand, but his next sentence stopped her.

"I guess I heard her."

With her mouth hanging open and confusion on her face, Kindle stared at him. "Her?"

"Yeah. Anybody who nags that much has to be a girl."

"Oh," Kindle replied, her mind rocked by his conclusion. She had always imagined Hux to be a man and suspected all the makers were similar to him. Thinking of them as anything more than one sort of person seemed strange, but as she remembered Ella's very different dragon and how each of the makers spoke in a unique way, it did not seem possible for them to be exactly the same. Now wondering what his dragon looked like, she eagerly asked, "Can I see your necklace?"

"Why?"

"Well, I never really thought about them being different—except the colors—but Ella's little dragon wasn't like mine, so I bet yours is different too." Kindle grinned, feeling a little silly about her next thought, but voiced it anyway. "And maybe it looks like a girl."

Tad's half-evil smile snuck onto his face as he drew his gem from under his shirt and turned so she could see it. Kindle gave him a funny look, mystified at his expression, but when she let the blue jewel fall into her palm and stepped closer to examine it, his grin made sense. The silver dragon did not strike her as male or female, just extremely ferocious. Its spikey head was thrown back in a sharp toothed, fiery roar, and its arched back and powerful legs were angrily tensed. Even the dragon's tail—a sleek curve ending in a ball of spikes—appeared ready to attack.

"Look like a girl to you?" Tad sniffed. Kindle turned her face up to answer but found it so terribly and wonderfully close to his that she had to step back before her brain would work.

"Um, yeah, er, I mean, no … uh, it just looks mean."

Tad turned the necklace to scrutinize it for a moment then snorted, "Fits. It looks mean and my maker's a nag."

Desperate to escape her momentary emotional spasm, Kindle turned to the river and conversationally asked, "You said it nags a lot?"

Tad also faced the water but, instead of answering, crossed his arms.

"Didn't you?" pushed Kindle. "I mean, say it nags you?"

He shrugged.

"Oh, come on, I told you all that about Hux helping me

remember stuff. I'm not gunna think you sound weird or anything if you tell me how it talks to you."

Tad glanced at her with narrowed eyes, but she could see the hint of a smile on his face. "I don't hear those voices like Ella, but yeah, it's bugged me a couple of times."

"Yeah?" Kindle encouragingly smiled. "Like when? I mean, I know when we were in Iteraum …"

His grin fully surfaced as he popped up two fingers. "Twice."

"What?"

"I told you guys about knowin' I had to go in that stupid castle, but you remember before that stupid parade?"

Kindle squinted in thought. "When Ella went in that tea place?"

"Nah, after that. When I found you standin' in the middle of the street."

"Oh."

"Yeah. Same thing. You know, like you said—thinkin' stuff you weren't thinkin'—only I get this feeling I need to go somewhere and don't know why."

His words seemed familiar, and Kindle tried to recall if he had said them before, but her own curiosity distracted her more. "Did you hear—um, *feel*—it telling you where to go any other times?"

"Yeah," he snorted then glared Ella's way. "The whole time we were goin' to that stupid Beryl or Aryl place and talkin' to that overstuffed nut job."

"To get out?" she wondered through her giggles.

Tad nodded as he smirked at her laughter.

"We should of listened," Kindle sighed as the serious consequences of their refusal to pay attention to him hit her.

"Ya think?"

"I'm sorry," she apologized as she recalled *she* had been leading them at the time. "I didn't know it was your maker telling you that, and I thought it'd be—"

"Forget it," he quietly broke into her avid apology. "It's not like it was you who wouldn't listen anyway." He began to sneer at Ella again, but Kindle caught his shoulder.

"Yeah, it was." She quickly dropped her hand as he glared at it. "Sorry … um, it was me who didn't listen. I thought everything would be okay, and it just seemed safer to go with Wissen … but I should of listened to you. I mean …" Kindle shook her head in amazement at how everything was incredibly meshing into one resounding truth. "That's what Ella said: we have to listen to our makers, and that's how we'll know what to do. And to do that, we *have* to listen to each other, and we *have* to believe each other when we say the makers are talking to us."

Tad began to nod, but instead, his lifted chin tilted sideways. "I dunno if I can trust *her*."

Kindle knew he meant Ella and determinedly sighed, "You can. I mean, I know we were wondering about her being a witch elf and all that, but down there and even with that rock guy she never quit trying to save us or make sure I was okay. She didn't leave me behind when that wall broke and I couldn't see where to go and even made that rock monster chase her so it wouldn't come after me. We can really trust her, I know we can."

She watched Tad's eyes slip back and forth and hoped he was thinking over her proof of Ella's loyalty. Finally, when Kindle was close to bursting with curiosity, he consented, "I guess."

Kindle beamed at him.

Trying his best to frown back, he grumbled, "She just better have some breakfast tomorrow."

She rolled her eyes and laughed as she wondered what it would take for Tad to stop being grumpy. Considering that staying up all night wouldn't help, she mumbled, "We should probably go back to sleep."

"Yeah," he grunted and started for the grass.

Kindle moved to sink back onto the bank but remembered his jacket. "Hey," she called as she slipped it off and held it out.

He glanced back but didn't move to retrieve it.

"You want it back?" she pushed, ready to return to sleep.

"I'll get it in the morning," he mumbled then flipped over so his back faced her.

Kindle blinked at him then the jacket. A small smile began to lift her mouth, but she bit her lips together to annihilate it and hurriedly lay down on the rocky bank.

$$EQ$$

Menthoshine sat drumming her long black nails on the arm of her throne. The repetitive cascade of clicks played on and on as they usually did when she remained still. Her unfocused eyes were glaring out into the darkness straight ahead of her. She appeared to be thinking, waiting, or both. After maintaining her brooding position and clicking for an enormous span of time, Menthoshine suddenly yelled, "Olivar!"

At first no one answered, but finally, a spider spun down close enough for the green light of her orb to illuminate its aerial bow.

"My lady?" he respectfully squeaked.

"What is your progress?" she hatefully demanded.

He nervously twirled his front two legs as he spoke. "The spiders are not tunnellers by nature, my lady. You must under—"

"Progress, Olivar," she growled.

He thoughtfully swung on his silk before answering, "Maybe halfway … or, by the new day, we will be at that point."

"Is that *all*?" Menthoshine questioned, her voice near bursting in outrage.

"Ma'am, ma'am," Olivar quickly soothed. "We are only small, lowly creatures, and this cavern was dug deep. Master Ben—"

"Do not speak of him!" shouted Menthoshine. "Or any of those beastly swine you disgusting arachnids treasure! They are all worthless, foul creatures who hate you! Now, back to work!"

"Yes, ma'am!" he anxiously peeped as he scuttled out of her sight. Once the light taps of his legs had faded, she settled back in her throne only to jolt forward again.

"Castrosphy?!" Menthoshine screamed. He did not answer, and she slid her eyes back and forth across the room. Then a clear voice—a female voice—called out, and Menthoshine stood to her full height as she snatched her staff. "Who's there?!" she commandingly shouted. "Olivia?! Arra?!"

She waited with bared teeth for the voice to reply. After only silence met her, a wrathful huff escaped her lips, and she started across the room.

"If I catch any of you—!" she began to threaten but suddenly halted. The green beside her had faded. Menthoshine glanced at her orb then jolted back from it in shock.

A small but growing, swirling blueish-grey cloud was rapidly spinning at its heart. When it filled about half of the glass sphere, a long gusting wind rose, and out of it a voice asked, "Was it you who called?"

The voice was light and airy like Castrosphy's, and although it contained crisp articulation rather than a hiss, it still caused Menthosine's fists to tighten.

"No," she resolutely spat, and very gradually, the wind and cloud ebbed out of existence. Menthoshine held her tense, distant stance until her familiar green lightning returned. Then she snatched the black wood of her staff, spun on the sharp toe of a boot, and stormed back to her throne. She jerkily sat and clicked her nails several times. Her mouth twitched up into a sneer, and after slamming a fist down on the armrest, she pushed herself up again.

"Bennickle!" she raged at the orb. "Ben, you wretched ogre— gah!"

Menthoshine rocked away from the orb as the lightning waned and a horrible scream rang out from it. Blocking an ear from the blasting sound, she wiped a hand over the glass, and as immediately as it had begun, the scream ceased. She huffed angrily, warily glaring at it. "Beast," she grumbled and turned her face from the familiar green glow. Her body had almost returned to the throne when a series of deriding hisses broke out. In an instant she deftly grabbed her staff, spun it in the air as she twisted, and brought it down like a club beside her throne.

"How! Many! Times!" she screeched, swinging it with every word. Finally, one of her hits propelled Castrosphy away from the throne and into view. His cloak shuddered to motionlessness, but the mocking hisses still floated from it.

"What, you roach?!" she raged as she blew forward to kick him. When her pointed shoe collided with him, he stopped laughing. "You disgusting, creeping roach—you know what that was, don't you?!" She slammed her staff over him. "What was it? One of Ben's little tricks? TELL ME!"

"Ssstrange thingsss."

"Cease your babblings, Castrosphy! I know you are far from damaged, so do not play!"

"The voice isss ssstrange thingsss."

Menthoshine halted her next kick and instead stepped back from him. "That was one of the children?"

"Yesss."

Menthosines's eyes narrowed. "And how, Castrosphy, do you know? Were you there? Were you with that ogre?! You know you cannot leave this place unless I order it!"

"The passst," he hissed as he floated upright. "She ssscreamsss much."

Menthoshine hautily raised her chin. "Was she with Bennickle? Why was she with Bennickle?"

"It isss misssty."

Glaring at his shape out of the corner of her eye, she rumbled, "It should not be."

"Perhapsss he hasss differencesss."

"Differences," she snapped as an intense sneer revealed her white teeth. With an enormous force, she knocked Castrosphy to the ground and then pressed her long, thin heel into him.

"And do you, my vile thorn, share these differences?"

Castrophy snickered, and she pressed harder against his cloak. "I *will* bring an end to you when the time is right."

He halted his laughter to breathe, "Hisss differencesss are hisss own."

Menthoshine released him but kicked his form away from her. As she turned to storm back to her throne, she avowed, "When I leave this wretched hole, you *will* remain by my side."

PRECISELY AS IT OUGHT

Kindle resisted the sunlight as long as she could but finally opened her eyes to see the glittering river flowing by. She watched it for a while, listening for any sound of Tad, Ella, or Andrew. A distant shout shocked her into full alertness, and she jolted upright to search for its maker.

"Cozy?" Ella's bright voice asked, and Kindle twisted to see her friend sitting behind her, slyly grinning. Kindle stared back, trying to figure out what was causing her playful smile. Only when Ella dipped her head and Kindle followed its incline did she understand.

"Oh!" Kindle blurted and flung Tad's jacket aside. "I was cold."

"Mmm-hm," Ella hummed and began to open her mouth, but Kindle pointed a warning finger at her.

"Don't."

Ella laughed at her giggled threat and sighed, "Alright. I've worked at the inn far too long to not know when a matter is not for me to go prying into. And anyway, I was only going to ask how you were."

Kindle almost argued with her assumption that something had happened that was not her business but decided it would be safer to remain silent on the point. "I'm fine."

"Are you sure?" Ella interrogated in a motherly manner. "Because all through Tortuosus Labyrinthos you claimed you were fine, and you most certainly were not."

"I really am," she insisted as she scanned the bank. "Where are Tad and Andrew?"

"They've gone to look for my bow and arrows," Ella replied as she moved closer to hold Kindle's hands.

"But what about Bennickle?" Kindle gasped in horror and tried to stand, but Ella pulled her back down.

"Kin, it's alright."

"No, Be—"

"Kindle," Ella firmly interrupted but smiled, "they will be alright. Bennickle's not after them. It's your and my necklaces he wants, and as long as we're here by the river, he and all those horrid goons of his seem to want nothing to do with us."

"Oh," she mumbled and relaxed then peered between the slender, lovely trees. "You think they'll find it?"

"By the sounds of it, I believe they have and are less than aptly attempting to catch a bit of breakfast. Now, you aren't shaking anymore, but how about walking? Can you manage that?"

"*Yeah*," Kindle exasperatedly replied and stood to prove it.

"Don't be miffed, Kin," Ella gently retorted as she also rose. "You were in a horrid sort last night, and I only wanted to make sure it has passed."

"Sorry. I just … I'm okay."

"And that is splendid." Ella glanced over her shoulder then slowly brought her eyes back. "What *did* happen? In Tortuosus Labyrinthos? Did Bennickle harm you or …?" Her voice faded as Kindle dropped her gaze. She did not want to chat about her mistake and the awful pain it had caused.

"It's alright, Kin, you don't have to say." Ella chipperly consoled. "How about a walk along this lovely river instead?"

"Yeah," Kindle mumbled, still distracted by all the distress Ella's question had evoked. As they walked along the bank and Ella began rambling about how she missed all the wonderful breakfast dishes her papa cooked, though, Kindle gradually escaped her melancholy and joined in with her own stories.

"Oh, man, and cinnamon rolls. Do you even know what cinnamon rolls are?"

"You eat rolls of cinnamon?" Ella incredulously questioned.

"No, they're rolls. You know, like, bread rolls? And they have cinnamon in them and icing on top. They're so good."

"That sounds much more like dessert than a proper breakfast."

"Well, you can eat them for dessert, but they're breakfast too. My grandma makes them every time we go see her and—"

A nearby yell ended Kindle's thoughts of warm, sticky rolls, and she and Ella exchanged alarmed glances.

"You think …?" Kindle breathed, wanting to believe the boys were fine but worried they were not.

Ella shrugged as she turned to the trees and called, "Andrew! Tad! Can you hear me? Are you two alright?"

Neither boy yelled back, but Kindle was sure she heard them talking and moving through the forest.

"Do you see them?" she asked Ella, but quite suddenly, a horse and rider appeared, and the two girls dashed out of their path. Nox powerfully leapt onto the bank where she and Ella had stood and sent pebbles and sand flying as he skidded to a stop.

"Tad, you—" Ella began in a chastising tone but stopped when he tossed her bow down to her. She briefly examined it then smiled up at him. "Thank you."

"Yeah," he unaffectedly replied.

In the next second, they all scattered. This time Nasah galloped out from the trees and much more naturally and gracefully halted. As soon as her legs stilled, she puffed in agitation and shook her head. Andrew, who had been clinging to her neck, quickly dismounted and almost ran from her. Kindle contained her laughter at his sick, terrified face but could not stop her amused grin. To disguise it she stepped to

Nasah's side and praised her for being a good girl.

"Oh, thank you! Both of you, really, thank you," Ella gushed, and Kindle leaned around Nasah's neck to see Andrew handing over her arrows.

"Yeah, and guess what?" Tad proudly asked and then, once they all turned his way, produced two dead squirrels. "Boom! Breakfast!"

"Marvelous!" Ella cried in delight. Kindle tried to be excited as well but felt too nauseous.

Tad rode over to Ella and tossed them at her feet. "Yeah, so that means you owe me two birds *and* two squirrels for dinner tonight."

"I told you I would catch your dinner when we found our way out of this forest," she seriously reminded him but then peered down at the animals and smiled. "But, yes, two each now."

Tad triumphantly grinned.

Kindle felt a flood of gratitude toward Ella. She hoped and believed that Ella's continued promise would convince Tad that she really was trustworthy. It wasn't much, Kindle knew that, but from the brief glance Tad shot back at her as they all headed down the bank, she almost knew it would be enough.

As Ella prepared and they all ate their breakfast, she and Kindle took turns narrating the previous day. When they neared her encounter with Bennickle's orb, Kindle nervously prepared herself to reveal at least part of what had happened, but Ella swooped in and told the event from her view. As Ella explained that she simply found Kindle and they continued through the tunnel, Kindle noticed Andrew's brow slightly draw together and wondered if he knew she had omitted something. Thankfully, he continued to silently listen until Kindle told of his rescue plan.

"And it was pretty awesome," she finished then turned to Andrew. "I mean, I didn't even know you could swim—um, sorry, that didn't sound nice … but you can and really good. Do you swim, like, all the time?"

Andrew avoided her eyes while he finished chewing his bit of meat. He considered what was left on his stick but finally lay it aside and mumbled, "I used to."

"Before you came here?" questioned Ella with sympathy, and Kindle wondered if he missed his home as much as she did but had simply never confessed it.

He shrugged and picked up his stick only to set it down again. "Before … my mom was a doctor, and twice a week she'd lead a water aerobics class for seniors. She wasn't paid for it, she just liked to. I always went with her and swam in the lanes the whole time."

Tad sniffed and deridingly questioned, "Your mom likes hangin' out with old people?"

"Don't make fun of my mom!" Andrew yelled as he sprang up and pointed a threatening finger down at Tad.

His loud, impulsive reaction left the rest of them staring at him in stunned silence. Kindle knew Tad's tone hadn't been nice, but it had been such a characteristic, trifling comment that she couldn't understand Andrew's anger. He so rarely showed any kind of intense emotion that Kindle had considered him unable to become genuinely upset. She peeked sideways at Ella to see if she knew the reason for his outburst, but she appeared just as shocked as Kindle felt.

Finally, Tad broke their stupefied standstill. "Chill, dude," he grumbled and returned to his breakfast.

Andrew lowered his hand but maintained his stance and red-faced glare.

"Andrew, sit down. It's alright," coached Ella.

Without taking his eyes from Tad, Andrew shook his head and with slight uncertainty yelled, "No! It's not okay! I don't care if you make fun of me, but I'm not going to let you make fun of my mom!"

Tad tilted an incredulous face up at him. "Dude, what's your problem?"

"Apologize!" Andrew demanded.

Tad snorted. "You gunna make me?"

"Andrew, really," Ella broke in, but neither boy seemed to hear her.

"Apologize," he commanded again but with less force.

Tad's face crunched into a sneer as he speared his skewer into the ground and also stood. "What? You gunna make me?"

"Stop it, both of you!" Ella rebuked, but they continued to glare only at one another. Kindle grimaced between them, doubtful they would listen to Ella.

"A–apologize," Andrew determinedly stammered, his face turned up at Tad's.

"What if I don't want to? What're you gunna do?"

Andrew's eyes momentarily searched his feet, then he picked up his chin and awkwardly raised his fists.

"Dude," Tad laughed, "don't make me smash your face."

For a moment Andrew seemed ready to take his advice but then determindedly set his jaw and planted a fist right in Tad's chest. Before Kindle's gasp of surprise, horror, and delight at Andrew's boldness could leave her mouth, they broke into a frenzy. Andrew and Tad immediately began throwing punches as fast as they could into one another, and Ella shrieked and jumped up.

"Stop! Stop! Stop!" she shouted at them, but Kindle could see they definitely had no intention of listening. She watched as Andrew tried to tackle Tad while avoiding his punches and they slowly tipped over before returning to their scuffle.

"Stop!" Ella cried again then shot an expression of confused disbelief at Kindle. "What is happening with them?"

Kindle shrugged, her own brain puzzled and thoroughly shocked.

Ella looked back at them then huffed, "No. This is obscene. Stop!" As she shouted her last word, Ella dashed around the dying fire and tried to find a free limb to yank. Very briefly, Kindle considered helping her break them apart, but she thought it safer to watch. The longer she sat and stared at the three of them, the better she felt about her decision. Ella did manage to capture Andrew's arm a few times, but overall, her attempts proved futile; both Tad and Andrew seemed just too ferociously determined to beat one another to be persuaded to stop.

Kindle knew Tad always jumped into every fight with

everything he had, but seeing Andrew match his vigor heightened her amazement and desire to watch. Just like Tad, and really even more so, Andrew was swinging and kicking with every ounce of rage and energy he possessed. After a few minutes of neither of them showing any sign of stopping or wearing down, Ella finally scooped up a handful of sand and rocks and tossed it at them. In the moment they flung their hands up in defensive surprise, she caught Andrew under his arms and dragged him away from Tad. As soon as they were fully separated, she rounded him and jammed her hands on her hips.

"Now, there was absolutely no reason for you two to go tearing at one another like uncouth beasts," she chastised, swinging her disapproving face between them. "You both were completely unreasonable. Really, you could have sorted things—"

"Hey, he started it," interrupted Tad from the ground, and Kindle thought she heard laughter in his tone. Apparently, Ella did as well because her face froze in disgust, and she swung her displeasure to him.

"This is not *funny*," she seriously sighed. "You two could have hurt one another and, more importantly, were snubbing what Azildor said about getting along with one another. Now, *both* of you come back to breakfast, and we will talk through this like civilized—"

"Pft. Nah, it's cool."

Ella gaped at Tad as he calmly stood. She whipped her flabbergasted face at Kindle, who felt just as dumbfounded and shook her head to signal that she had no explanation. Finally, Ella swung her eyes to Andrew.

"What—?" she started to question, but he lumbered up and took up a quick walk into the forest. Once he disappeared, Ella spun back to Tad. "Whatever can be going on in your mind to believe this is all *cool*? You both are completely heated—you beat one another for no fathomable reason, and now he's gone off on his own. He is clearly upset, Tad. That means everything is *not* alright. Now, go round him up and—"

"You really think he wants me runnin' after him?"

Ella crossed her arms, glanced at the forest, then sighed, "Well, no, but Kindle and I can't go in there."

"Maybe he wants to be left alone," Tad grumbled as he sauntered back to the fire.

Ella, still standing her ground, shook her head and exasperatedly complained, "This is ridiculous. Your thoughtless spat can't go on forever. We will never get to our destination behaving like this. You must—"

"Shut up!" he yelled back at her. "I told you it was cool, okay? Just leave the dude alone for a while, and we'll be back on your stupid schedule."

Kindle watched Ella take a deep breath as she recomposed her face. When Ella opened her eyes, she met Kindle's stare and tilted her head at Tad. Understanding her motion, Kindle gave her a slight nod, and then Ella turned and trekked down the bank. Kindle watched her friend's long auburn hair swing while she tried to think of exactly what information Ella wanted her to extract from Tad. Just as she decided that Ella probably wanted a promise of an apology, Tad lazily glanced over his shoulder.

"She want you to talk to me? Make me feel bad?"

"Um …" Kindle mumbled, realizing she and Ella were not as discreet as she had thought. A small, apologetic grin broke over her face, and she sighed, "Yeah—well, I mean, she wants me to talk to you, but I dunno about what." Kindle bit her lip for a moment then blurted, "That was really weird. I mean, Andrew."

Tad shrugged.

"What? You don't think it was weird? Just, like, how mad he got? I mean, he punched you!"

"Nah, most dudes get all tough if you make fun of their mom."

"Ugh, then why'd you do it?"

"Hey, I was statin' a fact."

"Well, he didn't think so. You could have just apologized."

"Why?"

Kindle rolled her eyes. "Um, I dunno, so he wouldn't have punched you, you guys wouldn't have fought, and everybody wouldn't be mad."

"You mad?"

"Well, no, but everybody else is."

"I'm not."

"Then why'd you fight him?"

Tad snickered, "Thought it'd be fun."

"Ugh! Seriously? Fighting isn't fun. It makes people mad and … and hate each other."

"He'll get over it," Tad assured her then threw his empty stick into the ash pile between them. She watched him eye Andrew's still half-full stick and uttered a disgusted noise.

"Don't you care that he's upset?"

"He'll get over it," Tad repeated, clearly annoyed. "Why do you and Miss Fire Pants think he's gunna fall over dead?"

Kindle almost snapped back an equally aggravated answer but decided to change her words. "We don't think he's gunna die. It's just … you made him mad, and when you make people mad, you have to apologize so you can … you know, be friends again."

"Who said we're not?"

Kindle blinked at him. She could not understand how Tad did not understand that a fight caused two people to become enemies and also did not know that Tad or Andrew had ever considered the other as a friend.

"What?" she finally questioned, and he gave her a funny look.

"What do you mean 'what'?"

"You just got done beating each other up—how can you be friends?"

"Exactly."

"Exactly?"

"We *just got done* beating each other up. That's how. It's over."

"That doesn't make any sense."

"Why not?"

"Because … I already told you: when people fight, they hate each other."

"*That* doesn't make any sense," Tad declared with finality, plucked up Andrew's stick, and commenced to tearing the meat off it.

Confused and frustrated, Kindle buried her face in her hands and huffed. When her urge to scream finally left, she picked up her eyes to see Tad was staring at her questioningly.

"Wuf wong?" he asked with a mouth full of food.

Out of disgust and annoyance at his oblivion, she turned her face to the trees and sighed, "Okay, so Ella's mad because you and Andrew are mad at each other, and I guess she wants me to get you to say you're sorry, but you're not sorry, and you guys aren't even mad at each other—and I don't know how you're not—so I dunno what to do."

She heard Tad snort and mumble, "Quit worryin' about what Ella wants."

Rolling her eyes back to him, Kindle huffed, "No, I—"

"Hey," he interrupted, pointing the almost empty skewer at her, "quit worryin' about what everybody else wants you to do. You even said it—whatever she's havin' a cow about isn't even goin' on. So if you really want somethin' to do, finish this." Tad tossed Andrew's stick at her then leaned back on his elbows. Kindle dropped her eyes to gaze at the lone piece of meat. Eating it did not enter her mind because it was too full of other considerations.

She did want to forget Ella's unspoken direction and believe that everything truly was fine but doubted Andrew and Ella were as unaffected as Tad. The image of Andrew red-faced and fighting like an animal that had been caged for too long still lingered in her mind and told her that he was definitely not fine. Kindle knew that even if he really was not outraged at Tad, he was upset about something. Her thoughts roamed around for any other cause of his anger but found nothing. Just when she had concluded that her comment about his swimming ability must have been the trigger that caused his snap, a nearby noise pulled her out of her musings. Blinking around, she saw Andrew taking a seat between her and Tad. When he noticed her staring, Andrew ashamedly lowered his face.

"Sorry," he mumbled. His word caused Tad to look around and then sit up. He obviously hadn't heard Andrew approach either.

"What? About that?" Tad laughed. "Forget it, dude."

Andrew picked up his face to examine Tad, and Kindle saw he had a black eye. After a few moments, Andrew gave an accepting nod.

"And nothin' against your mom, I was just sayin'," Tad explained, and Kindle deliberated if it was a sincere attempt to apologize. She watched Andrew eye him, probably pondering what she was, and then shake his head as a twitch of pain pinched his face.

"Are you okay?" Kindle blurted in concern. "I mean, I'm sorry if I said something." She abruptly silenced herself by biting her lip. He appeared on the verge of throwing up or crying. Thankfully, he did neither.

"My mom died," he whispered, "in a car wreck. Only a couple months before we came here."

"Oh," Kindle breathed as her face squished in sympathy. She rolled her lip in and out of her teeth, trying to think of something consoling or nice to say but finally abandoned the effort. When people were sad, she always felt compelled to speak but never knew what words would help. Peeking at Tad, she saw he had turned away from Andrew as well and wondered if he felt the same dilemma or just awkward. They all sat avoiding one another's stares for quite a while. Finally, Kindle chanced a glance at Andrew. His eyes were lifeless, locked in one place but focused on nothing.

"Do you want to talk about it?" she hesitantly inquired. Kindle knew it always helped her to pour out her thoughts when they overwhelmed her.

Andrew sighed and tried to give her a small grin but ended up frowning and shaking his head.

"That's okay," she quickly reassured him and fell silent.

"You want your squirrel?" Tad asked Andrew and caused Kindle to jump. Andrew gave him a puzzled look, and Tad tilted his head at the skewer near Kindle. "You got some left. You gunna eat it?"

Kindle nervously switched her stare between them, sure Andrew would rise up in anger or fall into tears at Tad's lack of sympathy. Andrew, though, followed his motion and calmly nodded.

Amazed, Kindle handed over the skewer.

While Andrew chewed it, Tad commented, "We gotta catch more squirrels. They're better than those puny birds."

Andrew nodded. "More meat."

"Yeah," Tad grumbled as he chucked a rock into the river. "Bet there's fish in there."

"We don't have a pole."

"Yeah … maybe we could stab 'em."

"Fish would feel the water vibrate."

Tad grunted as he tossed another rock.

The two boys ended their conversation, but Kindle continued to gape at them in disbelief. Nothing made sense about their behavior; they had just fought, and Andrew just had revealed an incredibly sad, intimate piece of his life, but they were now bantering like old men at a coffee shop. Their friendly, casual mood all at once delighted, frustrated, and confused her, and she decided to leave them before she impulsively yelled at or hugged them.

"I'm gunna go see where Ella went," Kindle informed them as she stood. Neither of them replied, and she rolled her eyes as she began to tramp away.

"Hey!" Tad called once she had walked a few steps. "Your sword's on Nasah."

"Um, okay," she sassily replied, still confused by his choice of subject matter.

He gave her a sneer and shrug that seemed to indicate that he thought *she* was acting strange and commanded, "Get it."

Done with his and Andrew's weirdness, Kindle trudged over to Nasah, found her sword, and then climbed onto her horse. She thought she heard Tad yell something as she rode away but ignored him. His and Andrew's inability to recognize all the strife they had dumped out on the bank annoyed her, and she knew talking to them would drive her into deeper frustration.

Keeping a lookout for Ella, Kindle urged Nasah into a quick trot. She wanted to find Ella before all her thoughts led her into an emotional spiral. What Andrew had revealed had caused her heart to cringe not only in sympathy for him but also in fear for her own family. Hearing about his life surprising him in such a horrible way prompted her to worry if something just as terrible was happening in her own life and family. Kindle knew that just because one person's mom died, not everyone's mom would also, but the reality that her life was churning on without her somewhere far away where she had no say in or knowledge of it scared her. If something—even something good—happened, she would be left out. If her family needed her help or to talk with her, she would let them down. An extra bitter guilt stung her as she remembered that her mom had told her she wanted Kindle's help at Mikey's party. Kindle bowed her head, incredibly regretful that she couldn't help her mom, eat her dad's burgers, or even watch Mikey and his friends demolish a half-melted ice cream cake. As her mind continued to ponder and mourn the memories and tragedies she might be missing, Kindle gazed down at Nasah's brown mane and stroked it to try to comfort her sadness. She so distracted herself with her horse's hair that she forgot her search for Ella and jumped when she heard her voice.

"Kindle!"

"Huh?" she breathed and looked up to see Ella striding toward her with concern covering her face.

"Whatever is the matter, Kindle? You look utterly downtrodden."

"Oh, um …" Kindle mumbled, trying to pinpoint a cause for her expression that she wanted to reveal. Admitting that she was rolling in possibly imaginary self-pity did not appeal to her, so she finally divulged, "Andrew's mom died."

"Oh my," Ella whispered, but then puzzlement scrunched her brow.

"Oh, well, not just now. It was before we got here—in Anelthalien—but … but that's why he got mad."

"Oh," Ella thoughtfully sighed. "So he returned. Did Tad apologize to him?"

"Um, kind of. They're not mad at each other anymore. They started talking about fishing."

"Fishing? Catching fish? With one another?"

"Yeah, I know, it was weird."

"So … they are alright, then? No averse feeling between them?"

Kindle heaved a long, weary sigh before answering, "No."

"But you're not?" Ella supposed. "What's worrying you?"

Wanting very much to spill her fears and frustrations but not sure of how to start, Kindle turned her eyes to the ground. "You wanna ride? I think I'm gunna walk."

"No, I'll stay on foot. Here, let's turn 'round and wander back."

Kindle slid off Nasah and then turned her in a circle. Ella came around to her other side and only had to send her one sympathetic, questioning glance for Kindle to burst.

"It's just that Andrew saying his mom died and being all sad about it made me feel really bad, and I started thinking about my family and, you know, if they're okay. And then I just, I dunno … what if they're *not* okay, and I won't know about it, and they get mad or more in trouble because I'm not there, and even if they are okay, they're still doing stuff without me, and … and I guess … I just feel like I'm missing out on my life, you know? Like I'm missing out on stuff I should be there for or stuff they need me for, and, I dunno, I don't want to not get to live my life."

She watched Ella thoughtfully examine the ground passing under them and wondered if she understood.

"Do you know what I mean?" she anxiously asked, doubting Ella fully knew how it felt to be plucked out of her life and dumped in an entirely different world.

"Yes," Ella seriously replied, "I've often thought of how I've been cheated of the life I ought to have lived."

The deep comprehension of her words surprised Kindle so much she momentarily forgot to move her feet. Ella glanced at her, and Kindle quickly tried to cover her shock.

"Yeah, um, yeah. That's what I mean."

"Kin," Ella sighed as a slight grin lifted her mouth, "did you not believe I would understand?"

Reluctant to truthfully answer, Kindle simply shrugged.

Ella's smile faded, and she stared off into the forest. "I don't remember if I ever really said, Kin, but my papa isn't truly my papa. He's quite hot-tempered and just as pale and red as any witch, but hasn't a bit of witch in his blood. My real parents left me. I did tell you of the old woman, didn't I? How she told me my parents loved me but couldn't keep me? That's the only way I know. For such a long time, I didn't want that memory. I didn't want it to be true and wanted to really be my papa's daughter because I felt that if that memory was honestly real, it not only made me something horrible but also meant that I was living the wrong life. As I said, I so often thought of how I should have grown up—where I should have lived, the things I should have learned, and the two people who should have cared for me. I never wanted to think on those things … but I did and very deep inside knew who I was and believed I really was robbed of so much that I ought to have had."

Ella fell silent, and Kindle stared down at her boots. She felt incredibly guilty for thinking Ella couldn't understand her struggle. The enormity of all that Ella had missed made her feel pathetic for whining about her few months apart from her family that she actually had a good chance of returning to.

"I'm—" she almost apologized but instead mumbled, "That's really bad."

"No, honestly, it wasn't," Ella instantly brightly assured her and, after chuckling at Kindle's dumbfounded blinking, explained, "It was quite awful—all I thought I'd lost—for a long while, but one day I was so overtaken by the unfairness and all I felt because of it that I told my papa about it. And, Kin, I remember it just as he told me. He sat me down in a chair and knelt down beside me and pointed his finger right at my nose. He said, 'Young lady, you are precisely where you ought to be and everything going on in your life is happening precisely as it ought to be. I found out a long time ago that we can't go thinking this and that is the way it ought to be because this and that never was. All that you're conjuring ain't the life you was to live—*this* is, right as it is happening right now.' He told me that, Kin, and I knew he was right. That all I had imagined about my real parents—whether it really did happen to them or not—was not the life I was meant to live. My life happened as it did and our lives are happening like this right now because they are supposed to be happening this way. Everything that's gone on has happened for some reason, and now you're not at your home and I'm away from my papa for some purpose.

"Ever since he told me that, I've known that every bit of life happens as it should—never wrongly or mistakenly or out of order—but I've never really understood how so many strange, mundane, and mad things can all be for some real purpose until now. You see, it's the makers, Kin. They've made everything, and not just the wood of these trees and things, but a plan and purpose for all of it and Anelthalien. There's no other way they could know what we must do before we've done it. Do you see? It must be quite like when my papa stews a soup—he takes all sorts of mad bits of this and that, and you can never see how it will all turn out, but once it's done and you taste it, you see how it all worked out. The makers aren't just guessing at where we need to go or what to do when they tell us to go somewhere or do something—they know precisely why we four are the ones here and how all the strange, mundane, and mad bits of this journey are exactly what we need when we meet them and have some reason we may not see until it's all done and worked out. Kin, all this *is* happening precisely as it ought, and we and Tad and Andrew are all precisely where we ought to be."

Ella inhaled deeply then let it out all at once as she smiled at her. Kindle blinked back, still processing the momentous idea Ella had unloaded on her.

"So … I'm not missing out on anything?" she slowly asked Ella.

"Nothing that you were ever meant to miss," Ella assured her.

Feeling more overwhelmed than consoled, Kindle slipped back into her mind and tried to sort out all that Ella had explained. Kindle clearly understood that she really was supposed to be in Anelthalien instead of school, home, or anywhere else at the moment and so she was really not missing anything, but the rest of Ella's conclusions were more difficult to grasp.

The idea that what they were doing and all they had done while in Anelthalien did matter was hard for her to believe. She could not fathom how something so horrible as Bennickle's orb or so insanely tedious as their talk with Lord Beryl was essential to their journey. Neither had brought anything except pain and trouble, and Kindle was almost positive if they had not happened, they would be closer to their destination. Ella's words about none of the events in their journey making sense until it was all finished rang in Kindle's head also, though, and pushed her to believe that they were somehow necessary. Kindle shook away the difficulty of accepting each bit of her time in Anelthalien as important and forced her thoughts to Ella's perplexing reasoning for her conclusions.

The makers knew about and had planned everything. Somehow that idea seemed even more far-fetched and frightening than the last. It meant that Hux, who she had been convinced was her friend, had planned for the man in Assula to stab her leg, Adlic to trick her, and even for the horrible wind and cold. Kindle put an arm on Nasah's neck as she wondered if she truly could trust Hux or her necklace. Peeking down, she saw the red gem bumping against her with each step she took. It seemed so innocent and unassuming, and staring at it made it harder to believe that it or Hux had planned to hurt her.

She tilted her head to see if Ella was watching her then questioned, "You really think they planned everything? I mean, the makers. You really think they wanted all the stuff we've done to happen?"

"I do," Ella slowly but confidently replied. "Kin, you've seen as much as I have that they know the exact path to get us out of a pinch. How could they know such incomprehensible things if they hadn't meant for it to happen all along?"

"Well, yeah ..." Kindle sighed. She understood Ella's line of reasoning but did not see how it meant that the makers had planned anything except the good parts of their adventure.

"What is it?" Ella encouraged.

Feeling guilty but too bothered to not speak her disbelief,

Kindle divulged, "Well, I get what you mean—that they know how to help us—but … but you think they planned all the bad stuff too?"

They walked a few steps before Ella replied, "Kindle, does it really make sense that the makers so precisely would know how to help us out of a mess if they didn't know how we had tangled into it? Do you see? If they planned everything, they wouldn't have only planned half of everything and …" Ella's face traveled to the forest, and Kindle leaned forward to see her eyes were unfocused, seeing something in her thoughts. Only a second later, Ella shook her head. "Apologies. And anyway, what if all these things that seem so horrid really aren't? I … Kindle, as I told you, I thought it horrid and unfair to be unwanted by my parents, but thinking over it now, I truly doubt I would have lived very long with it being so clear of what I am. And perhaps the makers knew that and so did something that seemed so horrid at that time to make sure I lived a better life … and lived at all so I could be here now and so I could have helped you three out of Beryl's prison and you out of Tortuosus Labyrinthos just last night. Do you see, Kin? All that's ever gone on in our lives has had some purpose, even what we think are the bad bits. The makers have planned it all for what's truly, in the end of it all, best."

"I dunno," mumbled Kindle, still not convinced. "I just don't get why they'd want to do stuff that hurts us."

"To keep us from what would hurt worse," Ella seriously answered. The locked stares, and her face melted into sympathy. "Kin, I know it's hard to see, but I'm positive that's why they have run us through all this—to help us."

"But why can't they just do it another way? You know? Like, why can't they just make it so only good things happen? Just … if they really care about us, why do all these bad things have to happen?"

After a silence long enough to make Kindle anxious, Ella finally answered, "I don't know, Kin. I don't know why it all has to be as it is, but I do know that it all *does* have to be as it is. It all *does* happen to help us somehow, and …" Ella glanced at Kindle. "And that's why I believe it's important you let us know what happened last night."

"What?" Kindle impulsively blurted, hoping Ella wasn't pursuing something she had imagined about her and Tad.

"Well, I suppose it wasn't really at night, but surely, Kindle, you know what I'm getting at—what happened to you in Tortuosus Labyrinthos."

"Oh," she sighed as momentary relief relaxed her. Her ease almost instantly faded, though. "Oh, um …"

"And, Kin, I honestly wouldn't nose in something I didn't believe I ought, but I could tell something more than just a bit of a fall had gone on when I found you. Kin, I didn't mention to the boys, but I saw a light."

Kindle bit her lips together and peered at Ella's pleading face.

"I know it was something important, Kin. I wouldn't ask otherwise."

"I know," sighed Kindle as she avoided Ella's gaze to think. It didn't bother her that Ella wanted to know what had happened, but she thought that Ella would chastise her for doing such a dumb act. She just did not think she could handle the reprimand intensifying the bite of the cold and wind that still lived in her memory. Determined to tell Ella that she might reveal the incident later, Kindle lifted her eyes, but they halted on the sight before her.

Tad and Andrew were not far away. They seemed to have finished snuffing the fire and packing the horses and proceeded to occupying themselves. Andrew was wading in the river, but Tad was attempting to smack all the sand off his jacket. He stood exactly where he had when they had talked during the night, and his position caused Kindle's mind to jump to the conversation.

Kindle almost laughed at what she had so adamantly explained to him. Her reasoning for why they could trust the makers almost perfectly matched Ella's reasoning for why every bit of life was as it was: the makers wanted what was good for Anelthalien and everything in it. As the two thoughts wove together into one full circle of connected realization, Kindle let her eyes drop to her necklace. The little golden dragon seemed to be not only looking at her but to be craning its neck in anticipation. It caused her to wonder if somewhere

Hux was waiting and hoping for her to stop forgetting and trying to disprove all that she had already worked out and knew to be true and instead just trust that it really was all true. She inhaled deeply, still feeling unsettled and somewhat confused, but then exhaled, "Okay."

CONTENTION

"And you're positive it was Bennickle's?" Ella quietly wondered, and Kindle nodded. She had just finished telling Ella and Andrew about the orb in Tortuosus Labyrinthos. Although she hadn't included as many details as when she had explained her experience to Tad, Kindle had tried to recount enough to help them understand the cold and the pain.

All morning she had been reluctant to release her story into the sunny air and Ella and Andrew's possible judgement. While they had finished erasing signs of their camp and decided who wanted to ride and walk, Kindle had successfully avoided Ella's eye. Once they started traveling, though, she found it much more difficult to keep her focus on the boys walking ahead and ignore Ella's urging glances. Finally, when the sun seemed straight overhead and Kindle feared they would stop and she would have to endure everyone's stares while she spoke, she decided to relinquish the truth.

Kindle had thought she would feel awful once Ella and Andrew knew her mistake, but now that she had, she felt much less burdened. Knowing that Ella's reaction was curiosity rather than condemnation also greatly comforted her.

"Yeah, I'm sure," she answered when she noticed Andrew listening. "It was that glowing thing he had when he talked to us."

Ella bobbed her head in comprehension.

"You said Bennickle was the earth spirit," Andrew commented in such a thoughtful, puzzled tone that Kindle knew it demanded an answer.

"He was, he absolutely was," Ella assured him.

"That globe made wind," mumbled Andrew and glanced up at her.

A sudden shot of pained offense ran through Kindle. "I'm not lying!" she protested and saw Tad shoot a bristling glare Andrew's way.

Their moment of upset settled when Andrew blandly replied, "I know."

"Why you callin' her a liar, then?" Tad challenged.

Andrew stared at Tad with subtle exasperation. "I didn't. I said that the globe made wind."

Tad glared back at him but in a confused way. His eyes ran over Ella, Kindle, and to Andrew again. "Yeah. So?"

"Bennickle is the earth spirit," Andrew explained, "but he made wind. That doesn't add up."

"I thought you believed me," Kindle whined, her hurt creeping back.

"No, Kin, I believe I see what he means. You saw a globe that really wasn't Bennickle's even though it *appeared* to be his. Right, Andrew?"

He uncomfortably wriggled his shoulders. "Not really."

"What?" Tad impatiently and Ella encouragingly demanded in unison.

"What if it wasn't Bennickle's globe? What if it was the wind spirit's globe? It sounds like it held a lot of power. What if all of the spirits have a globe they're keeping their power in?"

"Really?" Tad grumbled, unconvinced. He tugged on his necklace with his thumb. "I thought *these* were where they kept their power."

Andrew stared off over the river. "They don't have the necklaces anymore. So if the necklaces have their power, the spirits shouldn't have any power. Bennickle caused an earthquake, though, so they have to have some power left."

Tad sniffed, and Kindle doubtfully pinched her face.

"But what was it doing underground?" she argued, and they all turned to her. "I mean, Ella, you even said it down there—the wind spirit isn't gunna be hanging around underground. He's gunna be … I dunno, on a mountain or something. And nobody was around the globe, and Bennickle's the only one we ever saw, *and"* —Kindle swung her eyes to Ella— "Bennickle's staff was right by it."

Realization dawned over Ella's face before she apologetically smiled down at Andrew. "She's right, Andrew. It had to be Bennickle's."

Andrew shrugged. "Okay."

"Don't be miffed over it, Andrew," Ella told him. "It honestly is odd that a globe belonging to Bennickle created wind, and it honestly was a clever reckoning you had for it. It only … Kin, was there nothing else that happened? You saw no one? Heard no one?"

"No, nobody else was there. I even yelled a couple times to see if somebody was there."

"And not a soul answered?"

"No."

"Alright, Kin," Ella sighed but sounded satisfied. "I'm glad you told us all."

"Yeah," Kindle replied as she caught sight of Tad send a brief, questioning glance over his shoulder. Too eager to be done with reliving and mulling over the unsettling orb, Kindle let herself pretend she had missed his look. Thankfully, he didn't pursue whatever thought had caused his action, and all four of them fell into silence. Even when Kindle and Ella decided to walk and Tad jumped on Nox, they didn't say more than necessary. Only after what seemed like hours and Kindle's hunger took over her thoughts did she awaken all of them with a question of food. Ella immediately dismissed the idea of stopping before evening, and even though Kindle didn't want to accept her decision, she did want to keep herself from complaining and Tad from glowering, and so she struck up a conversation.

For a long while, she and Ella talked about their homes and families, but when Ella questioned Tad about his, Kindle hurriedly turned their chat in another direction. To her relief, her split decision to banter about school somehow fascinated Ella.

"All of you still have lessons? All day?" she almost laughed.

"You can't quit till you're 18," Tad grumbled.

Kindle gave him a look of disbelief before she told Ella, "Yeah, you go till you're a senior, and then you graduate. It's usually when you're 18 or 19."

Ella eyed her then asked Andrew, "Are they fooling me?"

He shook his head. "Twelve years and then most people go to college for about four."

"College?" she eagerly questioned as she swung her head around at them.

"School for stuck up rich kids," Tad sniffed, but Andrew contradicted him.

"It's specialized schooling. It's to learn how to do one specific career."

"Like apprenticeship?"

"Somewhat …" Andrew dropped his gaze to his shoes. "More reading, though. I think my mom went for 12 or 13 years and only spent the last few in a hospital."

"Did you say she was a doctor? What is that?"

Ella's question caused Kindle to grimace. She worried it might push Andrew into gloom or anger, but surprisingly, he grinned slightly and nodded.

"An orthopedist—a bone doctor. She was a bone mender. That's why she led the senior water aerobics. Exercise in the water isn't so hard on old bones." Andrew chuckled to himself and Kindle wondered if a hidden joke was embedded in his words. She peered at Ella's face to see if she understood but saw deep confusion. Realizing Ella probably didn't know anything about pools, aerobics, or old bones, she decided to slide into the conversation.

"That's really nice she helped old people." Kindle grinned at him, and his smile grew.

"She helped a lot of people."

"Was she quite lovely, then?" Ella wondered. "What all was she like? Of course, you don't have to say if you'd rather not. I only never had a mum, and it's wonderful to hear about each of yours."

Again, Kindle feared Andrew might retreat into silence, but he opened even more.

"She was great. She was nice to everybody and always worked hard to help people get better. She did work a lot ... but that's why she always took me to the pool with her."

Ella grinned at him then turned her gaze to the river. "So do you live near the sea?"

Andrew slid a confused glance at Kindle, and she shrugged. Ella's question seemed odd to her as well. Andrew dropped his searching eyes to his feet, but Tad found a response first.

"What? You think a pool's the ocean?" he snorted.

Ella stared up at him. "Do you mean the sea? Yes. What else would it be? You don't expect me to believe he means he swam 'round the pool of a fountain, do you?"

Tad narrowed his eyes and slowly, deridingly explained, "Swim-ing pool."

To keep them from diving into an argument, Kindle jumped ahead of his next words. "You guys don't have swimming pools? Like, huge concrete holes people fill up with water so they can swim in them?"

Ella sent her a smirk of disbelief. "Now you really are fooling me."

"No, seriously!" Kindle insisted, almost laughing at the fact Ella had no faith in the reality of a pool. "They're everywhere. And they're not just huge—lots of people have those round plastic ones in their yards. You guys know what I mean, right?" She looked between Tad and Andrew for support, confident one of them would help her. They both nodded, and she smiled at Ella.

"Yeah, people think actin' like a fish is fun," grumbled Tad then almost immediately muttered, "No offense, dude."

Kindle turned to Andrew as he expressionlessly nodded as if he had taken no insult at all. Baffled that Tad's insult had not ruffled him, she continued to examine him for any sign of anger but only found it on Ella's affronted and perplexed face.

"Tad, you can't speak to him like that," Ella parentally sighed up at him, and before Kindle could say any word to stop the retort she knew was filling Tad, he erupted.

"I didn't speak to him like anything! I said fish swim, that's it! So get off my case."

"Oh, Tad, don't be childish, you know—"

"It's okay," mumbled Andrew, but Ella only briefly paused her lecture.

"You know very well what you said and exactly why it was insulting."

"Hey, do you have ears? He said it was okay, so shut up. *Man*, don't you listen to anybody?"

Ella huffed, "*Really*. I thought we were past all this."

"You're the one who's makin' a big deal out of nothin'."

"I am not! You—"

"It's fine," Andrew softly growled, and Ella swung her head to him.

"Is it really, Andrew?"

They stared hard at one another as if waging a mental war. Kindle peered between them, waiting for one to surrender, but their standoff lasted long enough for her to become awkward. As she uncomfortably turned away, Kindle realized that they had stopped but Tad and Nox had continued to walk along the bank. Glad to have an escape from Andrew and Ella's seemingly endless silent battle, she slinked a few steps away.

"I'm just gunna … you guys can catch up," she mumbled and then spun and trotted away. Once she caught up with Tad, Kindle simply stared up at him expectantly.

He finally noticed her expression and grumbled, "What? *You* want me to apologize to *her* now?"

"No," she sighed, letting go of her irritation at him. Truthfully, Kindle had hoped he felt some remorse for arguing, but she also knew he really hadn't initiated it. "I just wish you guys wouldn't fight."

He eyed her for a moment then defensively muttered, "I didn't start it."

"I know, but … yelling at her really doesn't help."

"I wouldn't yell at her if she didn't act like I was some kind of criminal."

Unwilling to bash either of them, Kindle puffed out a long sigh. She twisted back to check if Ella or Andrew had won their glaring contest yet and saw they both still stood firm.

"How long you think they're gunna stand there?" Tad snickered, and Kindle turned to see he had followed her gaze back to them.

"I dunno," she quietly replied, rolling her eyes ahead. The constant fighting not only raked Kindle's nerves but also disheartened her. It seemed like they could only make headway in their journey for a short time before another silly argument yanked them to a halt. She wanted to shout at them and command that they quit being so annoying and mean but knew that would only place her in the fight as well. Desperate to find some method to end their disagreements that did not involve her tangling herself up in them, Kindle squeezed her eyes shut to think. Almost instantly, her toe found a rock, and she stumbled. An aggravated breath blew out of her mouth.

"Tired?" Tad questioned, stopping Nox.

"No, I—well, yeah, but I'm just so sick of you guys fighting. And I know it's not just you—"

"Yeah, it's her."

"It's *all* of you guys."

Tad glared down at her then slowly tore his eyes away as he asked, "You gettin' on?"

Kindle sighed, angry at everything—even at herself for being angry. "Yeah, sure."

He gave her a hand to climb up on Nox and then resumed their slow progress. They rode without speaking for a few minutes until Kindle began to seriously worry that she had offended him.

"I'm sorry."

"For what?"

"I dunno, for whatever I did to make you mad."

"I'm not mad."

"Oh, well ..." Kindle didn't finish her thought but instead pushed the heels of her hands against her eyes and took a deep breath. She couldn't pinpoint the exact reason why, but she suddenly felt incredibly full of a mob of overwhelming emotions. Sensing aggravated tears pushing to escape, she kept her palms pressed against her face. Crying embarrassed her, especially when she couldn't see the reason for it and knew no one else would either. Just when Kindle thought she had stemmed her tears, she felt Tad shift and knew she had been caught.

"What's wrong with you?" he bluntly asked, and she let her hands flump down onto her legs.

Blinking at the sky, she huffed, "I dunno, I dunno."

He squished his face in what seemed to be disgusted confusion, and Kindle broke.

"Ugh, I just ..." she choked, trying to keep her words intelligible. "You guys keep fighting, and it feels like we're not getting anywhere, and everything just seems like it's going wrong, like we're never gunna find the evil guy because we just keep fighting, and ... and it's stupid." Kindle dropped her face, unwilling to see what expression Tad had now or if he was even looking at her.

Immediately, her necklace caught her attention, and she fell into greater despair. "Ugh, I know," she moaned, "I know everything isn't really bad or whatever, and I know Ella said all this stuff matters, but I don't get how fighting and arguing and that stupid Bennickle and his stupid globe thing is important or is gunna do anything good. Everything just seems wrong and bad and like it's never gunna get better, and ... and I'm just so sick of it." Kindle ended her argument with the little dragon with a frustrated huff and shut her eyes to close out everything around her. She expected Tad to comment on her rambling, but he didn't, and for once she was grateful for his silence. Her mind felt too full and too conflicted to take any more input.

Deep down she knew Ella was probably right and everything would be fine and the makers would eventually show up and help. The current state that the four of them sat in, though, seemed so far from fine that it just agitated her to think that the makers had made everything happen as it had and could apparently choose to fix everything any time they wanted but had not yet. As Kindle kept her head bowed and stewed over the unfairness and seemingly pointlessness of everything, helpless frustration built up in her. She felt as if she could do absolutely nothing about their progress but desperately wanted to fight all that impeded it. Her desire grew and grew until she could not stifle it any longer. Ready to yell and kick until everything was fixed, Kindle let her eyes snap open.

Instantly, most of her rage morphed into guilt. The red gem was catching the sun's light, and the golden dragon was watching her. Its stare was so patient, quiet, and hopeful that she felt sorry for being angry at it and the maker attached to it. Looking at the dragon, she knew and pushed herself to accept that Ella had to be right. The makers were very slowly doing something important and would somehow eventually work out everything. Even though her necklace had reassured her, Kindle still felt the unsettling energy from her frustration and guilt. At first, she was tempted to chatter to relieve herself but decided it could annoy Tad. As she shook away the thought of him yelling at her to shut up and glanced up at the sky, an impulsive idea popped into her mind.

"You wanna fight?" she asked.

Tad slowly turned a questioning, leery glare back to her. "You're being weird. And not just normal girl weird."

Realizing that her words had sounded strange, she clarified, "No, I mean swords. Sword fight. I just … I dunno. I feel all frustrated and weird, and I need to do something."

He eyed her suspiciously. "Really? You think me takin' you down is gunna help?"

"Shut up," she retorted as she rolled her eyes but smiled.

Playfully arguing with him eased some of her disgust, and she kicked her leg over Nox and jumped to the ground. "C'mon," Kindle challenged as she unsheathed her sword. It felt wonderfully appropriate in her hand, and she gazed fondly down at its long metal blade. The sound of Tad's feet hitting the ground shook her from her happy examination, and she had just enough time to raise her sword before his slashed into its block.

"Really?" he asked again, this time with his evil but silly grin spread across his face.

Kindle gave him a nod. He instantly threw aside her block and returned with a new attack. When she barely caught it, Kindle realized just how much time had passed since she had practiced. For a moment, she wondered if testing her dusty skills against Tad was wise, but he was already slicing at her again, and she forgot her hesitations.

"You're gettin' slow," he teased as his sword almost met her head.

She forced his blade back. "It's been a while since we've practiced."

Tad smirked and then in a blink faked a slash at her neck, spun, and smacked her side with the flat side of his sword. "Dead," he laughed.

Fueled by embarrassment and determination, she whipped her sword from high to low and pushed his back. "Again."

She knew by his focused eyes and grin he understood and would do all he could to execute another swift victory. Before he could trap her in a defensive dance, she took the first strike. He easily deflected it, but Kindle smiled—she held the advantage. Channeling the array of emotions pumping through her into the fight, she was able to unleash several more swipes at him before Tad pulled one of his unfair stunts. When she jabbed, he twisted his blade around hers, forcing it down, then quickly snatched her wrist and yanked them into opposite spots. Kindle knew this trick and ducked as his sword breezed over her with all the momentum of their switch.

"Are you *trying* to cut my head off?" she tried to sassily snap but ended up panting in a laugh.

"Hey, whatever it takes to help you out," he defensively, jokingly retorted.

Kindle snorted and rolled her eyes then straightened up to stop another one of his head shots. After that they fell into a fairly even battle. Tad slashed a few dangerously close attacks, then Kindle took advantage of his brashness and aimed for whatever limb he forgot to protect until his strength put her in a defensive position again. They repeated the cycle several times before Kindle felt tired weakness begin to creep into her arms. As she took her turn blocking, she searched for any defeating opening but saw none. Tad was bold but not messy when sparring, and he always kept most of himself just out of her reach. Realizing that the only way she could win was to risk closing the space between them, Kindle dodged his shin attack like a jump rope and took the millisecond of his surprise to shuffle forward and strike.

Tad quickly mirrored her action; he threw up a block and bounded backward out of danger. Determined to not let him evade her, Kindle more confidently swung at him as she hopped closer. A sneer pinched his face, and Kindle instantly knew she was nearing a win as well as irking him. Afraid of making him sincerely angry, she unconsciously paused to think. Her mind had no time to consider her options before Tad's ferocious sword sliced centimeters from her leg. Instinct took control of her actions, and she struck forward to catch his arm on his upswing, but he saw it and recoiled down and back instead. In the second he did and exposed his right side, Kindle anticipated where he was headed, crouched to evade his powerful circle swing, then pounced.

He didn't see her low attack until her sword was a moment from his calf. Just as a triumphant grin began to form on her lips, Tad sprang up and back away from her swipe. Knowing her possibly only chance of winning had failed, her face began to fall, but as it did, so did Tad. The smooth agility of his backward bound ended when his feet met the river's edge. As if someone had yanked a rug from under him, his feet slipped forward, and he tumbled back into the water. Kindle gasped a shriek but then realized another opportunity to win had appeared. She hurriedly gathered herself up and ran forward to deliver her winning strike, but just as her foot hit the water, Tad's leg collided with her ankles. The world around her momentarily blurred and then exploded in a splash. Her hard landing knocked the air out of her lungs, and she coughed and thrashed in the shallow water, trying to orient herself. As Kindle rolled on her back and propped herself up to drink in the air, she realized her fingers no longer held her sword. Before she could move her hand to search for it, cold metal slid under her chin.

"Dead," Tad's voice proclaimed behind her. Kindle rolled her head back to find him. He also was panting and soaking wet but grinning.

Seeing his glee, she couldn't hide her smile as she unwillingly consented, "Okay. Dead. Now help me find my sword."

"Ha! Double dead!" he yelled and swung her sword over her head to poke her stomach.

"Double dead?" she laughed and snatched it from him. "You can't be double dead."

"That's right, 'cause *you* are!" he gloated and finally took his weapon from her throat.

Kindle rolled her eyes at him as he sloshed up to the bank. "Okay, whatever."

"What? You gunna be a sore loser? You were the one who wanted to fight."

"No, I just ..." she paused to giggle as he shook his shaggy hair like a dog.

"What?"

Kindle peered down at her boots then decisively concluded, "That was fun."

"Tad! Kindle!"

The shout caused them both to twist around. Nasah was galloping toward them with Ella and Andrew on her back.

"What's happening?" Ella worriedly questioned as she pulled Nasah to a stop near Tad. "We heard fighting and shouts. Are you hurt? Did those monsters come back?" She hopped to the ground, swinging her anxious, expectant face between them.

"Yeah, she's double dead," Tad snickered, tilting his head Kindle's way, and she groaned at his sarcasm.

"What?" Ella demanded, even more worried. "What's gone on? Kin? Are—?"

'I'm fine," she interrupted and pushed herself up to join them on the rocky bank. "He's kidding, Ella. I'm fine."

"What was all the ruckus, then? We both heard it," she interrogated, gesturing at Andrew, who was carefully climbing off Nasah.

"What do you think it was?" Tad grumbled as he wiped the water from his sword with his shirt. Sensing the instigation in his tone, Kindle breathed a deflated sigh; they were going to dive right back into an argument. Tad, though, glanced at her then mumbled, "It was just us. Sword fighting."

Shock jumped on Ella's face. "Whatever for? I thought at least you two weren't at odds."

"We were just practicing," Kindle quickly explained, and relieved comprehension replaced Ella's shock.

"Of course, Kin. I apologize. All this bickering and being chased and such has gotten me wound as tight as a bag of minas. Of course you were practicing." Ella sighed a smile onto her face. "And that's brilliant—we do need to keep our skills sharp. Good, alright …" Ella searched the ground as if hunting for her next words, and Andrew slinked into their circle.

"We should stop for the night," he slowly suggested as if trying to calm and direct Ella.

"Yes," she quickly agreed then softly grinned at him. "Yes, Andrew, you're very right. I'll go make a fire if …"

Andrew nodded then looked to Tad. "Are you coming?"

"What? Hunting? Pft—yeah!" he eagerly replied and sheathed his sword. "Where's the bow?"

"Here." Ella handed it to him and her quiver to Andrew. "Be safe, you two."

"Yeah," Tad offhandedly replied and then raced off between

the trees. When he and Andrew had disappeared, Kindle sat beside Ella. She could tell that her friend was troubled but did not know if the reasons truly were the encounter with Bennickle and their arguing. Sure that Ella would talk to her about whatever was bothering her but unsure of how to begin the conversation, Kindle simply asked, "You okay?"

"Oh, Kin," Ella dismally sighed and rocked back from the fire she was lighting to plop on the ground. "Now even Andrew's told me I boss too much … and you know he's right about most everything."

Since she couldn't think of any comforting words, Kindle sympathetically grimaced.

Ella nodded at her expression and continued, "Well, he really did not quite say I boss too much. He told me that he could think and speak for himself and didn't need me to. Of course, he was well-mannered about it and not at all in a temper, and I couldn't find a rebuttal at the time, but, Kin, honestly, I *know* he can think and speak for himself."

"Yeah," Kindle commented, hoping Ella wouldn't ask for more input.

Ella leaned forward to tend to the fire but sank back again. "Do I act as if he can't think or speak? No—I apologize—do not even answer. I know he would not have said it if he didn't have an honest reason for thinking it." She huffed and returned her hands to the waiting sticks. "It's only that I've explained to you all that it's only natural for me to help and take command of things. I honestly don't mean to overstep into bossing and belittling."

"Yeah, I know."

"But I do, Kin, don't I?"

Kindle wrestled with the truth before deciding to say, "Boys don't really like to be told what to do … at all. You know, if you tell them to do something, they just do the opposite. Like, my brother won't ever get out of my room if I tell him to leave, but he won't ever come help me with anything if I tell him to."

Ella considered her words for a while then wondered, "Do you mean it would be best to say the opposite of what I mean to them?"

"No, um … I just … I guess I mean you just need to let them … figure stuff out."

"Think and speak for themselves, you mean?"

She meekly shrugged and nodded.

"Alright," Ella conceded. "I'll honestly try not to boss and direct. I only didn't realize I did so much. Well, Tad's spoken about it, and—it's not that I don't trust his opinion—it's only that he's been quite against me this whole while we've known one another."

Conflicted at her words, Kindle dropped her eyes. She had no intention of voicing her thoughts until her necklace caught her attention. "Hey, um …"

"Yes?" Ella prompted.

Kindle heard hope in her voice and knew she wanted a better conclusion to her conflict. "Um, me and Tad … last night I told him all the stuff that happened in the Labyrinthos—and not just the stuff that we did but, you know, about the makers and everything. And I told him that we could trust them—that we *had* to trust them—and … and that we had to trust each other." She peered up to check Ella's expression and saw the hint of a smile on her rapt face. Kindle grinned and continued, "And he said he's gunna trust you. Well, I mean, I had to tell him how you saved me like a million times down there, but after that he said he'd try. So, I guess it's not like you shouldn't ever help us out because you're really smart and most of the time you're right about stuff, especially when you listen to your maker, but … but we've got makers too, so just listen to us too."

Ella beamed at her. "Of course, Kin. Of course I can listen to you three. I suppose you've pinpointed it, though," she sighed as she turned her smile to her necklace. "I've heard him so clearly that I've almost forgotten it isn't only me knowing what to do and that you all have a maker just as real and as right as mine. I am sorry for that, Kin—I don't know everything, and I will listen to you three."

Amazed at Ella's honesty and that she—the one who seemed most attuned to her maker—apparently struggled to discern his voice from her own thoughts, Kindle blinked at her. She wanted to ask when or how she had mixed her thoughts with her maker's voice, but before she could form the question, their silence was disrupted.

"That would be dinner," Ella laughed at the yell as she turned to the forest.

"Yeah," Kindle tried to laugh as well but couldn't hold her false grin while still in her thoughts.

"Kin," Ella seriously whispered, and she gazed at her friend's face. "Thank you for talking to him on my behalf. I could not have done that on my own."

"Oh, um, you're welcome, but it's not really a big deal."

"It is. You proved to him that he could trust me, or try to at the least," she laughed. "And I know you're the only one who could have done that, and you didn't have to. I'm grateful, Kin, I am."

Feeling as if Ella was praising her for much more that she actually did, Kindle shrugged but nodded to accept her thanks.

"Hey, c'mon! Where's the fire?" Tad yelled, and they both twisted to see he was proudly carrying a squirrel their way.

"You've already caught one! Fantastic!" Ella cried and popped up to receive it.

"Yeah, so skin it and spike it," he replied and then turned back to the trees.

"Are you going for more?" Ella quickly asked.

"Nah, you guys share that, and I'll go find some leaves to eat," he dryly remarked then jogged out of sight.

Ella swung a confused face from the forest to her. "He was fooling … wasn't he?"

Kindle giggled at her inability to read his blatant sarcasm and kindly sighed, "Yeah."

RUMBLINGS

The rest of the evening passed by much better than Kindle would have dared to hope. Tad and Andrew continued to find squirrels while Ella prepared them, and Kindle made herself busy away from the dead animals. Once the boys had brought back their seventh and eighth squirrels, Ella convinced them to stop and eat what she had already roasted. During their meal, Ella apologized several times for not providing anything more to eat, but Tad finally interrupted her and told her she could make up for it when they found their way out of the forest. After that, they began a debate about how much game Ella owed Tad. The seriousness of their trivial argument entertained Kindle, and when she leaned back to enjoy the friendly deliberation, she noticed Andrew was also chuckling at them.

"Tad, you cannot even eat nine squirrels. You would make yourself sick."

"Pft—these things have hardly any meat on 'em. They're like chicken nuggets, and I can eat twenty of them easy."

"I can hardly believe anyone would have the patience and stomach to pluck and eat twenty chickens."

"*Nuggets,*" he emphasized as he held up a piece of meat that resembled the size and shape of a fast food nugget.

"Why would anyone put nougat in their chicken?" Ella demanded. "That sounds absolutely revolting."

Tad barked a laugh at her disgusted face and snickered to his small audience, "She doesn't get it."

"A chicken *nugget* is a small piece of breaded chicken," Andrew patiently explained to Ella.

"Yeah, just like that big," added Kindle as she pointed to the bite Tad was still holding.

"Oh, well, if that's all a nugget is, then of course you can eat twenty."

"Ha! So you agree you owe me twenty birds—"

"That was not a consent—"

"And ten squirrels."

"Nine."

"Ten."

"Oh, alright, ten. But I haven't any inkling how that tenth one snuck in."

"He didn't sneak in. He knocked, and I let him in."

Ella furrowed her brow in confusion, and the rest of them laughed.

"He's joking, Ella, he's joking!" Kindle assured her as soon as she could collect her giggles.

"Oh." Ella made an attempt to grin but still appeared perplexed. She shook her head and turned a genuine smile to Kindle. "You're finished. Do you want to have a few rounds of practice?"

"Um ... sure," she slowly replied. Truthfully, Kindle felt like doing nothing but laying on the bank, but Ella had asked so hopefully that she couldn't reject her. Ella immediately sprang up and trotted a short distance from the fire. After sending a weary glance at Tad and receiving a snicker, Kindle sighed and dragged herself up and over to Ella.

The first few minutes of their match brought Kindle some relief—Ella was even more out of practice than her. Her speed, skill, and ferocity were nowhere near the intensity of Tad's, and so Kindle let herself enjoy the slower, more precise strike and block routine they slipped into. They wordlessly took turns attacking and defending until Kindle let what should have been an easily deflected swipe strike her.

"Ugh," she groaned even though Ella really hadn't hit her very hard.

Ella lowered her weapon and kindly smiled. "You're tired, aren't you? Go on and lie down, you've been a brilliant contender long enough."

Kindle considered arguing, but her weariness pushed her to instead gratefully accept Ella's observation. "Yeah, okay. Thanks," she mumbled and trudged back to the fire. As she tossed her sword and then herself between Tad and Andrew, Ella called to them.

"Either of you two want to practice?"

"Nah!" Tad instantly replied. He was reclining on his elbows and looking very satisfied about it.

Andrew, though, heaved a deep sigh and mumbled, "Probably should."

Kindle watched him gradually stand and trudge away to find his sword. Once he disappeared from her immediate vision, she eased down on her back and closed her eyes. The bank didn't feel as rocky as the previous night, and she wondered if it was due to fatigue or a smaller number of rocks. Her mind was so worn that it didn't dwell on the quandary but began lazily and sporadically replaying bits of the events from the day.

"How long?" Tad's voice whispered and pulled her out of her subconscious.

"Mm?"

"How long till he drops his sword?"

Kindle lifted her heavy eyelids and saw he was bending his neck to watch Ella and Andrew. She turned to examine the pair then closed her eyes again. "I dunno."

"C'mon, you're not fallin' asleep, are you?" he teased and lightly kicked her foot. "It's not even dark yet, and that over there is gunna be gold. Comic. Gold."

"'S almost dark," she mumbled.

"Boom. Dead," Tad hissed, and Kindle took the great effort to see that if Ella had intended to harm Andrew, she would have just speared him through the heart.

"You guys are weird," she half-consciously told him and rolled her head over to shake it at Tad.

He laughed, and even though Kindle guessed it was due to her dull state, she still felt compelled to lethargically argue her case.

"No, seriously … you fight and then be friends … and then make fun of each other and be friends … weird."

She heard him chuckle at her again.

"Seriously," she muttered as insistently as she could while giggling herself and losing her battle against sleep.

Kindle's eyes broke open and darted back and forth. She didn't know what had woken her up but felt sure something outside of herself had. The extremely dark bank, river, and forest in her vision, though, held nothing unexpected. Picking up her head to investigate all her surroundings, Kindle saw that Ella rested not too far from her but the boys and horses were sleeping just under the trees. After turning her head a few times to assure herself that no other life existed nearby except her slumbering companions, Kindle lay back down.

She was swimming down into peaceful rest when a low, distant rumble pulled her back up into consciousness. Its familiar sound placated her; it must have been what had roused her and meant nothing more than a possible rainstorm. She almost let herself dive right back into her pursuit of sleep, but a sudden thought alerted her to sit up and examine the sky.

Every night since leaving the Chokmah's, the dark, silky dome above had glittered with stars and a moon, but for the first time it held nothing but shadows of voluminous clouds. Rainclouds meant rain, and thunder meant a storm, and together they guaranteed that she would be drenched. Kindle frowned up at the clouds as another rumble rippled through the air. She didn't want to get up and find some way to sleep under something that would keep her dry but even more did not want to be pelted by cold rain. As Kindle considered waking up the others to warn them and gain their help constructing a tent, her eyes fell on the river. She sighed. Many times she had heard adults warn her to stay away from water during storms. Knowing and realizing that it would be dangerous to do anything except shelter in the forest but also that Ella would never chance entering it due to a good reason, Kindle decided to settle for the edge of the forest. Dragging up her tired body, she trudged over to the horses and tried to think of anything in their saddle bags that would make a decent tent.

Another louder grumble of thunder shook the forest, and Kindle halted to stare up at the sky. Besides the black expanse of clouds and occasional rumble, no other signs of a storm had arrived yet. No wind shook the trees or brought the smell or chill of coming rain, and no lightning cracked or flashed. Kindle squinted around in the darkness, trying to hear raindrops hitting the river or feel the breeze she expected, but the night remained quiet and still. A fear that perhaps the sound was not thunder slowly crept into her mind and pulled her eyes to the forest. Sure she was about to see a rock monster, Kindle held a fist over her mouth as she leaned back and forth to peer between the trees.

In the middle of a slow, bending sidestep, she froze. Her eyes had not spied the monster she expected but a small, distant light. It quickly disappeared from sight, but Kindle knew she had not imagined the little green illumination. For a few minutes, she remained motionless as her mind sped in a million directions. The light had been so lovely and unique that it piqued her curiosity. She felt compelled to discover what it was but at the same time feared getting any closer to it. In the same moment that she debated to run away from or closer to it, Kindle wondered if she should wake up Ella, Tad, and Andrew and warn them that something loomed nearby. She lowered her hand from her mouth and glanced back at her friends. The thunder had not disturbed any of them, and seeing them so peaceful made her reluctant to stir them for what was likely nothing.

"It's nothing," she whispered to reassure herself and eased back to the packs by Nasah to start her search for a rain shield. As she approached her horse, Nasah raised her head then stood.

"No, no. Shh, shh," Kindle breathed but smiled and stroked her wonderfully intelligent friend. She knew Nasah understood her lingering fear of the light and would not rest until she had shaken it.

"It's okay," she sighed more to calm herself than Nasah. "It's just some stupid light, and it's g—" Kindle's word evaporated as she peeked up to confirm it. The green light hovered straight ahead of her, this time absolutely still. As she lifted her entire face to stare at it, a very loud, close tremor of thunder shook even the earth under her feet. Nasah whinnied in agitation, and Kindle tore her gaze from the light to calm her.

"Wha's tha?" Andrew's voice mumbled, and she twisted to see him. He was laying only a few feet away, rubbing his face. Kindle held her breath as she waited for his next action. She hoped he would miss her presence so she wouldn't have to explain herself but also hoped he would notice her and have an explanation about the light or a solution to the brewing storm. Before Kindle could decide which she wanted more, he was blinking up at her.

"What are you doing?" he mumbled.

Too shaken to fabricate a lie, she admitted, "The thunder woke me up."

"Thunder?"

"Yeah, I think it's gunna rain."

He buried his sleepy, confused face in his hand for a moment then slowly asked, "Rain?"

She nodded. "Um ... do you think we should make a tent?"

"Okay," he vaguely mumbled as he dropped his face back down onto his arm. Kindle waited for him to rise or give a direction, but after a few minutes, his long breaths told her he had fallen back asleep.

As soon as Kindle realized he was not stirring, her eyes

snapped back to the forest. The light still shone out from between the trees, but it seemed larger. A knot of dread twisted in her stomach. Whether or not she wanted to discover what the green glow was, it was coming to them. Without thinking over any more options or possibilities, Kindle dashed to the bank to grab her sword, hurried back to Nasah, found and attached her reins, and then mounted her horse. Nasah huffed in objection, and Kindle felt the same displeasure of riding bareback but did not want to give the approaching person or thing time to reach the bank. She cast one more look around at her unconscious companions then urged Nasah forward.

As Kindle wound through the trees, she tried to ignore the fact that she had no idea what to expect. Instead, she focused on the three totally unprepared and unarmed friends she could possibly be saving and the weight of her sword at her side. Even though she *hoped* that the light would belong to just an ordinary trader or traveler, she doubted it would and wanted to stop it—whatever it was—from discovering all of them. The closer she rode to the light, the more Nasah resisted her signals and prods.

"C'mon," Kindle begged as Nasah halted and stomped her hooves. "C'mon, Nasah, don't be scared," she tried to whisper calmingly but heard her anxiety and wondered if she should turn them around. Just as the idea entered her mind, Nasah retreated a few steps and then began to turn. A sudden fear of opening her back to an attack grabbed Kindle, and she pulled Nasah's reins, but the horse tossed her head and continued her motion.

"Fine," Kindle hissed and slid off her. "Go back."

Nasah did not hesitate to obey but trotted away as quickly as possible through the trees. Seeing her leave filled Kindle with abandonment as well as renewed terror, and she spun to face the light.

It had vanished. Her heart beating, Kindle whirled in a circle to find it but saw only the outlines of trees. Everything was quiet and still. She tried to force her internal state to assume the peace around her but feared that she had made a very rash, foolish decision and would pay for it at any second. After one more quick glance around, Kindle started to carefully walk backward toward the bank. All she wanted to do was escape the forest, but she still felt opposed to turning her back to the light and its silent carrier. A twig snapped under her own heel and shocked her into tense paralysis. With her eyes squeezed shut, Kindle assured herself of the sharp sound's innocence and released a long nervous breath. She almost felt ready to resume her backward walk when a blast of thunder boomed overhead and she lost all her nerve and pivoted to sprint back to the river. Her ready feet hit the ground only once and then danced back to steady her.

The green light as well as the person holding it stood only a few trees away. Now that Kindle could clearly see the light, she knew she had made a horrible decision. It wasn't just an odd flame or lantern but ferocious yet silent green electricity striking the inside of the glass orb that contained it. Although it held a different kind of storm, it greatly reminded her of Bennickle's globe. Her instincts told her that he held it, but her eyes showed her otherwise.

The hand wrapped around the staff that held the orb was thin, smooth, and white—so ghostly white that the green lightning flashes reflected over it like momentary veins. The hand and orb began to slip out of Kindle's terrified stare, and she realized that the person holding it was moving in a slow circle around her.

Too scared to move her feet, Kindle let her head turn to keep the person in her sight. Even though she knew it could not be Bennickle, Kindle did not know what sort of person held the staff since a black cloak completely covered him or her. As the person continued to walk, the visible hand, thin outline, and the long dragging hemline of the cloak pushed Kindle to believe it was a woman. Her long cloak and languid pace also convinced Kindle that if she broke into a run, the woman wouldn't be able to catch her. She took a deep breath to prepare for her escape, but as if the woman sensed her intention, she halted.

"Going somewhere?" a beautiful but chilling voice whispered. Knowing that the voice had to belong to the woman, Kindle instead stifled her screaming urge to run and shuffled her feet to face her. Very gradually, her hood began to turn. Kindle wriggled in discomfort as a sliver of white waxed into view.

"Frightened?" the woman almost chuckled as she tossed her chin up to push the hood off her head. The face that proudly examined her captivated and terrified Kindle. The woman's face was just as devoid of color as her hand except for her shockingly green eyes and full red lips. Her long black hair and boney face seemed so old and worn but so vibrant and smooth that she reminded Kindle of an evil vampire queen. An impulse to hide her neck seized Kindle, and as she acted on it, her fingers graced her gold chain.

"I'm not giving it to you," she choked. Touching her necklace had reminded Kindle of the much more real danger of the spirits wanting their marks.

The woman frowned in disgusted confusion then fully faced her to eye her up and down. Then, much quicker than Kindle had believed possible, she strode forward until only a foot existed between them.

"What?" she demandingly spat.

Kindle knew she should give an immediate answer, but her mind seemed to have switched off. All she could do was gape at the woman and the angry lightning beside her.

"Are you incompetent?" she impatiently rumbled, and Kindle suddenly found her voice.

"No, I–I'm not giving you my necklace."

"Oh," she lazily replied with a sniff. "Your spirit stone or mark or whatever vile name you want to title it? No, if that's what I was after, I'd simply rip it off your neck."

Her response stunned and frightened Kindle but not as much as the terrible succession of hisses that reached her ears. She peered around the floor of the dark woods, but the woman's reaction brought her attention back up. A sneer had rolled back her upper lip, and she twisted her neck as if wrenching a crick out of it. With what seemed like great effort, she angrily whispered, "I *ordered* you to remain *silent* and unseen."

Kindle almost apologized even though she had not heard the woman order her to do anything, but just a second after she finished her menacing reminder, the woman deftly spun around. She swiped her staff around with her, and a dull *thud* told Kindle that someone else was the cause and recipient of her words and anger.

"And remain on your face, you filthy roach," she warned then whirled to glare at Kindle. "Who are you? What is your name?" she growled with narrowed eyes.

Kindle did not want to answer but, after viewing the woman beat someone who disobeyed, felt she had no other option. "Kindle. My name's Kindle."

Without even waiting for Kindle to finish, she interrogated, "And where is your home?"

"I, um … I don't—"

"You don't live in Anelthalien." The woman's eyes glittered as she completed Kindle's sentence. Her knowledge about Kindle seemed to delight her, but it disturbed Kindle. Great discomfort welled up inside her, and she felt herself leaning in the direction of the bank. The woman caught her slight motion and flicked her eyes between Kindle and her desired escape route. Kindle feared she would snap at her for trying to flee, but instead, an evil grin slowly picked up her lips.

"Are the three others close by?"

"No," Kindle impulsively lied. She did not want the woman to know anything about Ella, Tad, and Andrew.

"Liesss," an eerie voice hissed, and Kindle shivered. It was a much too familiar sound.

"Infernal wretch!" the woman screamed, and as she did, a powerful crack of lightning momentarily illuminated everything in green light. Kindle hunkered against the overwhelming noise and then tumbled backward into a tree as the creepy hooded figure floated around the woman. Its appearance startled Kindle into a panic, and she attempted to stand, draw her sword, and scamper away at the same time. Her terror switched to amazement, though, as the woman slammed it aside with her staff.

"You are not to go near her or any of the children!" she yelled, and a roll of quaking thunder harmonized with each word. "You slime! You revolting, disobedient, greedy slime!" With each insult the

275

woman threw another vicious hit into the creature. Her abusive rage horrified and sickened Kindle so much that she almost felt sorry for the black lump that finally fell still. Once it did, a bolt of lightning flashed and a torrent of rain simultaneously began. Kindle blinked in surprise and then, realizing the woman had transformed into a blur in the downpour, sprang up to dash away. After only a few steps, a force hit her shoulder, and she found herself pinned against a tree.

"You knew him!" the woman screamed inches from her face as Kindle felt her fingernails dig into each of her arms. "Where have you seen him?! How did you recognize him?! Speak!"

"Iteraum! Iteraum!" Kindle cried, vainly trying to escape her tightening grip. "He wanted our necklaces! He tried to kill us!"

The woman breathed a disgusted sound then spat back "*Us?! Does that mean you were lying to me?!*"

"Wha—uh!" Kindle shrieked as a stinging palm slapped her face.

"Where are they?! Where are the others?!" she demanded, but Kindle violently shook her head and continued to struggle. "Answer me, you foolish girl!" she raged and shook Kindle. "Answer—!"

Suddenly, the shaking ceased, and Kindle felt her arms fall out of the woman's hold. Fearful that she was about to receive a blow from the staff, she tossed her arms over her head and braced for the impact. A wild scream of pain caused her to drop them and squint through the rain. The woman had backed only a few steps, so Kindle could see the chocked shock on her face and arrow sticking out of her neck. They both stared at one another with gaping mouths for a few seconds. Then the woman snatched her staff and swung it to smash another arrow out of the air. The woman darted forward and pushed the black staff against Kindle's throat but called, "You may have won this pathetic wretch, but you can't save all of Anelthalien! This storm has only begun!"

At her last word, she abruptly released Kindle and blew away. Just as she faded, Tad appeared at her side and demanded, "Where'd she go?!"

Relieved to see him, Kindle smiled and panted, "No, no, we

gotta go."

Tad's face started to morph into objection, but the woman's voice distracted him.

"To the east, Castrosphy!"

Before Kindle could register what she had said, Tad dove in the direction of her yell.

"No!" Kindle cried, but he had already disappeared. She started to draw her sword but heard an aggravated growl and halted. "Is she gone?"

"Yeah!" he angrily called back. "Stupid hag! I had her!"

She breathed out a long sigh and pushed her sword back into its sheath. Another shout from him caused Kindle to jump out of her ease. "What?! Are you okay?"

"Yeah," he grumbled as he returned. "Just wish all these idiots would quit running away like a bunch of pansies." He glared up at the rain for a moment then shook his hair out of his face and flatly mumbled, "C'mon. Ella's about to have a cow. Don't wanna miss that."

"Hey, I'm sorry," Kindle worriedly told him. She knew a large part of his aggravation was her fault.

He halted and squinted at her. "For what?"

"Just coming out here and thinking I could take care of it by myself and being stupid again and waking everybody up anyway," she confessed in a rush and then prepared herself for him to consent.

Tad did not agree with her. He shut his eyes and mumbled, "I hate this stupid rain."

"I'm sorry," Kindle mumbled.

"For what?! You didn't make it rain!" he snapped, and Kindle shrank back from him and started for the bank. She still felt rattled from the woman's wrath, and his yell only shook her further. Everything seemed to be wrong once again, and this time it was completely her fault. If she had not followed the light, she would not have met the woman and they all would be asleep. Realizing that she had made the same mistake of following a strangely lit orb two nights in a row, embarrassed shame coupled with her guilt, and Kindle stopped her trek to hide her emotion. Just feeling the raindrops all over her made her feel worse and better. The falling water seemed to know her sadness and encouraged and disguised her tears so she could fully allow herself to feel and also release all her pent-up pain and guilt.

Kindle cried in the downpour long enough that her mind began to wonder if the others were looking for her or had decided to leave her like some smelly piece of refuse. Gazing up, she immediately found her answer. Tad was leaning on a nearby tree, soaking wet and glaring at the ground. An apology for everything almost tumbled out of her mouth, but out of fear of being yelled at, she kept it to herself. A constrained breath escaped instead, and Tad lifted his glare to her.

"I'm—" she began, but his expression twitched, and he looked away. For a moment she thought he was so sick of her that he didn't even want to hear her talk, but then he spoke.

"I didn't mean to, you know, yell in your face," he told her with difficulty. "I just hate this stupid rain."

Glad he didn't hate her but avid to not let him feel as if he had done wrong, Kindle blurted, "No, it's okay, it wasn't that. It's just … I feel so stupid and pathetic, like I can't do anything but get in trouble and make all you guys save me. I just feel so stupid and pathetic."

"How's it make you pathetic if a bunch of nut jobs are huntin' us down?"

Kindle bowed her head at his question. The argument in it really did make a point that threatened her desire to wallow in self-pity. Finally, she admitted, "I dunno … because it's always me. None of you guys have walked right up to them like some idiot. I mean, if I would have just stayed away from Bennickle's globe and that lady's globe—"

"Kin. They're *hunting* us. They were gunna find us whether we walked up to 'em or not."

"Well, then doesn't it make me stupid to just go up to them?" she retorted, not sure why she felt so determined to argue against herself.

Tad shot her a look that echoed her own thought but contended, "No."

"Well, what's it make me, then?" she sighed, frustrated at herself for half-hoping he would just give in and agree with her.

"I dunno, but why not run up and stick 'em before they stick you?"

Kindle blinked at him and wondered if from his boy perspective he truly did not see her as foolish but somehow strategic and brave. She sighed and mumbled, "Well, I didn't stick anybody. You did."

"Who cares who cuts these freaks up as long as somebody does it?"

"I just feel bad that … that everybody has to keep rescuing me," Kindle struggled to say then quietly admitted, "It makes me feel weak."

Tad didn't speak for so long that she believed he finally would agree with her, but when she peered at him, he mumbled, "Yeah, well, just be glad you got somebody who'll cut up all the nut jobs for you."

Unsure if his vague statement should lift or drop her spirit, Kindle simply stared down at her boots. Curiosity to know his true thoughts slowly built up inside her, and she carefully asked, "You think it's okay to be … you know? I mean, it doesn't make me useless or annoying or anything?"

Tad sniffed a laugh. "Hey, if it wasn't for you, I'd never get to cut anybody up."

His joke spiked her, and she dropped her head in dejection.

"Nah, seriously," he sincerely mumbled, "you're not useless."

Kindle turned a hopeful but hesitant face to him. She didn't want him to just say what he thought would make her feel better. "Really?"

"C'mon, you think me and Ella and Andrew would still be runnin' around this place together if you weren't around to tell us to shut up and get over ourselves? Nah, we wouldn't. We wouldn't be anywhere near here, and we wouldn't ever get to that evil guy. We'd start cuttin' each other up."

Kindle stared down at the forest floor. Tad was too frank to just flatter or placate her, and so she knew he was telling her the truth.

Finally believing that perhaps her actions had not ruined everything and rendered her useless, she began to turn a smile to him but her eyes halted in the middle of their ascent. Somehow her necklace was sparkling in the dark under the raindrops covering it, and its gleam widened her smile. She wrapped a hand around it and stepped nearer to Tad.

"Thanks … um, you know Ella told me that all this stuff is happening for some reason. Like it's all gunna work out for something good, and that the makers are doing it all, so that's how we know it's all gunna work out, but, um …" She shook her head and opened her fist so Tad could see her gem. "But, um, maybe they also—you know, the makers—also picked *us* for some reason. Like, we each have some kind of purpose, and they knew we would need each other to make it all the way to the evil guy and his throne and … do whatever we've got to do."

"Your maker tell you that?" Tad asked, and for a second Kindle thought he was mocking her. When she met his eyes, though, she knew he was serious.

"Yeah, I think so," she admitted and then, catching sight of his roaring silver dragon, wondered, "And did–did yours tell you to come find me … again?"

Tad followed her gaze then smirked. "Yeah."

SPLINTERED

Menthoshine ripped the arrow out of her neck and flung it at Castrosphy. "You vile, lying parasite!" she screamed at him then glared up at the rain falling on her. Clutching her staff in both hands, she raised it high over their heads. A sneer of frustration started to curl up her lip, but she suppressed it. Just as her entire face melted into calm, a loud crack burst through the air and a million threads of green electricity wove a dome above them. Menthoshine heaved a satisfied sigh and returned her attention to the ground. Castrosphy stood at her feet, closely examining the arrow she had thrown at him.

"Stealing again?" she rumbled through bared teeth and sent a swift kick up through the arrow into his hood. "How dare you! How dare you disobey my orders to keep yourself from sight!"

Castrosphy squirmed on the ground but laughed animated hisses.

As she started to raise her staff, Menthoshine's nose flared in hatred. Instead of swinging it at him, though, she kept it at her side and began to pace around him like a wolf closing in on its prey. "And not only did you disobey me tonight—that girl knew you. And,

Castrosphy, do you know what she screamed out when I asked just exactly *how* she recognized your disgusting presence?" She continued to silently circle him as if waiting for an answer. After a few minutes, Castrosphy let out a new round of chilling laughter, and Menthoshine halted to scream, "Do you?!"

"The prinssse, the prinssse," he chortled in sinister glee.

"No, you insipid slug!" she screamed, and a green bolt from the dome struck the ground beside him. "She knew you from *ITERAUM* where you tried to take their necklaces!" Menthoshine stalked up to him and dangerously whispered, "Was the wretch lying?"

Castrosphy attempted to roll over, but she pinned his hood in place.

"Don't you dare turn your face to me! Now answer, cretin! Was she *lying*?!"

He said nothing but continued his laughter as he wriggled under her hold.

Menthoshine gave an infuriated roar and picked up her staff only to smash it down on him again. "Traitor! Filthy, detestable, sneaking *traitor*! You want nothing more than your own glory and reign! You believe yourself better than me! You believe just as she did that I am nothing—only a weak placeholder—a latent, slowly rotting, worthless corpse! DON'T YOU?!" Menthoshine let out a furious shriek and brought a collection of green spikes down on Castrosphy.

He twitched for a few seconds then finally fell still and quiet. Her uncaring green eyes briefly surveyed him, then she whirled around to take up her prowling circle again. While she paced, her frown twisted and her eyes roved around as if she was participating in an unheard debate. Very gradually, her mouth shifted into a malicious grin, and her gaze settled on the lightning swimming in her orb.

Only when Castrosphy stirred did she turn her eyes out of her thoughtfulness and onto him. Slowly, she steered her path to his shivering cloak and placed her boot on it. Bending down so her face hovered just a foot from his form, she whispered, "I *will* fulfill the legacy of the evil reign, and you will *not* live up to yours."

OBSCURE

When Kindle and Tad emerged from the trees, Ella and Andrew met them with a blanket umbrella.

"Are you alright, Kin?" Ella immediately asked, and Kindle nodded as she wiped her face dry and took a corner of the blanket. Since Ella knew nothing about the terrible woman or the hooded creature, Kindle felt her friend's question only pertained to the storm.

"I'm fine. Just wet," she assured Ella's unconvinced, concerned stare.

"Whatever did you go in the forest for? We—"

"Lost an arrow," Tad interrupted and stuck Ella's bow in her face.

With her mouth still open, she took it and then her quiver from him. After glancing over the arrows, she corrected, "Two. Two are gone. What were you shooting at, Tad?"

He didn't answer but slid his gaze to Kindle. A happy rush of trust and gratitude toward him filled her. She knew he was silently asking if she minded that he reveal what had happened. Even though she very much didn't feel inclined to talk about her mistake of following the green orb, Kindle knew Ella and Andrew wouldn't belittle her for it and so gave Tad a small nod.

"A stupid hag," he viciously answered, and shock took over Ella's face.

"An old woman?!" she incredulously cried. "Tad! Whatever impulsed you to shoot at an impaired, old woman? And *twice*?"

"Was it an old woman?" Andrew calmly questioned, and Kindle felt glad that he knew better than to take Tad's insults literally.

"I dunno how old the chick was, but she needed somebody to shoot her in the face."

Looking exasperated and confused, Ella questioned, "Tad, did you shoot a chicken or a woman in the face?"

"Oh, man," he chuckled then looked to Andrew. "Dude, help her out."

Andrew contained his amused grin and quickly explained, "'Chick' is just a slang word for a girl. He meant that he shot a girl, not a chicken."

"And I got her right in the throat, not the face." Tad smirked, but his grin darkened to a sneer as he grumbled, "Her stupid face was too busy screamin' a bunch of crud."

Ella squinted questioningly at him but finally shook her head and sighed, "Kindle, what happened?"

At first she considered telling Ella that she was too tired to talk about it but shrugged off the urge to lie. Kindle knew she wouldn't be able to sleep with the woman still fresh in her mind and would have to eventually explain anyway, so she heaved a sigh and divulged every detail.

When she reached the point of her story when Tad bolted after the woman, Kindle paused to consider if it was necessary for her to relate her crying episode to Ella and Andrew. To her relief, Tad cut in and she didn't have to make the uncomfortable decision.

"And I had her! I was two seconds from sitckin' her, and then poof—gone."

"She disappeared?" Ella half-asked, half-mused.

"Yeah, her and that stupid mystery midget."

Ella's face briefly pinched at his insult but returned to thoughtfulness as she hesitantly asked, "What was it that she said, Kin? Right before then?"

"Um … I'm not sure. It was like 'to the east catastrophe' or something. It didn't make any sense."

"Do you think something's happened in the east?" Ella worriedly wondered and peered at each of them for an answer.

Kindle felt anxiety twist her stomach as she digested Ella's question. The two most eastern dots on their map were Letum and Garrick Kingdom, and Kindle knew which one concerned Ella. Not wanting to push her into a panic, Kindle simply shrugged and honestly admitted, "I don't know. I don't even know if that's what she really said."

"Well, whatever she said, we're not gunna figure it out standin' here like a bunch of wet idiots," Tad grumbled and glared up at the completely saturated blanket.

"Yes, you're right," Ella agreed as she followed his stare. "How about it, you three, do you feel as if you could sleep in this downpour or should we press on?"

Kindle indecisively peered at Andrew then Tad. Both options sounded miserable to her, and she didn't want to be the one to blame for picking either.

Finally, Tad grumbled, "Whatever gets us out of this stupid rain." They all exchanged a reluctant but agreeing glance before accepting the inevitable chore of loading their horses in the rain. Kindle was sure that everything they possessed would be soaked through, but when she poked her hand in the sacks as she loaded them, she found that the ones the Cifra had given them were dry on the inside.

Very soon, they had managed to toss everything, including themselves, on Nasah and Nox and were trotting down the bank. Riding through the dark, rainy night caused Kindle to feel extremely unsettled. She knew that they were still in the same land and nothing except the time and weather had shifted, but she felt as if they had been dumped into a completely new, much more dark and dangerous world.

The tall white trees loomed like silent, unyielding sentinels on one side, and the dark river stretched out like a chasm full of bullets hitting metal on the other. The relentless downpour even shadowed Nox into nothingness and distorted Ella and Andrew into floating, ghostly outlines. Kindle stared up at the sky to see if the storm showed any hint of dwindling but found nothing that gave her hope. It was dark, very dark, and every bulging cloud seemed to mock her desire to be dry, warm, and resting. Pulling her eyes from the antagonistic view above, Kindle instead let them fall on her necklace. When she held it up to her dripping face, the golden dragon watchfully stared up at her and its wings still appeared ready to fly. Its bright, unwavering presence comforted her, and she determinedly gazed at it so her mind wouldn't wander to and fret over the storm and all the enemies and danger that seemed to be closing in on them.

Before she realized her sleepiness was overtaking her, Kindle felt her head bob and jolted up to keep herself on Nasah.

Tad lazily twisted to see her. "You sleepin'?"

"Trying not to," she sighed. "I'm just so tired. It feels like I didn't even sleep at all."

"You did," he assured her with a chuckle. "Snoring the whole time they were fightin'. You missed some good comedy."

"I was snoring?" she moaned, embarrassed.

"Nah, made that up. But you were sleepin' hard."

She half-heartedly shoved him and sighed, "I hope this rain quits soon."

"Yeah," he emptily agreed then spurred Nasah to catch up with Nox. When Kindle saw that Andrew was somehow asleep while sitting straight up, she had to contain her giggles so she wouldn't wake him.

Ella turned a kind but very weary face to them and asked, "Are you two holding up?"

"Barely," replied Kindle.

"Yeah, but better than him," grumbled Tad, tilting his head at Andrew. A wicked grin curled up on his face, and he yelled, "Hey!"

Ella gave a long, patient sigh then murmured, "Why?"

"Had to," he snickered as he turned to see Andrew. "So how

long till we get out of this stupid forest?"

Andrew blinked in annoyance a few more times then shook his head. "The map shows a lake in the middle of Xylina Forest. We haven't gotten to the lake yet."

Tad grunted, and Kindle felt his agitation. She did not want to stay another minute in the forest but sensed that Andrew's answer meant they wouldn't escape it for days.

"And ..." Andrew started to add but grimaced at the river instead.

"What is it, Andrew?" Ella prompted, and he returned his melancholy expression to them.

"And on the map, four rivers meet the lake from each direction, so unless we find a bridge or some way to cross the lake, we'll be stuck following the north river up to ... I don't remember the name, but the town that sits up between Xylina and the Ledyard Mountains. They should have a bridge near the town." He finished so meekly and miserably that Kindle knew he hated admitting the forecast as much as she hated learning it.

"Well, let's hope for a bridge or boat or shallow bit, then," Ella replied so cheerfully that they all turned a questioning stare to her. Seeing them, a slight smile broke over her face, and she admitted, "Well, if we must pass up that way, we'll have to pass by Garrick before we reach Letum, and ... I honestly can't say that is incredibly disheartening."

Ella's confession caused Tad to groan, but it sparked some delight in Kindle. Ever since Ella had first told her about the massive kingdom by the sea, Kindle had been curious to see it. Immediately, her imagination spun together her expectations of what the Lighthouse, Ella's papa, and the waterside market would look like, and she also smiled.

"That would be neat," she told Ella, whose grin widened.

"We couldn't stay," Andrew quickly cautioned and dragged the cheer off their faces. "If we do have to go north, we'll already be taking more time than we planned to get to Letum. Azildor told us to get there as fast as we could. Wasting time could mean not stopping the new evil reign."

"Of course, Andrew," Ella somberly agreed. "I only meant that we would see if the kingdom was alright or if—" Her voice abruptly ceased as if she had been interrupted, and she turned all her attention to steering Nox. Kindle understood that no external force had silenced her but the fear of the terrible woman's final words had. She tried to pull some reassuring words together in her groggy mind but found it also slipping into anxiety.

"Do you think she was one of the spirits?" she unintentionally wondered aloud and received a bemused look from Tad.

"Who?"

"Oh, um, I just … that woman. Her globe thing was like Bennickle's, so I just thought she might be a spirit too."

"That would be all four," mumbled Andrew, and they all stared at him. He dipped his eyes and explained, "Bennickle, the little monster, the woman, and the fire spirit … if the fire spirit really is dead."

"Yes, *if*," Ella repeated. "But we haven't a clear view of if any of those suppositions are certain. Well, I suppose Bennickle made himself known, but none of the others have. Kindle, the woman never said her name or who she was at all?"

Kindle thought over all she had said and remembered something odd. "No, and … when I told her I wasn't gunna give her my necklace, she acted like she didn't want it or care about it at all. She just kept yelling at me to tell her where you guys were."

"So you *don't* think she's a spirit, then?" questioned Andrew, clearly hungry for clarification.

Kindle, though, didn't feel like she could give him any. Her own mind was still spinning around in confusion, and so she shut her eyes and shrugged. "No?"

"So we only know of one spirit who's after our necklaces?" Andrew tried to conclude.

"Oh," sardonically laughed Tad, "don't forget the mystery midget. He's huntin' 'em too."

"Tad, stop calling it—or him—that," Ella gently chided then

sighed. "We could go over and over all of this again and again, but I hardly believe we'll understand any more of all this madness. It might be best to just accept that we haven't any inkling of what's churning all 'round us."

"Yeah, we do. Rain," muttered Tad, and Kindle cracked a smile in the middle of a yawn.

Ella even gave him a slight grin as she retorted, "Yes, Tad. We can at least be certain of this rain." Kindle watched her face slowly sadden before she breathed, "I do hope it ends."

ꞓꞺ

The rain did not end. No matter how many times Kindle fell in and out of sleep, she always opened her eyes to the same miserable sheet pouring on them. Each time she jolted awake, the compulsion to ask what time it was seized her, but she never acted on it. She was positive that Ella, Tad, and even Andrew were just as disoriented by the unchanging darkness and their lack of sleep as her. Once when she stirred awake, she heard Ella's voice singing through the roar of raindrops. Remembering how cheerful her songs were, Kindle tried to listen, but after catching a few words, broke her focus. Whether Ella was trying to match the gloomy downpour or not, it sounded more like a funeral dirge than a bubbly pub tune.

She almost tumbled back into sleep, but when she rolled back her face to check the sky for change, her mind pushed against her weariness. "Morning?" she groggily mumbled.

She watched Tad's head tilt slightly, then he grumbled, "Who knows."

"Sky looks lighter."

"Mm," he vaguely grunted, and Kindle tried to blink back her lingering stupor.

"Hey, let's switch. Let me steer."

"Nah."

"But you've been awake all night."

"So have you."

"No—I've slept some. Now you shou—ahhh!" Kindle's hands flew over her shriek as her eyes widened at the sight in front of them. Without any sound or tremor of warning, a cluster of trees had exploded right beside Ella and Andrew. The force and wooden shrapnel had pushed Nox to the ground and sent Ella and Andrew tumbling into the river.

"What?!" Tad yelled while Kindle's scream still lingered in the air, but before either of them could say or do any more, a rock monster—bigger than any Kindle had seen yet—tumbled out of the space and bellowed a roar that shook every inch of Kindle. Nasah reared up at the thunderous sound, tossed her head and reins out of Tad's grip, and bolted into the forest. They both scrambled to find something to cling to. Tad grabbed the saddle as she threw her arms around him.

"Nasah, stop! Nasah, go back!" Kindle frantically cried. While she very much did not want to face the rock monster, every fiber in her wanted to rescue Ella and Andrew from danger.

"Stupid horse!" Tad yelled as he tugged the saddle in vain frustration. "C'mon! Quit! Stop! Whoa!"

At his last command, Nasah slowed to a walk and then began wildly stomping the ground and throwing her head. She suddenly reared back, and they both tumbled into a pile on the ground.

"Stupid horse, forget you!" Tad angrily shouted as he kicked his way back from her hooves.

"She's scared!" Kindle defensively cried, also hurrying to escape the mud under Nasah.

Tad swiped the mud from his arm as he stood. He started to turn toward the bank but paused to ask, "You comin'?"

Her mind racing too fast to think over a decision, Kindle snatched a look at Nasah and then the trees they had just raced through. "Yeah," she breathed, and he grinned fiercely then sprinted away. Kindle scrambled up and ran after him as fast as her cold, wet, stiff body could. Sitting on her warm horse, she hadn't realized just how miserably tense and frozen the rain had left her limbs and now struggled to gain speed. When she finally reemerged on the bank, though, her adrenaline and movement had pumped her blood through every inch of her. Ready to dash to Ella and Andrew's aid, she pivoted to run their way but smashed into Tad.

"Wha—?" she began to question his stillness, but the amazing scene ahead of them stupefied her as well. A ferociously churning, towering wall of sand, rock, and fire was barricading the rock monster against the trees. The creature was lumbering right and left and madly swinging its fists into the mass of flaming debris, but it continued to shove the giant creature backward. The monster roared then spun and shattered the trees poking it so it could take a running start at the wall. Sure the rock monster would crash through it, Kindle held her breath, but before it could even finish its ambush, the wall surged forward, caught the monster in the air, and threw it down into more innocent trees. When the quake from its fall subsided, Kindle looked up from her feet and almost squealed in triumphant joy. Now she could see that just on the other side of the wall, Ella was standing with raised arms, and the flames whipping through the tornado were surging from her hands.

"C'mon!" she cried to Tad, who was still gaping with a slight smirk on his face. Kindle grabbed his arm to shake him into movement, and they sprinted to Ella.

"Stand back!" Ella shouted as soon as she spied them. "This is wonderfully dangerous!"

"Yeah!" laughed Kindle as she and Tad joined Andrew in the shallows of the river. The curve of the incredible wall shielded them not only from the monster but also from most of the pouring rain. Kindle grinned up at the wildly spinning airborne sand and rock, grateful for and baffled by it all.

"How're you doing that?!" she cried over the rushing fire and clatter of the rain behind them.

"I haven't any inkling!" Ella merrily shouted back, but then a tremor shook the earth under them, and her face fell into seriousness. "What's going on over on the other side?! I was sure he had been knocked flat with that rumble a moment ago!"

"He was!" yelled Tad then shot off down the bank with an eager grin.

Kindle almost shouted for him to come back but was afraid she would only draw attention to him. To her relief, he very soon spun around, momentarily surveyed the scene, and then raced back.

"He's up, and he's *mad*," he reported with such vicious joy that Kindle rolled her eyes. She could not believe he was enjoying being attacked.

"What should we do?!" she asked Ella but received only a head shake.

"Swim?" Andrew's soft voice suggested, and she and Tad whipped around to face him. Andrew dropped his gaze to their wet feet and weakly explained, "The other rock men wouldn't go in the water."

Suddenly, a new gritty noise accompanied by a roar erupted above them, and they all turned their attention skyward. Kindle gasped and stumbled back in horror. Half of the monster's face was jutting through the churning wall. An urge to follow Andrew's suggestion seized her, but her fear, amplified by the creature's gruesome expression and howling, kept her rooted.

"Nah, c'mon!" Tad shouted and jolted her from her frozen terror. He was tripping up the bank away from them.

"Tad, what are you doing?!" demanded Ella.

He stopped to point up at the monster, who was slowly retracting its face. "That guy's not backin' down, so we gotta scram!"

"He will catch you if you run!" Ella argued, and he threw his arms up in frustration.

"And he's not if we stand here?! C'mon! We have to go *this* way *now*!"

Kindle nervously flipped her eyes between the two, waiting for one to comply. They glared at one another in heated frustration for a few seconds, then Ella's face abruptly snapped into comprehension.

"Yes! Yes, Tad! Go! Kin, Andrew, go!" she cried, and Kindle jumped in surprise but followed her command. Tad, though, hesitated.

"You too!" he shouted at Ella.

"No, I'll—!"

"Come on!" he yelled and dove forward, snatched the arm she was waving at them, and pulled her from her flame and the flying debris. Expecting the blockade to crash down and the rock monster to come tumbling at them, Kindle spun and bolted. Tad and Ella quickly caught up to her and Andrew, but none of them slowed. The only thought that pulsed through Kindle was to put as much distance as possible as quickly as possible between herself and the gigantic monster. An urgent curiosity to see just how much space existed between them pulled her gaze over her shoulder. Even though the heavy rain was still blurring their surroundings, the sun definitely had risen somewhere above the storm, and so Kindle could make out what stood behind them. Instead of showing her the monster, her brief glance revealed that the sand and rock barrier still shielded them from it. A mix of amazement and hesitant relief washed through her, and her legs decreased their fear-driven pace.

"Guys!" she tried to yell through the rain and her short breath. Ella and Tad had run too far ahead to hear her yell, though, and Andrew only gave her a fleeting glance before returning his eyes to the mushy, slippery ground. Realizing that none of them would ease their race against the rock monster to see that it wasn't chasing them, Kindle regathered her will to run and keep up with Andrew.

Glad for but mystified by the existence of the churning wall, Kindle kept snatching glances back at it as she ran. She had thought that Ella had created it with her fire, but now wasn't sure what power was holding it aloft. The only explanation she could fathom was that it was another weird phenomenon of Anelthalien. However, something about the way it seemed to be guarding them pushed her to believe it was not just a natural occurrence.

Andrew suddenly slipped, and her mind snapped out of its wondering. He fell so near her that to avoid stomping on him, Kindle leapt over him and almost lost her footing as well.

"You okay?" she asked as she regained her balance and bent to see him. He turned a pained, dirty, but unscathed face up to her, and she offered a hand. After blinking at it a few times, his expression jumped to fearful alertness, and he scrambled to push himself up.

"Hey, he's not after us," Kindle assured him, and Andrew froze in mid-stand to whip his gaze backward. "Well, I mean, all that sand and stuff was still in his way after we started running."

He returned his eyes to her to give her a questioning stare.

"Really," she argued with his unspoken doubt. "I know it sounds weird, but I saw it. And if he was still chasing us, he already would of crushed us."

Andrew's eyes darted around in thought, and finally, he nodded. "We would have felt him running after us," he concluded as he straightened.

Kindle smiled, glad that he didn't think she was dumb, and nodded. "Yeah, exactly."

"We should keep going," he replied, trying to lean around her, and Kindle's boost of confidence deflated.

"Oh, yeah, sorry."

"It's fine," he mumbled as they resumed their path at a walk.

After only a few steps, Kindle's mind roved back to the strange barrier, and she asked, "What do you think it was? That thing? I mean, I thought Ella was making it, but maybe it was a sand tornado or something."

Andrew grinned slightly, and Kindle feared he thought she had said something silly.

"Well, what do you think it was?" she retorted with annoyed defensiveness. She knew Andrew was smarter than her but didn't want him to make her feel dumb because of it.

He eyed her for a moment then informed her, "I wasn't laughing at you. I don't know what it was."

"Then … what were you laughing at?"

The grin reappeared as he shrugged and admitted, "Almost nothing here makes sense."

After trying and failing to see the humor in his sentence, Kindle wrinkled her nose and questioned, "What?"

"The weather doesn't follow a pattern, the rocks and ground

are alive, necklaces talk … none of it makes sense."

Even though Kindle still didn't see the humor in his explanation, it quelled her suspicion that he was deriding her. "O…kay," she relented and decided to stop questioning him. They trudged along in silence until a rumble lifted both of their eyes upward.

"Was that thunder?" Kindle quickly and hopefully asked, but when another tremor reached not only their ears but also feet, her hope vanished. Her wide eyes met Andrew's for half a second, and then they simultaneously broke into a wild sprint.

Even though the rain obstructed the bank behind them, Kindle was certain that the rock monster had somehow pushed through the protecting wall. Part of her wished she could see exactly how much distance separated them and their pursuer, but another part of her was thankful that she could not see its terrifying figure. Every few seconds Kindle tossed a glance over her shoulder to check if the monster was close and that she had not left Andrew. He was much slower than her and seemed to be having trouble keeping his completely saturated tennis shoes from slipping and popping off his feet.

Feeling annoyed at his shoes, Kindle gasped, "Take 'em off!" She didn't hear him respond or react but didn't look back to see if he had followed her advice. The rumbling was growing in its force, and she knew that meant the monster was nearing them faster than they could escape it. For a few moments, her mind frantically searched for a better plan, but after slamming into the only other and just as dangerous routes of the river and forest, it focused back on running as fast as possible.

An ear-blasting roar exploded through the sky, and Kindle chanced a peek behind her. Andrew, although he had fallen behind, was still in her sight, but Kindle's eyes also caught the misted outline of the rock monster. Alarm spiked through her, and she turned her face ahead just in time to see a blue-green blur rush right into her path. Before she could come to a full stop, she smashed into it.

"We have to go! We have to go! He's right behind me!" she shrieked as she fought Ella and Tad's restraining arms. "We have to—!"

"Will you quit?!" Tad angrily shouted, and shock froze her. His blue eyes were especially icy as they bored into her, and her panicked brain could not understand why.

"He—" she started to plead, but he huffed and dragged her forward just a few steps.

"We're not goin' anywhere," he grumbled, and her determination to flee abruptly switched to a compulsion to latch onto his arm. They stood just an inch from open air. The ground ended and turned a sharp angle down into an unmeasurably high drop-off. As her eyes quickly assessed the vast, hazy space, she realized that they stood at the top of a rushing waterfall. Kindle started to wonder how she hadn't heard it, but Tad pulled her away from the cliff as Andrew smashed into their group.

"It's a waterfall, Andrew," Ella hurriedly explained as he blinked terrified eyes around at them.

"Waterfall?" he panted.

"Yes, and it is much too steep and high to travel—we need another way," she almost begged in a rush as her eyes drifted to the steadily sharpening figure of the rock monster.

"We go in the forest, we lose it, bam, done! I told you!" Tad retorted, and Kindle felt his hand tighten on her arm.

"Tad, we—" Ella began to argue, but Andrew interrupted.

"Wait."

Ella glanced at their now almost clear enemy and cried, "It's right there, Andrew, we cannot—!"

"Wait," Andrew quietly, fearfully repeated, squinting up at the creature. For two horrifying seconds they all stood frozen, watching the oncoming monster. Kindle's brain and body seemed to go numb as she sensed death sweeping toward her. Her heart was beating so frantically and her lungs were so drained of air that everything seemed to slow and hush to a silent standstill.

Then, just when the monster raised its gigantic leg over their heads, every sight and sound flooded back into existence.

"Run!" Andrew yelled, and they all dove into the shelter of the forest. Kindle felt air sweep past her back and then tumbled into a pile with the others as the earth violently quaked right behind them. Almost simultaneously, an enormous roar shook her whole body, and she pushed her hands over her ears. The shaking and bellow slowly subsided until finally, all she could feel and hear was the rain and her companions' ragged breath.

A Steep Expense

Very cautiously, Kindle unshielded her ears and lifted her head. She saw that the others also lay hunkered on the grass at the edge of the forest. She twisted around and gave a small gasp. Not even a foot away, a humongous depression had appeared on the bank, and water from the river was beginning to trickle into it.

"Oh," Ella's voice breathed, and then she appeared at Kindle's side. "It almost crushed us," she whispered, shaking her head in disbelief.

"Are you nuts, dude?!" Tad loudly laughed, and Kindle spun to see his face. His tone sounded angry, but his half-giddy, half-evil grin was shining at Andrew.

"If we would have ran sooner, it probably would have just followed us," Andrew calmly replied as he stood and stepped down into the giant footprint. His eyes searched it, the river, and then the cliff. "How did you know about the waterfall?" he slowly questioned and leaned past Kindle and Ella to see Tad.

Tad wrinkled his face into a suspicious frown. "I saw it. It's right there."

"No," Andrew sighed, shaking his head. "When you told us to run instead of swim. You knew we would have fallen over the waterfall if we swam."

"I didn't know the stupid thing was here," Tad grumbled in return as he joined Andrew on the sunken bank.

"You knew we had to come this way," Andrew insisted, and Tad rolled his head back in agitation. Kindle anticipated another fight stirring, but Ella's voice broke into the tense air.

"And that's all you knew, wasn't it?" she gently asked, and Tad whipped his narrowed eyes to her. Unfazed by his glare, she trotted down between the boys. "Was it just like the few times before when your maker urged you along? Telling you where you must go, but no hint as to why?"

Comprehension hit Kindle from several directions as she watched Tad squint down at his necklace and Ella smile at hers.

"It was your maker," Kindle sighed in wonder, and they all turned to her. "I mean, I dunno if it was just like every other time—it nagging you—but you went exactly where we needed to go. And that sand tornado …" Kindle gave Ella a prompting nod.

"Yes, Kin. That was my maker."

"Not you?" asked Andrew, looking bemused.

"No, not at all," she laughed. "I thought we were at an end, and then I heard my maker's voice tell me to raise my hands, and when I did, all that rose up as well. It wasn't any of my doings—it only appeared that way."

"And that's why it stayed up!" Kindle cried, happy that, unlike Andrew's face showed he still believed, everything *did* make sense.

"It stayed up?" Ella repeated with cheerful amazement.

Kindle eagerly nodded. "Yeah, it did! When we ran, it just stayed there and—"

"Gave us just enough time to get away," finished Andrew in a deeply somber, thoughtful voice.

"Um, yeah," agreed Kindle, deflated by his tone. Realizing how much the makers had helped them greatly delighted her, but Andrew's gloom caused her to feel as if her joy was mistaken. She wanted to ask him how being saved could make him so grumpy, but knew her question would be rude, and so withheld it.

Tad, though, sniffed and muttered, "What? You sad about not gettin' stomped?"

Andrew shook his head but kept his eyes on the ground and remained silent.

"Whatever," Tad grumbled and strode over to the edge of the drop-off. "So, what now? We just stand here waitin' for an elevator?"

Ella slid Kindle a confused glance but replied, "Well, do you suppose we could make our way down that cliff? Do you see a footpath?"

"Nah, looks like the only way down is the way big and ugly took," replied Tad as he stuck his chin out to peer down.

"To fall?" Ella questioned, and after receiving a bland expression from Tad, she nodded and sighed, "Alright then, that does not sound pleasant ... Andrew? Have you any inkling?"

He finally peered up from his musing to stare around at them. "Hm?"

"Andrew, what has you fretting?" Ella kindly asked, but when he simply stared at her, Tad rudely called to him.

"She wants to know how we're gettin' down this stupid waterfall."

Andrew blinked at him then Ella as his mouth awkwardly opened and closed. Finally, after a long, painful silence, he admitted, "I–I don't know."

Kindle felt her heart sink. She had been sure his brain would conceive a clever plan but now thought she understood his dismay. Even though the makers had helped them escape the monster, they now stood trapped. The precipice was too high and sheer for them to navigate, and traveling through the forest meant risking meeting Bennickle again.

"Where do we go?" she whispered and searched the nearby

trees as if they held the answer. Slowly, her gaze traveled down to her necklace, but just as she focused on the golden dragon, a voice—one she had never heard before—distracted her.

"Excuse me. I believe I can help you."

·· ℰℚ ··

Bennickle heaved a great sigh as two creatures made entirely of mud ushered in two men wearing blue tams with ridiculous pink puffs wobbling atop them.

"Where is Aryl?!" the shorter, much fatter one loudly demanded. "Aryl! Tell these mud men we can walk on our own! Tell them we are capable, Aryl!"

The second man whipped his nose at the loud man and much more quietly cautioned, "Lord Beryl—"

"Aryl! Tell Wissen to never address Lord Beryl! Aryl!"

"Stop," Bennickle directed in his deep, slow voice, and both men fell silent to twist their heads around the almost black room.

"Who—?!" Lord Beryl began to shout, but Bennickle interrupted.

"Greetings."

"Greetings," replied Wissen, sticking his nose in the air as if he intended to sniff out who had spoken. "And who is it that I and Lord Beryl, the ruler of Aryl, have the opportunity of hearing but not seeing?"

"My name … matters not."

Wissen sniffed loudly. "Perhaps this dark and enigmatic façade is compensation for a lack of authority. Lord Beryl is—"

"Quiet," Bennickle rumbled, and Wissen snapped his mouth shut.

However, Lord Beryl opened his. "Aryl?! Aryl?! Wissen is doing a poor job, Aryl! Perhaps we discontinue his service?! Yes, Aryl, fine idea, you're right! He couldn't even keep four children locked up for one night! Yes, Aryl, and the tax collection never adds up when—"

"Four children?" asked Bennickle, and his orb brightened slightly.

"Aryl?! Did you hear, Aryl?! This secretive fellow is interested in my spies as well, Aryl! Do you think we should tell him, Aryl?! Mm … hmm … yes, Aryl, he likely does! We should, Aryl! It is a good idea to trade his riches for information, just as those children! Hmm … no, Aryl, I don't suppose he has shinys like the spies. The girl said they were marks of the makers—an elite line of jewelers, no doubt."

"Marks?" Bennickle leaned forward in interest, and the now even brighter light emitting from his orb touched his face.

Wissen flipped his wide, fearful eyes at the earth spirit then back to Lord Beryl. "Stop your foolish banter," he hissed. "You will vomit everything the man wants, and we will not even have our lives to barter."

"Aryl! Tell Wissen to only address you! Tell Wissen to end his disrespectful conduct!" yowled Lord Beryl to the darkness above. "Tell him his service *is* discontinued as of now!"

Wissen waved his nose in fury, but Bennickle eased back into his stone seat.

"Aryl," he slowly said, also gazing up, "we will … do business."

"Aryl! The man wants to trade, Aryl! Ask him, Aryl! Ask him what he will give!"

"My entire kingdom … for information."

"He has an offer, Aryl! Should we take it?! Yes, Aryl, it is a whole—"

"Lord Beryl! You are not even aware—!"

"Tell Wissen he is discontinued!" cried Lord Beryl and pounded a meaty fist on his striped pants.

"Who were … the children, Aryl?" Bennickle softly directed, and Lord Beryl fell back into his musings.

"Aryl, he wants to know who the four spies were! Perhaps he wants spies as well! No, Aryl, it does not matter. He will not have a kingdom if he has our spies. And, Aryl, they were not good spies, remember? The girl was set on some mission already. Not at all good, Aryl. And we will be the ones to profit anyway!"

"Mission?" Bennickle prompted, and his orb intensified its glow so much that it revealed his entire intimidating form.

Wissen sucked in a breath and shuffled back, but one of the mud creatures shoved him forward again. "This is erroneous!" he cried.

"Ignore him, Aryl!" Lord Beryl demanded to the wall that had appeared on his right. "You know he is discontinued, Aryl!"

Bennickle lifted a hand toward Wissen and commanded, "Take him." Immediately, one mud creature snatched Wissen's arm and pulled him out of sight. When the echoes of his furious ranting finally died, Bennickle returned his gaze to Lord Beryl and promised, "The children's mission … for my kingdom."

"Aryl! He says the deal is still hot! What do you suppose, Aryl?! Yes, Aryl, you've already said that. Hm … mm … no, Aryl, I do not know what his concern is about their current mission—perhaps, Aryl! Perhaps he is a spy as well on an opposing mission! Yes, Aryl, an opposing spy—that will teach those children to flee as free agents! Now, Aryl! Tell him what she said … yes, the small one! Tell him, Aryl, about her babblings of an evil king and their mission to destroy him! Tell him all about that magic stone they're seeking and how they'll save the whole land!" Lord Beryl laughed the last few sentences as if he believed they were ridiculous and continued to chuckle once he finished.

Bennickle, though, kept his face as still as stone. Only after Lord Beryl began chatting to Aryl about dinner did Bennickle stir. "Satis…fied?" he quietly inquired, and even though no voice answered, he lifted a silent hand at the remaining mud creature to remove Lord Beryl. The round man allowed himself to be dragged away by the creature as he continued to debate with Aryl.

Bennickle shut his eyes but otherwise remained stoic.

"You failed us," an airy but grave voice breathed, and Bennickle cracked open his eyes to see his orb. No face floated in it, only a bluish-grey cloud.

"They have ... power," he coldly replied.

"Of course they do, Bennickle, but so do you. At least ... I thought you did."

Bennickle's jaw ground back and forth, but he did not take his turn to speak.

"Calm yourself, Bennickle," the voice breathed, "and redeem your place by telling me where Menthoshine is."

For a few seconds, Bennickle simply glared at the cloud. Very gradually, his dark eyes began wandering around, surveying every inch of space while not seeing the room around him at all. Finally, his distant gaze reached the far wall, narrowed, and slid back to the orb. "Not home."

"Yes. I know. But *where* is she?"

"It is difficult."

"Difficult?" the voice questioned in a crisp, dangerous tone. "Just as it was difficult for you to communicate with me when I told you of our dear flame's wanderings? Just as it was difficult for you to pour more of yourself into our investment? Difficulty, for you, Bennickle, seems to be more a pattern of selfish reluctance than a matter of ability. Am I correct?"

He did not answer.

"Where is the girl?"

"It is difficult," Bennickle resolutely repeated.

"It should not be—would not be if you had invested as you agreed," the voice practically hissed in disdain.

"I did."

"Then, again, I must assume your difficulty is a cover for selfish reluctance."

"Silence offers me ... no benefit."

The voice blew away its bite in a long sigh then whispered, "Bennickle, you do understand what that man revealed, don't you?"

"They will be ... where she is."

"No, they will seek where she *should be*. And seeing as how the uncooperative girl has escaped your prison and not divulged her location, we must assume she understands as much as we do and will use that against us. We must find her. We must find *them*."

"I will donate … no more lives."

"You lost one man. Make a new one," the voice emotionlessly spat. "I am not concerned what life it requires from us; we will have our life in the end. But, Bennickle, for that end to result, you must locate them."

Bennickle turned his face to the tunnel his mud creatures had disappeared through. His jaw worked thoughtfully, and at last he answered, "It is your … investment. I am done."

"No, you are not. Your selfish tendency has invested you just enough that whether you choose to continue or not, your hands are already secured as the ones with all of Anelthalien's life hanging in them."

Author Note

Thank you for reading *Earth Quaking*. I would so appreciate hearing what you thought of this book and the first book in the series, *Anelthalien*. Please leave a review on Amazon, Goodreads, Christianbook.com, your blog, Instagram, or Facebook. Reviews help authors so much!

I would love to hear from you and connect online. Find me on these sites:

Web page: https://www.hapruitt.com

Instagram: https://www.instagram.com/hapruitt/

YouTube: https://www.youtube.com/channel/UCILV2H57QT_wDTYP4Y6bBDA

Facebook: https://www.facebook.com/AnelthalienHAPruitt/

Goodreads: https://www.goodreads.com/author/show/19930566.H_A_Pruitt

Amazon author page: https://www.amazon.com/H-A-Pruitt/e/B081LKTKXF/ref=dp_byline_cont_pop_ebooks_1

If you would like to learn more about the story behind *Anelthalien* and *Earth Quaking*, please subscribe to my YouTube channel HAPruitt Anelthalien.

Thanks

I owe all the credit of this story to God. Without His gracious intervention, I never would have known this beautiful land of Anelthalien even existed. God gave me every word, every scene, and every amazing moment in this far away land. I only heard the story first and wrote it down—my Maker is the Author.

I also owe the credit of this entire book's creation to God. If He had not urged me to publish it, supplied every bit of ability and means necessary, and continued to encourage and abundantly provide, I would not have even started. I am so thankful that God fully supplied for the mission He gave me and that He gave it to me at all.

God has used so many people to bring me His abundant provision.

Scott,

I could fill pages with all the ways I am grateful for you, but since you particularly appreciate humor, I'll keep this entertaining. Thank you for contributing to Tad's vocabulary. I don't know if you ever actually said "mystery midget", but you are the ever-flowing fountain of wit and sarcasm (and borderline offensive) in our home. Thank you for watching hours of random old TV shows so I could lay (excuse me, *lie*) on the floor armed with a Q-tip and pencil to draw my illustrations. Thank you for not asking questions when I asked you to take a weird picture or video for illustrations or marketing (and for repeatedly taking down the curtains for my costume). Thank you for reminding me that only grammar sticklers like me care if I use the correct form of "lay" or "lie". And thank you for every day praying for me, loving me, and reminding me to just quit being scared and do what God has called me to do. You have a contagious, fierce fire in your heart. I love you.

Brenda,
Thank you for expressing your eagerness to read book two nearly every time you saw me. I so appreciate your help with proofreading, and I so enjoy listening to all your postulations about the other books. Thank you for all the prayers, cards, and time you have given me. And, no, I don't have the third one typed yet. Please keep asking.

Alexandria,
I am so grateful that God led us to find one another. Your support as a fellow author who understands the fears, obstacles, joys, and technical innerworkings of being a Christian author has been the exact encouragement I have needed time and time again. Your stories have strengthened my faith, your personal messages have brightened my days, and your prayers have comforted my heart.

My author friends,
Niki, Erica, Effie, Kimmie, Jessica, and all of you authors who have encouraged me, joined my launch team, prayed for me, reviewed *Anelthalien*, or shown kindness in any way—thank you. Having author friends who show the love of God and remind me that the story God has given me truly does matter is so motivating and encouraging. Thank you.

Mt. Etna,
Thank you for being the best church family ever and for relentlessly praying for me and *Anelthalien*. I so appreciate all of you.

Reader,
Thank you for joining this adventure with me. I appreciate you giving your time to read *Earth Quaking*, and I hope God has given you precisely what you need through it.

9 781737 230908